MW01122825

BLOOD BROTHERS

A Novel of Courage and Treachery On the Shores of Tripoli

E. Thomas Behr

This is a work of fiction. Names, characters, places, and incidents either are the product of the author's imagination or are used fictitiously, and any resemblance to actual persons living or dead or to historical events is entirely coincidental.

ISBN: 1456527304
ISBN-13: 9781456527303
Library of Congress Control Number: 2011900402

The Mediterranean

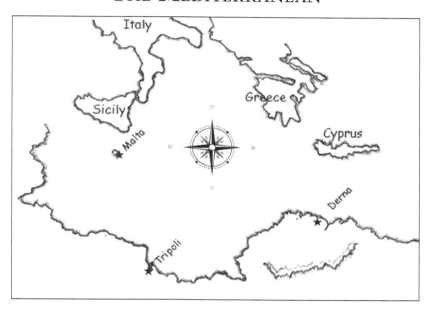

THE *USS EAGLE*

The fictional *USS Eagle* has a historical counterpart in the *USS Nautilus*, a topsail Baltimore schooner built by Henry Spencer and purchased by the navy in 1802 to support the war effort against the Barbary pirates.

The *USS Eagle* has a real counterpart in the *Pride of Baltimore II*, a replica of an 1812 Baltimore privateer, Thomas Boyle's *Chasseur,* that wreaked havoc on British shipping from 1814 to 1815. The *Pride II* beautifully reproduces the graceful lines that made these ships so fast, and as privateers, so lethal. As Baltimore's Goodwill Ambassador since her commissioning in 1988, The *Pride II* has sailed almost 200,000 miles and visited over 200 ports in 40 countries in North, Central, and South America, Europe, and Asia. A fitting testimony to her speed and sailing qualities are the many races she has won, including the 2000 Transatlantic Tall Ships Race. To learn about this marvelous ship, go to www.pride2.org.

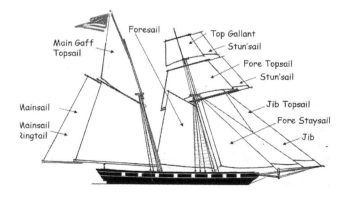

INTRODUCTION

For over three hundred years, the Barbary pirates of Morocco, Algiers, Tunis, and Tripoli preyed on merchant shipping in the Mediterranean, seizing ships and raiding seacoast towns. The men and women they captured fortunate enough to have wealthy friends could hope to be ransomed; those less fortunate were doomed to a harsh life as slaves or concubines in their captors' brothels.

Preoccupied by their own wars on the continent, the European powers solved the problem of the corsairs by bribery in the form of yearly tributes to the Barbary states in return for safe passage for their merchant ships.

When America gained her independence from Great Britain following the Revolutionary War, she lost the protection of the British flag. The thousands of American merchant vessels in the Mediterranean became lucrative new targets for the North African corsairs.

The American government followed the pattern established by European countries: paying tribute. By the time Thomas Jefferson took office as president in 1801, the price tag for securing peace with the Barbary States had climbed to $1.3 million.

Outraged at the constantly increasing demands for payment to ensure the safety of American merchant shipping, President Thomas Jefferson ordered a small squadron of US Navy ships to sail to the Mediterranean to protect American interests. "Millions for defense," was the popular cry, "but not one cent for tribute."

No sooner had the American fleet arrived in the Mediterranean than Tripoli declared war on the United States. The ruler of Tripoli, Pasha Jusef Karamanli, demanded a new treaty priced at $225,000 and an additional $25,000 in yearly tribute.

The war sputtered along for three years under a series of ineffectual commodores. Then, in September 1803, the US Navy's new commander in the Mediterranean, Captain Edward Preble, burst on the scene like a bomb thrown into a ship's magazine. The young American captains in his command, "Preble's Boys," burned the *USS Philadelphia*, which had been captured by the Pasha of Tripoli, and under Preble's leadership, launched a series of devastating naval attacks against Tripoli.

Preble's bold conduct of the war found a ready supporter in the person of William Eaton, former Army Captain, Indian fighter, and US Consul to Tunisia. His plan was to attack Tripoli from both land and sea, launching a coup that would put a pro-American ruler, Hamet Karamanli, on the throne of Tripoli. But before Eaton could bring his plot to reality, Preble was called back to the United States, to be replaced by a new commander, Commodore Samuel Barron.

CHARACTERS

IN THE MOHAWK VALLEY

HENRY DOYLE (*Okteondon*): Raised by the Mohawk tribe of the Iroquois Nation before the Revolution, he left America to serve under his Muslim name, El Habibka, as a British spy in India, the Middle East, and Africa—now war leader of the Tuareg people in North Africa.

JOSEPH BRANT (*Thayendanega*): The most influential of the Mohawk chiefs and Henry's closest Mohawk friend—as comfortable and effective in a London drawing room as at an Iroquois council of war.

SUSAN DOYLE: Orphaned as a child, she was rescued by Sir William Johnson, eventually became his mistress, and bore him a son, Henry Doyle.

SIR WILLIAM JOHNSON (*Warrahiyagey*): British agent for central New York state and self-styled "Lord of the Mohawks"—adopted by the Mohawks, he fought to preserve their independence.

TIYANOGA: Mohawk leader known as Chief Hendrick and longtime staunch ally of Sir William Johnson.

WITH THE AMERICANS

WILLIAM EATON: Former US Army officer and Consul to Tunisia who leads the march across the Libyan Desert to attack Derna and place Hamet Karamanli on the throne of Tripoli.

EUGENE LEITENSDORFER: Soldier of fortune who joins Eaton as his adjutant and travels with Eaton to Cairo in search of Hamet Karamanli.

PETER KIRKPATRICK: Captain of the *USS Eagle* who accompanies General Eaton to Cairo and joins the march to Derna.

THOMAS CHRISTOPHER: Peter Kirkpatrick's First Lieutenant on board the *USS Eagle.*

ISAAC HULL: Captain of the *USS Argus,* commodore of the US Naval squadron supporting General Eaton.

PRESLEY NEVILLE O'BANNON: US Marine lieutenant who accompanies General Eaton to Cairo and joins the march to Derna.

JOHN DENT: Captain of the *USS Nautilus and* member of the naval squadron that attacks Derna.

STEPHEN DECATUR: America's first great naval hero and Peter Kirkpatrick's boyhood friend.

COMMODORE SAMUEL BARRON: Commander of the US fleet in the Mediterranean whose support for Eaton's mission shifts with the winds.

SAMUEL SMITH: US Secretary of the Navy whose support for Eaton is equally tenuous.

TOBIAS LEAR: US General Consul for North Africa opposed to Eaton's mission.

ROKKU: Lear's Maltese secretary.

THE BRITISH

BURTON GREY: British Admiralty agent.

SIR SAMUEL BRIGGS: British Consul in Alexandria favorable to the American mission.

CAPTAIN VINCENTS: British soldier attached to Brigg's mission.

JAMES DACRES, British navy Lieutenant and Peter Kirkpatrick's friend.

The minute I heard my first love story,
I started looking for you, not knowing
how blind that was.
Lovers don't finally meet somewhere,
they're in each other all along.
Rumi

For JoAnn

TURKS, EGYPTIANS, ARABS, AND TUAREGS

DIHYA: Henry's Tuareg lover and warrior princess of her people.

HAMET KARAMANLI: Deposed Pasha of Tripoli whom Eaton intends to restore to power.

PASHA JUSEF KARAMANLI: Current ruler of Tripoli who seized control of the country in a coup against his brother Hamet Karamanli.

KOURSCHET AHMET PASHA: Turkish Viceroy of Egypt .

ALI: Egyptian Dragoman assisting Eaton's voyage up the Nile to Cairo.

IBRAHIM: Egyptian beggar hired by Leitensdorfer as a spy.

ACHMET: Egyptian boy hired by Leitensdorfer as a spy.

IBN HASSAN and KHALID: Former officials under Hamet now serving as his unpaid emissaries.

SHEIK EL-TAHIB: Bedouin sheik hired by Eaton to transport the army's supplies in the desert march to Derna and recruit Arab soldiers for Eaton's army.

SHEIK MUSTIFA BEY: Commander of the Tripolitan forces in Derna.

SHEIK HASSAN BEY: Commander of the Tripolitan relief force sent to defeat Eaton's army.

OTHERS

SALVATORE BUFUTTIL: Hamet's agent in negotiations with the Americans.

DON JOSEPH DE SOUZA: Spanish Consul General and Pasha Jusef Karamanli's negotiator with the Americans.

LEON FARFARA: Pasha Jusef Karamanli's banker.

CHAMEAU: French agent.

TAL-PATANN: Maltese spy working for Chameau.

From the Journals of El Habibka
Everything in the world of existence has an end and a goal. The end is maturity and the goal is freedom. For example, fruit grows on the tree until it is ripe and then falls. The ripened fruit represents maturity, and the fallen fruit, freedom.

Nasafî

CHAPTER 1
ও MALTA 1804 ও

If I needed someone to slit a throat or steal a purse, Eaton thought, I would come here to find him.

William Eaton had arrived early for that evening's rendezvous with the British agent, Burton Grey. Grey had picked a bad place for their meeting—the Sedum Tavern—in a bad part of Valletta harbor. In the daytime, the square was a fish market. At night, other things were bought and sold.

The lengthening shadows cast by a fading sun played across the centuries-old weathered stone buildings fronted by awning-covered stalls. Eaton stood, unnoticed, in a boarded-up doorway, his cloak pulled tight against the damp cold rolling in from the harbor. With the approach of twilight, merchants were shuttering their shops and their customers were fleeing the square. Eaton watched as patrons entered the tavern: sailors from the ships of twelve nations crowding Valletta's harbor, dock workers, pick pockets, thugs, cutthroats, and whores. A bright-eyed rat looked up from his supper of fish scraps on the shop table next to Eaton. Eaton nodded a greeting: paying a visit to your two-legged cousins, I suppose? Above the doorway, rust stains like dried blood streaked downward over the stone from a crude iron hook in the wall. I wonder what has hung on that hook, Eaton thought. Fish—or men?

Eaton looked at his watch, then eased quietly from his hiding place into the tavern and stood in darkness near the door. He pulled back his cloak to free his pistol, his eyes passing carefully over those patrons he could see in the candle-lit gloom. A few moments later, his aide Eugene Leitensdorfer came through the door, spotted Eaton, and joined him by the entrance.

Before they could begin speaking, an angry quarrel broke out at a nearby table. A British navy captain jumped to his feet and cried out to his companions, "I say, if you stand for this you ought to be damned. You may as well hang a purser's shirt from the rigging to let all know you are no better than lubberly merchant captains begging assistance from true men of war! I move that all of you that are true Englishman shall rise with me from the table and throw these brazen Yankees into the street with the vermin and dogs where they belong!" He gestured at a group of noisy American sailors at the far end of the table.

Expecting the room to erupt into a fight, Eaton and Leitensdorfer retreated further into the shadows. Before the first blow could be struck, another British officer interceded. "Gentlemen," he cried, "We make too much of an inconsequential trifle. If a man is insulted by one of his own kind, he must seek satisfaction. But here," he said, pointing to the Americans, "where the offenders are worthless, the abuse is innocent. I pray you," he said, gently guiding his drunken fellow officer back into his seat, "let this pass." His words had the desired effect. The Americans resumed their own conversation and the crisis passed. The noise inside the tavern returned to a subdued murmur of voices.

"That would have been an inauspicious start to our evening here," said Eaton. "But who would have imagined a sensible British officer in a place like this?"

"He may just have counted the number of Americans they would be fighting and didn't like the odds," Leitensdorfer replied. "The Englishman Burton Grey should be here shortly. Let's hope he is more agreeable. Come, I've arranged for a place where we won't be disturbed." He led Eaton through the crowded tavern to a small private room to the right of the bar. They settled in behind the deeply scarred, stained wooden table. "We can talk in confidence here, but with the doors open, watch whoever enters," Leitensdorfer said. Eaton nodded, then left the table to go to the bar, returning with four wine glasses.

As he sat down, their English contact arrived at the tavern. Leitensdorfer went to him, spoke briefly and led him back to their table. Without waiting to be introduced, the Englishman greeted Eaton with a brief, diffident nod. "Mr. Leitensdorfer and I share an acquaintance, sir. But you would, I assume, be William Eaton?"

"Your servant, sir," said Eaton, coolly matching the Englishman's neutral tone. "Mr. Grey, I believe we may call you?" As Eaton rose to greet Grey, he noticed their disparity in size. He looks like a terrier, Eaton thought—or a ferret. I will need to handle him carefully.

"Grey will do quite admirably for our purposes; my real name obviously does not concern you," said the Englishman, sitting down wearily. "Is there anything drinkable in this hovel?"

"I would be surprised if there were," said Eaton. "So I took the precaution of bringing a bottle with me: a 1783 Leacock and Spence Madeira. I trust you will find it acceptable," he said, knowing that it was, in fact, superb. Gesturing at the table, he continued, "We have paid for glasses. May I pour you one?" Grey picked up the bottle, inspected the label, and then nodded.

Their glasses filled, Grey began. "As I will disclose to you shortly, the French have wind of what you are proposing and seek to frustrate your intentions. But we still lack one member of our group, the gentleman whom you seek as a—what is the word you Americans might use—as a scout who is quite familiar with the desert terrain of Tripoli. By all reports, he is a man of considerable parts, quite gifted in the languages of this region. My contacts in London recommend him with the greatest of confidence and are sure of his discretion. Some mention was made, as well, of his accomplishments in the military line as a leader of Arab cavalry and irregular forces. But I must confess I do not know the man. You will need to make your own assessment."

Almost as the words left Grey's mouth, a tall man approached their table. Leitensdorfer sprang to his feet. "Why gentlemen, upon my word! This is the very scout Mr. Grey's good services have procured for us. May I name Henry Doyle to you?" As he nodded to their new arrival, Eaton realized that he could not swear exactly when the man had entered the tavern. It was possible that he had been there all along, observing them in silence.

"*As-salaam ahlakum,* Eugene," Doyle said in Arabic, embracing Leitensdorfer.

"*Wa ahlakum as-salaam,*" Leitensdorfer replied. "And peace be with you."

Doyle turned to the others at the table. "Good evening, gentlemen. Mr. Leitensdorfer I know. Mr. Grey and I have not had the pleasure of an acquaintance, but I know who you are, sir." Eaton caught the slight edge in Doyle's voice behind the formal politeness. As Doyle sat down, they could see his face more clearly now in the flickering light of the candle, his strong features marred only by a scar across his left cheek running under his ear but missing his neck. Doyle noticed Eaton's scrutiny of his wound, caught Eaton's eyes and nodded.

"Yes, it was a close shave. Some unpleasantness serving with Tippu Sultan in India, back in '85. So you are William Eaton, I presume?" Doyle asked. "If you will forgive such familiarity in a stranger, sir, I would take the liberty of mentioning we have a mutual acquaintance of an academic sort. I believe, if I am not mistaken, we are both graduates of the Wheelock's fine school in New Hampshire, although you, I would guess, had the pleasure of studying with the son. My tutor was that godly old man, his father Eleazer." He smiled at the look of recognition that crossed

Eaton's face. "We seem, neither of us, to have traveled too far from *vox clamantis in deserto.*"

"You are surprisingly well informed, sir," said Eaton.

"An affectation, to be sure," Doyle replied. "A foolish matter of pride. I humor myself in thinking good information may have kept me alive all these years. But if I am not being overly bold, I believe we have business to discuss?"

"If you will forgive some boldness on my part," said Eaton, "It seems you are an English agent who fought in India, speaks Arabic, and went to Dartmouth College before the war, when most students were Indians. And you have studied my background. Mr. Grey promised us a very capable resource; I would say he has kept his word. But if I may ask, are we secure here?"

"We are alone," Doyle said. "I followed you from your lodgings. You were, of course, careful, and knowing your destination, I could lag behind and notice anyone attempting to trail you. Then I waited, undiscovered, for the good Mr. Grey here to join us. No one followed you either, sir."

Grey bristled, "I make it my business, sir, never to be followed if I choose not to be."

Doyle responded with a smile, this time somewhat less warm. "Since I make it my business never to be seen when I follow someone, it would appear that our gifts have complemented each other's."

"I have no wish to quarrel," said Grey, holding Doyle's gaze steadily, "at least in this place at this time." He paused, then added, "At another time, you might find me more accommodating." Doyle gave him the slightest of nods in acknowledgement. "But permit me to say, sir," Grey continued, "I wonder at your confidence. Some men might call it presumption."

"Indeed they have, sir," Doyle answered, "but not a second time."

God help us, Eaton thought. These two may be at each other's throats in a minute. He looked at Grey again. The Englishman's narrow face had become even more pinched with anger. Eaton exchanged a quick glance with Leitensdorfer. He sees it too, Eaton thought.

"Gentlemen." Eaton intervened in a strong, commanding voice. "Gentlemen. I pray we may turn to the matters before us." When he had Grey and Doyle's attention, he continued, as if their tense exchange had never happened. "The enterprise we are about involves Hamet Karamanli, brother of the current Pasha Jusef Karamanli, who usurped Hamet—the same Pasha who also holds Captain Bainbridge and the crew of the unfortunate *Philadelphia* as hostages. My government has authorized me to find Hamet, lead an expedition to restore him to the throne, and free not only the American hostages but all Christian slaves."

"And the fine thing that would be," said Doyle, then turning to Grey, "May I ask the Crown's interest in this American gallantry?"

"My role here is merely to make introductions then disappear from the scene," Grey said to Eaton, ignoring Doyle. "I have letters with me to our consul Sir Samuel Briggs and his aide Dr. Francisco Mendrici in Alexandria. They are wholly in favor of the plan, and will provide whatever assistance their means make possible, particularly in locating Hamet, of whose whereabouts we have now only rumors. We hope the success of this venture will be annoying to the French. Despite Bonaparte's disgraceful abandoning of his army in Egypt, they still have power in this part of the world and are capable of considerable harm to my country's interests."

"I had the pleasure of knowing Dr. Mendrici from his days as the chief physician of the Bey of Tunis," Eaton said, "when I was the American consul there. Both of us departed rather precipitously at the same time. In my case, it was from a lack of congeniality with the Bey; in Dr. Mendrici's case, as it was reported, from too much congeniality with one of the Bey's wives. But I am certain he is an excellent gentleman for all of that." Eaton beamed at the Englishman. "May I say, Mr. Grey, how grateful the United States is to receive such support from Great Britain against a country and dictator who has shown himself to be no friend of either of our nations?"

Grey acknowledged the compliment with the slightest of nods, his lips lifting up in a narrow smile that was taken back almost as soon as it had been offered.

"To return to our purposes, gentlemen," Eaton continued, ignoring Grey's response, "Mr. Leitensdorfer will travel with the army as my chief of staff, since he knows the country and its people and speaks the languages." He turned to Doyle. "We need, as well, a group of scouts to guide us across the desert. It was suggested that you, sir, might provide such an advance force."

"My Tuaregs will serve the purpose splendidly," said Doyle. "The Bedouins fear them and let them pass in peace wherever they go. For my involvement, the traditional face veil worn by Tuaregs serves admirably in the way of disguise. The only way you remove a Tuareg's veil is by taking it off his corpse." He suddenly rose to his feet, "I apologize for the interruption, gentlemen, but I seem to be caught short. Quite likely some bad mussels I ate. Perhaps you will excuse me for a moment?" He slipped away from the table and melted into the gloom of the tavern.

Grey refilled his glass and disappeared into his own thoughts. Even in the candlelight, Eaton could see the barely restrained anger in Grey's fingers gripping the glass. If he's not careful, he'll break the damn thing, he thought. For all he notices us, we might as well not be here.

Some minutes later, Doyle reappeared at the table and sat down again. "If I may continue, gentlemen," Doyle began, "we will need of course, Mr. Eaton, to review your plans in detail. But there is one other matter we should discuss. I am pleased, honored, in fact, to be part of a mission so motivated by the highest of ideals, but sadly, my purposes require that I be compensated for my services. A low, crass thing, to be sure, but there it is," he added, with no sign of embarrassment.

"For my own person, sir," cried Eaton, "I believe that there is more pleasure in being generous than rich. Man wants but little, and that little not long. But here we make war, and war calls for money and men. Whoever wishes to make war must spend without thought and take no account of the money. We will find a way to compensate you appropriately, sir!"

"You are very good, I'm sure," replied Doyle, "but it may be others are prepared to help in this matter as well." Turning to Grey, he asked, "May I assume the usual relationship with London will be honored in this affair, with the same arrangements made with my bankers in Leghorn, the Baccris?"

"You have my word for it," Grey snapped. "That should be enough."

"Then I am your man," Doyle said to Eaton.

"So we are settled," Eaton replied. "We will be in Alexandria in two weeks' time, weather permitting. I wonder if we might rendezvous there, perhaps at Mr. Briggs' residence?"

"Alexandria it is, gentleman, with the blessing. But do not expect to see me as I am here," Doyle said. "Once I set foot in Egypt, I too become a Muslim. Do not look for me; I will find you. Now, forgive me for what could easily appear to be an insult," he looked at Grey, the insult quite clear in his tone, "but as I did when you came, I will linger behind to make sure you are not followed. Please take it merely as a matter of my staying in practice, no more than that. Since we have been here, two men have entered and made a great deal of pretending not to notice us. And they have been speaking French. They might be innocent, or they might not. I believe I should engage them in conversation to ease my own mind of its suspicions. So farewell, gentlemen. Good hunting to us all. *Ma'a salama,*" he added with nod at Leitensdorfer. Wrapping his black cloak about him, he moved into the darkness of the tavern, then disappeared.

"A man of some considerable parts, indeed, Grey," Eaton said. "Your London contact could not have chosen better for us." He gave Grey a friendly smile. "I should think a man would be careful in crossing him."

"I personally am not recommending him, you understand," Grey said. "He was suggested by Whitehall based on prior service to the Crown. I must tell you, however, that he now works as a hired spy—or assassin. We still purchase his services when we need them—but so do many others. Whether he is reliable, or just a self-serving adventurer, is a decision you will need to make. But you Americans are making a lot of noise in the Mediterranean these days—coming it quite high as a world power, I might say. I trust you will have the wisdom to make your own decision."

He trusts us to make asses of ourselves, Eaton thought, but continued looking at Grey with a warm, open smile. "Once again, Mr. Grey," Eaton said, "you are far too generous in your compliments—too kind, indeed. But we thank you nonetheless. As a young nation, we have fought but one war against a major power," Eaton paused for a moment, "which we had the good fortune, happily, to win." Grey grimaced as if he had just bitten down on a rotten fig. If anything, Eaton's smile was even more engaging. "For all that, I do not question that we have more to learn. Perhaps you might tutor us."

"I know Henry Doyle," Leitensdorfer interjected. "I will tell you, Aphra Behn could not have written a stranger history for him. I boast, I will admit it, of my own adventures, but Doyle puts me to shame. While he works always for whom he chooses, for his own reasons, he is utterly, absolutely reliable. In a word, I would trust him with my life—and have."

"And so you will have to," said Grey, rising from the table. "I have done my part. What you make of Doyle or he makes of you is your business. I bid you good evening." With that he left them, shouldered his way through the crowded tables to the door, and stepped into the darkness outside the tavern.

"He might at least have thanked me for the Madeira," said Eaton, looking at the remains of the wine in the candlelight. "He drank enough of it."

CHAPTER 2
ॐ MALTA 1804 ॐ

Doyle stood outside the tavern. The square was now cloaked in darkness except for a single guttering lamp at the tavern's door. He watched Grey leave first and head toward the surrounding maze of narrow, cobbled streets, lit only by the occasional burst of light from an open door or window, usually accompanied by music and laughter, or sometimes by voices raised in anger. At this hour, the streets leading out of the square were empty.

One of the Frenchmen who had been watching them exited the tavern and followed after Grey. It was the big one, taller than himself, and probably twice his weight. Gelada, Doyle thought. No notion of a fair fight. Doyle let Gelada pass, then stepped out and called in a soft voice, *"Pardon, M'sieur. Vous désirez...?"* Gelada turned, and in that instant, the hilt of a throwing dagger blossomed in his throat. Gelada looked at Doyle in angry surprise, took a step towards him, then crumbled to the ground. Doyle stepped to the body. A sharp pull to free the blade completed the work.

Grey heard the scuffle, turned and ran back toward the noise. He saw Doyle standing over the body. Grey knelt down in the dark trying to look at the man's face. "You know him?" he asked.

"Gelada," Doyle said. "They call him 'The Bull,' or more properly, called him. Easy to see why. He's a French agent, as you might have guessed."

"You might, at least, have spared him so I could talk with him," snapped Grey.

"Or I could have let you attempt to deal with him yourself," said Doyle. "No offense, of course, but I would have liked to have seen you attempt *that*. Happily, now you can make your way home in safety. I trust you can manage that?"

Grey glanced up at Doyle, saw the look in his eyes and the bloody knife in his hand, and thought better of the retort he had intended to make. "I'm sure I'll make do," he said. "Perhaps you and I will meet again."

"It would be my pleasure, at any time and place of your choosing." said Doyle. "Now if you'll excuse me, I have a body to attend to." Grey rose and headed back up the street toward his lodgings without a word.

Doyle wiped the knife on the man's cloak and dragged the body into the shadows. I should scalp him. That would certainly create a stir in the morning. Well, his purse will do, Doyle thought. One more robbery in a part of town accustomed to dead, looted bodies. I will probably regret not having taken care of Grey in the bargain.

Doyle walked back to the tavern. Above the square, the looming walls of the fortress stood out against a moonlit, cloudy sky. Doyle stepped back into the blackness under the market stall nearest the tavern's entrance to wait.

Several minutes later, Eaton and Leitensdorfer emerged among a boisterous group of sailors. The sailors shattered the quiet of the evening with their singing as they staggered down an alley leading to the harbor.

Some die of constipation, some die of diarrhea.
Some die of deadly cholera, some die of diphtheria.
But of all the dread diseases, the one that we do fear,
Is the drip, drip, drip from the chancred pr--k of a British Grenadier.

Americans, Doyle thought. The new, rising power in the world. Not what you'd call an improvement. He saw his two colleagues head up the hill towards their hotel. The second Frenchman he had spotted in the tavern dropped in behind them. Lapin. Gelada's little rabbit. He'll be easier to deal with and far more talkative. Noiselessly, Doyle followed the three men as they turned up a steeply climbing street toward the fortress. Lapin took a double-barreled pistol out of his pocket and held it down at his side. Ahead of him, Leitensdorfer dropped something, and, in the process of picking it up, spotted the Frenchman shadowing them. Smoothly done, thought Doyle. The two continued their way up the hill, wrapped in conversation, but now, he guessed, talking about the Frenchman behind them. They are both professionals, aware of the danger, and will not have seen me behind them. Tricky, he thought.

Doyle soundlessly closed the distance between himself and Lapin, now some ten paces behind his prey. He stretched a long dagger across the Frenchman's throat. Lapin came to a startled halt, not daring to look around at the person holding the blade.

"Gentlemen," he called ahead. "We have a guest."

Eaton and Leitensdorfer spun around, both now holding pistols.

"Well, my friend, you do show up in the damnedest ways," Eaton commented.

"Your servant, sir," Doyle replied. "It would seem that our party has grown by one. Your friend, Gelada" he continued, addressing Lapin, "is lying several streets away in the gutter with his throat slit. Be careful in your own movements unless you wish to join him. Now be a good sport, and give my companions your pistol." The Frenchman immediately complied.

"General," continued Doyle, "perhaps you would do me the honor of allowing me to have a few words with this fine chap. I may be able to convince him to talk freely by methods that might be uncomfortable to you."

The men exchanged glances. "By all means," Eaton replied. "You know our concerns. I am sure he will make a clean breast of things with appropriate persuasion. So deal with him as you think best. If there is any pressing news to be gained from him, you know where we lodge. If not, we will meet again at our rendezvous." Then he looked directly at the Frenchman. "God speed all of us on our coming voyages. *Adieu, M'sieur. On ne pourrait pas dire 'Au Reviour.'* Come, Leitensdorfer. The evening has been long and more of that excellent Madeira awaits us, assuming of course, your Mussulman religious scruples will not compel me to drink alone."

When the two had gone some distance up the hill, Doyle moved Lapin into a dark alleyway several yards ahead and spoke quietly with him. Whatever bluster of resistance Lapin might have offered drained from him. When Doyle had gotten all the information the Frenchman could provide, he lifted Lapin's chin up to look in his eyes. "I'll give you what you and Gelada would have given the Americans," he said, "but spare you the beating that would have preceded it." With that, he slit the Frenchman's throat in a single, quick slash, wiped his dagger and dropped the body in the alley.

He started up the street that led to his rooms near the Upper Barraca Gardens, by the old castle of the Knights of St. John. The slightest breeze from the harbor would not have moved more quietly or invisibly along the dark streets.

From the Journals of El Habibka
To be a Sufi means to be a lump of sifted earth with a little water sprinkled on top.
It means to be something that neither harms the soles of the feet nor leaves a train of dust behind.

Ansari

Eaton and Leitensdorfer sat in Eaton's sitting room enjoying more of Eaton's Madeira. Eaton had taken rooms in Searle's Hotel with a balcony overlooking the arcades of the Upper Baracca that gave a commanding view of Valletta's Grand Harbor. The harbor was now dotted with the riding lights of ships at anchor, like fireflies in the darkness. Beyond, bathed in shadow, were the looming walls of the fortresses of St. Angelo and Isola. "So, Leitensdorfer," Eaton began, "what could you tell me about this Doyle fellow—that is, within the scope of what you think proper to reveal?" And what you think proper to reveal about yourself, Eaton thought.

"Of course, general," Leitensdorfer replied. "I was being deliberately cautious with the Englishman Grey. I would observe that one cannot easily guess where the interests or allegiance of such a man might lie. I'm speaking of Grey, of course. I have no doubts whatsoever about Doyle, and you can trust me to be frank in my assessment."

And so say all true men, thought Eaton, and all false liars. "So you served with Doyle, I take it, in the siege of Acre?"

"I have told you about my experiences as a Muslim Marabout," said Leitensdorfer. "Some of my efforts at, shall I say, faith healing among the faithful, had produced less than auspicious results among the inhabitants of Istanbul. It seemed prudent for me to leave the town for a while. Jezzar Pasha was recruiting men in Acre, and so I signed on with the Turks. Napoleon's army was near at hand, as well, but unfortunately, I had left their service rather abruptly. General Menou knew me by sight, if by a different name—I think I called myself Carlo Hossondo then—so I decided I would be better off facing a French army than a French firing squad. May I inquire what you know of that siege, general?"

"It was all the talk of Tunis when I was the consul there," said Eaton. "A brilliant victory for Jezzar Pasha, with no small degree of help from Sir Sidney Smith and the British Navy—and a crushing blow to Napoleon's dreams of making himself the ruler of all the Middle Eastern lands. Had Napoleon succeeded at Acre, the Syrians might have joined him in rebellion against their Turkish masters; then there would have been the devil to pay."

"I was with the first Turkish relief force that the French met at Mount Tabor," said Leitensdorfer. "This was the flower of Napoleon's Army, still untouched by the plague that ravaged them later, and they carved us up as a chef would an *aiguillette*."

"They must have been well *entranched*," laughed Eaton

"We got no joy from the meal they served up to us," responded Leitensdorfer, sharing Eaton's pun. "Had it not been for Doyle, I would have been surely killed—or captured, leading to very much the same outcome once I was recognized as a deserter. At that time, Doyle was still working for the English and was attached to Smith's diplomatic (actually, his espionage) mission to the Sublime Porte in Istanbul. But he showed up on the battlefield as quite a different character, El Habibka, the celebrated leader of Bedouin cavalry."

Leitensdorfer reached across the table, and using wine glasses and silverware, laid out the deployment of the opposing armies at Mount Tabor. "The French had crushed our center, here; we were in the process of being completely overrun. Napoleon, true to form, had ordered Murat's cavalry to collapse our left flank and throw the entire Turkish force into rout, when El Habibka, excuse me, Doyle counter-attacked." Leitensdorfer pushed a knife across the table. "His Bedouins hit the French like a hammer. Quite remarkable—one so rarely sees the backs of French cavalry. I was stranded in the ensuing mêlée, and Doyle saw me alone, with the French infantry rapidly approaching. He swooped down, plucked me onto the back of his horse, and saved my life. During the retreat, we spent several days together. He told me a little of himself—no more than he wished to disclose, I'm sure. When we parted, my whole life's story was open before him." Leitensdorfer paused for a while, then looked directly at Eaton.

"I have led an adventuresome life," Leitensdorfer said, gauging Eaton's reaction as he spoke. "Some might call it irresponsible or disreputable, even immoral. I am who I am, and I take no personal shame in that. What strikes the oyster shell does not damage the pearl. So I judge a man's character, general, by how he judges me."

"Like the quite proper Mr. Grey?" Eaton asked. Or me, he thought.

"Of course." Leitensdorfer snorted. "One would not have imagined how much contempt could be so thoroughly expressed in so few words. But I take no notice of him. He is like the thirsty dog who approaches a pool of water and sees a dog staring back at him. The more he barks and growls to scare the other dog away so he can drink, the more ferocious the other dog becomes, until he finally gives up and goes away thirsty."

"Well," said Eaton, "Speaking of angry dogs, Doyle certainly did not take to him. I thought the two of us were close to being asked to serve as seconds to their duel. Grey seems hard enough, but were odds laid, all my money would go on Doyle, pistols, swords, or any other weapon."

"On the whole, Doyle doesn't think well of a certain class of Englishmen. Something soured him when he was in India."

"I would say there's a certain class of Englishmen one would like to thrash with one's cane. But Doyle's background puzzles me. He apparently was raised in America. He has served the British, but it would seem he now follows Islam."

"As for that, we are both converts to the true faith of the Prophet, blessings upon him, although I suspect both our motives and the depth of our piety differ. We do share the painful fact that both of us underwent the obligatory circumcision to become a Muslim in both faith and physical appearance. Mine,

I confess, was a self-administered operation—with a razor." He grinned as Eaton reflexively winced. "His, I believe, was carried out by softer, gentler hands."

"I think I shall remain true to my stout Congregationalism," said Eaton with another involuntary shudder. "But to return to our point, I take it you are comfortable with the choice of Doyle as our chief scout?"

"As I said at the tavern, I can think of no better choice. It remains to be seen what he thinks of us."

"That will unfold in time," said Eaton, leaning back in his chair. "Come, the evening draws to a close, Leitensdorfer. I see your glass is empty and the bottle stands by you. Pray do not require me to finish it myself."

CHAPTER 3
❧ MALTA 1804 ❧

Early the next morning, before the street vendors had made their appearance, a small, chubby man made his way quickly along the alley that led to the ancient market of St. Ursula, ducked through the first of the arches under the portico, and rapped sharply on a small side door with the hilt of his dagger. He waited patiently, knowing at this hour, Chameau would be in and would hear his knock.

After several minutes, a grated window in the door slid open. "Who is it?" Chameau asked sharply from the blackness behind the door.

"Tal-Patann," the man answered.

"I told you never to come here by daylight, you fool!" Chameau said. "And your knocking must have drawn eyes and attention. Come back at your usual time."

"I have news," Tal-Patann said. "It cannot wait until the evening. The street is empty and I was not followed. Be quick and let me in."

After a few more moments, the door opened just enough for Tal-Patann to slide into the dark hall of the warehouse, stacked high with barrels and crates. He followed Chameau to the center of the building where the early morning light was already piercing the high, slotted windows. Chameau sat down at his desk and glared at him through puffy eyes. He's had a bad night, it seems, Tal-Patann thought. Well, others have had a worse one.

"Your news?" Chameau asked.

"I do have news. Interesting news. May I assume you have money?" said Tal-Patann.

"Always the money, damn you! I think you would sell your sister if the price was high enough."

"I don't have a sister," Tal-Patann replied, "and from the talk one hears, a little brother would be more to your fancy." Then, glancing around at the barrels around him, he added, "But as for the money, you know we Maltese have a saying, *Min ma jbossx, jifsa.* The man who complains most about farts lets out the silent stinkers. I assume you do not grow poor in this business. As for me, I think the purse of a timid man neither increases nor decreases. So I am not timid."

Chameau reached under his desk, took a key on a chain around his neck, opened a strong box, withdrew the customary fee and shoved it across the desk to Tal-Patann. "Remember what you Maltese also say, the seller has one eye, the buyer a hundred. Your news had better be worth it."

"Judge for yourself," Tal-Patann said, pocketing the money. "Gelada and Lapin followed the Americans to Sedum, as ordered. They left the tavern and were found earlier this morning by the watch, both with their throats cut."

"Lapin I can understand, but Gelada, he is a ferocious man. Surely there was a struggle?" Chameau said.

"No way to know, but the spies I had posted by their lodgings reported the American party returned safely, by all accounts unharmed and in good spirits."

"So two men are dead and we still know nothing."

"Whatever they learned died with them. But when you hear who else was at the meeting, you will, at least, better understand how they died." Tal-Patann paused and looked at Chameau.

"You are a scoundrel," Chameau said, as he once again opened the box and threw more money across his desk.

"Yes, but I am *your* scoundrel. I took the precaution of having someone watch the watchers. There were four men at the meeting. Eaton we expected; he was accompanied by the renegade Leitensdorfer."

"Who the devil is that?"

"A pretentious fraud, some men say. He professes to have been a Capuchin monk who converted to Islam. He has wandered throughout the Empire as a Mussulman holy man calling himself Murat Aga, casting out devils and effecting miraculous cures, I have no doubt, with passages from the Koran and fervent mumbo jumbo. He has served in the Austrian, Turkish, and French armies—and deserted from each. He may, for all that, be of service to Eaton. He is quite fluent in Arabic, Turkish, Coptic, and English and has traveled throughout Egypt. He can pass, with his newly adopted religion, as a local. But to continue, Eaton and Leitensdorfer were joined by another man my contact did not know, a rather unpleasant creature of no apparent account. But my man knew the fourth, from his service at Acre. It was El Habibka." He paused to let the news sink in.

"El Habibka? Here in Malta? That would explain Gelada. But I had heard El Habibka had retired, or disappeared. This American meddling is not his business."

"The Americans are not afraid to spend money. El Habibka has been bought before."

"But why him? This changes things. He has resources we do not fathom."

"You know the world is a wheel, men are the spokes, and the devil does the spinning. Some have called El Habibka the devil. Certainly you French had more of him at Acre than you wished."

Chameau rose from his desk, dismissing Tal-Patann as if he were no longer there, and walked into the sunlight now streaming through the windows above. He pulled out a small cigar, lit it, and, for a while, watched the smoke rise into the dust-flecked sunlight.

"We will make no more attempts on the Americans here in Malta. With El Habibka guarding their backs, it would be throwing away useful lives. We have other, less risky means we can employ." He crossed to his desk, took out the strong box, and this time with less truculence, counted out a significantly larger sum and handed it over to Tal-Patann.

"The Americans' commodore, Barron, is a helpless, bed-ridden invalid," Chameau continued. "He has, to our good fortune, turned all matters over to their envoy, Lear. This Lear is no more than a child in these affairs, an imbecile, a glutton for all the lies we may feed him about Eaton and Hamet Karamanli. You will contact our agent," he wrote a name on a scrap of paper which Tal-Patann read, then handed back. "See that you place a trustworthy man on Lear's staff and bring me news. El Habibka or no, there is mischief we can do them. Now go."

CHAPTER 4
⤳ THE MOHAWK VALLEY 1770 ⤳

The boy sat in the secret hollow of a huge red oak, feeling the roughness of the jagged bark merge into his bare skin. He let his mind empty out, becoming quiet and open to the forest around him. A beetle, foraging for food, crossed over onto his leg. He felt the pull and release of its tiny claws on his skin as it worked its way across his body to move further up the trunk. As he quieted, the sounds of the forest around him began to come to life, the way the morning sunrise gradually turns dark shadows and unrecognizable shapes into bright, familiar clarity.

Old Grandfather *Tiyanoga*, the Mohawk chief, had been his first teacher. The earliest lessons he could remember had been about quiet patience, letting the forest come to him. White men walk through the forest with their eyes on the ground, their tongues flapping, and their ears closed, *Tiyanoga* had taught him. When a warrior or hunter walks, he sees with his feet, listens with his eyes, and looks with his ears. Now the Mohawk way of moving silently, effortlessly through the woods, feet feeling and adjusting to avoid the snapping twig or rustling leaf, senses open and mind empty, was as natural as breathing.

He remembered waiting for hours by a deer path, letting his spirit become one with the rhythm of the forest, merging into the space around him, so that small animals ran past him or over his legs as if he had been just another stone. When a deer finally passed next to him, he reached out his hand and touched its glossy side, with no more pressure than a yielding branch.

His mother, Susan Doyle, was white, and his white name was Henry Doyle. The Mohawks called him *Okteondon.* His mother lived on a small farm, a mile from Johnson Hall, home of the great English chief, Sir William Johnson, whom the Mohawks and their Iroquois brothers called *Warrahiyagey.* Since he could remember, the Mohawks had been his people, and Joseph Brant, whom the Mohawks called *Thayendanega*, his best friend. He had never known his father. Some people said he was *Warrahiyagey's* son. Others cruelly said his father was a marauding Cherokee, or worse, one of the evil spirits, the *Jo-Ge-Oh*, who lived in the north. His mother had said that his father was a great chief, who would one day proclaim him as his son. When he had killed his first deer, and *Warrahiyagey* had marked his face with its blood, his heart had burst with the question he could not ask, "Are you my father?"

Once again, the boy's mind drifted into his dream.

He was looking again at the countryside around Fort Johnson, but now from a great height. He felt his heart beating rapidly as his shoulders effortlessly drove feathered wings.

Around Fort Johnson the longhouses of the People were all gone. The great forest that once had stretched as far as the eye could see was broken, the land stripped bare by hundreds of small farms. White men with horse-drawn plows worked the fields the People had once tended by hand.

His vision leapt ahead of his sight. Now he flew over ugly brick buildings stretching along both banks of the river, spewing smoke into the air and fouling the water with their waste. This time, the sun seemed to gather its light into a single, impossibly bright cloud that drifted down until it was right before him. Without a thought, he flew directly into the brightness.

When he came through the light, he was looking at a wilderness of sand, empty of trees, water and life. Far to the south, mountains, ragged as broken, rotten teeth, rose from black, rock-strewn soil. His eyes caught a glimpse of a dark, motionless speck miles away to the east and his brain said "food." His wings, now huge and powerful, drove him downwards toward his prey. As his shadow spread across the figure on the ground, sharp, taloned feet stretched out to grasp it.

When the dreams first began, he had gone to Corn Silk, the *arendiwanen*. Are my dreams real, he had asked. She had answered, "The dream world *is* the real world, *Okteondon*. This life we have here is no more than a shadow world. White men have forgotten how to dream, so they live always in the shadow world, ignorant and blind as stones. They have opened a great wound between the earth and sky and lost the part of themselves that is one with all created things. They pray to an absent god to take them back to the real world. In dreams, you live in the real world and find the great spirit in yourself."

"But are my dreams true? Do they tell of what must happen in the future?"

"There are many kinds of dreams," Corn Silk said. "Some are big, some little, all come from your spirit. If you think false, you will dream false. If true, then true."

"But how will I know when I dream true?" Doyle asked.

"In a true dream, every sense, every part of your spirit lives in that dream. There is no separation between the dream and the dreaming and the dreamer. But you ask too many questions. *Serihokten.* Go away and stop pestering me or I will turn you into a rabbit and cook you for dinner."

His mind gently slid back into the present. Nearby, two birds paused in their nest building as the chattering sound of a pine squirrel fifty yards away changed into angry complaint. Further, deeper into the forest, the song of another bird and the croaking of the frogs by the small creek several hundred yards away had stilled. The boy couldn't actually *see* the fox that had noiselessly stepped to the edge of the creek, but he knew it was there.

So he heard the approach of the visitors long before they broke out of the woods on the Schenectady road and turned their horses past Johnson Hall toward the Fort. Beneath him, on one side of the steep hill, flowed the river. Fort Johnson, with its many barns and outbuildings, was directly in front. The long houses of the Mohawks were next to the creek to the west. Everyone came here to seek *Warrahiyagey*'s counsel and to ask for his help—the people of the Iroquois, the white settlers, and the British chiefs in their fine clothing.

Becoming invisible to the white settlers in the forest around Johnson Hall had been easy. Their minds were so busy with themselves they saw almost nothing anyway. It was a good game, taking fifteen minutes to stalk them until he was standing next to them, then pulling on their jacket or sleeve. Some laughed in surprise, some cuffed him away in anger; few ever saw him approach—or leave. He had learned that white people focus on what they expect to find; becoming part of what they, themselves, didn't notice made him disappear.

A big table had been set up in front of the house, between the two block houses. Some soldiers, easily spotted by their red coats and tall, pointed caps, stood lazily on guard in front of the house, their rifles stacked in tripods. Servants, and occasionally a red-coated officer, were busy at the table or running back and forth from the house.

Already, the chiefs of the Mohawks and the other Iroquois Nations were gathering in a circle around the fire, some standing and talking, others spreading blankets and furs on the ground and sitting, sachems in front and the war chiefs behind them. Now *Warrahiyagey* appeared from the house and began talking to each group of chiefs. The boy gently lifted himself up from the tree and climbed back down to the ground. He would listen to the talk of the men around the fire. There would be long speeches, punctuated by frequent cries from the People, "We hear!" "We understand!" After the speeches were completed and the Nations had spoken with one voice, the presents would appear. Gold medals, lace-trimmed hats and silver buckles and buttons for the sachems and war chiefs: blankets, kettles, salt, and seed corn for the women; bright hair ribbons, new tomahawks, knives, and guns for the men and, of course, rum. Barrels of rum. By the time the men were all drunk, a boy should be careful not to be seen or found underfoot.

Doyle sat in a creek cooling his aching legs and feet. The creek fed the Tennessee River near its convergence with the Mississippi. On the morning of his twelfth birthday, Joseph Brant had woken him and told him to pack a small fletch for a journey. Joseph Brant, *Thayendanega* to the Iroquois people, was ten years Doyle's elder, his mentor, and a Mohawk chief. Doyle was careful in the questions he asked.

For the past two days he and Brant had been traveling through the far western reaches of lands claimed by the Iroquois but also serving Cherokees and Shawnees as a hunting ground. They had been the snap of a twig or the sudden glimpse of movement in the trees away from deadly encounters with their enemies. Since they had left Johnson Hall, Brant had kept to a killing pace, a mile-eating lope that was more like floating through the forest around them than running in it.

Brant squatted down next to him by the creek bank. "You are wondering why we came here," Brant said, asking Doyle's question for him. "I saw this place in my dream. Here is where you will meet your spirit animal. He's already met you in your dream. You know him; now you need to recognize and understand him. Our journey here was to prepare you for that meeting. You ran past the point of exhaustion, thirst, and hunger without complaint; with a head full of questions, you kept silent; surrounded by our enemies, you were untroubled by fear. I think you're ready."

Brant led Doyle away from the stream deeper into the forest into a sunlight-speckled glen. At the edge of the glen rose a huge, ancient basswood tree. The carved face in the tree was old—very old. The bark had been burned around its edges long ago, but as the tree had continued to age, new growth had scarred over the edges, encircling the mask in a ridge of gnarled burl.

Its metal eyes, the copper now a dull green, stared back at Doyle above a grotesquely large, broken nose. Its mouth was twisted into what Doyle thought could be a laugh—or a scream. It had been washed by countless rains, but Doyle could see traces of its red coloring.

As they neared the tree, Joseph asked, "What do you see?"

"A face. A False Face."

"You are wondering why it is still in the tree," Brant said.

Doyle nodded. "I thought after a False Face is created and brought to life with tobacco, it is cut from the tree and its maker brings it back to the village to join in the healing of the people."

"You understand correctly. But this False Face is different. It was carved by *Tiyanoga*, when he was younger than I am now. *Shagodyowehgowah*, the Healer and spirit of the False Faces, told him to leave it here, that someone was coming who would have need of it."

"And I am that person," said Doyle.

"You are. *Tiyanoga* didn't know when he created it who you would be. He just knew you'd come." Brant reached into his pouch, and took out a deerskin-wrapped bag of corn mush and spread it gently over the mask's lips. He went into his pouch again and took crushed wild cucumber berries and rubbed them as gently over the eyes.

"Bring me firewood," he said to Doyle. Doyle returned with dry twigs and branches. Brant lit a fire at the base of the tree. When the fire was burning strongly, he gave his offerings into the flames: tobacco and dried red dogwood leaves. Lighting his pipe with an ember, he blew smoke into the False Face.

"Sit by the fire," he told Doyle, "empty your mind, and then tell me about your dream." He squatted down to watch Doyle.

Doyle closed his eyes and drifted back to the vision of flying over the Mohawk valley, transformed into the farms, cities, and factories of white men. In his previous dreams, the images had been blurred and distant, as if he were seeing them through a veil of time; now they were clear and distinct. He was *in* that world. He described the dream to Brant as he relived it. Again he entered the bright light and came out into a strange, hostile wilderness empty of people.

"What are you seeing?" Brant prompted quietly.

"First, a speck on the ground in the distance. I'm hungry. It could be food. I get closer and it's a wounded young bird. Maybe a baby eagle."

"What do you want to do right now?"

"I want to save it."

Brant gave Doyle time to come out of his dream, then asked: "How do you feel now?"

"My shoulders are sore."

Brant just laughed. "You have told me what you saw. Who was doing the seeing?"

"I was—and a bird was."

"Was there a difference between you and the bird?"

"No."

"You have met your dream spirit, *aswe'gai,* the hawk. The more you seek him in your dreams, the better he will serve you." Brant paused. "I try to explain how we Mohawk dream to my London friends and they just laugh as if I were a child speaking nonsense. 'That's all very good as far as it goes, Brant. Now why don't you dream up a hot wench for my bed? Or the next winner at Ascot.' So I laugh with them and my fear for our people grows."

"I saw the Mohawk Valley stripped of the forest and inhabited by white men. The People were gone. Is that a true dream?"

"It is my greatest fear. So long as *Warrahiyagey* lives, we are safe. The treaty he has forced the English to accept will preserve our home. But you see the number of English settlers who pass with their wagons through our lands on their way west. We have what they prize more than their souls: land, and the money they can wrench from the land. We will never stand against them in battle. The white death of smallpox they brought with them has killed half of all the People; the black death of rum will do, in time, for the rest. When *Warrahiyagey* dies, and he's an old man, the treaty and our protection die with him."

Doyle was silent for a while. "And what of the rest? The flight to a strange world and the bird I rescue?"

"That you will need to find out from your dream spirit. How do you feel about rescuing the little bird?"

"I want to do it."

"Then that's enough to know for now. White men mock our dreaming because it yields more questions—not the answers they seek. You need to learn to be patient with an important question until the answer becomes clear." He stood up.

"Now give me some pemmican from your fletch. It was hard work bringing you here and I'm hungry." They ate at the base of the huge basswood tree. Doyle felt as if *Tiyanoga*'s False Face was

30

staring at him—evaluating his spirit. When they had finished, Brant kicked out the remaining embers of the fire. "We'll rest tonight," he said. "Then you get to lead us back to Johnson Hall. I hope you know the way." Doyle fell asleep into his dreams. *Tiyanoga's* False Face spoke to him as he slept. "Where are you going? Who will you be when you get there?"

He had no answers.

CHAPTER 5
❧ THE MOHAWK VALLEY 1776 ❧

Susan Doyle heard the knock at her door and looked up from where she had been working on her mending by the fire. Her dog, who would normally have given notice of a stranger's approach, had gotten up and padded to the door. Susan noticed his tail was wagging and his hair lay flat on his back.

She stood by the door, lamp in her hand, and called out, "Who's there?"

"Henry," was the reply.

She slid back the heavy bolt and swung the door open. For close to a year now, she had been latching her shutters and locking the door at night. The dog leaped with joy over her visitor as he entered the room, licking and nuzzling the outstretched hand.

Her son entered the room. She could see that at sixteen, he already had his father's size, confident charm, and piercing dark eyes. He was dressed, as always, like a Mohawk warrior.

"Hello, Mother," he greeted her. "I just returned. *Thayendanega* told me you wished to see me." The Mohawk chief, Joseph Brant, frequently used her son on scouting missions, in spite of his years. The Oneidas called him "Fox who moves without a shadow," and the Onandagas called him "Young hawk who sees many looks." Doyle explained his long absences as hunting trips, although game was now becoming scarce throughout the Iroquois Nation. Susan suspected Brant was using her son to gather intelligence for the war that many felt would drench the Mohawk

Valley in blood. Almost a year had passed since the fighting started at Lexington and Concord then grew into broader rebellion. All along the valley, men were taking sides, and families dividing, often bitterly, in their loyalties.

He entered the cabin, closing the door behind him. His mother's glance darted to his belt, looking with dread for scalps. There were none, she noticed with relief.

"Please sit, Henry," she asked. He settled on the bench near the fire, relaxed, yet poised at the same time. How strange, she thought, not to know one's own son. His father, whom he now so closely resembled that others must have noticed, had been all sunlight and warmth when he had captured her heart. Her son was dark, like a cloud.

"You are becoming a man; the Mohawks already treat you as one. It is time to tell you about your father." She imagined she saw his face tighten almost imperceptibly around his eyes. "As I tell you, please do not judge me too harshly. You have grown up among a good people who loved you. You cannot know the fear of being alone, friendless, without food, facing a winter of starvation. I've told you when I was no more than twelve, my father was killed by marauding Cherokees on a hunting trip with the Mohawks he had befriended. My mother and I were left penniless, with winter coming, and in danger of starving. Sir William provided for us, gave us this farm clear of debt, and helped us survive the winter.

"When I felt the stirrings of womanhood, he came to me. We became lovers." She paused for a moment. I am his mother, she thought, and he's still a boy. Why am I so ashamed? She made herself go on. "I see the look on your face. It was not that way. Sir William has had many women, more than I can think of, before me and after me. Not a one was ever raped or taken against her will. And he has many children. You know John, Guy, and his children by Molly Brant: William, Joseph, the girls."

"And I am another of his bastards," he interrupted harshly.

"I know. I know. Try to see it as it was then. You must feel the desires of manhood now within yourself. In him that desire burns like a fire, unquenchable. How can I tell you this? It draws women to him; I have felt its own flame inside me. In other men, love and lust are somehow separated, just as their spirits are divided and often at war. With him there is no separation—one embraces the other in his nature."

"When I was little, Mother," Doyle answered, "believing what you told me, that my father was a great chief whose name you could not divulge, how deeply I wished my father might be *War-rahiyagey*—Sir William. When I slept, that was my dream; when I woke, that was my prayer. Was he kind to me, when he troubled to notice me? Of course, but he was that way with all the children of the Mohawks—his and everyone else's. It was *Tiyanoga* who taught me as a little boy to hunt and track, to bear myself as a warrior with honor, and to respect *Deganawida's* Great Peace among the Nations. Were I to claim a father now, it would be *Tiyanoga*."

"Henry, please hear me. At Sir William's suggestion, I gave you to the Mohawks to raise so you would have a family. Molly Brant herself adopted you into her clan. But we are white people, not Iroquois."

"No, Mother," he responded sharply. "I am *Haudenosaunee*, the People of the Long House, of the Bear Clan of the *Kahniankehaka*, the People of the Flint and Keepers of the Eastern Door."

"But your father *is* Sir William Johnson. He wishes you to bear his name."

"And will *you* then become his wife? You know Molly Brant. She has managed to ensure that Sir William returns at night to sleep in *her* bed. She would never permit that."

"Nor do I want it." She made herself look him straight in his dark eyes. "You know Samuel Kirkpatrick and know he is a good man. He has asked me to become his wife and I have said yes."

"So whose son shall I become, Mother? One of *Warrahiyagey's* many bastards; Henry Doyle, as the white men call me; or *Okteondon*, my *Haudenosaunee* name?"

"You must choose, as I have. War is coming to this land, Henry. You hear the talk around the council fires. Sir William is old and failing in health. He cannot keep the Nations together. Joseph Brant is telling the tribes to stay loyal to the King. The Oneidas see no other hope than to ally with the settlers who flock into our valleys. Even we English are divided, some loyal to the crown, some bitterly opposed. Nicholas Herkimer and the Tryon County Committees of Public Safety are already talking of rebellion. Samuel Kirkpatrick and I are moving back to Philadelphia to be with his people," she persisted. "Will you come with us?"

"And then, I suppose, take his name?" The bitterness went suddenly out of his voice and his face softened. Some of his father's light shown now in his eyes. "You do what you must do, Mother. I will stay here with the *Haudenosaunee* who raised me. They need me. You and Samuel do not. He is a good man and he will care for you. I am glad of that." He paused for a moment. "And I agree you should leave; the sooner the better."

The Susquehanna
April 1780

Henry Doyle heard the approaching rider coming up the trail toward the Rebel's camp long before he could see him. The rider was walking his horse cautiously. He was well aware, Doyle guessed, of the Iroquois and Loyalist rangers who had been raiding General Sullivan's Rebel army since it left its base camp in Easton and headed north along the Susquehanna River toward the Iroquois villages and rich farms in New York. His dream spirit, *aswe'gaí,* had alerted him to the rider's approach several hours before. Now he waited patiently by the deadfall he had rigged across the narrow trail. The rider came into view. As Doyle expected, it was a dispatch rider, in the blue uniform of regular Continental troops. The rider moved slowly along the trail, alert, Doyle thought, but not fearful, his pistol held at the ready. He had tightened and lashed his equipment so that he and the horse made no sound. Not that that mattered, of course. Doyle had easily heard the other animals in the forest grow quiet as the man approached and passed them. The Rebel might as well have been singing at the top of his voice.

He came to the place where Doyle had arranged the fallen tree across the trail. It looked like an accidental blow down from the trees Sullivan's axmen had cleared to open the trail through the forest. As Doyle had planned, the rider dismounted, pulled a second pistol from his saddle holster, thrust it in his belt, and paused for several minutes to listen. The forest was silent. He then stepped carefully to the left of the trail to step over the tree trunk. Doyle, a few yards away, cut the rope, releasing the deadfall's tension. The branch exploded into the dispatch rider's chest, knocking him to the ground. Doyle sprang from hiding to seize the frightened horse's bridle and tie the horse to a tree. He went back to the unconscious Rebel and felt for a pulse. That worked, Doyle thought. He's still alive.

Doyle picked up the rider's weapons, lifted and tied the rider to the horse. After removing the obstruction from the trail and all signs of the deadfall, he led the horse down a side trail to a small glen a mile away, well out of earshot of the Rebel's camp. He stripped the man naked, tied him to a tree, lit a fire in front of the tree, and waited for the man to regain consciousness. The rider was handsome, in his thirties, Doyle guessed, blond and clean shaven, with surprisingly little body hair. Doyle noticed scars from several wounds on his body.

He watched, with curiosity, as the man slowly gained consciousness and grappled with his situation. He will have no memory of being hit by the branch, Doyle thought. One moment he is in control of his life and future; the next, he is helpless. This man will not enjoy his helplessness. Then the prisoner's eyes found Doyle, squatting on his haunches a few yards away. What he saw was a Mohawk warrior, face fiercely painted in black and red stripes, tomahawk and scalps at his belt. The rider just glared defiantly at Doyle without a word.

He is preparing himself to resist me, Doyle thought. Good. A brave man is easier to reason with than a coward. He walked to the prisoner's saddle bags, took out a pipe and tobacco, lit the pipe with a twig from the fire, then stood in from of him, smoking, regarding the man as calmly as if they had just met in a tavern.

"So, what's your name?" Doyle asked, a friendly smile now lighting his face. He knew the man would be disconcerted to hear flawless English coming from a savage. "Your saddlebag says 'M. Wilson.' Are you called Matthew, or Martin, perhaps?"

Almost in spite of himself, the prisoner replied, "My name is Mark."

"Well, let me tell you how things stand, Mark. When a man is captured as you have been, his first thoughts are confusion and surprise. I watched you search in your mind to understand how you got here. Then the mind tries to deny what the body tells it. It races around, looking for ways to escape what is inevitable. Know that there is no escape and there will be no rescue. No one saw you taken, and no one will follow you here." He paused to allow his prisoner to come to terms with that reality.

"I see you are a warrior who carries the scars of many fights; I am sure you have killed many enemies. Men die in war. We both know you are a dispatch rider, and so you cannot be allowed to live. You know what we do to prisoners. Between the fire and the skinning knife, death can be a very slow business." Doyle watched the Rebel's face tighten. That's helpful, Doyle thought. He knows.

"So the only question you have to consider now, my friend, is how you will leave this life. There is no other bargain to be made between us. You are already dead. Your choice is dying with long, slow pain, or a warrior's quick death. I see you are a brave man, but pain, over time, can strip bravery away from the strongest man until the only thing left is pathetic begging for the pain to stop. It just takes time, Mark, and we have plenty of that. I really would prefer to spare you that disgrace."

Doyle paused again, and stretched the pipe toward his prisoner's mouth. It was so instinctive a gesture that Mark took the pipe, drew in and exhaled a mouthful of smoke, then, in anger and confusion, jerked his head away.

"I'm curious about the contents of your dispatch case, Mark. Oh, by the way, you can call me Henry. I could, of course, try to lift the seal carefully with my knife, and could probably replace it without signs of tampering. But since I intend that these dispatches reach General Sullivan, it would be better that the dispatch case appears still unopened. I'd appreciate your help."

"You know I can't tell you that," Mark cried. "I was just given the sealed case and my orders. I have no idea what the dispatches contain." Doyle caught the note of apology in his voice.

"To be sure," Doyle answered. "But officers talk all the time and soldiers listen. I know the size and strength of your army. I don't mind telling you that there is no notion of opposing you. We haven't the men and can expect no help from Niagara. Our cause is lost here. But I want to alert the women and children of our villages in time to flee to safety."

"The same safety you savages offered the women and children you butchered and raped in Wyoming and Cherry Valley?" Mark snapped back at him. "Those massacres spurred General

Washington to retaliate. You have brought this destruction on your own heads."

"The Mohawks had no part in those massacres," Doyle replied hotly. "That was the work of the Butlers. They are dogs; their actions disgrace their manhood. I spit on them." He turned away to regain his composure. "My people wanted none of this war. We sought to remain neutral. That choice was taken away from us. Now our only hope is escape. I want to buy time for that to happen before your army brings fire and death to our homeland."

"I simply don't have the information you want," Mark replied. Then, looking Doyle straight in the eyes, he added, "If you're going to kill me, just get on with it."

Doyle nodded in silent agreement. "You're right. It's time. I made you the promise of a quick soldier's death. A man's family should know he has been buried properly. When I'm done with my business I'll make sure your body can be found by your troops. Give me something—a password, perhaps—so I can keep my promise."

"For the good it will do you, the password I was given was 'Lafayette and Liberty.' You'll have to decide if I'm telling you the truth."

"I think you are, my friend." With that, he drew his knife, quickly slid it up under the sixth rib into the heart, and held Mark's body next to his until the spirit left it. He cut down the body, buried it, and marked the grave, burning sage as he offered prayers to the four winds, so that Mark's spirit would return safely to the earth. Then he carefully washed his face in the nearby brook, dressed in the officer's uniform, skillfully lifted the protecting seal of the dispatch case, and began to read the papers inside.

The Mohawk Valley
October 1780

Doyle ran back toward the village at full speed, dreading what he might find. He and his Mohawk brothers had been fighting a hopeless, retreating battle against General Sullivan's army of 3,000 Continental regulars and militia. For three months, the Rebels had worked their way north from the Susquehanna, leveling every Mohawk village they had come to. The Mohawks, their crops destroyed and homes torched, fled toward safety in Canada. In the panic to leave, a group of women and children had been left behind, with the Rebels' advance scouts near the village.

He slowed down and moved cautiously as he neared the crest of a small hill overlooking the village. Besides his knife and tomahawk, he was carrying the Kentucky long rifle he had taken from a dead Rebel, two pistols, and a large-caliber Hessian Jaeger carbine on his back. In the village, 50 yards away, a group of four Rebels, all militiamen, had gathered the twelve women and children into a clearing.

"Kill 'em all," the leader, a big, red-bearded man, shouted.

"Even the children?" another asked.

"The children especially," he roared. "Kill 'em before they can breed. But keep this one alive for a while." He grabbed a young girl, perhaps no more than 13, and ripped the front of her shirt open. "Look at those fine little titties, boys. This one will amuse us while we burn the village."

Doyle primed his rifle, rested the barrel on a tree branch, took a breath and shot the leader through his left eye. He dropped like stone, an easy shot at this range. Then, running forward through the trees, he yelled a Mohawk war cry. The startled Rebels glanced wildly around, looking for the source of the shot. Spotting the smoke, one fired his musket in the direction of Doyle's first shot, another at the sound of his cry. By now, Doyle was thirty yards closer, still barely visible among the trees and foliage. He unslung the Jaeger musket. Not trusting its accuracy, he gut-shot another Rebel. Predictably, the remaining Rebels, now panicked, fired again at his new location. Grabbing his pistols and yelling war cries, he rushed them, bounding down the hillside.

One man continued fumbling at reloading his musket, while the other paused for a moment, then dropped his weapon and started running down the trail from which they'd come.

Doyle missed with his first pistol shot, but hit the reloading Rebel in the chest with his second as the man was frantically pulling his ramrod free. Doyle continued to race after the one fleeing survivor, yelling to the women and children to start up the hunting trail to the west of the village.

Within fifty yards he had closed the distance to twenty feet, and without breaking stride, threw his tomahawk with enormous force. The tomahawk buried its blade in the man's back and he dropped like a stone. Doyle paused for a moment over the man's body, quieting his breathing, cupping one ear forward and tilting the other downward, like a deer, listening for sounds of approaching troops. The forest was still silent. He yanked his tomahawk out of the man's back, kicked him over, pulled his knife, and with three quick, practiced cuts, scalped him. Then he scooped out the man's eyes with his knife point and ripped open his britches and castrated him. He'll enter the spirit world blind—and no longer a man.

He paused briefly in the village to scalp the other three, without worrying to make sure they were dead. This will slow down pursuit, he thought. He stripped two of the men of their muskets, ran quickly through the village, scooping up some dried corn and pemmican, then, collecting his weapons, hurried up the trail after the women, pausing only to reload at the crest of the hill.

In under a mile, he caught up with the party, and guided them to a deer trail leading to a waterfall they knew well, about a mile away. After he had armed them and set them on their way with the promise to rejoin them for the trek to the north, he carefully erased all signs of their leaving the main trail.

He ran up the trail to just before it bent to the left, took a shawl he had removed from one of the women and snagged it on a branch where his pursuers could easily see it. Several hundred yards later, he dropped one of the powder horns he'd taken from the Rebels, carved with the dead man's initials. Then he left the trail, covering his tracks as he went, and headed for his rendezvous with the women and children by the waterfall. He felt sure he would never see this village again.

Ft. Niagara, The Western Territories
November, 1780

Henry Doyle stood by the open gate, in the drenching rain, as the last of the Mohawks, almost all women and children with a few elders carried in litters, dejectedly struggled into the British fort at Niagara. They had left a homeland in ruins, burned by the order of the man Washington whom the People would forever after call *Caunotaucarius*, "destroyer of villages."

Doyle sloshed through the mud to the British officers' quarters. The one sentry, huddling under the eaves for shelter, considered challenging Doyle, took a look at the death written in his face and thought better of it. Doyle kicked open the door, and without ceremony or greeting to the British and Loyalist officers in the room, placed his rifle against the wall, threw off his sodden cloak, and walked to the fire to warm himself. He spoke in a low voice, staring into the flames.

"I have brought in all I could find, *Thayendanega*. The old ones who died on the march we buried as decently as possible."

Joseph Brant strode to him and put a brother's arm around his shoulders. "The People thank you, *Okteondon*. But know that this destruction will not go unavenged. The Butlers, Johnsons, and I are planning counterattacks even now, beginning with a raid this winter to punish the Oneida for their treachery. The Senecas under Red Jacket are wavering and will need to be urged to stay loyal to the Crown. We are speaking with the Mingo and Shawnee; their hearts are strong and their young men eager for Rebel scalps. There is much work for you."

"There is no more work for me, here, my brother." He turned and looked Brant in the eye, the anger in his face replaced by a bleakness as cold as the chilling rain outside. "The council fire of the Onandagas at *Kanadaseagea* no longer burns. The people of the Six Nations fight each other, and *Deganawida's* Great Peace is broken. It's over."

"Come with me, little brother," Brant replied. "We must talk together." He turned to the officers around the map-covered table in the room: "Gentlemen, please continue without me." Then, to Doyle, "Can I give you something? Food? Something to drink?" Doyle just shook his head. They walked together to an inner room where the young warrior, in some ways still a boy, in others an old, old man, collapsed into a chair. He had held himself together for days, rarely sleeping, to keep those who depended on him strong. He felt now as if all the life had been sucked out of him.

"No one is more deserving of our thanks than you, *Okteondon*. But even if you do not travel the war path again, there is so much to do here. We have a new nation to build in Canada. The fire of the Nations will be relit. I have promised that with my life."

"You must let me go, *Thayendanega*. You graciously made me one of you. I will never forget the People, or the pride I feel being *Haudenosaunee*, or your friendship, but some part of me burned to ashes in the fires we left behind us."

"But where *will* you go? If the Rebels catch you they will surely hang you, and thanks to the incompetence, laziness, and stupidity of the generals the British have sent here to manage this war—I say this for your ears only—the colonies are lost." Henry nodded in agreement. There might be a chance of holding the west, but British rule in the colonies was over, especially now that the damned French had entered the war on the Rebels' side.

Doyle sat in quiet for a while, Brant respecting his silence. Finally Doyle spoke. "I know my father is Sir William Johnson. I may go to Ireland to find out where he came from. After that, I don't know."

"Then my brother, permit me to help you. Take a day or two to rest, then come to me. There are people in London—Lord Melbourne of the Admiralty and Sir Joseph Blaine come to mind—who would be pleased to meet you and could suggest a number of paths for you to follow. With the letters it would be my greatest honor to write, they will welcome you, and if desired, open doors for you. But know this. I have often thought that there was no more sorrow left in the world for me to know, but your departure will leave a wound in my heart that will never heal."

"And mine," said Doyle, looking up at his friend.

Doyle shut his eyes as the stored-up fatigue and sadness washed over him. Brant waited until Doyle was asleep, draped a cloak from the wall over him, and blew out the candle on the table next to Doyle. The room was dark now, with only the flickering light of the fire's embers playing along the walls. Brant silently left the room and closed the door behind him.

From the Journals of El Habibka
Cross and Christians, end to end, I examined. He was not on the Cross. I went to the Hindu temple, to the ancient pagoda. In none of them was there any sign. To the uplands of Herat I went, and to Kandahar. I looked. He was not on the heights

or the lowlands. Resolutely I went to the fabulous mountain of Kaf. There was only the dwelling of the legendary Anqa bird. I went to the Kaaba of Mecca. He was not there. I asked about him from Avicenna the philosopher. He was beyond the range of Avicenna. I looked into my own heart. In that place I saw Him. He was in no other place.

Rumi

CHAPTER 6
❧ ALEXANDRIA 1804 ❧

Peter Kirkpatrick, newly appointed Master Commander of the United States Navy's *Eagle,* stood on her quarterdeck as his ship cut through the sea's foaming crests toward Alexandria. His body instinctively rolled in rhythm with the Eagle's surge, spray from her bow glistening in the bright sunlight each time she bit cleanly into a wave. A fresh westerly breeze on the starboard quarter drove her at close to thirteen knots.

A man would have to be a brute indeed, he thought, not to feel a certain affection for his first command at sea, however crank she might actually sail. For Kirkpatrick, assuming command of the Eagle was instantly requited love. A Baltimore topsail schooner, built by Henry Spencer with the characteristic sharp ends that gave these famous ships their speed, *Eagle* could out-and-out fly. Her fourteen guns, four long 9-pounders and ten 24 pound carronades, made her the match for almost anything the Pasha of Tripoli might put out to sea—or any other of the villainous Barbary pirates.

The starboard watch had just finished holystoning the deck, washing and flogging it dry with extra care and extra speed, and were enjoying a few rare moments of relaxation before the change of the watch. Kirkpatrick had watched the men at work. They were, he was pleased to acknowledge, a splendidly trained crew after more than a year in the Mediterranean under Dickie Somers, before Somers' tragic death aboard the *Intrepid* in Tripoli harbor just months before. He had died when the *Intrepid,* rigged as a fire ship and sent into Tripoli harbor, had mysteriously exploded, killing all aboard. Now, as Somers' replacement, Kirkpatrick at times felt he shared the captain's cabin with the ghost of his close friend.

Taking command had been awkward. Peter Kirkpatrick, Dickie Somers, and Stephen Decatur had grown up in Philadelphia together and joined the navy at the same time. In 1801, their first year on station in the Mediterranean, Kirkpatrick, along with other American midshipmen, had been rudely accosted by a group of Royal Navy officers. When the insults became more than Kirkpatrick could bear, he called the loudest and most obnoxious of the Englishman an infamous scoundrel and damned liar and knocked him to the ground. Only when cards were exchanged for the inevitable meeting did he learn that his man was a skilled duelist and deadly shot who had stood up on five previous occasions and killed his opponent each time.

Decatur, of course, had offered to be his second. When he met with his English counterpart and was asked to agree to the usual pistols at ten paces, Decatur responded, "Pistols, yes, but at *four* paces." The English officer objected, "Good Lord, sir, that looks like murder, not an affair of honor." Decatur countered, "Not murder, to be sure, but certainly death. Your man is a professional duelist. This will narrow the odds, and the honor will sort itself out when the smoke has cleared."

On the following morning, the English officer, quite unnerved at the pistol staring him in the face just twelve feet away, fired too soon and his shot missed Kirkpatrick by inches. Kirkpatrick held his aim, breathed as Decatur had reminded him, aimed low, and shot his man dead.

Four hours later, the *Eagle,* now sailing broad on the starboard tack, approached the entrance to the eastern harbor of Alexandria reserved for foreign vessels. His gun crew stood ready for the obligatory salutes for the Admiral's flag on a Turkish frigate, the Turkish Viceroy of Alexandria, and the various warships in the harbor, including the *USS Argus,* commanded by Isaac Hull, under whose leadership Kirkpatrick would serve. Looming due south just ahead of them they saw the long mole guarding the harbor, the whitewashed walls and gun emplacements of the Quaitbey Fort to their right, and the imposing minarets of the new Abu El-Abbas Mosque soaring above in the city beyond the harbor.

Kirkpatrick turned to the quartermaster at the wheel. "With this wind, let us have a straight run through the harbor entrance, Mr. Fox, then we'll make for an anchorage north of the Kasr El Teen wharf. The old sewer empties into the harbor south of the wharf, and I want none of that. At low tide you're swimming in offal."

"Aye, aye, sir. Due south it is and nothing off."

The *Eagle* surged proudly through the entrance, then came sharply into the wind to make for her anchorage. In the midst of the pleasure of hearing his nation's flag honored by the Turks and British, Kirkpatrick noted, with instant anger, that his salutes had deliberately been ignored by the French frigate anchored in the harbor. "The devil," he exclaimed. "I'll see him damned for that!"

"Mr. Fox, I believe that Frenchman is blocking our easy passage past the wharf to our anchorage. Steer two points leeward, if you please, and no higher." The *Eagle*'s bow swung to the left as her crew trimmed her topsails to keep them drawing full. "Mr. Fox, what do you make of our heading now?"

"I'd say, sir, that if the Frenchy don't move, on this course we'll split her in two just aft of her catheads."

"Fine," said Kirkpatrick. We'll see what iron these Froggies have in their bellies."

The *Eagle* lifted and drove toward the French ship, for all apparent purposes intending to ram her. Kirkpatrick had the satisfaction, as the distance between the two ships narrowed rapidly, of watching the men on board stare, then point at the American ship on its deadly collision course, then, at the very end, scatter in panic.

"She's slipped her cable, sir!" cried the forward lookout. Sure enough, the French frigate had cut her anchor line in desperation and was drifting sternward.

"Now, Mr. Fox," said Kirkpatrick, "let us shave her bowsprit as close as we ever may and pass her smartly."

"Aye, aye, sir. A two-razor shave it is." The *Eagle* turned ever so slightly to windward to surge past the French frigate.

Kirkpatrick spotted the French captain in the foredeck of his ship, his face red with anger. Kirkpatrick called out. "If we meet again, should you forget to honor our flag, the sound of cannon will announce not a salute, but the arrival of shot and grape. I have had the pleasure, sir, of removing the French flag from the defeated *L'Insurgente* with my own hands. It would be a pleasure to do the same with your fine ship!"

Whistles and catcalls erupted from onboard the *Eagle*, and some of the topmast hands went so far as to expose their buttocks, patting them as they roared in laughter. The crew of a Danish frigate, lining the rails, cheered lustily and waved their hats as the *Eagle* passed. Kirkpatrick's first impulse was to stop the foolery immediately. On the verge of crying out the command, he paused. They need their moment of pride, he reflected. Within a minute, without his bidding, his bo'suns had restored order.

Once safely past the French ship with open water and a good anchorage ahead, the *Eagle* gracefully came into the wind. His men, trained to think with their captain's mind, acted in a practiced blur of superb seamanship, and the *Eagle* glided to a halt, anchors dropping smoothly and sails furled as if she were on parade. That was for you, Dickie, he said to himself.

The *Eagle*'s crew watched as the French frigate slowly spun in the wind and finally dropped anchor in the foul water beyond the Kasr El Teen wharf. Kirkpatrick turned to the officers around him. "Let's see how they enjoy wallowing in shit."

From on board the *Argus*, Captain Isaac Hull and William Eaton had watched Kirkpatrick's arrival. "Well," Hull remarked, "I see Captain Kirkpatrick has joined us, with his usual flair. Make signals for the captain of the *Eagle* to report to the commodore," he ordered. Then turning back to Eaton, "Orders or no, Kirkpatrick would be at my cabin in moments, eager to find out what's afoot and how he can serve. It appears that he was just as displeased by the French captain's disrespect of the flag as we were, although his method of communicating that displeasure was a bit more direct than ours."

"May I take it then," Eaton asked, "that this young gentleman's martial spirit is as consistently fiery as this display to the French might suggest?"

"That would be, at the very least, an understatement," Hull answered. "He is criticized at times for rashness. Commodore Preble kept him close hauled, but not so tight as to destroy his natural zeal and energy—a lesson the crews of the Turkish gunboats he so successfully boarded and captured in hand-to-hand fighting learned to their dismay."

"Then he is a welcome addition to our enterprise, indeed," cried Eaton. "When the issue is a matter of arms and not prating diplomacy, a commander's boldness and unquestioning resolve will carry the day. Give me a man of action, unencumbered by self-doubt, and there is nothing that may not be attempted with good hope of success. His leadership among his men and the dismay he creates in the breasts of his foes are worth more than a division of lukewarm troops! When I was with General Wayne in the Ohio country, fighting the Shawnee, the example he set for his men was worthy of Caesar and Alexander ...."

"I should dearly like to hear of it," Hull interjected, before Eaton could continue. "However, perhaps you will forgive me if I make the ship ready for Kirkpatrick's arrival? It sounds like a tale worth more time and attention than I can give you in this moment. By your leave, sir?"

Kirkpatrick mounted the side of the *Argus* to the ritual skirl of bo'sun pipes and cadenced clatter of Marine arms, saluted the flag and quarterdeck, embraced his fellow officer and friend, Isaac, and bowed respectfully to Eaton. Both men were large, imposing figures: Eaton with the hard physical strength of a former army officer and Indian fighter, Hull already surrendering to the portliness that on more than one occasion had caused his tight regulation britches to split in the midst of hand-to-hand combat boarding enemy ships.

Ducking their heads, the three men crowded into Hull's day cabin. In a ship of the line, the cabin would be called the captain's coach; on the *Argus*, it was more like a donkey cart. Since Hull and Eaton had commandeered the two chairs, Kirkpatrick perched casually on the breech of a carronade.

"Let me share with you, Peter, the notes of my and General Eaton's meeting with Commodore Barron," Hull began. "Our written orders are no different than they have been for months: the *Argus* and *Eagle* are to call in Alexandria and Smyrna to convoy any ships we may find in these ports to Gibraltar and the safety of the open sea. Our secret, unwritten orders direct us to launch a combined land and sea invasion of Tripoli that will restore the rightful ruler Hamet Karamanli to the throne and free the American hostages now held in abject slavery by his brother, Pasha Jusef Karamanli."

"And with Hamet as the new Pasha of Tripoli, friendly to America," Eaton added, "the United States will gain a naval base in Tripoli to support America's growing commerce in the Mediterranean. We will bring this war against the Barbary pirates to a triumphant conclusion and establish America as a power to be reckoned with in this part of the world."

"We will only know what ships will be available once the campaign is launched," said Hull, "but our plans call for a frigate, most likely *Constellation* with her heavy guns, *Argus, Vixen,* and *Hornet.* Since the *Eagle* is reputed to be the fastest boat in the fleet—although I would offer that claim needs still to be proven," he added, smiling at Kirkpatrick, "you, Peter, will serve Mr. Eaton as his naval liaison."

"If I may offer my observations, sir," Kirkpatrick turned to Eaton, then paused to glance quickly at Hull to gauge his reaction, "this plan sounds like the very best thing. I mean no disrespect to Commodore Barron, whom we know is troubled greatly by the illness that has kept him pent up in Malta. But under Commodore Preble we had the Tripolitans on their knees. The passive blockade we have commenced since Preble's departure has given these scoundrels breathing space and rekindled their foolish arrogance. I cannot but think this stroke will dish them for good and all, and allow us to lead Captain Bainbridge and the other hostages out from captivity in triumph! A splendid plan, sir. I am honored to be able to play a part!"

"And I thank you for that," replied Eaton. "If I may say so, America has been brilliantly served by Commander Preble. The enterprise of this judicious and gallant commander has effected astonishment on his foes. With the small force under his command, he has stamped an impression on the Barbary mind that will not be erased this generation and has placed the character of our arms to its proper consideration among the neighboring nations." He paused for a moment, "Excepting, of course, the French. They seem to be somewhat backward in their lessons, as my old teacher would have said. Although," he nodded to Kirkpatrick, "you have taken them to school quite admirably this morning."

Their meeting concluded, both captains watched as Eaton descended the side of the *Argus*, nimbly jumping into the pitching ship's cutter waiting to ferry him back to the wharf. The *Argus's* cutter pulled away, to cries of "Pull lively, now! Put your backs to it!" from Hull's coxs'un. Kirkpatrick turned to his friend.

"If I may be permitted to share a notion that just entered my mind," Kirkpatrick said, "are you troubled, Isaac, that our real orders are merely verbal?"

Hull had already gained a reputation for being a precise, thoughtful man. He considered his response carefully before speaking: "If I may speak frankly, Peter, and intending no criticism of my commanding officer, I for one would have preferred these orders to be written, and that Commodore Barron's support had been less ... well, less tenuous." He exchanged a look with Kirkpatrick. "I fear what is said verbally may be as easily unsaid. We are sailing into dangerous, unknown waters. I trust our compass to be true," he nodded respectfully at Eaton's figure in the now distant cutter, "but I would feel better if we had clear, accurate charts to guide us."

Kirkpatrick, with the easy thoughtlessness of a small boy, stepped on the carronade near them and swung a step up into the rigging, from where he looked down on his friend. "Well, whatever the seas, we are sailors, Isaac. But what do you think Eaton made of me?"

"You mean did he find you rash, impetuous, and wholly ungovernable when you nearly re-opened our recent war with France this morning?" Hull chuckled, then added more seriously, "We both know how you plagued Preble with your headstrong ways, Peter. Another commodore would have broken you or removed you from command. Preble rode you hard, but trusted you to take over Dickie Somers' ship. Have you ever considered why he did that?"

"I wish I knew," said Kirkpatrick.

"Let me venture a guess then," said Hull. "Come off your perch up there and walk with me." Kirkpatrick jumped down easily, and the two captains walked toward the stern of the *Argus* in unconscious harmony with the roll of the ship in the retreating tide. Hull placed his arm gently on Kirkpatrick's shoulder. "My father served with Preble in the Revolution and was imprisoned with him when they were captured together. From what he told me, I suspect that in you, Preble saw an image of himself as a young man. Eaton, like Preble, is a man of action and a careful judge of men's character. It may be that he sees more in you than you can yet glimpse in yourself." Catching the look on Kirkpatrick's face, Hull continued. "If I may be permitted to speak more personally, Peter, I believe a man's father shapes, one way or another, who a man becomes. Every man walks his path in life in his father's shadow. For some—many, I suppose—their father's shadow is always before them. They walk in it, for good or ill. Others turn into the sun and walk away from that shadow; but if they were to look at their feet, they would find the shadow still there and just as securely attached. Is it possible to conceive, Peter, that since your father died shortly after you were born, you are a boy seeking to find your father's shadow in others?"

Kirkpatrick considered his friend's question for a while without responding, then asked, "What about you, Isaac? Where is your shadow?"

"As you know," Hull answered, "my father died while I was still young. He never recovered his full health after the heartless treatment he received in that damned British prison hulk. But I went to sea with my father at age nine, and for five wonderful years, we were together. Much of what I know of the sea, ships, and the men who serve them I learned from him. To answer your question, Peter," he said with a laugh, "my father walks alongside me. He's there when I need him but he's not in my way as I go forward."

CHAPTER 7
❧ PHILADELPHIA 1797 ❧

If the gang of rowdy, ill-mannered boys who followed the young Stephen Decatur—"Decatur's wolf pack"—had been an actual brood of wolf cubs, Kirkpatrick would clearly have been the runt of the litter. A year or more younger than Decatur and two years before his growth spurt would begin, Kirkpatrick was fittingly called "shrimpy," "skinny," and names worse than that—when the boys deigned to notice him at all. Invariably, his attempts to join them caused him to be angrily chased away.

Kirkpatrick lay in his bed, fully dressed, at 9:00 in the evening. As the sounds of church bells across Philadelphia arguing over the proper time faded into silence, Kirkpatrick heard Decatur's rallying cry, the call of a wolf, strong and clear in the night air among the empty streets and warehouses surrounding the navy yard. Doyle darted out of bed, ran to the window, lifted the sash, and let himself out onto the roof below, crabbing rapidly across it until he reached the eaves and could lower himself down to the ground by the drainpipe. He sprinted as fast as his legs could move towards the Philadelphia Navy Yard: the rally point for Decatur's gang. Kirkpatrick ducked quickly through the hole in the fence the boys had opened and hid behind a large pile of discarded cordage where he could see the gang's headquarters— an abandoned cooper's shop. Minutes later, once he was certain all the gang members had entered the shop, Kirkpatrick crept to a gap in the shop's broken siding where he could observe without being seen. This time he was determined to stay hidden and just listen.

Inside, Decatur quieted the happy babbling of the boys around him with a loud "Avast, you swabbies! Hear this! Now hear this! Attend to orders from the quarterdeck!" Decatur hopped agilely on top of an old locker to address his crew. "Tomorrow night we begin with a proper cutting out expedition, as bold and daring as ever taken against the tyrannical English or any other foe. I mean to take the *United States* for my own and run my flag up her mast!" and with that he yanked his straw hat off and waved it above his head to a chorus of cheers. Kirkpatrick listened to Decatur's plan, then headed home as quietly as he had come.

The next evening, Decatur led the gang out of the cooper's shop. Ducking behind buildings and scurrying through shadowed open spaces, they reached the bow of the *United States*, moored to the wharf. The *United States* was one of the navy's newly commissioned frigates, built in the Philadelphia navy yard and launched a week before. She was now in the first stages of rigging, with her aft mizzenmast raised and stepped with its shrouds in place. Even without most of its rigging, the oak sides of the ship rose above them like a dark fortress in the moonlight. Decatur ordered Dickie Somers to reconnoiter the watchmen in their hut twenty yards from the stern of the *United States*; Somers returned at a bent-over run to report that as expected, the two watchmen were well into their evening companionship with a jug of whiskey—with no thought to anything going on outside their hut.

From where he was hidden on the wharf a few feet away, Kirkpatrick watched Decatur and the rest of the boys shinny up the thick hawser of the *United States'* bow mooring line to the hawse hole where the line left the ship. They reached up to the bowsprit fore chains and climbed aboard, Decatur calling "shhh!" to quiet their excited, whispered chatter. When Kirkpatrick was sure Decatur and his gang had all gone aft to the base of the mizzen mast in the rear of the ship, he climbed aboard and hid amidst the piles of gear on deck. Kirkpatrick looked upward to the top of the mizzen mast. It rose to the mizzen top, a broad platform from which the mizzen foremast would be supported. Above the mizzen top, a single temporary spar had been rigged to aid in raising the mainmast in the middle of the ship.

"That's where I will fly my flag!" said Decatur to the boys around him, pointing to the naked wooden spar above the mizzen top, swaying back and forth with the rolling of the ship.

"But Stephen," Dickie Somers objected. "There's no rigging—no shrouds to climb!"

"I care not for that; I'll shinny up it like a monkey," said Decatur, then added, "Somers with me. Perkins—clap an eye on the watchmen's hut and warn us if anything stirs." With that, Decatur and Somers mounted the ladder of mizzen shrouds on the far side of the ship away from the watchmen's hut, and rapidly scaled up to the mizzen top. Oblivious to the movement of the spar as the ship rolled, Decatur shinned up to the peak, then looping an arm over the forward guy rope, pulled off his straw hat and held it against the spar. Yanking a knife from his belt, he drove the blade through the hat brim deeply into the wood. He slid back down to the mizzen top, embraced Somers as they both admired Decatur's "flag," and the two boys scurried down the shrouds, barely able to contain their laughter. When they reached the deck, the rest of the gang broke into loud "Huzzahs!" "Nobly done!" "The finest thing!" as they clustered, cheering, around their leader.

They didn't need Perkins to alert them that their shouting had roused the watchmen. The two watchmen stumbled out of their hut, wooden clubs in hand, looked for the source of the noise, and immediately spotted the boys at the base of the mizzen mast. "Get the hell off that ship, you damned little weasels!" one yelled, "or we'll skin the hides off ye and nail them to the mast!"

Decatur quickly gauged the distance forward to the bow line they had used to board the ship and the now running watchmen and yelled, "Abandon ship. Every man for himself!" He then stepped to the aft taffrail, poised on top for a second, and dove cleanly into the water below, followed with shouts and catcalls by the other boys. "Look y' here, old Deadeye," Decatur called from the water to the head watchman. "Your ship's been captured! If you want to strike her new flag, climb up and do it yourself. We'll come back after you're good and drunk and warp her out to sea!" The watchmen hurled scraps of wood and metal at the boys to no effect, and then settled for curses as Decatur's gang swam to safety on a nearby pier. Kirkpatrick stayed hidden aboard the *United States.*

Kirkpatrick waited until the wharf was quiet again, then made his way aft to the mizzen mast. The wind had picked up, and the *United States* was pitching even harder in the heavier swells. He pulled from his pocket the long winter scarf his Aunt Bessie had given him for Christmas, a startlingly ugly thing of blue, red, and white wool that he had worn only once to school, to the resounding mockery of his classmates. You'll grow into it, Aunt Bessie had cheerfully said as Kirkpatrick had stared at its impossible length. I'd need to become a giant to do that, he'd thought. Winding the scarf loosely around his neck, Kirkpatrick climbed the shrouds to stand on the swaying mizzen main top, grasping a guy rope for balance, the deck now fifty feet below. Above him, the spar reached another thirty-five feet up to Stephen's hat, now gyrating back and forth as the ship rocked. I can't do this, was his first thought. I must, was his second, and he started up. The ascent terrified Kirkpatrick; his arms and legs, shorter than Decatur's, could just reach around the spar, which was getting more slippery as the moist sea breeze increased. Another foot up, he kept telling himself. Don't look down; don't look down!

After what felt like a timeless battle to inch upward, he finally got to the top and saw Decatur's hat, firmly fixed to the spar. Kirkpatrick tried to link his arm over the same guy rope Decatur had used, but realized in a spurt of fear, I can't reach it! He clung to the swaying top, and took a deep breath, forcing his racing thoughts to become quiet. Use the ship's roll! The idea popped into his mind, unbidden. Kirkpatrick unwound the scarf with one hand, squeezed even tighter against the spar, and as the ship's roll pushed him forward, passed the scarf around the spar with both hands—just catching it in time to desperately tighten his grasp as the backward swing of the spar began. Taking advantage of the ship's steady rocking motion, Kirkpatrick hastily tied three hitches around the scarf and snugged it tight against the spar just below Decatur's hat, then paused to recover himself.

He allowed his eyes to lift away from the spar toward the watchmen's hut, now no larger than a doghouse eighty-five feet below him. To his horror, he saw one of the watchmen walk outside the hut. Kirkpatrick froze against the spar. Above him, his scarf gaily danced its full length in the wind. Kirkpatrick was clearly, ridiculously visible in the moonlight. Don't look up! Kirkpatrick prayed. His prayers were rewarded when the watchman stretched, walked to the side of the hut, urinated against a pile of rubbish, and came back inside, never taking his eyes off the ground. With the spar's roll to help him, Kirkpatrick slid down to the mizzen maintop, dropped through the lubber's hole in the center of the top to reach the mizzen shrouds, and descended to safety once again on the deck. A few minutes later, he was racing along the wharf back to the cooper's shop and Decatur's gang.

Kirkpatrick burst into their meeting and strode up to Decatur. "Able bodied seaman Kirkpatrick reporting for duty, sir!" he cried, in as deep and grownup a voice as he could manage, and gave what he imagined was a proper salute, right knuckle to his forehead. He was greeted with jeers from the startled gang. "Did someone fart? I heard a noise." "Look here, Decatur, we really must board up this shack. Any kind of rat or vermin can come in as they please!" "Pop back into whatever hole you came out of, Skinny, and stay there!" "Get the hell out of here, pipsqueak, before we strip you, beat you, and send you back to your Momma, naked and bawling." Decatur just looked at Kirkpatrick in silence.

"What do you mean to tell us, Kirkpatrick?" he asked. The room quieted.

"If you go to the *United States*, now," Kirkpatrick replied, "you will find a broad pennant below your flag. You will recognize the colors."

"The devil you say," cried Decatur. He took another look at the expression on Kirkpatrick's face, then hopped off his perch and ran for the door. "Follow me, boys!" What they saw as they spilled outside the shop was the mizzen mast and spar of the *United States*, majestically rising over the roofs of the surrounding buildings, with Decatur's hat at the peak now bright in the moonlight, and Kirkpatrick's scarf trailing triumphantly in the breeze beneath it.

Decatur was the first to come back into the shop, his face now lit up by a huge grin. The boys crowded excitedly around Kirkpatrick, and Decatur put his right hand on Kirkpatrick's shoulder. He looked Kirkpatrick up and down, then met his eyes. "If that isn't the damnedest thing I've ever seen," Decatur said. "Welcome aboard, shipmate. Welcome aboard."

CHAPTER 8
ᖚ GIRABUB, SAHARA 1804 ᖚ

The long knife whispered through the wall of the tent in which Doyle was sleeping. A shadow, even less than a shadow, slid into the tent and knelt by Doyle's head, watching the relaxed rise and fall of his breathing for several minutes, then laid the razor-sharp knife almost weightlessly across his throat.

Doyle rose slowly to consciousness out of his dream. He had been flying over that same barren wilderness he had seen in his visions as a child. (He now knew that the black, rock-strewn wasteland of his dream was, in fact, the western edge of the Hoggar Mountains that lie south of Tripoli.) Doyle thought in the language of whatever people he was with at the time, but he still dreamed in Iroquois. His spirit bird, *aswe'gaí,* the hawk, had watched the stranger enter his tent, but had sensed no danger and given no alarm. Doyle waited until his spirit consciousness and his body consciousness were one again and he could just feel the pressure of the knife blade on his skin.

Then he opened his eyes, and in the foulest language of the Tuaregs he could manage, greeted his guest. *"Matalid, Dihya.* You certainly do like to play your games, don't you?"

Dihya laughed in return, then threw aside the knife. Clasping his face, she bent down and kissed him with almost angry passion, her long black hair billowing over both their heads like a tent. She pulled away, finally, to catch her breath, leaned back on her elbow, and looked at Doyle intently. He couldn't read what was behind her gaze.

"Let's see what kind of gift you brought me," she said, and picked up her knife again and slit the caftan he was sleeping in from his chest to below his knees.

"Typical," she scoffed, carefully but playfully flipping his still flaccid penis with the flat side of her knife. "Like every *Franzwazi*, all talk and promise but no action. What is this *sujuq sagheer* you offer me after all these weeks of separation? This is not a gift. This useless, contemptible thing is an insult. I would cut it off and feed it to the dogs but they would not bother with it."

"Dihya, my *Tizemt,* my lioness. Perhaps it is because you have not greeted him properly with the ritual kisses of friendship, as the customs of our people say we must do."

"As usual, you worthless *idi,* you make me do the work," she answered, bending over him. "I hope there is life left in this beast. I have a long journey to take and I intend to ride hard to get there."

Several hours later, Doyle woke first from sleep. While they were sleeping, Doyle's servant had quietly slipped into the tent and put fresh water, tea, bread, dates and figs on a table next to them. He looked at Dihya, seeing her, as he always did, with new eyes—as if they had made love for the first time. She lay on her back, her lips slightly parted, the suggestion of a snore puffing her lips as she exhaled. Her hair now tumbled wildly on the cushion around her. She was totally, nakedly, trusting and vulnerable.

His eyes followed the path his tongue often took to the bullet scar on the left side of her chest. He could see the white, raised ridge of the old sword wound on her left leg. She had been named by her people *Dihya Damya* after her ancestor, the "*Kahina,*" the warrior queen who had fought the Arab invasion almost a thousand years before.

When Doyle first joined the *Kel Tamacheq,* the Tuareg tribes-men had welcomed him with the hospitality afforded any Muslim guest, along with the natural curiosity to learn about someone who claimed to be a war leader. He asked and was given permis-sion to join a scouting party of twelve Tuaregs sent to investigate thefts from the tribe's herds to the east. After two days hard rid-ing, they found their quarry, a group of twenty or so Chaaba raid-ers leading a herd of stolen Tuareg livestock. They had left the open desert behind them and entered a tortured landscape of tall, twisted, wind-carved pillars of striped stone. When they spotted the pursuing Tuaregs, the Chaabas clustered facing the Tuaregs about five hundred yards away.

"What do you expect them to do, Joba?" Doyle asked the Tuareg party's leader.

"They are more numerous, Sidi. I think they will want to protect what they have stolen. They will attack us and hope to drive us off." As the words left his mouth, the Chaaba raiders kicked their camels into a lumbering run at the Tuaregs, shout-ing and waving their spears.

As befitting a visiting chief and Sufi Marabout, Doyle had been given a servant for his use. He had taught the boy to prop-erly load his rifles. With the boy next to him, Doyle took one of the three rifles he had brought with him, carefully gauged the wind and elevation, and at four hundred yards, shot the lead-ing Chaaba out of his saddle. Then, firing as rapidly as his serv-ant could reload, he continued bringing down whichever Chaaba surged into the lead. After seven Chaaba had been shot, the charging raiders pulled up, now no more than thirty yards from the Tuaregs. The Tuaregs had watched Doyle's marksmanship with amazement, and then pleasure, shouting triumphantly as yet another Chaaba rider went down.

"Now, Joba," Doyle said, "I think I've evened the odds and taken some of the fight out of them. Let's teach them a lesson."

With that, leaving his rifles with his servant, he unsheathed his sword and led the Tuaregs in a charge after the fleeing Chaaba.

The Chaaba killed or dispersed, Doyle and Joba led the captured herd of camels homeward. "That was impressive, Sidi," said Joba, his eyes above his veil sparkling with pleasure.

"The people I most wanted to impress were the Chaaba. It's not enough to discourage your enemies from attacking you. You need to discourage them from even considering it."

Within a month, Doyle had been put in command of the tribe's fighting men and immediately started training them in European tactics. The first supplies of modern weapons began arriving shortly after. Through it all, Doyle had noticed Dihya watching him at a distance, polite at meals and social gatherings, but no more than that. One evening, after he had been with the Tuaregs for three months, she came to his tent unbidden, dismissed his servant, and sat down beside him.

"You are good at what you do, *M'Touga*," she said, using the clan name he had given the Tuaregs as his. "Let me tell you why I am here. Among the *Imaqzighen,* the ruling class of our people, women choose their men. I have decided to choose you." And that was that. They had been lovers now for almost a year. He watched her gently drift into consciousness. As she woke, he turned to the small of table and poured her a cup of tea. As she drank her tea, she looked at him thoughtfully.

"So, you will serve the Americans. Do you not hate them?"

"Hatred is a luxury, Dihya—actually, a weakness—for someone who kills as often as I do—and need to do. Of course I hate what they did. The Mohawks of my childhood were the strongest of the six tribes of the Iroquois Confederacy. From the border of Canada to the Delaware and westward into Ohio was all Iroquois land, united in *Deganawida's* Great Peace. The American, Franklin, used our form of cooperative government to help design the democracy Americans are now so proud of. But there was no promise, no treaty that would keep the land-hungry American colonists from destroying our towns, burning our crops, and driving us off the land that had been our home before memory. So if Eaton and the Americans die of thirst and starvation in the desert trying to attack Tripoli, or if Pasha Karamanli slaughters them in battle and impales the survivors on the walls of Tripoli, I will shed no tears. No. I don't serve them. Probably better to say that I use them."

"But the killing," she said. "I have killed in the red rage of battle, as have you, but much of the killing you do is without passion. Cold, without mercy."

"I might ask, Dihya, that when you kill in anger, what is doing the killing? You, or your anger? When I kill without emotion, I have no excuse that protects me from my deeds, nor does it matter that the ones I kill are themselves killers, with blood on their own hands. I am the one doing the killing, not my anger."

"You remember that when Ali, son of the Prophet, blessings be upon him, fought with an enemy chieftain and finally disarmed him, he was about to strike the killing blow and the man spat at him. Ali returned his sword to its sheath and spared his enemy's life. His foe asked him: I don't understand. You were about to kill me but when I spat at you in defiance, you stopped. Why is that? Ali said to him, I would have killed you in fighting for the sake of God. When you spat at me, I became angry. Had I killed you in anger, I would have become a murderer. I will fight for God but I will not commit murder for the sake of my pride.'"

"Ah, you Sufis," Dihya laughed. "You can spin anything on its toes. So Ali killed for God, blessings upon Him. What do you kill for?"

"I kill to keep your people free. Let the blessings be on them."

"Well *that* I can understand." She reached across and pulled Doyle back onto their bed. "I accept that you can kill without passion. You had better never make love to me that way!"

They lay among the pillows in bed that evening, a down comforter pulled up against the deepening desert chill. They had been quiet for a while. Men remember their first love, he mused. I also remember my first killing—the Rebel dispatch ride—Mark, I think his name was. Had I spared him, he might be in his fifties now, with children to honor him and perhaps grandchildren at his knee. I buried him with the same respect for his spirit's journey to the afterlife I might have paid to a fallen brother, and kept my promise to let his people know where he was buried. I haven't done that for a long time now.

Dihya stirred next to him. Sensing that she wanted to speak, Doyle turned toward her. She leaned over, kissed him, and asked, "You have loved other women before me, haven't you?"

"Yes," said Doyle. "I have," trusting she would not ask the next, impossible question.

She didn't, but her next question was more painful for Doyle: "What happened to them?"

"You know I don't like to talk about the past," Doyle said.

"I know," Dihya replied, but left the question still open between them.

"There was only one other," Doyle said. "Fatima, the daughter of Tippu Sultan, the ruler of Mysore in India. Tippu defeated the British at Seringapatam and forced the treaty of Mangladore on them pledging England's noninterference with his realm. The British sent me to befriend him, infiltrate his court, and report on his plans. Since I was already becoming well known as El Habibka and both of us were Muslims raised in the Sufi tradition, I was sure to be welcomed; and so I was. Tippu took me in, treated me as a son, and I served him loyally in his struggles for the next few years against the Rajah of Travancore. Meeting Fatima and falling in love with her—it just happened to both of us. Our hearts overruled our heads."

"Or perhaps," said Dihya gently, "her heart and mind were one with yours."

"Well, yes," acknowledged Doyle. "They were."

"And you had no children?"

"She said she wasn't ready. I think she saw what I saw: that the British would not stop until they had conquered Mysore and added Tippu's wealth to their empire. Our child would have been born into a dark, troubled world."

Dihya watched the pain enter his face and waited patiently to let the surge of memories pass.

"I lost my childhood people when the Americans destroyed the Mohawks." Doyle continued. "Who would have thought such hurt could come into a man's life twice? Tippu Sultan was not a saint; he fought to protect his people against the consuming hunger of an insatiable enemy the best way he could. But he was not the monster Wellesley and the British painted him to be, either. For a few years, Fatima and I had a life together."

Dihya paused, but finally asked the next question she knew she must ask, for Doyle as much as for herself. "And you couldn't protect her?"

"No, I couldn't," Doyle echoed, the bitterness plain in his voice. "I knew what forces the British were gathering against Tippu: an army of twenty six thousand British and Sepoy troops of the East India Company with as many from their puppet regimes in Hyderabad and Marathas: fifty thousand men to Tippu's thirty thousand, and all hungry for the spoils from his plundered kingdom."

He looked into Dihya's eyes: "I was played for a fool, *Tizemt*, and took the bait. While I was in Bangladore, seeking to negotiate a last-minute treaty with Wellesley that would preserve Tippu's kingdom, the British and their allies had already launched their attack from Bombay. I went to bed in the evening believing I had succeeded. I awoke the next morning to the sound of drums mustering Wellesley's army to march against Mysore and link up with the forces already besieging the city. When I confronted Wellesley, his explanation was, 'Policy, my good fellow. Policy must trump personal feelings. Don't you see? We needed you out of Mysore before we attacked. You should thank us for that.' Then he dismissed me, just another bothersome colonial gone native."

"And Fatima?" Dihya asked in a whisper.

"I begged her to leave before the war broke out. She knew her place was with her people, regardless of what might come. Of anyone," Doyle laughed ruefully, "I certainly understood that. Fatima died alongside her father when Wellesley broke through the fortress walls and sacked the city. And I was far away, unable to protect her. I was told later that when the British went to bury Tippu and his slain family, a monstrous storm struck: gales of wind and drenching rain fiercer than anyone then alive had ever known—as if nature itself had joined in the grief of his fall. It cannot possibly have been stronger than the storm that raged within me."

"And does that storm still blow within you now?" asked Dihya.

"I don't know. Perhaps it has passed; perhaps this is a momentary peace in its calm center, with the worst yet to come."

"Then, *Igider*," said Dihya, and she drew herself closer to him, "I will ride out that storm with you."

Doyle lay quietly beside Dihya as she settled back to sleep. His vision of Fatima returned. He saw her again, lying on the funeral pyre surrounded by flowers, her death wounds covered by her jeweled robes. I dreamed of Fatima before she died, he thought, on the pyre with her father. I didn't see myself next to her. I was not meant to die at that time. So is this my destiny, now, here with Dihya and her people? Or is something else planned for me? When I try to look into our future together, it is veiled from me. All my life, I have followed the path unfolding before me in my dreams, without concern for where it will finally lead. But the thought of a life without Dihya is terrifying. I have never feared for my own safety. Will my fear for our safety cripple me?

Only when he emptied his mind, allowing his heartbeat to match Dihya's slow, peaceful breathing, did Doyle finally fall asleep. In his dream, he saw a red-tailed hawk that had been circling above them rise higher in sweeping circles and fly west.

From the Journals of El Habibka

Your love lifts my soul from the body to the sky
And you lift me up out of the two worlds.
I want your sun to reach my raindrops,
So your heat can raise my soul upward like a cloud.

Rumi

Chapter 9
❧ Alexandria 1804 ❧

Burton Grey and Sir Samuel Briggs, the British Consul for Egypt, sat in the open veranda on top of the English consulate in Alexandria, located on the *Place Des Consuls* with a fine view of the eastern harbor. The two men were shielded by an awning that provided some relief from the oppressive sun, Briggs in loose, Arab-style linen trousers and knee-length shirt, Grey clearly uncomfortable in his wool suit. "So Grey," Briggs inquired, "What direction can you provide us in working with the Americans?"

"We must, I think, allow ourselves to take the longer view in this," Grey said. "As decisive as Nelson's and Sidney Smith's victories were, and as shamefully abrupt as was Napoleon's abandonment of his army in Egypt, we have merely frustrated, but not stopped his ambitions. The tyrant sees himself the next Alexander, and having subdued most of Europe, like Alexander, he looks eastward toward India. His army may be gone from Egypt, but his agents remain. At present, they maintain a sham neutrality in the struggle for supremacy for Egypt between the Mameluke viceroy and Mohammed Ali's Turks, betting on both horses in the race, if you will. But as soon as the victor appears, they will rush to do him honor and buy his allegiance."

"And as you've informed me," said Briggs, "within the next few months, the French will be sending a prince's ransom, worth perhaps as much as two hundred thousand pounds, to await the

73

declaration of victory between the Mamelukes and Turks. That treasure, I should think, would do better in our hands. May I ask what plans are afoot to relieve the French of this largesse?"

"To be sure, you may ask, Sir Samuel, but I must not respond," said Grey. "We have plans for that treasure which, by your leave, I must keep to myself for yet awhile."

"But, without any intention to correct you," said Briggs, "we have capable agents here in Alexandria, men who know the country and the players in the game. Please forgive what may sound like mere petulance on my part, but it strikes me as a grave error for Whitehall politicos and functionaries to attempt to manage such matters as this from afar, knowing nothing of the local situation. It is not policy; it is mere meddling."

"Meddling, you say? Meddling? Indeed," Grey snapped back. Briggs recoiled from the sudden anger in Grey's eyes. "Perhaps you should reconsider before tarring me with that brush," Grey retorted. I have been called many things, Sir Samuel. A meddler in matters I do not understand has not been one of them."

"A thousand pardons," quickly replied Briggs. "Surely I meant no offense to you personally, none at all. It was merely my zeal and loyalty to our cause that was speaking. But this is an ancient part of the world, deep in its cunning and treachery—a very pit of vipers. I have seen it consume both the well intentioned dreamer and the impetuous fool, bringing their plans, and often their lives, into ruin. Will you not share with me at least the broad outlines of what you intend so that you might benefit from the knowledge I and my people might contribute to its success?"

"In due time and measure, Sir Samuel. But might I observe that where you know, you are usually known, as well? In a place like this, where the very breezes that bring us comfort here on your veranda seem to carry our words—and even our thoughts— wherever they blow, a secret is that thing that is known to one man and shared with no one else. The same intelligence that brought us word of the French treasure bound for Alexandria has also hinted at leaks within your organization. However staunch your own loyalty and fervent your zeal—I have no doubt of either, to be sure—your work is carried out by men for pay, and what gold can buy, gold can corrupt."

"Damn me, sir," Briggs interjected. "Without meaning to instruct you in your duty, if you have knowledge of treachery in my organization, should you not tell me?"

"Specific information, no," Grey said, and sat back in his chair dismissively. "But there is, how shall I say it, an odor of betrayal, a whisper attaching itself to this business, that I suggest we heed. I pray you see things from Whitehall's perspective. I will confess there are grand plans launched in London that turn out to be chimeras—the worst kind of enthusiasm based on utter ignorance. At the same time, I am sure we have both seen clear and sensible strategies fail of their purpose when they are executed by self-interested, unprincipled men. That, too, is an old story. Difficult as it may be, I beg you will allow us, absent the comfort of knowledge, to proceed in trust. But there is a second matter to discuss, and that is our support for Eaton and his Tripolitan adventure."

"Indeed," said Briggs. Hardly a discussion, he thought, his temper heating beneath his carefully polite outward expression. He lectures me like a schoolboy. Damned pragmatical, absolute little shit. Briggs rose, went to his desk, and pretended to look through papers while he let Grey stew in his chair. Finally, after several minutes, Grey coughed impatiently. Briggs looked up at him over the rim of his reading glasses.

"I might say that trust is a road that runs two ways," said Briggs, "I will have to trust that you know your business, and as it turns out, mine. But as to the Americans, frankly, it is hard to know what to make of them. To be sure, under Preble, they did display a surprising degree of courage and resolve, but all that in the balance, they are still a third rate power."

"They may prove a useful annoyance to the French in their machinations in Egypt," Grey said, "but we have another, perhaps graver concern in Tripoli, and that is Pasha Jusef Karamanli. His imperial ambitions are lesser in scope than Napoleon's, but just as strongly felt. The American's attacks and blockades have merely demonstrated what all will soon recognize: the days of unchecked Barbary piracy are over. That means Pasha Karamanli needs other sources of revenue to ensure his hold on his kingdom and avoid being deposed and strangled by his own subjects. That source is slavery."

"If I may be allowed to contribute some information," Briggs interjected, interrupting politely, "Pasha Karamanli has already begun by subduing the Awlad Sulayman tribe of bandits that had controlled the roads to Fez and replacing their sultan with his creature—Mohammed al-Mukni—who has doubled Pasha Karamanli's profits from slaves and gold dust from the south. We believe Pasha Karamanli intends to conquer all of North Africa and gain a monopoly on the entire slave trade."

"Yes, yes, of course" said Grey, waving his hand as if to brush away Brigg's words. "The French would happily support him in that venture, had they the means. An alliance between Napoleon and Pasha Karamanli could be devastating, especially if the French-Spanish fleet under Villeneuve gains ascendancy in the Mediterranean. It would suit our purposes nicely should the Americans succeed in deposing Pasha Jusef Karamanli and replacing him with a pro-American puppet—his brother Hamet—especially if we show ourselves to be America's friend and continue to fan their distrust of the French.

"And what news is there of Villeneuve?" Briggs asked, deliberately changing the subject to give himself time to think. "We heard of the escape of his fleet from Toulon, and nothing since."

"More words in the wind, I'm afraid." Grey said. "When I left, London was in a frenzy over daily rumors that Villeneuve's fleet had been spotted in the Channel, on its way to support Napoleon's invasion of England from the Low Countries. It is the Armada all over again, with alarm bells ringing and signal fires set ablaze at each new sighting of the Portuguese fishing fleet or the emergence of a low line of clouds to the south. Less excitable heads say that Villeneuve, with Nelson in hot pursuit, means to draw us into an unequal fight on Villeneuve's terms, where the combined French and Spanish fleets, with their advantage in ships and weight of metal, will prevail over Nelson's cunning. We must wait, I fear."

"And *trust*, I suppose?" said Briggs, allowing the irony to color his question. "Well, as to the Americans, may I assume that we are to give them as much support as we can, without seeming to take sides with either the Turks or Mamelukes?"

"In so far as your judgment deems appropriate, Sir Samuel."

"But can you assure me that Government, at least, is firm in their backing of the American's designs on Tripoli?"

"I can tell you Admiralty is. There are certainly others with power and influence, including the Sovereign, who wish nothing more than the restoration of the colonies to English rule and view Americans as no more than traitorous rascals to be frustrated and balked at every turn. For them, any increase in American power or prestige would be a very unwelcome outcome. So you must rely on your discretion."

"I see. If you will permit me to speak plainly, I understand I am to support the Americans without appearing to support them and ensure their success so long as they are not truly successful— while also frustrating the French without appearing to take sides in Egyptian affairs. And all that at the peril of my own reputation? Damn me, sir, but had such a message been conveyed to any Pasha or Dey in the Levant, the messenger would have been instantly impaled."

"Which is why, Sir Samuel, we must always be glad we serve a constitutional monarchy and not the Turks." Grey allowed himself a small smile. "You have the latest ciphers. As soon as I have information I believe I can share with you, count on me to do that." With that Grey rose. "I think we draw near the hour of your meeting with the Americans. They must not see me here. Might there be a place from which I could listen, unobserved?"

"I will meet Eaton in my private study. There is a long balcony outside the windows of the study. I should think from there you could overhear everything." And roast in the sun while you're doing it, Briggs thought with quiet pleasure. "I will have a servant take you there."

CHAPTER 10
❧ ALEXANDRIA 1804 ❧

A few minutes later, Eaton arrived at the consulate, to be warmly greeted by Briggs. "A pleasure, sir," Briggs said, his normal open cheerfulness restored by Grey's departure. "Might you join me in my study?" Briggs led Eaton upstairs, past the obligatory portraits of monarchs past and present looking down from the walls, along a dark, narrow hallway toward his private quarters. He opened the door to his study and gestured for Eaton to enter. The room, perhaps twenty feet wide and nearly as deep, was a delightful surprise—an explosion of light, actually, streaming into the room from two floor-to-ceiling French doors letting out to a balcony. The doors were open, covered by lace curtains now stirring with the seaward breeze just beginning to bring relief from the mid-day heat.

One learns a lot about a man from the space he retreats to and the objects that give him comfort, thought Eaton. This is no antiquarian's cluttered study nor a recluse's dark retreat. He paused to admire the rich carpet they were standing on by the entrance. "I am an amateur when it comes to carpets, Sir Samuel, but may one say this is quite splendid? True Persian *Bahtiyar*, if my eyes do not deceive me?"

Briggs allowed himself a smile of genuine pleasure, and then pointed to the carpet under his desk near the back wall. "I'm rather fond of this one, too," he said. "Sixteenth century *Lician*."

Eaton admired the rich patina and intricate latch hook medallions of blue, dark wine red, ivory and earth tones. "The finest thing!" he exclaimed. "Would I be correct in saying that particular deep terra-cotta hue marks it as a *Yoruk?*"

Briggs nodded his appreciation. "You would be right. If I may be allowed a philosophical observation, I would say the freedom of these people finds its expression in the subtly of the design. I suspect that's why it so appeals to me."

Eaton's eyes travelled to an elaborately carved low table on which Briggs had carefully arrayed a few choice treasures. "The table I recognize—Moroccan, surely—I would say from the Atlas Mountains?"

"*Amazigh*," Briggs affirmed. "But tell, me," he said, walking over to the table and picking up a silver amulet on a chain and handing it to Eaton: "What do you make of this?"

Eaton lifted the amulet, a hinged oval box nine or ten inches wide on a three foot chain, to let the light play across the turquoise stones and silver intricate filigree. "Astounding," he smiled.

Briggs answered the question in Eaton's eyes. "It's an equestrian Koranic amulet. *Bukharan*, I believe. It would be worn around the neck of a horse in wedding processions, with appropriate passages from the Koran inside to bless the fortune of the bride and groom."

Eaton held it closer, to admire the detailed silverwork, gently placed it back on the table, and looked around the room at the other objects hung on the walls. "I could spend hours here, Sir Samuel, enjoying your collection." He turned to a sword, hanging on the wall next to them, with gold overlay on the blade and a finely carved ivory handle, and studied the inscription on the blade. "If I can make it out, the inscription seems like a *tughra*," he shifted the angle of the blade for a better look, "for Sultan Mahmud II." He read the Arabic: "*Mahmud Han bin Abdulhamid mazaffer daima:* Mahmud Khan, son of Abdulhamid is forever victorious."

"As, in their imagination, are all conquerors and despots," replied Briggs. "I hang it here as a kind of *momento mori*— a reminder of the brevity of our lives and the futility of our dreams. But come. I know you have matters of concern to discuss." He led Eaton to two chairs away from the windows with glasses and a bottle of wine on a small table next to them. "Let me offer you some hospitality and explore how we may be able to assist you."

As they relaxed in their chairs, Briggs began. "Mr. Eaton, I would be most pleased to afford you and your staff the welcome and courtesies of my consulate here, should you need a base of operations. Our friendship is already well known to the French, and they are spending money quite liberally to frustrate any attempts you might make on Tripoli—so your public presence here can only add to their current truculent state of mind. Although, I must say, yesterday's amusing episode with the French frigate, which I had the distinct pleasure of watching from my balcony, cannot but have put them in even fouler humor, if that were possible."

"I have long thought, Sir Samuel," Eaton replied, "that any moment spent frustrating or irritating a Frenchman was time well spent. To our purpose, however. If I may be permitted a summary to supplement what Mr. Grey may have told you, Washington has pledged a thousand stand of small arms, some field artillery, and $40,000 on loan to Hamet. Our attack will be a coordinated effort involving a combined force of Hamet's allies, mercenary troops hired in Alexandria, and American sailors and Marines, all supported by the firepower of the navy.

"I have it on the best confidence," Eaton continued, "that the loyalty of Pasha Jusef Karamanli's Turkish and Bedouin troops is secured by the slenderest of threads. Like the Scottish usurper in Shakespeare's play, Pasha Karamanli's borrowed robes now hang upon him like a giant's clothing on a dwarfish thief. The least push, if sustained resolutely, will unseat him and bring the disaffected flocking to their rightful ruler's banner."

With an appreciative laugh, Briggs broke the silence that followed Eaton's outburst. "Would you permit me to observe that you Americans are quite astounding? This part of the world, so old in its history and beliefs, has never seen anything quite like your energy and dash. I beg to repeat my congratulations on the service you have so far rendered your country, and the hair-breadth escapes you have had in setting a distinguished example. Your bravery and enterprise are worthy of a rising nation. If I were to offer my opinion, it would be that you have done well not to purchase a peace with the enemy. A few brave men have, indeed, been sacrificed, but they could not have fallen in a better cause. And I even conceive it advisable to risk more lives rather than to submit to terms which might encourage the Barbary States to add fresh demands and insults."

"Very kind. Very kind, indeed," Eaton replied. "I fear you do us too much honor. We are a young nation sprung out of a new, boundlessly fertile soil, yet we come from sound and true English stock. But compliments aside, could you, in all goodness, tell us how things now stand in Alexandria?"

"It is all at sixes and sevens, large wagers placed but no flow to the game," Briggs said. "Nominally, of course, Egypt is still ruled by the Sublime Porte, and the Ottomans have certainly not relinquished their claim to sovereignty. But Napoleon's devastations, followed by our successes, have utterly weakened any actual control the Ottomans might have. Now Egypt is like a scrap, and a poor one at that, over which fierce dogs fight. I tell you in all frankness it is at odds over which side will prevail, the Arnaut Turks led by Mohammed Ali—Albanians, actually, not Turks at all—and the Mamelukes. And this is not a gentleman's fight. The Mamelukes, at present, are quite out of sorts over the murder of many of their leaders by the Turkish Admiral, who invited them on board his flagship to discuss peace then sent them to eternal peace in paradise by means of the strangler's cord."

"That comes as no surprise," remarked Eaton. "Nothing can be more fluctuating and capricious than the government in this country, except the disposition of the slaves over whom it dominates."

"And the population does suffer," Briggs continued. "Between starvation, floods, and the Turks, I do not wonder but that the Egyptians must believe Moses has reappeared with his plagues. And now the man who would have played Pharaoh has fled back to France with his tail between his legs. At the very least, you will need to meet and charm over the Turkish commander here. Given the opposition of the French, some gifts will, of course, be in order. I share with your government the belief that tribute money is a poor expedient in achieving safety for one's merchant shipping. But bribery, well, bribery is the coin of the realm throughout the Mediterranean, followed closely by flattery—the more fulsome the better."

"So I have found, myself," Eaton said. "Like Cassius with Caesar, when I tell a Dey or Pasha I admire him because he hates base flatterers, he says he does, being then most flattered. For our purposes now, while I am uncertain about Hamet Karamanli's whereabouts and status, it seems inevitable that he will need a *firman* granting him safe passage out of Egypt before he may think of setting foot on his soil."

"We might be able to help in the matter of locating Hamet, although joining forces with him may well prove troublesome." Briggs responded. He arose from the table, walked to a window overlooking the harbor, and paused for a while. Grey would have me feign support for the Americans, Briggs thought—and deceive them. That's the strongest argument for doing the opposite. If I must trust a man, it would be Eaton.

"I wonder," Briggs said, turning back to Eaton. "Would it be too presumptuous of me to offer a suggestion? Now is the hunting season, and while civil war rages around us, Europeans are able to maintain the pretense of civilized pursuits. What would be the outcome, do you think, of my offering you and some of your men the diversion of a hunting expedition up the Nile? Birds abound at this time of year, and it is not inconceivable that one might encounter an African lion or two. You could proceed to Rosetta, below Cairo, accompanied by my aide, Captain Vincents. He has received the same information about your intentions as I have, and I trust you will find him a frank, open-hearted, generous soldier, quite in harmony with your desires. From Rosetta, with his assistance, I do not doubt you could arrange to secure *marches*, river craft quite like the *dhows* one sees here in Alexandria, to take you up the Nile to meet with Hamet."

"Perfect! The very thing," cried Eaton. "We are settled then." He rose to make his departure, taking Briggs' arm as they headed to the door." Sir Samuel, I cannot properly express my gratitude for your assistance, but I am sure of its consequence: confusion to Napoleon and defeat for his creature, Pasha Jusef Karamanli."

Having shown the Americans out, with the warmest professions of support, Briggs returned to his study to find Grey waiting for him, collapsed in a chair. Grey had taken off his coat and was fanning himself with his handkerchief. "So," Briggs said cheerfully, "I trust you were able to overhear our conversation."

"I almost died of the damned heat. I stood it for ten minutes and then had to leave the terrace. You might as well have placed me in an oven."

That was my intent, Briggs thought. "How unfortunate," he said. "But you have spent time with Eaton. Pray tell me what you think of him?"

"I tell you what it is. When it comes to Americans, I try not to think of 'em at all. What a universally smug, unmeritoriously arrogant, graceless pack of garrulous non-entities it is! As if their twenty-five years of contentious existence had elevated them to the rank of first among the great nations of the globe. What did Dr. Johnson say? 'Rascals, robbers and pirates. They are a race of convicts and ought to be thankful of anything we offer them short of hanging.' They have, some of them at least, mild pretensions to learning and the outward show of culture. But as for ever encountering an American gentleman in the true sense of the word, I think one would have a better chance meeting up with a unicorn, a hippogryph, or some fabulous creature from the Arabian Nights. No, Sir Samuel, unless compelled by my duty to the Crown, on my own devices I should never choose to speak with an American, game with one, drink with one, and most certainly never dine with one of 'em."

"Permit me to say," replied Briggs, the politeness gone from his voice, "while we are in a life and death struggle with the Corsican, we *must* look to assist them, the bellicose speeches by some of our Lords in Parliament notwithstanding. I had the less than pleasurable experience of fighting against Americans in the War of Rebellion. At first, they were little more than rabble; a joke, actually. We crushed Washington at New York and Long Island early in the war. We would have squashed the entire insurrection at that point had not General Howe been a poor copy of his brother the Admiral. General Howe was more interested in conquering Mrs. Fanshaw's resistance to his advances than the Rebels. We let them off the hook, and in time, the Americans learned how to fight us—and beat us. Saratoga was no joke. Neither was Yorktown."

"Tut! Tut!" injected Grey, waving his hand as if brushing away a bothersome insect. "What is next? Washington, who won but one small skirmish on his own at Trenton in five years of war is now to be cried up as another Alexander the Great? Yorktown wasn't a joke; it was sheer folly on the part of Cornwallis and Graves."

"That may be as it is," said Briggs, "but we lost the war. And to speak plainly, I fear war between England and America will come again. Our navy's insatiable hunger for more trained, skilled seamen for the French war will bring us to blows with the Americans sooner or later. I, for one, will rue that conflict. Savages they may be, if one is of Dr. Johnson's mind, or damned traitors, as some of our Tory leaders insist. But I agree with Eaton: if England were to find a loyal ally in this world, it must be America." He glanced at Grey to gauge his response. I might as well be talking to the Sphinx, Briggs thought. He shrugged his shoulders. "So then, if you would, pray tell me, Grey, what *you* make of the American's plans."

"Audacious, or fool-hardy—with Americans one doesn't know. Americans will passionately cry up a war before it is declared; they have yet to demonstrate the stomach to sustain war until victory has been won. So whether Eaton's plan has the full backing of government in Washington remains to be seen. President Jefferson launched this war in 1801. For the first years, it languished in half-efforts carried out in a desultory fashion, with the blockade of Tripoli as its only accomplishment, and a meager one at that. Americans cry 'millions for defense, but not one penny for tribute.' They have, in fact, already spent almost a million on a poorly conceived, poorly conducted war, thousands of miles from their homeland, without anything to show for it. To be sure, they halted attacks on their shipping by the corsairs, but they would need a much bigger fleet to effectively blockade Tripoli's commerce. When the news of the disaster of the *Philadelphia* arrived, it had the effect of turning the murmurs appeasement into a shout for peace from the anti-Jefferson party within their Congress. Then just when the clamor was shifting opinion toward conclude the war, Preble arrived on the scene, destroying the *Philadelphia* and relentlessly hammering Tripoli with naval bombardment, as you so—ah, graciously acknowledged in your comments to Eaton."

Grey went to the sideboard and poured himself a glass of sherry. "The Americans, in their ignorance, cannot conceive of how close they were to gaining the release of their prisoners had Preble remained in command. Now Preble is gone, to be replaced by Barron, whose resolve is still untested. The cry for appeasement and a peace treaty to free Captain Bainbridge and the other unfortunate prisoners will be heard again in many quarters, not the least being among the supporters of the Secretary of State, Madison. He has his eye squarely on the presidency when Jefferson's current term is over. If *anything* is hanging by a slender thread, it may well be Jefferson's continued support for this war."

"Little good can come of it when politicians play at war," Briggs replied. "But this scheme, so outlandish on the surface and so ill-conceived in its support for Hamet, whom I am sure you will agree is the worst sort of self-indulgent weakling, may yet succeed—because of Eaton. I have conducted my own inquiries into his history and character. We would do well to take him seriously, and so should the French, and so, especially, should Pasha Jusef Karamanli. We have much to learn about Americans, but if you will forgive me, I believe we need to start seeing them as they are, faults and strengths weighed all in the balance, and not as a rabble of debased Englishmen. This Eaton exemplifies that principle. From humble beginnings, he put himself through school, mastering French, Greek, Latin, philosophy, and mathematics in the process."

"And acquired a highly irritating fondness for punctuating his oratory with quotations from the Bard, I might add," retorted Grey.

Ignoring Grey, Briggs continued. "He has served both as a regular infantry officer and a scout—one might more properly say, a spy—in General Wayne's successful war against the Indians in the west, where by all accounts, he added any number of savage languages to his linguistic skills. His service as the American consul to Tunis equipped him to negotiate effectively with the various Muslim factions here in North Africa, Turk, Mameluke, and Arab alike—which negotiations, I might add, are carried out in capable Arabic." He added as an afterthought, "You do not speak that language, I believe."

Grey's look revealed his answer: why should I?

More for his own sake than any attempt at changing Grey's bias, Briggs continued: "America finds ways to use a man like this. It could be said that when we English find an officer of bold enterprise, like Sir Sidney Smith or Cochrane, we disparage and seek to ruin him—precisely because he does not act as an English gentleman *should*. Let us not forget that had Nelson's audacity not carried the day in Aboukir Bay and Copenhagen, he would have been censured, perhaps cashiered. Perhaps even, like poor Byng, shot *pour décourager les autres,* if I may be permitted to change Voltaire's gibe. Who knows? The Americans may tire of this venture yet. But I believe that if anyone can pull off so improbable a mission, Eaton is the man for the job." Briggs rose and walked to the door of his study, indicating that their conversation was finished, and paused by the door. "You have your work to do. I will attend to my business. I bid you good day."

CHAPTER 11
⮞ THE NILE 1804 ⮜

Thanks to Sir Samuel Briggs' generous support, within a week Eaton and his party were afloat upon the Nile, headed south toward Cairo and their eventual meeting with Hamet Karamanli deep in the Egyptian desert.

The first boat carried the Americans under their own flag. The party consisted of Eaton, Kirkpatrick, one of Hull's midshipmen, George Mann, and an American Marine lieutenant, Presley Neville O'Bannon. They were supported by six servants, all hand-picked for their reliability and skill with musket and sword, a dragoman named Ali, and Eaton's mysterious janissary, Katir Al-Hareeq.

They were escorted by a second boat flying the British flag, commanded by the British consul's secretary, Captain Vincents, a bluff, no-nonsense infantry officer, and an equally well-armed group of soldiers and servants. At Vincents' suggestion, in addition to muskets, pistols, swords, and a plentiful supply of ammunition, they had equipped each boat with two 4 lb. swivel guns.

Kirkpatrick had, naturally, been put in charge of their *marche*. He found the boat sailed easily enough with its low draft and single huge lateen sail. Small wonder, thought Kirkpatrick, since they've had thousands of years to perfect how to navigate this river.

Each bend in the wide river was a new discovery as they sailed past wheat and sugar cane fields, already blooming in the rich black silt from the spring's flood, the deep brown of palm trees lining the river, with grey rolling hills and desert always in the distance. Every few miles they passed small, dun-colored villages, mean and depressing in their poverty, the villagers crowding the river bank to gape at the strange flags and unfamiliar travelers.

Once, when they pulled close to a small town, somewhat larger than the villages they had passed, the people, accompanied by the evilest half-wild dogs Kirkpatrick had ever encountered, crowded around their boat, crying out and begging for alms. Later, Ali their dragoman explained to Kirkpatrick that they had been calling for the English, for the love of God the Merciful and Compassionate, to return and take control over the country and free them from the terror of the Turks.

Three days into the voyage, just before they reached Cairo, they watched from two hundred yards off shore as a large band of Arab bandits methodically looted a village of its camels, buffalo, and cattle as its people cried piteously for mercy and aid. From inside the village they could hear high-pitched screams that grimly suggested the Arabs were not limiting their depredations to robbery. At the general's suggestion, seeing a huge flock of ducks ahead of them they and the British boat following them discharged several volleys from their muskets and even a round or two from the bow swivel guns in the general direction of the birds. The birds rose with an immense clamor, momentarily darkening the sky. The display had its intended effect on the marauding Arabs, who let them sail on in peace. Only after their flotilla had passed did the Arabs take to their boats to begin robbing the river craft that followed them.

As the slow, sun-drenched days unfolded, Kirkpatrick found himself drawn to Lieutenant O'Bannon. They were both of an age, with the same unquestioned confidence in their ability to act decisively and to lead men into danger. In contrast to his quick temper, Kirkpatrick found O'Bannon's Virginia-bred charm and easy manner disconcerting at first then irresistible. It would be as hard to be angry around O'Bannon as it would to be afraid.

"So, Peter," O'Bannon asked one evening as they prepared their evening bivouac ashore. "What do you think of our mysterious companion, the general's janissary Katir Al-Hareeq? It doesn't help that he muffles himself in his burnoose so that one can see little more than his black eyes, but I, for one, find him unfathomable. I tried my French on him to no avail. It got little further than 'The sun is very hot today,' 'The boat swims quite fast now,' or 'How does one call that strange beast over there?' but of course, I couldn't make sense of his response."

"You're right about his French, Presley," said Kirkpatrick. "It's execrable. But I notice him and the general deep in conversation when we stop at night, away from the others' hearing. I'm quite at a loss to imagine what language they are using unless the general converses in Arabic or Turkish. Then there's this other thing about him. I awoke at first light this morning and couldn't get back to sleep, so I went for a walk. You remember where we camped last night with the palm trees above us on a bluff? Well, I climbed almost to the top and there I found him, in the grove of trees, alone, doing what looked to be a slow, sustained dance. At times his postures looked like he was grasping or repelling some enemy I could not see—although I would swear *he* saw him. At times he looked for all the world like some animal or bird—a stork, perhaps. I forgot all about myself and just watched him. I was spellbound. When he finished, in a posture I might imagine to be one of prayer, he walked back to camp—right by me. When he passed me, he just smiled at me—not with his face, to be sure, because of his veil, but with his eyes. He looked straight into me." Kirkpatrick shook his head. "The damnedest thing, Presley. I wonder what he saw."

"He is, sure, a strange creature," said O'Bannon. "But I tell you what it is about him. Al-Hareeq is a deadly shot. You remember the other day when we were potting crocodiles along the bank for sport—you had your eyes on the river. By signs and grunts, mostly, he let me know he would fancy a wager for the best out of five, but firing at the crocodiles *in* the water, when only their eyes and snouts are visible. So we set about it, with Ali loading for us. I am no slouch with a musket, but he beat me four to five, and each of his was a clean kill. It cost me a fine dirk of German steel. But it gets more interesting than that. You know the Kentucky rifle I brought aboard, a gift from my father-in-law Daniel Morgan, the Revolutionary War General. In the politest way, given our limitations in communication, he let me know he would like a try with it. Feeling I owed him the favor, I let him take a shot. He picked it up, readied and loaded it as if he'd handled such a weapon all his life, then, as easy as kiss my hand, raised it and killed a small animal, a fox perhaps, some one hundred yards away. A fine shot."

"An enigma," agreed Kirkpatrick. "But have you seen him practicing with those throwing daggers of his? He and the general were taking odds with tomahawks and knives at thirty feet. There was no advantage between them. Katir Al-Hareeq's a man I would not want on my bad side, or at my back. Bad French or no, I greet him with a hearty *bon jour* each morning."

"Well, enough of him for now," said O'Bannon, looking over to where their servants had been setting up that evening's camp. He went into their cabin and returned with his bedroll and pistols, checking the pistols' priming before placing them in a bundle to carry ashore. "It appears from the aroma that Ali has been successful with those fine perch he caught today. A bit of that fish and some of Consul Brigg's estimable wine would settle my spirits most admirably."

Doyle and Eaton had gone to a knoll beyond earshot of the rest of the expedition, now gathered in small groups around the evening fires on the bank of the Nile. The last rays of sunset that had flamed across the western sky like biblical pillars of fire now began to paint their faces in soft violet light. Out of respect for Eaton, Doyle had removed the veil from his face.

Eaton's years in government service in North Africa had made him a helpless coffee addict. So he was especially gratified to learn that his janissary insisted on preparing coffee for himself and Eaton the traditional, thrice-boiled Arab way. Doyle ground the beans—the finest Yemeni and Ethiopian blend—boiled the dissolved sugar, added the coffee and cardamom seeds, then poured the finished mocha into the intricately carved *finjans* he had brought with him. As they drank their coffee, the general regarded Doyle thoughtfully, Doyle sitting quietly and easily under his scrutiny.

"I would not presume to open the chapters of a man's life unbidden," Eaton began, "or pry into the secret recesses of his past. Yet you said something when we first met, a reference to the Wheelock's school, that has stirred my curiosity." He waited for a response from Doyle, and receiving neither an invitation nor a rejection, continued. "If you studied with Reverend Eleazer Wheelock, that would place you at Dartmouth in the 1770s. By the time his son John had taken over as school head in 1779, you would have left. We both know the Wheelock's commitment to educating Indian youth; I wonder what your association with the..."

"Savages?" Doyle asked.

"Indian youth, I would prefer to say. If I may be so bold, when you were practicing with the tomahawk you had borrowed from Lieutenant O'Bannon, I noticed you threw it with the full arm, not with the forearm and snap of the wrist as others are apt to do. Surely that is a skill learned from natives." Then he switched to fluent Iroquois. "You carry yourself with the pride of the *Haudenosaunee*. I wonder if you were raised among them?"

Doyle replied in Iroquois, "Your eye is good. I am of the Bear Clan of the *Kahniankehaka*. *Tiyanoga* raised me and *Thayendanega* was my teacher."

Eaton recognized Joseph Brant's Mohawk name. I must be careful here, he thought. "In my time with the Oneidas," Eaton continued, "fighting the Miamis in the west, there was talk of a great scout among the Mohawks, *Okteondon*, called by many the bravest and fiercest of a brave and fierce people. I wonder if you knew him as a child?"

"I knew him well," Doyle said. "He was killed in the war. That time is now dead to me."

A man may kill time, Eaton thought. The feelings that accompany one's past do not die so easily. He looked at the low hills around them, stretching away into empty, unending desert. We are tiny, inconsequential specks in this vastness, he thought. And we are placing our lives in the hand of a man who has every reason to hate us. Eaton refilled his *finjan* with more coffee from the pot over the fire, sat back down, and watched as the fire's coals gradually winked into graying embers. Doyle, next to him, sat in patient silence.

"So you have journeyed here, from the *Haudenosaunee* of the Mohawk Valley to the nomads of the trackless desert," Eaton said. "Unless my curiosity has become an impertinence, may I wonder how you are now among the Tuaregs?"

"If you were a proper Englishman, general, or for that matter were I," Doyle laughed, "your interest in my personal affairs would be insufferable. Happily, neither of us can claim that level of civility. You are, after all, an American, and I ..." Doyle shrugged his shoulders and Eaton joined him in laughter. "I first learned of these mysterious, proud people, the Tuaregs—in their own language the *Kel Tamacheq*—years ago on a mission to

Algiers for the English. I was impressed by their ferocious independence and intrigued by their matrilineal culture. Like the Mohawks of my childhood, women were highly respected, serving as the keepers of inherited wisdom of the clan. So I arranged to spend some time in Algiers with a man who had been a captive of the Tuaregs and had only escaped back to his people a few years before. When I asked him what these people looked like, he told me most Tuaregs of the ruling class, the *Imagzighen*, are tall, like myself, and white complexioned where their skin is not exposed to the sun. Many have black hair with black, brown, or hazel eyes. He thought I could pass for Tuareg myself—and that's just what I did. I learned to speak their language, and when the time was right, joined a caravan out of Algiers bound for the desert to the south to trade camels with the Tuareg. I was introduced as a warrior chieftain from the clan *M'Touga* of a race of *Imagzighen* who lived across the great salt water. After five years and many battles, I rose to the rank of war commander over all clans. But enough of me. Let us turn back to your business, general."

Eaton opened up the map he had procured in Cairo, spread it on the ground, and knelt over it with Doyle.

"We leave Egypt and go along the coast to attack Derna, here." Eaton traced a line across the map. "Captain Hull will meet us at Bomba," he pointed again, "with supplies. Pasha Karamanli's fort and garrison at Derna is the door to all of Tripoli. Conquer Derna, and the rest of the country lies open before us."

Doyle let out a low whistle. "That's five hundred miles, general: a damned hard march if I may say so, and a damned dry one, too. So let's see—you will have to cover forty miles to your first water; it is a well, here," Doyle pointed to the map and Eaton circled the spot. "It is clearly found along the main coastal caravan route; the first sight of habitation you will encounter. Be sure to reload your water containers, however; it is a ten hour march to the next water. Here," pointing to another point on the coast, "you will find abundant water—deep cisterns. Then it is a dry march for one hundred miles to Massouah castle. There is water again at Oz Kerr, another day's trek. From there you will need to head inland, skirting these mountains to the south. For this part of your journey until you reach Bomba, another two hundred and fifty miles, water will be scarce; you'll need to trust that one of our people will be available to guide you. Does that degree of trust make you uncomfortable?"

Who's testing whom? Eaton wondered. "I don't command you," he said, selecting his words carefully, "and have no thought of managing the march to Derna on my own. Hiring local Arabs to guide us would be folly. What other choice do I have but to trust you?"

"You are a brave man, general," Doyle laughed, an open look of appreciation in his eyes. "Many would call your bravery mere folly."

"Fear is an indulgence that a man on a desperate mission must never surrender to," Eaton answered. "If I do not believe in myself, how can I expect others to follow me? But fear and careful planning are quite different. My men will expect me to lead them to water, and they will rely on that trust to conquer their own fear. I must not fail them. You have commanded men many times," he said, looking directly at Doyle. "You know what I'm talking about."

Doyle nodded in agreement. "I do, general." I reached him on that, thought Eaton.

"I pride myself in being an apt judge of character," Eaton continued. "I have this opinion of you: you say what you will do, and you will do what you say. I need no further reassurance. But I do need guidance. We are appointed to meet up with Hull and the *Argus* at Bomba. When must I head north again to pick up the coastal route?"

Doyle and the general spent the next hour plotting Eaton's line of march. Their coffee finished, they watched the blackness of a moonless night roll toward them, a sky full of stars in its wake. Eaton's mind drifted back to his time in the Ohio country years ago with a trapper who had raised a wolf for a pet. Eaton was sitting by the fire as the trapper fed the wolf scraps from their meal. The wolf looked up at him with his yellow eyes. The message was unmistakable: "I may be friendly; I am not tame."

From the Journals of El Habibka
If you cannot stand a sting, do not put your finger in a scorpion's nest.

Saadi of Shiraz

CHAPTER 12
☙ CAIRO 1804 ❧

O n December 7th, the party had reached Bulla, a small village just below Cairo. They pulled up to the river wharf, as had become their practice, with all weapons at the ready and Captain Vincents' *marche* fifty yards off shore to provide covering fire from its swivel guns if needed. There they were met by a party of five men armed with muskets, a brace of pistols per man, and wicked-looking swords with crossed hilts that reminded Kirkpatrick of the Crusader sword of Richard the Lion-Hearted he had seen in London. They were mounted on fine looking camels, *méhari*, bred for speed, with several more *demi-méhari* carrying supplies. The men were all fit looking, but their faces were completely masked by dark blue veils worn over their faces above their white bur-nooses. Kirkpatrick noticed that the townspeople, who normally would have swarmed over their boat, kept a respectful, even fear-ful distance.

"Who are these men?" he asked their dragoman Ali.

"Tuaregs. The 'Forgotten of God,' we call them," replied Ali. "It is death to oppose them."

Their mysterious companion, Katir Al-Hareeq, disembarked and joined the Tuaregs, one of whom led a camel for him to mount. Kirkpatrick noticed with surprise, then recognition, that among the weapons provided for Katir Al-Hareeq on his mount was a Kentucky rifle not unlike the one he had used to such advantage on their voyage. Without a word of farewell, Katir Al-Hareeq mounted. The party kicked their camels into movement to the accompaniment of loud braying protests. Within moments they were out of sight, and the *marche* was pushed back into the river to resume its journey to Cairo, just a few miles ahead.

Word of their arrival had obviously traveled ahead. As they approached the wharf for foreign ships, they saw it crowded with a company of armed men.

"Whose soldiers are these?" asked Kirkpatrick.

"They are janissaries of the Turkish viceroy Kourschet Ahmet Pasha," said Leitensdorfer. "I would guess that they're here to greet, rather than attack us. Given their numbers, let's hope that is the case." As Kirkpatrick nosed the boat into the wharf and dockmen handled the mooring lines thrown to them, he studied their viceroy's troops. They were rough-looking, long-mustachioed Turks clad in baggy white trousers that stopped at the knee, with embroidered red waistcoats over white shirts. They wore red circular hats with turbans wound around them in the shape of a pyramid.

Each man carried pistols stuck into the broad sash around his waist, a curved sword, a musket slung over his back, and crossed cartridge belts over his shoulders and chest. Their officer, who now came forward to greet them, was distinguished from his troopers by a wide turban richly decorated with jeweled brooches.

After some conversation with General Eaton, Captain Vincents, and their dragoman Ali, they were welcomed to the city and permitted to make their way to the British consulate with the viceroy's janissaries as an escort. Kourschet Ahmet Pasha had sent richly caparisoned horses to transport their group to the consulate.

For their entry into Cairo, the officers had attired themselves in their best dress uniforms—well brushed with brass brightly polished. General Eaton, for the first time, donned a costume he had created for this mission: a military cut, high collared black jacket with gold epaulets, a black hat topped by a white ostrich feather, all of it set off with a red sash and a gold presentation sword Eaton had been given by the Dey of Morocco when they were on better terms. Leitensdorfer had chosen a plain Arab burnoose and head scarf covering his face.

They passed along main thoroughfares lined with a Noah's ark of humanity: soldiers and officials in various types of array; merchants in lavishly embroidered waistcoats and brightly colored pantaloons; Bedouins cloaked in plain, long, flowing white burnooses; local workmen in a single length of cotton cloth wrapped around them like a Roman toga; and beggars—an overwhelming swarm of beggars. Men of every age, barely clad in rags, some clearly former soldiers, often with one or more limbs missing—wretched creatures with open sores and every imaginable sign of illness. And hordes of small children, often as maimed as the men they scurried around.

Kirkpatrick turned to Eaton. "I must say, sir, this is not the fabled Cairo of the Pharaohs I had expected."

"Grand Cairo," Eaton said, "differs from the places we have already passed only as the presence of the tyrant stamps silence on the lips of misery with the seal of terror. Pale wretchedness and dumb melancholy stalk here! Egypt has no master, just the most frightful despotism. The Turkish soldiery, restrained by no discipline, seize with the hand of rapine everything for which their passion creates a desire."

As they rode, Kirkpatrick noticed that the crowds, while keeping the respectful distance owed to people of status and rank, were intensely curious.

"Do all visitors to Cairo receive this much attention?" Kirkpatrick asked Ali, riding next to him.

"No indeed. They expected to see the red Indians we have heard about."

"I do not see any women here," Kirkpatrick remarked.

"Do not worry, young sir," Ali responded. Pointing to the latticed second *story windows* above them, he added, with a laugh, "rest assured the women of Cairo are seeing you."

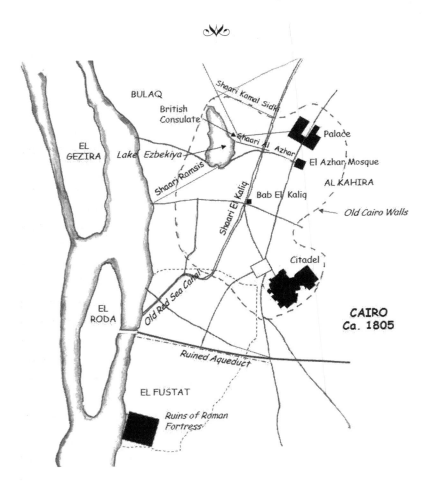

Two days were devoted to receiving state visitors and returning visits from their quarters in the British consulate, agreeably coordinated through Ambassador Brigg's efforts. Meanwhile, Leitensdorfer had disappeared into the city. On the evening of the second day, he returned to report to Eaton. "I have news, general," he said, looking around at the other Americans and British officials enjoying the sunset's glow from the consulate veranda.

"Let's go for a walk," Eaton responded.

Once they were on the street, Leitensdorfer led them to the corner of a quiet café at a table out of earshot of other patrons.

"So what news of the elusive Hamet?" Eaton asked eagerly when they were comfortably seated.

"I've located Hamet's former ex-governors, Ibn Hassan and Khalid," Leitensdorfer replied. "From them we know where Hamet is. But extricating him may be a problem. Hamet, unfortunately, seems to be grasping at straws. He and the followers still loyal to him have joined forces with the Mamelukes against the Turks. I can't imagine that news will be welcome to Kourschet Ahmet Pasha. Worse, Hamet and the Mamelukes have managed to get themselves trapped. They're being besieged in Miniet, a village in upper Egypt, by eight thousand Arnaut and Levant Turks. The saving grace is that his aides, Ibn Hassan and Khalid, swear they know how to reach him and manage his escape. I've asked them to join us here in an hour."

After three hours waiting in vain, Eaton's patience had been replaced by testy irritation: "We are on a fool's errand here, Eugene. Had Hamet's people crawled on hands and knees to get here, they would have appeared ages ago." He waved aside Leitensdorfer's attempt at an apology. "I appreciate your efforts, Eugene, but we are not dealing with proper Englishmen, methodical Prussians, or punctual Swiss here. The more often an Arab swears by the Prophet to keep his word, the surer you can be he will break it. We are done here."

As Eaton started to rise from the table, Leitensdorfer caught his attention again. "Begging your pardon, general," Leitensdorfer said, "but I think there is another problem. Once we have located Hamet and somehow freed him from the Turkish forces that have him trapped in Miniet, we still need to get him out of Egypt and into Tripoli."

"I know. I know," said Eaton, relaxing with a sigh back into his chair. "And granting that safe passage lies with Kourschet Ahmet Pasha here in Cairo. I must find a way to win him to our side—in spite of Hamet's allegiance with his enemies. But one insurmountable obstacle at a time. You must locate Hamet's emissaries and free him from Miniet. He may be a mere puppet, not a grand actor on the stage of history, but if we can't put *someone* on stage, there is no play. This whole plan collapses without him."

Chameau's agent Tal-Patann had been working on Ibn Hassan for a half hour. For his work, Tal-Patann had selected one of the abandoned hovels of Fusat in the northern section of Cairo—all that remained of the old city that had been burned and destroyed during the Crusades. Hamet's former aide was now already near death, his eyeless face a ruin of burns and cuts inflicted by a heated knife blade. The two thugs who had kidnapped Ibn Hassan and Khalid watched Tal-Patann's efforts with a professional curiosity.

"He has worked too quickly," remarked one, now that Ibn Hassan's screams had diminished to a wordless blubbering of pain so that normal conversation was again possible. "It is permissible to take pleasure in one's efforts, but this Christian dog is clearly an amateur in the business. This man will be unable to tell him anything now that his tongue has been removed. He is already standing on *sirath*, the bridge that will take him to Hell."

"*Bismillah,* but thou art in error," retorted his companion. "By the Beard of the Prophet, doest thou not see that this *Franzwazi,* may jackals despoil the graves of his ancestors, is a true artist? This first man was tortured to inspire the other to speak fully and in truth. Clearly this first one knew nothing, or he would have babbled like a baby. It is the other who knowest what the *Roumi* is seeking. Observe. Thou will see I have judged correctly."

Tal-Patann now turned to Khalid, setting his knife back in the fire to re-heat, and pulled a rough stool next to Khalid so he could speak face to face. Khalid was drenched in sweat and the stench of terror rose from his body. "This is a simple matter," Tal-Patann said. "You can avoid the suffering you have just witnessed by telling me everything you know about the Americans' plans to find Hamet and bring him to Alexandria. You may begin talking now."

After half an hour of questioning, Tal-Patann had the information he needed, and ended the conversation. "Dispose of these two," he said to his companions, "and meet me tomorrow at sunset in the old Roman city by the aqueduct. I will have more work for you. The Americans are being helped by a man named Leitensdorfer—here in Cairo he goes by the name Murat Aga—he is their eyes, so we must remove him. Once they are blind, their own folly will destroy them."

CHAPTER 13
๛ CAIRO 1804 ๛

With all the disorder in the country, there was still splendor in the viceroy's trappings of power. At eight o'clock on the appointed evening, Kourschet Ahmet Pasha sent a heavy escort to the British consulate to convey Eaton's party to the palace. Ahead of the procession, bearers with flaming torches lit their way through the dark streets. When they reached the palace, two ranks of well-armed troops snapped to attention. Shaky as his power might be, the surroundings of the Sublime Porte's Viceroy of Egypt were still magnificent.

They entered a small piazza with three long cloisters that disappeared into the darkness. Out of the fourth whitewashed wall, a fountain gushed into a marble basin. Around them soared fantastically carved columns of marble and equally ornate cedar buttresses. Mounting a wide stairway whose blue tiled walls shimmered in the torchlight, they crossed through a passageway open to the outside air and entered another hall upon whose walls were hung handsomely decorated swords, scimitars, shields, and spears. Eaton kept his face carefully expressionless as he met the stares and saw the whispered conversations of the scores of guards they passed. These people may be curious about us, he thought, but they would slaughter us all in an instant. They've been killing Christians for a thousand years. He tried desperately to memorize their path in case they needed to escape. After a dozen more turns into the maze of the viceroy's palace, he gave up.

They pushed through a tapestry covering a small door and entered the viceroy's private audience chamber. Viceroy Kourschet Ahmet Pasha sat within a luxurious palanquin on tasseled silk cushions. Thick Persian carpets covered the floor and gracefully filigreed Moorish arches of carved cedar rose to the ceiling. The viceroy was attended by richly dressed officials, most of them older men with long grey beards, more guards, and two slave boys, employed in fanning the viceroy's face—one obviously of European parents. Their comeliness suggested to Eaton that they might have other, less innocent duties to perform in their master's service.

As befitting his station, Kourschet Ahmet Pasha did not rise to meet his guests. With a great show of laughter and smiles, he graciously welcomed his visitors, bade the party join him, and made a place for Eaton next to him on the cushions within the palanquin. Like nothing so much as a fat, jolly spider, Eaton thought, luring his prey into his lair with affability, waiting for his moment to pounce.

"It is a great pleasure, general," the viceroy said, speaking in French, "to see with my own eyes these Americans of whom so much is being said these days." His round face split in a jolly laugh, exposing uncommonly fine white teeth. I'm surprised they're not pointed, thought Eaton.

"Your pleasure, sire," Eaton answered, "is only surpassed by the honor we feel to have the great privilege of meeting so renowned and powerful a prince as yourself." Then, in a carefully contrived sop to the viceroy's Ottoman pride, he added in Turkish, "*Günaydın, Pasha Bay. Tanıştığımıza memnun oldum.* We are honored and pleased to be granted this audience with you."

"*Hoş bulduk.* To the contrary, the pleasure is mine," said the viceroy. "*Yolculuk nasıldı?*"

"It was a pleasant journey, thank you. *Kabuk geti.* I just wish my Turkish were better," said Eaton, happy that the long hours of practice with Leitensdorfer had actually given him the cultivated accent and musical intonation of an Istanbul grandee. "I am quite comfortable conversing in Arabic, if that would please you," said Eaton, knowing of course, that for a Turk, it wouldn't. "But I wonder if your Highness might prefer that we speak in French so that my colleagues might benefit from our discourse?"

"French would be fine," said the viceroy. "On the whole, we were quite pleased to see the French leave, and even more pleased with what they left behind." He clapped his hands, and servants instantly materialized with wine for their guests. Eaton knew that Kirkpatrick could follow the conversation in French, and that Leitensdorfer, of course, could attend to what the viceroy was both saying and not saying. He also knew that Captain Vincents, like any other good Englishman of his class, never bothered to learn foreign languages in the confident belief that regardless of where one traveled in the world, all that was needed was English, spoken slowly and loudly.

Eaton directed O'Bannon to bring forward the gifts be had selected for the viceroy. "May I have the honor of presenting Lieutenant O'Bannon? He is an officer in our Marines, of whose exploits at Tripoli in destroying the Pasha's navy I am sure you have heard." O'Bannon, his pride fully up to the task, stepped forward, and laid the gifts at the viceroy's feet. He stepped back, looked the viceroy squarely in the eye, and snapped his very best salute. The viceroy's gaze momentarily hardened with curiosity as he regarded the Lieutenant.

Eaton first presented large gold medallions of President Washington for the viceroy to give to his chief ministers, knowing that a tyrant like Kourschet Ahmet Pasha must continuously repurchase the loyalty of his servants. These were followed by finely polished, glittering gemstones from the northern and southern states, the elaborate headdress of a Cherokee chief, and his principal gift, a gold-embossed Kentucky rifle with matching powder horn.

"This is the weapon, Highness, that defeated the British armies. You will see it fires four times farther than your best musket, twice as accurately, and in spite of the small size of the ball, kills with deadly force. In our war against the British, it was our practice to begin a battle by killing all the enemy's officers hundreds of yards before their troops could engage us in musket fire. They complained, of course, that this sort of practice was ungentlemanly. But a warrior like yourself knows that the business of war is killing and the purpose of war is winning. Cut off the head and the beast dies. Permit me to add that the lieutenant is a master with this weapon. It would be our pleasure to arrange a demonstration for you."

"*Hay, hay,*" the viceroy replied. "*Herhalde.* Of course." He looked again at O'Bannon, this time with an almost feral interest. "So tell me about America and the Americans," the viceroy urged. Oh, I surely will, thought Eaton.

"Imagine if you will, Highness, that the Prophet, blessings be upon him, had brought not only the boon of Islam to Africa, but, with the will of God the All Merciful and Compassionate, the gift of rain. You have seen, after a rainstorm, the desert briefly blossom in bright flowers. Imagine then a thousand years of rain, turning the barren wasteland of North Africa into green fields, forests, and pastures like those you must have known as a young boy in Turkey. That will give you some concept of the richness of America." Eaton noted the viceroy's rapt attention. Let's see who the real spider is and who is the fly, he thought.

"See, if you will," Eaton continued, his voice now flowing with the poetry of his images, "a fertile land of farms and fields stretching as far as from here to the very source of the Nile and westward to Algiers. Beyond this abundant cropland lies an enormous forest. A man could ride into that forest westward for weeks and never reach its end. In places, the forest is an impenetrable wilderness, inhabited by ferocious beasts. In others, tall trees reach skyward beyond the understanding of man, as if one were in such temples as the ancient Egyptians built, but in this place raised by the hand of God, not man. And thanks to our great President Jefferson's purchase of Louisiana from the French, America now reaches to the shores of the Western Sea, an expanse greater than from Cairo to Morocco. He sent out explorers and they tell of broad grasslands and plains stretching beyond the limits of sight, majestic mountains, great rivers, and herds of antelope and buffalo more numerous than the stars in the sky. If I may be forgiven the pride in such a statement and be allowed the great humility that must accompany that pride, it is if God the All Merciful and Compassionate had given us Paradise for our home." He paused to allow the effect of his speech to work its way into the viceroy's imagination.

"And what of the people you found there? The Indians? What sort of people and warriors are they?"

"All the world, Excellency, from Christendom to Islam, remembers the ferocity of the Mongols who brought such devastation to the civilized world. These people are of the same race. I have faced them many times in battle and there is no braver nor more cunning foe. In their mastery of their surroundings they are the equal of the Chaaba." Eaton deliberately mentioned the one race of Berber nomads that were the Tuareg's equal in navigating the trackless desert—and feared by the Turks. "Fortunately for us, like many primitive people, they are independent tribes, and can be turned against each other with little difficulty. They can be defeated by well-trained, well-armed troops."

"And what of these troops? We were told by the French that America was a nation of shopkeepers and tradesmen, and that it was they who won your war against the British for you."

Eaton lifted his head and raised his eyebrows in scornful disdain: *"Güldürmek beni. Şaka etmek."* That would be a joke from anyone but a Frenchman. Tell me, Highness, if, like the King of

England, you owned a land as rich as I have described, would you let it be taken from you by the French? But I am sure you have heard of Americans from your counterpart in Tripoli. What does Pasha Jusef Karamanli say of us?"

"He says the French lied, and instead of meek shopkeepers, America sent Preble to bombard his cities into rubble and a band of Christian dogs, fierce and cruel as the tiger, to kill his brothers and burn his ships in the dark of night before his eyes." He nodded toward O'Bannon, who had remained at stiff attention, his eyes fixed on the viceroy. "If I may ask, how many Marines do you have like this one?"

"We have a force of thirty thousand Marines, as skilled at fighting on land as on sea." Eaton lied easily, increasing the size of the United States' total Marine Corps ten-fold. "They are backed by an army of eighty thousand men and a million citizen militiamen, each one passionately devoted to his country's defense, each hardened in constant warfare against our Indian foes. But know, Highness, that there is another difference between Americans and Europeans. They seek conquest and domination; the United States does not unsheathe the sword for spoils but to vindicate rights."

"Let us then talk about these American rights you seek to vindicate," said Kourschet Ahmet Pasha. "I was told you come here on a hunting expedition. I wonder if you are hunting not harmless birds but an elusive desert lion?"

"It is true, Highness. The usurper Jusef Karamanli has become a watchword for faithless cruelty to both his enemies and his people. When he stands at the gates of Paradise, he will be sent spinning to *Iblis* without mercy or compassion. By restoring Hamet Karamanli to his rightful throne, we protect our merchants from his brothers' banditry."

"We will consider these things further. It is true that a brother should not take up arms against a brother."

"I would welcome our further discourse, Highness." A good start, he thought. Then an inspiration hit him.

Eaton took an American gold dollar out of his pocket, portraying on one side the American eagle, surrounded by the words "In God We Trust." Presenting it to the viceroy as a gift, he asked the viceroy's translator to read the English words on the coin.

"In departing," Eaton said, "I wish to point out, Highness, the affinity of principle between Islam and American religion, both being founded on the supremacy of *one* God rather than a *Romish* trinity. Both religions, your Highness, enjoin the universal exercise of humanity, and both forbid unnecessary loss of life. Restoring Hamet will end the bloodshed in which Jusef Karamanli has soaked himself and drowned his helpless, suffering people. Better a Hamet Karamanli in Tripoli ruling his people in peace," he added as a final shot, "than a stateless monarch with his followers seeking his fortune in your realm of Egypt."

Once their party had returned to the safety of the British consulate, Eaton met with Leitensdorfer in his room. "How do you think it went with the viceroy," he asked.

"I think you will have your *firman* granting Hamet safe passage in another meeting. He was quite charmed by you, I would say. But tell me, your description of America was enthralling. Does such a place actually exist?"

"In our dreams, certainly. What we make of it in reality remains to be seen. But yes, the dream is compelling. I struggle to find ways, Eugene, to explain America properly to Europeans who live on land, as masters or servants, that has been owned by *somebody* for thousands of years. To have in front of you an entire continent with untold natural riches, uninhabited except for small clusters of native tribes—to possess one's own land, servant to no one—small wonder we fought for our freedom and now seek to bring the gift of freedom to others. You must come to America one day, Eugene, and become your own master."

"I think I will. Yes. But since we speak of freedom, we still have Hamet's to manage. I've given up on his emissaries, Ibn Hassan and Khalid. They have simply disappeared. Give me a few days. I may have another plan to rescue Hamet."

CHAPTER 14
❧ CAIRO 1804 ❧

The following day, Kirkpatrick was sitting in the room in the British consulate he and O'Bannon shared. The strong light of the late afternoon sun beat through the window above his chair. Leitensdorfer had mentioned to Kirkpatrick his intention to recruit soldiers from among the hundreds of Greek mercenaries in Alexandria, and Kirkpatrick had thought it might be useful to speak enough of the language to give them orders. As he struggled to work his way through the Greek grammar Leitensdorfer had loaned him, he now regretted his enthusiasm. Kirkpatrick lifted his eyes from the book when he heard a discrete knock on the door. He quickly, but quietly, rose from the chair, crossed over to the dressing table and picked up his pistol, checking its priming before going to the side of the room away from the door opening. He called out, "Come."

Leitensdorfer entered the room, carrying a large bundle under his arm. He noticed Kirkpatrick's pistol, still held at his side, and said, "I applaud your caution. We are in the British consulate, but Cairo is still Cairo."

Kirkpatrick replaced the pistol on the dresser and hurriedly gathered up the clothing and books scattered on his bed, apologizing as he did for the clutter. "Forgive me; the room is quite a shambles. I wasn't expecting visitors. Might you have a glass of sherry with me?"

As Kirkpatrick poured sherry for them, Leitensdorfer picked up the *Iliad* and began paging through it. "I commend you on your energy, captain. If I may ask, how do your lessons go?"

"Not well, I fear. All those years I spent with Homer seem to provide me with less advantage than I had hoped."

"You could not wish for a better theme for your studies, to be sure. Perhaps, one day, poets will recite, 'Sing, O Goddess, the wrath of America.' But for now, if you would not find a suggestion completely out of order, I wonder if you would not be better served by laying Homer aside for the time being and approaching modern Greek as its own spoken, rather than written, language. For your purposes, as well, perhaps a reliance on the imperative to the exclusion of the optative mood for orders and commands would make things a bit simpler. But I have no doubt you will master all this on your own. I actually have a different matter to discuss with you if you have a few moments."

"I certainly appreciate your assistance with modern Greek; it's all a jumble to me. But how may I be of service to you?"

"What I wish to share with you is of the most sensitive nature imaginable. Would you be at all amenable to walking with me outside on the patio?"

Leitensdorfer and Kirkpatrick made their way to the veranda overlooking Lake Ebekiya, where most of the European government officials and merchants lived if they could afford it. To the west were the remains of Napoleon's home and headquarters. At this hour, the lake was crowded with pleasure craft, their white sails bright in the sunlight against the green of the gardens at the lake edge. Before beginning, Leitensdorfer looked around to ensure that their conversation could not be overheard.

"The issue at hand," he said, "concerns our delightfully cheerful, helpful dragoman, Ali. It appears that he may be less affable than he seems, and quite a bit more dangerous. I cannot reveal to you the intelligence that raised my suspicions about his character, but I took the precaution of having him followed the past few days, each time by two street ruffians. His business took him to the run-down area of the Askar, to the south of us near the old aqueduct. I made my own inquiries. It seems the shop he called on twice is that of an herbalist: a Syrian who specializes in the kinds of potions barren wives will avail themselves of in order to produce a child—and pregnant mistresses will use to cause exactly the opposite effect. Not surprisingly, he also specializes in poisons. It is quite likely that Ali ..."

"The devil, you say," Kirkpatrick interjected. "Why, we must go immediately to the scoundrel's quarters and confront him with his treachery!"

"By your leave, captain," Leitensdorfer continued, as if he hadn't been interrupted, "I suggest, as an alternative, that you and I follow him this evening when he is free of his official duties. We may be maligning his motives—although I doubt it. But if his purposes are nefarious, it cannot be but that he is acting with a confederate or a sponsor. I think, given the larger scope of our affairs, that we might do well to know more about our enemies before we deal with Ali."

"You are right, I'm sure. So how may I be of assistance?" Kirkpatrick felt the familiar rush of embarrassment, as much at his intemperance as what he took to be patient, polite condescension on Leitensdorfer's part.

"The bundle I brought with me, now at the foot of your bed, contains the costume of a Mameluke: grey cap, red pants, red slippers, a large white blouse, brocaded vest, the customary chainmail shirt to be worn under the vest, which, God willing, you will not have need for, and a burnoose to go over all. With your dark skin and covered face, by evening you will pass well enough. You will need to arm yourself with a brace of pistols, a sword—your naval cutlass should answer—and a dagger. I will be similarly garbed. So accoutered, we may move through the meanest neighborhoods in Cairo without fear of threat or challenge. If seven in the evening would be agreeable to you, I have arranged with Captain Vincents to have the hallways clear so we may make our departure to the street through a back door without being spied upon."

"I am your man," Kirkpatrick replied. As Leitensdorfer rose to leave, Kirkpatrick added, "I apologize for my interruption moments before, colonel. I meant no disrespect."

"None taken," said Leitensdorfer. "Do not think of it. I had much your same energy when I was a young man. But then, I was just like beeswax in the honeycomb that has no notion of the candle it will become, the flame, or the final guttering wick. If one fully understood things as a young man, there would be nothing to learn."

"I would be happy to learn from you."

"Oh, you can find better teachers than I," Leitensdorfer laughed. "I'm only like a donkey loaded high with the books of the old masters. The books may contain wisdom, but the donkey is still a donkey. I will see you at seven tonight." And with that, he left.

Several hours later, Kirkpatrick and Leitensdorfer were seated deep within the shadows of a European-style café across from Ali's lodgings in a *foondouk* near the British consulate. Leitensdorfer pointed to a filthy, nearly naked, one-armed beggar sprawled in the gutter next to the wide, crenellated doorway through which Ali would exit. "That's one of our hired spies this evening, Ibrahim. We cannot see the other, Achmet, yet another ubiquitous Cairo urchin, but for the reward he was promised, I am sure of his compliance." As he spoke, a very scarecrow of rags and visible bones appeared before them, his disheveled appearance brightened by shining eyes and a sparkle in his face that, were the grime washed off, might have been called beautiful.

"*As-salaam ahlakum,* Effendis. Hast orders for thy worthless slave, Achmet? Art ready to command me? Know there is no purse so tightly guarded that Achmet's fingers cannot steal, nor no sleeping throat safe from Achmet's knife in the dark."

"No, my child," Leitensdorfer answered in Arabic. "Thou must help us as before in being a shadow to the traitor Ali."

"That worthless eater of camel dung begotten by *Idris* himself on a mongrel dog?" the boy snapped back. "I pray thee, worships, hast not a Frankish enemy I may slay? The Franks killed my father and despoiled my sister so she killed herself in shame. I swear by the innumerable names of the Prophet, blessings upon him, that I mayst not call myself a man until my knife has tasted Frankish blood."

"Colonel," Kirkpatrick interjected. "In God's name, what is this fiend in swaddling clothes you have procured for us? My Arabic is far from perfect, but I recognize the words for 'kill,' 'knife,' and 'blood.' Surely this fledgling assassin cannot be more than ten years old."

"Twelve, I would say," said Leitensdorfer. "Starvation is your great enemy of health. And if the brightness of Achmet's eyes does not mislead me, he is already no stranger to the hashish of professional assassins. Beggar children grow old early in this place just as surely as they are fated to die early. But do not overly grieve for his misfortune. I have it on good report that his father sold him into slavery to the Albanians, from whom he escaped by poisoning his master. As for his sister, far from killing herself in shame at the loss of her virtue, she was mistress to a French Major during their occupation. When they left, she was sold to a British Brigadier, who kept her very well indeed, then sold her again when the British left, to a rich Lebanese merchant in Alexandria, at an appropriate profit, given her reputed gifts in the art of venery."

Kirkpatrick looked at the boy standing in front of him. He was clothed in rags. Ugly looking sores dotted his legs. "Ask him, then, I pray you, to tell us what he will do with the gold you give him? May that not change his prospects for the better?"

"I already know the answer to that question. The gold will go to his mother. He wishes no greater employment than serving in one of the better sort of bathhouses that cater to the wealthy citizens of Cairo. His duties there will include washing his customers, scraping their skins clean, anointing them with scented oils, then providing whatever additional services their desire may require. He will follow his sister into the ancient trade. But no tears for him, I think. In this world, prostitution is a better fate than starvation or the bastinado at the hands of a Turkish police officer."

Almost as Leitensdorfer finished speaking, Ali emerged from his inn and headed down the street at a fast, pre-occupied pace. Leitensdorfer threw a few coins on the table and they set off in pursuit. They made their way along the Shaari' Al Azhar, following Ibrahim, who stayed within eyesight of Ali. Their miniature murderer Achmet raced ahead, melting in and out of the crowd of people taking advantage of the cool of the evening for a promenade or concluding that day's business before the curfew.

They passed several large *kasariyas*, open markets providing everything from food to household items, and side streets leading to the smaller *suqs*. The same extraordinary mix of wealthy Turks, Albanians, Jews, Arabs, freemen, slaves, and beggars swirled around them. True to Leitensdorfer's prediction, their appearance caused the crowd to give them all the space they needed, and Leitensdorfer's fluent Turkish and Arabic prevented confrontations with other soldiers. As they walked along the Shaari' Al Azhar, Kirkpatrick was struck by its width, so unusual in an ancient city of labyrinthine streets and alleys. It seemed as if a giant hand had scooped away all the houses and shops on either side of the roadway, creating a boulevard 50 feet wide. "Tell me, colonel, if you please, how this street came to be so grand in its dimensions. As I look more closely, it seems that the principal instrument of civic improvement here has been artillery fire."

"Your eyes don't deceive you, captain. We are in the midst of one of Napoleon's attempts at urban reconstruction. I was here at the time, although the less said of the circumstances the better."

As they walked, still keeping their quarry in sight, Leitensdorfer recounted the story of Napoleon's failure. The military victory was easy enough. Napoleon brought the pride of the *Grande Armée*—seasoned veterans of a dozen great victories in Austria and Italy—and his most trusted staff officers: Kléber, Murat, DuPuy, and the others. The Mameluke army that Murad Bey sent out against the French was cut to pieces at Imbala. Napoleon, his army, and the scientists he had brought with him to study Egypt from the perspective of civilized, educated Frenchmen, expected to be greeted by the local populace as liberators from centuries of Mameluke despotism.

It started out quite hopefully: French cafés along the sidewalks, French soldiers and officers walking around like heroes and paying more money for the simplest things than anyone in Cairo could have imagined. Local merchants thrived, and the French, on their best behavior, began making friends with the Cairenes. Meantime, Napoleon seized key strong points around the city to place his artillery and garrison his troops to control and overawe the population.

Recognizing how vulnerable his army would be in close-quarter house-to-house fighting, unable to maneuver and coordinate with his superb artillery, he decided to open up the city streets to create artillery fire lanes and make room for his equally superb cavalry to operate. It was a terrible miscalculation.

Napoleon tried to clear the area around his headquarters at Ezbekiya but wound up disturbing graves in a local cemetery. He started widening the Shaari' Al Azhar and other roads linking his headquarters to the citadel by levying taxes on the buildings that would be spared. Both measures stirred up a hornets' nest of protest. It was just a matter of time until the hot heads in the Al Azhar mosque rebelled against the infidels. After that everything was sadly predictable. General DuPuy's division, sent to put down the insurrection, was ambushed and nearly massacred. DuPuy lost his life in the process.

Napoleon countered by firing into the Azhar and its approaches with his artillery from the citadel. To make matters worse, he commandeered many of the nearby mosques in order to use their minarets as cannon platforms. He then attacked the Al Azhar Mosque and university and dispersed the rebels with great loss of life among both the dissident students and local population. His cavalry rode into the mosque and desecrated that holy place in every gross way imaginable.

From that day on, he was constantly at war with the local citizens. It didn't matter that they were fighting the best trained, most thoroughly equipped army in the world with whatever weapons they could steal or improvise—including infernal devices constructed from the munitions Murad Bey had left behind in his headlong flight after the debacle at Imbala. It didn't matter that the French had freed them from the savage thievery and violence of their rulers. Nor did it matter that during the frequent power struggles among the Turks and Mamelukes, local inhabitants had, themselves, taken sides with one or another of the feuding factions. None of that signified. Cairenes were defending their city, their faith, their pride, and their way of life from a foreign invader. Napoleon wound up sneaking out of Cairo in the dead of night back to France, leaving the remains of his army to be decimated by disease and the local populace until the English invasion three years ago ended it all. The surviving French were delighted to be able to finally surrender to an actual army.

"So," Leitensdorfer concluded his story, "I would say Napoleon's entire three-year sojourn here in Cairo offers a world of lessons for potential conquerors, especially if they happen to be Christians imposing their will on a Muslim populace. Strange how in seeking to prevent what we most fear, we bring destruction on ourselves by our very actions. Like the king in the story," he mused, "whose astrologers told him a calamity would befall him on a certain day. So he built a house of solid rock, sealed himself in it, and posted guards outside. When he was safe in his refuge, he looked around and saw a small opening through which light appeared. He sealed it up to protect himself, and thus turned his house into the tomb in which he died. As we contemplate our adventure with Hamet, we would do well to remember ..." He stopped in mid-sentence. "Eyes sharp, captain. We turn here."

At the Bab El Kalig, one of the gates of Saladin's original fortress and a favorite spot for Mameluke rulers to impale their enemies, they headed for the maze of *khans* and *caravanserais* that sprawled beneath the looming walls of the citadel. Of necessity, they closed the distance between themselves and Ali. He seemed so intent on his purpose that he didn't look behind him to see if he were being followed.

They were now in the medieval part of the city, picking their way through a warren of small, cobbled streets between buildings whose extended upper stories blocked the last rays of the fading sun. Merchants' wares jutted out of the stalls, lining the street and spilling into the center of the roadway itself. The crowded space made everything around them closer and busier. They were assaulted by a din of voices crying out around them, a riot of color, and a collision of a hundred different smells.

Leitensdorfer took out a cane with a camel's hair whip on the end, and cursing in harsh Arabic, cleared passersby out of their way. They could barely make out Ibrahim continuing to work his way through the crowd querulously seeking alms, at first ahead, then in back of Ali. Achmet had disappeared once again.

"With goods so accessible, such crowds all around, and all business conducted on a cash basis," Kirkpatrick said, "I am surprised that there seems to be so little thievery."

"You will find your answer every time you pass a man with his right hand cut off," Leitensdorfer answered. "Justice here, whether supplied by Turk or Mameluke, is quick, harsh, and summary. "When a Mameluke or Janissary severs the hand of a thief or an innocent man accused of stealing—it all amounts to the same thing—the punishment is doubly cruel. Among a people who use their right hand exclusively to consume food and their left to cleanse themselves from the natural results of digestion, a one-handed man lives in a world of perpetual shame, disgrace, and moral, if not actual, filth. Unless, of course, the officer who serves as both judge and jury decides the crime is serious enough to merit taking the man's head and not just his hand. I must tell you if, dressed as we are, we encounter an outraged merchant with a thief in custody, be prepared to use your sword without compunction, or our disguise will be revealed as a sham."

Suddenly they saw Ali duck into a *wakala*, a small inn for merchants and travelers, built around an open court. Its gateway, like so many others that Kirkpatrick had passed, was a surprisingly ornate, delicate filigree of carved plaster, a poor man's version, Kirkpatrick thought, of the comparably intricate wooden carvings he had seen in mosques and palaces. Ibrahim sat down by the door and began begging passersby for alms. As if bidden, Achmet reappeared. Leitensdorfer directed him to follow Ali into the inn and note his movements while they stayed hidden.

A half hour later, Ali emerged. Leitensdorfer told Ibrahim to follow him and report back, then turned to Achmet. "What did those bright eyes of yours see, my child?" he asked.

"Truly, *Effendi,* Achmet sees with the eyes of *Hubal* of the red carnelian."

"Then let me cast my arrow at your feet, mighty *djinn,* and tell me where it points," answered Leitensdorfer. Instead of the ritual offering, he placed another coin in Achmet's open hand.

"That *yebnen kelp* Ali spent time talking with a man at a table under the broken lamp in the corner." Achmet spit in the dirt, careful to miss both men's feet. "*Omak zanya fee erd.*" Kirkpatrick caught the words for 'son of a dog, monkey, and mother.' "Thou mayst find him easily. He's a Jew."

"Go in peace, my child," Leitensdorfer said, then looked at the boy again, reached into his purse and gave him another coin. Achmet looked back at Leitensdorfer, kissed the coin, and disappeared in the crowd.

"He doesn't think highly of Ali," Kirkpatrick said. "I recognized at least some of what he said."

"Of course," Leitensdorfer answered. "In all fairness, neither do we. Besides, Achmet will say whatever he thinks I want to hear. But let us speak with Ali's mystery companion." He thought for a moment. "Normally, the sight of our uniforms would cause any man to talk in order to save his skin, or his head. Egypt is not Algiers, or Syria, however. For reasons I don't quite understand, Jews are respected here—and sometimes feared." He paused again. "Captain, I will do the talking, as I must, but you can be helpful. I have seen your temper flare in anger. If you could stand behind me, with that anger inside you, and sear him with your gaze, then you become the fire that will burn him to cinders and I will be his protection. Could you possibly do that?"

Kirkpatrick nodded, and they walked inside the arched door of the *wakala.* The Jew was easy to spot, in his long black cloak and three-cornered cap. They walked up to the table where he sat reading what might have been a prayer book. He ignored their approach. Kirkpatrick let his mind drift back a year ago to the fight with the Tripolitan gunboats when James Decatur had been treacherously killed while accepting the feigned surrender of the Turkish captain. The American's revenge had been bloody and merciless on the remaining gunboat crews. Kirkpatrick imagined the slash with his cutlass that would take off the head of the Jew seated in front of them, then looked up. What looked back at him as he met the man's eyes was black, violent hatred. He would kill me if he could, Kirkpatrick thought, still meeting the man's eyes, but he knows he can't, and that thought is driving him mad with rage. He instinctively pulled back his cloak to free the hilt of his sword.

Leitensdorfer acted as if he hadn't noticed. "*Masaa el kheer,*" he greeted Ali's contact politely. "We are looking for a man who sells herbs and potions such as women might use when they wish to be with child."

"There are many such men in Cairo."

"We are looking for one who just finished talking with a man named Ali," said Leitensdorfer.

"That, too, is a common name in Cairo."

"You know what we are and what we can do," said Leitensdorfer, as calmly as if they had been discussing the weather on a pleasant day.

"Yes. I know what you are and what you can do." If anything, thought Kirkpatrick, the rage boiling out of the man's eyes, in an otherwise expressionless face, intensified. Kirkpatrick had never felt so much in the presence of danger in his life.

Leitensdorfer nodded appreciatively in agreement and then suddenly changed the subject, again as calmly as if he were chatting with an old friend. "There was talk, while the French were here, of Napoleon's desire to go to Jerusalem, rebuild Solomon's Temple, and restore the city to the Jews. I wonder if you heard of it. It was quite the cry among Cairene Jews and Coptic Christians."

"Men will talk of anything that pleases them. Whether it is true is of no consequence."

"This man, Ali," Leitensdorfer said, "who talked with another man who sells herbs, works for the English. If they control Palestine, as they seek to do, the restoration of the Temple may wait another thousand years."

"We Jews understand waiting." The anger suddenly seemed to leave the man's eyes, and they became dead and cold, like the eyes of a shark.

Leitensdorfer just stood there, holding the other's stare. After what seemed an endless, empty moment to Kirkpatrick, he continued. "You have an unusual amount of rage in you, my friend, and beneath that rage I now see an even greater depth of sorrow and pain. I would guess your rage and pain nourish you. They keep you alive. What happens to your rage and pain if my comrade here," he gestured back at Kirkpatrick, "were to immediately cut off your head? I must tell you he lacks my deep respect for Jews."

"What do you want?" the man said.

"I want to know what it was that Ali, the English spy—who, I think, equally detests Jews—took with him when he left here. Actually, because I know your business—in this place, it is a trade like any other—I know what you sold him. I would rather know what he planned to do with it, if that's not too much to ask." Leitensdorfer added pleasantly, "A name would be helpful."

The man took a scrap of paper from inside his cloak, produced a crude pencil, and wrote quickly. "I don't tell secrets or share the confidences of my customers," he said, then shoved the paper across the table at Leitensdorfer and shrugged his shoulders. "This scrap of paper might have been blown by the wind from anywhere. Anyone could have written it; anyone could have picked it up." He turned back to his book. Kirkpatrick felt as if he and Leitensdorfer had just been not only dismissed, but actually erased from the man's consciousness and soul as if they had never existed.

Without a word, Leitensdorfer turned and headed for the door of the *wakala,* Kirkpatrick close behind him. As they left, the man spoke in a soft voice, but loud enough for both of them to hear, "*Yabn deen el kalb.* The god you worship is a dog."

As they entered the street, Kirkpatrick let out his breath. "That was ..." he struggled for the words.

Leitensdorfer finished his sentence. "That was Cairo, and Egypt, and this whole cursed piece of hell on Earth. These people have hated and killed each other since Moses claimed the promised land for God with the blood of slaughtered Canaanites. When will it stop? Not in a thousand more lifetimes, or, I suppose, until the second coming of Christ or Mohammed or Messiah. When I see what is done in their names, I wonder why any of them would bother returning."

CHAPTER 15
∾ CAIRO 1804 ∾

Ibrahim followed Ali back to his lodgings, waited a half-hour to make sure he didn't re-appear, then walked rapidly along the Shaari' Kamal Sidki, alongside the old walls of Cairo. He ducked into a small café and took a seat. He was joined moments later by Tal-Patann.

"Ali has been discovered," he said. "The Americans know about the plot to poison them."

"And you know this how?" Tal-Patann asked.

"They pay me to follow and inform on Ali; he thinks I am watching his back to make sure he is safe. They pay me more money, I might add, than you do: two piasters a day."

"What do we Maltese say? *Il-flus taghmel il-flus; il-qamel taghmel il-qamel.* Money begets money, and fleas beget fleas. You, it would seem, have an appetite for both, as well as the stench that accompanies both money and fleas."

"Amuse yourself with insults, if it pleases you," Ibrahim said. "I have nothing but time to spend, and the Americans have nothing but gold."

"For a man who eats and wipes shit with the same hand, you speak boldly," said Tal-Patann.

"I lost my hand serving your French masters. Boldness suits me. But were we not speaking of Ali?"

"See that he delivers the poison to our contact in Kourschet Ahmet Pasha's kitchen," Tal-Patann said. "Then find a way to kill him. He must not be permitted to talk to the Americans."

"Do you Maltese not have a saying: you must kill the spider to get rid of the cobweb? He told me the Americans will be going back to their boats tonight to prepare for tomorrow's feast. I will arrange to ambush Leitensdorfer and the American captain and see to Ali myself. In the dark of night a friend's knife can bite as deeply as an enemy's."

At dusk, Kirkpatrick and Leitensdorfer, with Ali to guide them and three servants carrying torches, exited the consulate and started toward the Shaari' Ramsis that led to the Bulaq docks. This time, Kirkpatrick and Leitensdorfer were dressed as Arabs. It was the custom in Cairo for both Turks and Mamelukes to demand that Europeans get out of their way. If Europeans were mounted—on donkeys or asses, since only Muslims were allowed to ride horses—they were required to immediately get off and bow in obeisance. Often as not, those demands could be accompanied by a beating if the response wasn't deemed to be quick or respectful enough. The British had solved the problem by going around Cairo on horseback, dressed as wealthy Arabs, so that, alone among the Europeans, they managed to preserve both their dignity and their safety. Kirkpatrick and Leitensdorfer had borrowed Arab robes from their British hosts but had decided to go on foot to attract less attention. Given the time of night, the darkness around them, and their present company, they carried their swords and a brace of pistols each. They worked their way through a series of crowded streets, and each time they turned a corner, Kirkpatrick momentarily pivoted, walking backward for a few paces.

"This walking backward," Leitensdorfer said, "surely this must be a special maneuver of naval officers. An ex-infantryman like myself would have no conception of performing such a trick."

"No, I am just studying where we have come from, so that if we needed to make a quick retreat back to the consulate by ourselves, I might have some sense of where we needed to turn. Intersections don't look the same when one retraces his steps."

"Bravo," said Leitensdorfer. "I applaud your foresight. Let us hope it is not needed."

I wonder what his opinion of me is, Kirkpatrick thought. I feel like a little boy around him, always saying or doing the wrong thing. I can't tell if he is just being jovial or is laughing at me. Certainly I give him reason enough, at times, to consider me a fool.

They turned left on the tree-lined Shaari' Ramsis. Unlike the narrow streets crowded with shops and residences through which they had passed, they were now walking along a broad avenue lined on both sides with well-tended gardens: vegetable gardens, Kirkpatrick supposed, from what he could see in the moonlight that made its way through the thick canopy of leaves above them. The avenue was surprisingly unpopulated; from being jostled by crowds as they left the consulate in the European quarter, they were now alone. Leitensdorfer slowed his pace a little, allowing Ali and two of their servants to walk ahead of them.

"I was wondering if you were thinking, as I am, that this would be a perfect place for an ambush," Leitensdorfer remarked, now that they were out of Ali's hearing. "When we left the consulate, did it seem to you that our redoubtable dragoman up ahead there seemed a bit more skittish than usual? Without making too much of a show of it, you might wish to have one of your pistols to hand."

Kirkpatrick looked quickly behind him. Ibrahim was now nowhere to be seen. A half mile ahead, they could see the buildings that lined the Nile, by which they would turn yet again to reach the river, their boats, and the security of the armed men who guarded them.

The attack came a few moments later, from a dense grove of palm trees to their right. Kirkpatrick saw Ali draw near the grove then appear to nod his head. Three men burst from the darkness in front of them, one of them engaging Ali, who had drawn his sword. Their servants dropped their torches and ran into the relative security of the gardens.

"This will be just a feint," Leitensdorfer cried. "Stand by me and have your pistols ready!" Sure enough, two other ruffians appeared from the trees, right where they would have been had they run to Ali's assistance. "I have the one on the right," said Leitensdorfer, aiming and shooting as the words left his mouth. Leitensdorfer dropped his man with the first bullet. A fine shot, thought Kirkpatrick, especially in the dark. He hit his man, wounding him and causing the wretch to disappear into the blackness from which he had emerged. They spun around to go to Ali's aid and saw him lying in the road, a dead or wounded robber next to him, and Ibrahim standing over both of them, a long curved dagger in his hand. As they ran forward, Ibrahim leaned down with his knife and finished off their wounded assailant. Kirkpatrick knelt by Ali and felt, without success, for a pulse. A wide stain, black in the dim moonlight, spread slowly over his chest.

Leitensdorfer nudged the dead attacker with his foot. "Pity this one died," he said to Ibrahim with a pointed look. "I would have liked some words with him."

"No offense, effendi, but these kind know nothing. Just a hired dog."

"All the same, it would have been useful to know who hired them. I suspect there were other motives here beyond robbery." Leitensdorfer leaned down over Ali and went through his garments, finding his purse, which he pocketed, and nothing else. "This may tell us something. Ah well. Be so good, Ibrahim, to call back our servants so we can get on with our journey."

"What of the bodies?" Kirkpatrick asked.

"There are two-legged dogs and four-legged dogs," Ibrahim answered. "Tonight it is the four-legged dogs that will eat." Then he turned, called into the fields around them, and two of their servants re-appeared, sheepishly gathering up the still guttering torches they had dropped. With Ibrahim now leading, they resumed their way toward the boats.

※

On the afternoon of their last evening in Cairo, Eaton and his party gathered in the drawing room of the consulate to discuss the farewell dinner Kourschet Ahmet Pasha had arranged in their honor. "So it seems," Eaton began, "we will be deprived of the charming social graces of our dragoman Ali. Well, he made love to that employment." Eaton helped himself to a large portion of figs, nuts, and dates from the plate in front of him, then passed it to the others. "I expect that *he* is already at supper, not where he eats but where he is eaten. But it is a pity, colonel, that Ali perished in the fight. One might have wished your man Ibrahim was less resolute in his defense or that Ali was more skilled at saving his miserable life. Now this Ibrahim—from what you and Captain Kirkpatrick tell me, he is not to be trusted either."

"I think not," Leitensdorfer responded. "I have released him and, as you know, the boy Achmet as well. I must tell you, general, that was the noblest gesture you made: emptying your own purse into the boy's pockets. In a place where a laborer may make as little as half a piaster a day, he received a princely sum."

"I looked at the poor wretch, thought of my own children safe in America, and blessed God for their safety. It was the least

I could do. But in any event, colonel, may I assume that the plot to poison us tonight goes forward?"

"I fear so," said Leitensdorfer. "The written information we received from the man we questioned turned out to be useless. We were too late to prevent Ali from delivering his deadly package to an accomplice here in the palace, of whose identity we are sadly in ignorance. If the attack on our lives is to be made at all, it must be this evening. We are untouchable in the British consulate, thanks to their increased security, and in two days we head back to Alexandria to effect the union with Hamet."

"So how do you suppose their foul scheme will be carried out?" Kirkpatrick asked.

"It cannot be through the medium of the food or wine we are served," Eaton answered. "Poison is so highly regarded by Turks and Mamelukes alike as a device for regime change that Kourschet Ahmet Pasha employs a food taster. Besides, the communal nature of meals, in which all dip with their hands into the same pot, would mean that any attempt on us would, inevitably, gather the Pasha into its lethal snare. The French, and I must agree with the colonel that their hand is at work here, would lose far more than they could ever hope to gain by the Pasha's death. I must confess that the late Ali's departure has left me quite confounded as to how he intended that our deaths would be effected. I suppose all we can do is watch the servers with great care. But we attend a state dinner in which, poison or no, we must continue to impress his highness with our civility."

Eaton turned to the others: "Please permit me to remind you and Lieutenant O'Bannon to feed yourself only with your *right hand*, and to do that only after you have washed it in the lemon water the servants will bring to the table. I am reminded of my first days as the minister to Tunis, in an occasion no less ceremonially portentous as this, when, to my great chagrin...."

"You say we must wash our hands *before* eating, and out of a separate, rather than a communal, bowl?" Kirkpatrick cried.

"That *is* the custom," Eaton replied, just barely hiding his displeasure at having his story interrupted.

"But then that's it, general!" said Kirkpatrick.

"Pray forgive me, but that's *what?*" said Eaton.

"The poison, do you see? Not the food, but the water! Poison the water, and when we use it to wash our hands, and then eat with that same hand...."

"Damn me for the greatest of fools! Of course you're right! We could raise a general cry of 'poison' and that would certainly frustrate the Frenchmen's purpose, but it would hardly advance our own, and the resulting inquiry could easily lead down paths we might not wish explored."

"Perhaps I have a solution," said Leitensdorfer. "They may provide two or three washing bowls for our party. Knowing their customs as I do, it is likely they will be filled by a servant with a single ewer of water. Should there be a fortuitous accident.... "

"And we have just the man for that task," Eaton said, turning to Kirkpatrick. "Might we take advantage of your unfettered, irrepressible nature, captain—I mean no disrespect, of course— but might you not be able to manage some appropriate clumsiness with the servant bearing the water for our use, perhaps in the guise of enthusiastic thoughtlessness—as innocuous as possible, to be sure?"

"You can count on me to manage it," Kirkpatrick replied, aware of the gentle reproof that Eaton had included in his request.

That evening found them once again in the viceroy's palace, this time in a huge banquet room, the Americans seated next to Kourschet Ahmet Pasha and his closest advisors in the place of honor. Kirkpatrick struggled for several minutes trying to figure out how to comfortably arrange his long legs under the low table before them, then gave up and awkwardly knelt on his heels. My knees will never make it through dinner, he thought. As the servants brought in the first of the many dishes that would comprise the feast, Kirkpatrick debated how best to carry out his assigned mission. His thoughts were interrupted by Eaton who rose to his feet, bowed ceremoniously to Kourschet Ahmet Pasha, and gave his brief speech of thanks in Turkish carefully rehearsed with Leitensdorfer. The viceroy then launched into a lengthy speech of welcome, like Eaton's, in Turkish. Eaton listened attentively, sympathetically, and approvingly while Leitensdorfer translated in a soft voice to Kirkpatrick, sitting on his left. Leitensdorfer didn't bother offering assistance to Captain Vincents, who sat, eyes and attention focused far away, as placidly as if he were back in his beloved Shropshire woods listening to the pleasant chattering of chipmunks.

"If I understood you properly," Kirkpatrick whispered to Leitensdorfer, "He just spoke for a half hour, in the most eloquent language, saying utterly nothing."

"I would say your understanding is perfect, captain," Leitensdorfer replied.

"Then he could surely run for election as the mayor in any city of America," said Kirkpatrick. "He'd win in a landslide. But tell me, I know they can't poison us with food, but these strange dishes might taste like poison. What are we eating?"

"That is feta cheese and spices," he pointed to one of the appetizers in front of them, "called *beyaz peynir ezmesi*. Next to it you will recognize tomatoes, garnished with garlic, lemon, and mint. I would guess the rice dish to also contain chicken, apricots and walnuts. That purplish looking dish is *pathcan kavurma*, fried eggplant in a tomato-onion sauce topped with yoghurt."

"Yoghurt?" asked Kirkpatrick. "I think I'll pass."

"Certainly it is not a taste Westerners are familiar with," Leitensdorfer said. "But you should enjoy the main dish, lamb killed this evening and cooked at the table. It is part of a ritual, going back, we believe, to the sacrifice by Abraham of his son Isaac, in which God, the All-Compassionate, intervened. Ah, but your moment has arrived." Leitensdorfer gestured to where servants, as they had expected, were walking around the large table pouring lemon water into the washing bowls.

"Then watch this," said Kirkpatrick. As soon as their two bowls were filled, Kirkpatrick cried out, in Arabic that made Leitensdorfer wince, something like "Good health on all! We Americans grate you with greetitude!" and having everyone's startled attention, plunged his left hand into the bowl.

The resulting silence was shocking. Leitensdorfer instantly began loudly berating Kirkpatrick for his utter disregard for manners and hygiene. Kirkpatrick jumped to his feet, overturning both the food dish next him and the wine that had been set out for the Americans and English.

With evident embarrassment, Eaton turned to the viceroy next to him, and apologized. "This is unconscionable, excellency! The boy is just a junior officer, without any sense of breeding or manners. I apologize from the depths of my soul for this affront to your hospitality and graciousness. He will be properly punished, I assure you. Colonel," he addressed Leitensdorfer, "Get rid of that foulness." Leitensdorfer immediately set their empty washing bowls on the floor behind him. Eaton turned back to the viceroy. "Excellency, forgive me, but may we redeem ourselves?" He gestured to the washing bowl in front of the Pasha, who, quite at a loss, merely nodded his head. As Eaton passed the bowl to Leitensdorfer he said sternly to Kirkpatrick, "Your right hand, you fool! Put your left hand near that bowl and I'll cut it off myself!"

Kirkpatrick sat down, feeling the scorn and contempt of the room fixed upon him. As the commotion subsided and the viceroy and his guests turned to their meal, he sat alone in his misery.

"You did well, captain," Leitensdorfer said, leaning close to Kirkpatrick so their conversation would not be overheard.

"Then why do I feel like such a wretched fool? Even when I do what was asked of me?"

"Perhaps you expect too much of other men," said Leitensdorfer.

"What do you mean?"

"You want them to give you what you are not willing to allow yourself to have. That's like a man trying to fill a sieve with water."

"I know I would like the general to respect me," said Kirkpatrick. "And you, colonel," he added after a pause.

"A wise man will see who you are and respect you for that. As for the rest, those who praise your success or who criticize your failure, they are fools. Taking meaning from what they say is like seeking truth in the braying of an ass. As for the general's criticism of you, remember that no one throws stones at a barren tree."

"I'm still not sure I understand," said Kirkpatrick.

"Good." Said Leitensdorfer. "Good. Accepting one's ignorance is always the first step toward wisdom. Let me ask you: do you find it troubling to be torn between confidence and uncertainty, pride and despair?"

"Sometimes the pain I feel is almost unbearable."

"Yet you withstand it. Consider this: that God turns you from one feeling to another and teaches you by means of opposites, so that you will have two wings to fly with—not just one. And besides, our failures are useful. If a man doesn't trim his beard regularly, pretty soon it grows so luxuriant it starts thinking it's the head." He looked at Kirkpatrick kindly. "Here is some more wisdom: when you are hungry, eat. The lamb is perfect—the very best thing to rouse one's spirits. Give me your plate."

Tal-Patann had chosen the Suq el Nahhasin next to the mosque of Qalaun for his rendezvous with Ibrahim the following evening. He waited impatiently for his agent's arrival, quite oblivious to the beauty of the mosque that rose before him.

"Our meeting was set for an hour ago," Tal-Patann said when Ibrahim finally made his appearance. They walked into the mosque's courtyard. In its shadows they could talk and be neither seen nor, at this hour, heard. "So our poison plot came to nothing."

"It turned out there was no way to safely administer it, and the man in our pay on the inside was terrified of Kourschet Ahmet Pasha's wrath. We naturally considered and rejected an attempt involving the food and wine. The tyrant is well-protected against poison—as well he should be. Some thought was given to placing it in the water bowls in which the Americans would clean their hands, but that was rejected as well. If sufficient poison were placed in the bowls to kill them, every time they re-dipped their fingers into the common dishes, they would have spread death around the entire table. It seems the Americans, from following Ali, suspected foul play in any event. That buffoon of a navy captain, in the pretext of giving a toast to the Pasha, conveniently managed to overturn everything, water bowls, wine, and food. I hear from my contact that the Pasha's response was polite, but icy. The Americans were quite mortified, but there's no advantage to be gained from that. The Pasha is interested in their gold, not their manners."

"A pity mortification isn't mortal," said Tal-Patann. "Especially since you so badly botched the assassination attempt on the

Shaari' Ramsis. I wonder whose side you are really on, mine or the Americans?"

"I take their money, but I despise them. Send me to Alexandria after them, and I pledge on the names of the Prophet, peace be upon him, that I will do for them as securely as I silenced Ali."

"Well, there is that," said Tal-Patann. "Ali's mouth is stopped, at least. I will consider your offer—and what it will cost me in more money. Leave me now. I will follow a few minutes after you depart." *Qabda trab u harja f'wicc kull ma kelli,* he said to himself. No more than a handful of dust and shit on the remains.

Ibrahim rose to his feet, walked through the courtyard into the *Suq,* and headed down a side alleyway. He never saw the two men who stepped from the shadows as he passed, grabbed him, stabbed him several times, and robbed his body. After ensuring his orders had been carried out, Tal-Patann worked his way through side streets to the nearby Sibil Abel Rahman Kikhiya, checking behind him and doubling his path to make sure he was not being followed. Damn Leitensdorfer's meddling, he thought. Without El Habibka to protect them here in Cairo, I thought they'd be easier prey.

CHAPTER 16
❧ THE NILE 1804 ❧

The next morning, Eaton's party made their departure from Cairo for the voyage back to Alexandria. Leitensdorfer and Eaton stood for a while on the bridge connecting the Bulaq with El Gezira Island, deep in conversation. Eaton had managed to secure the desired safe passage for Hamet, and Leitensdorfer was now charged with managing his escape from Miniet. Leitensdorfer and Eaton parted with an embrace, and the general scrambled down the embankment to where their boat was waiting.

After the general came on board and the lines were cast loose, Kirkpatrick let the current guide their *marche* into the river, steering carefully through the crowd of vessels seeking access to the port. After some tense minutes during which Kirkpatrick was acutely aware of the general's presence beside him, they cleared the narrow channel between Bulaq and El Gezira Island and found themselves again on the broad reaches of the Nile. As on their trip up the Nile, Captain Vincents' party followed them. Though the day was sullen and overcast with low dirty gray clouds presaging rain, Kirkpatrick felt as if he had been released from prison. Back in command of a boat, he felt more comfortable and competent. But his mood still matched the weather.

O'Bannon took a seat next to Kirkpatrick after the general went forward to consult his maps. "You look a bit mopish, brother," he offered.

"It's not that I'm not pleased to leave Cairo in our wake," Kirkpatrick answered. "There's such sorrow here. Everywhere we walked, we stepped in the dust of thousands of years of death and misery—and I've had the strangest dreams. In the worst, I found myself wandering in the cellar of the consulate. I came upon a small iron door. Following an impulse I could not explain, I swept aside the rubble surrounding the door, pushed it open with some difficulty, and, taking a torch with me, entered.

"I was in the first of a long series of storerooms, one leading into the next, lit by chain-suspended bronze chandeliers depicting mythological beasts. There was no sign of another human being; I was quite alone. All around me, the sides and shelves of the room were jammed with furniture and household items. Next to me was a lacquer-finished mahogany chair with a slender, curved frame embellished with ormolu highlights. As I looked around me, all I could see were hundreds of similar pieces: marble-topped pedestal tables with claw feet, sleigh beds, secretaries, commodes, armoires, all lavishly decorated with sphinxes and other Egyptian motifs or the laurel-encircled N and Bee of Napoleon. In a corner were piled a huge stack of busts, Roman-style, a few still on their pedestals, but most fallen and even shattered on the floor. Near them was a tall, lavishly decorated white gilded mirror. When I looked into it, I found myself being reflected in another room, this time ornately Turkish, much as we saw in the Pasha's palace.

"I turned to retrace my steps and found myself looking at a stone fountain. As I watched, the water from the fountain turned to blood and started gushing over the floor. I jumped back, in fear that blood might touch any part of me or my garments. I found myself running down a flight of steps, the walls around me now turned to stone and brick. I had dropped my torch somehow, but there was enough light from oil lamps set in sconces on the walls to see by. As I ran, the walls turned from rough stone to faces—

skulls, actually—I was in what seemed to be an enormous cata-comb: the wall decorations, the objects around me, even the chan-deliers were now made from human bones. I tripped and fell, and must have been rendered unconscious. When I came to, the cata-combs had given way to desert. I was lying wounded and helpless in the sand, the shadow of some huge bird circling over me. That's when I awoke. So, Presley, do you think I am quite mad?"

"Not at all. I don't dream, or I don't remember my dreams if I do. And as I listened to yours, I'm rather glad that I don't. Your dream has almost the feel of a vision, and you certainly don't need to explain to an Irishman what it means to have the Sight. Given your dream," he continued with his characteristic, open laugh, "are you sure you want to leave the comfortable world of the *Eagle* at sea and join Eaton's march through the desert?"

"More than I can tell you, or even explain. Something is com-pelling me to be a part of this mission, if Eaton will still consider me."

"Well, so long as you're willing to enter and become part of your own vision, I, for one, would be glad of your company. I'll willingly take your part with the general. You may lack some of the tact of a politico, Peter, but there's nothing wrong with your sword arm or your spirit in a fight."

"I thank you for that." Both men lapsed into silence as the *marche*, moving easily with the current, glided north towards Alexandria. They passed another of the wretched villages they had seen on their way upriver to Cairo. This one had clearly been raided: many of the small hovels the inhabitants lived in were burned, and for once, no crowd of people and mangy dogs rushed to the river bank to stare at them.

"Tell me, Presley," Kirkpatrick asked, "what do you think of this mission to put Hamet on the throne of Tripoli?"

"As a rule, Marine lieutenants don't have opinions. Thinking is above our pay grade. But if you were to be asking me as a friend,

I'd say from what I've seen of Turks and the local Bedouins, I wish we had better allies. Their loyalty lasts until they've spent the money we pay them—worse than the scourge of beggars in Cairo constantly scrounging for money. And in case you haven't noticed, they hate us as infidels. So it's odds what happens first—killing us or robbing us."

Eaton had wandered next to Kirkpatrick and O'Bannon and overheard the end of O'Bannon's comments. "Excuse me, gentlemen," Eaton said, "for intruding on a private conversation. I don't wonder that you disparage the Arabs who will serve as both our foes and our allies. One must, of course, hate one's enemies—even turn them in our minds into creatures that are less than human. If we don't hate them, how else can we kill them with the ruthless savagery war requires? But these Arabs are also our brothers in arms, their strange ways and heathen religion notwithstanding. I have spent years among them. At their worst, they richly deserve the opprobrium we Christians so readily heap upon them. All too often one finds that they have no sense of patriotism, truth, or honor—and no attachment where they have no prospect of personal gain. Poverty makes them thieves, and practice makes them adroit at stealing. Yet taken at their best, they possess a savage independence of soul, an incorrigible aversion to the mindless drudgery that we call discipline, a sacred adherence to their laws of hospitality, and a scrupulous obedience to their religious faith and ceremonies.

"So I invite you to consider: if any of us were judged solely by our faults, which if us would escape hanging? If we assume no worse of them than they of themselves, they may pass for very honorable men. And we have this in common: that as strange and primitively heathen as their religion may seem to us, ours is no less inexplicable to them. I remember a conversation I had with an Arab sheik of liberal and noble disposition whom I had befriended when I was in Morocco. When we departed, he said, with every indication of sincerity and genuine concern, that 'it was a shame for such a fine fellow as I to be barred forever from the blessings of heaven because of my lack of faith.' His words, of course."

On an impulse Kirkpatrick asked, "So what *do* you have faith in, general?"

"My mission and my men," Eaton answered with a smile at both of them. He paused for a moment. "Then this: I served in the war that gave America her freedom. So many good men suffered so much— your Grandfather Morgan among them, lieutenant— and so many paid the ultimate price—like your father, captain— that I must believe their sacrifice mattered. I must believe that the freedom all of us fought to establish was worth what it cost, not just for us but for all oppressed people. I have faith in that."

CHAPTER 17
❧ THE NILE 1804 ❧

That evening, O'Bannon sat in the *marche's* sheltered afterdeck finishing a letter by lamplight, oblivious to the shouting nearby as they enjoyed the now-ritual nightly cockroach races. Hull's midshipman, George Mann, had contrived to bring back a monstrous specimen with him from Cairo who was soundly thrashing all comers, to cries of "foul" from the other players who claimed the race was for Alexandrian-bred insects only.

Dear Father Heard:

What sad news your letter brought me, and all Americans. I, as all who loved him, must take solace knowing that Grandfather Morgan is now at peace in the bosom of the Lord, the suffering and pain of great age lifted from him. For all our conversations together, there is so much I would have wished to tell him. Forgive me if I say that for my generation, you, he, and your comrades in arms are giants—like the heroes of myths who, one by one, depart the land and country they created by their sacrifice, leaving us poorer for your departure.

It seems we are to march to attack Derna, 500 miles across the desert. I wish I might have talked with Grandfather Morgan of his exploits in the war: how he held his men together on that incredible trek to Quebec through the wilderness in the midst of winter, going days without food, to launch an attack against a fortified town in a driving snowstorm. It looks like I will be facing a similar challenge myself.

Thanks to the kindness of Captain Hull and the confidence I have earned from General Eaton, I will be given the command of the Marine detachment. I think I will be tested as an officer in ways I cannot imagine. I hope I am worthy of the name O'Bannon.

I struggle to convey to you my sense of Cairo. I had expected majesty; all I saw was misery. If you recall the hunting trip to the Dismal Swamp we took after my first tour of duty in the Mediterranean in '02, you will have a sense what we experienced. As we pushed deeper into the swamp, it felt to me that we had left the known world behind and were entering another world in which nature had first gone wild, then from wildness collapsed into ancient ruin. I'll never forget your comment as we journeyed each day deeper into trackless, sodden desolation: This must be like the world before the Flood. Small wonder God destroyed it. Cairo is the same desolation, this time of human nature. But I really must not continue; it is too dispiriting. Cairo is behind us and our mission in front of us. And I will have both a companion in that mission and a new friend as well.

On our voyage south to Cairo, we were accompanied by Captain Kirkpatrick of the Eagle, who commanded our boat. Kirkpatrick and I are now fast friends—thick as thieves, I would say, but in Egypt, that is a description of general employment, not a figure of speech. He is from Philadelphia. You may well have known his father, Samuel Kirkpatrick, a major who served in the siege of Yorktown with the Pennsylvania Brigade. I have written before of my opinion of our naval officers: they seem either to be heroes like Preble, Porter and Decatur or scrubs like Dale and Morris. Kirkpatrick seems destined to be one of the heroes, if he lives past thirty years of age. He has the true Scotsman's famous short fuse: easily blown into flame with no water tub alongside to douse it.

While we were in Cairo, we were walking home one night, later, it turned out, than we should have been, and were accosted by a brigands intent on robbing us—or worse. Kirkpatrick has picked up some Arabic and thinks what they were yelling was "Death to the

Christians." I know Mother Abigail is not pleased with my attendance at church when I'm home, and I would agree with her that I am a poor Christian when it comes to that. But it seemed a bad time to argue the point with them. I dispatched the one who set on me with little difficulty. Their work with a sword is all hack and slash; they have no notion of the use of the point. When I turned around to come to Kirkpatrick's aid, I couldn't find him. Then above me I heard fierce cries and suddenly a body, one of our attackers, came hurtling through the air from the roof above and plummeted to the ground just steps from where I stood. Kirkpatrick had chased the remaining three through a doorway, into a house past the terrified inhabitants onto the roof, where he made short work of two of them. The third leapt to his death rather than face him.

General Eaton had no end of amusement when he heard the tale. "For sure we are blessed to have among us hotspur of the north, he that kills me some six or seven dozen heathen at a breakfast, washes his hands, and says to all: Fie upon this quiet life! I want work!" I could make no sense of it, but Kirkpatrick thought it was something of Shakespeare's. Kirkpatrick wasn't sure if the general was mocking him or not; he's quite concerned that the general think well of him. But there was no mockery from the ruffians he killed. Kirkpatrick will be serving with us on the mission to Tripoli, as pleased as a little boy at Christmas when he heard the news from General Eaton. I will be glad to have him at my side, temper and all.

I have formed a better opinion of General Eaton on our trip to Cairo. He stood watch with the rest of us, made sure we were all fed before he ate, and showed no airs or haughtiness in his dealings with the men who accompanied us. He and I had many long hours in conversation working our way upriver against the current. He was gracious enough to tell me, with no touch of false pride, about his service against the Indians in Ohio and the Spanish in Georgia. As Grandfather Morgan would say, he has seen the black dog and looked it in the eye. I think he knew I needed to take his measure, and he mine, if we were to serve together. The more I get to know him, the happier I am to have passed his test.

So now we are heading back to Alexandria to wait for Hamet Karamanli's arrival. Somehow the general talked the Pasha into giving Hamet a safe conduct pass to reach us. Whether his word carries this far with the local Turks remains to be seen. Eaton says the Froggies are doing everything they can to thwart us—they attempted to poison our whole party in Cairo but Kirkpatrick literally overturned their plot.

I fear this letter has turned into a terribly confused ramble, but then it matches what we seem to be doing here. I will close with my love to Alice, and my duty to you, sir,

Your son-in-law, Presley Neville O'Bannon.

CHAPTER 18
ﻦ MINIET 1804 ﻦ

After bidding farewell to Eaton and the others, Leitensdorfer had set about the task of finding and freeing Hamet. Now calling himself by his dervish name, Murat Aga, Leitensdorfer had secured the services of a Sudanese servant, Afid, he had used before in Cairo. Afid had two great virtues: he was a giant, strong as an ox, and he was mute, his tongue having been cut out years before when he was captured and sold into slavery. And since he was convinced Leitensdorfer was a powerful magician, his loyalty was unshakable.

Leitensdorfer and Afid departed Cairo and raced across the desert, never stopping, feeding their camels balls of meal and eggs, and sleeping lashed in their saddles. On the fourth day, as they approached Miniet, the sound of gunfire alerted them to the location of the Turkish siege lines. They dismounted and crawled close enough to observe the Turkish deployment.

"Afid, look there," Leitensdorfer pointed toward the city's eastern edge. "Thou wilt notice the Turks have neglected to fully encircle their Mameluke enemies. Follow their tent line." Both men's eyes traced the rough semicircle of Turkish tents and troops until they came to a gap of at least a mile between two rough, deeply gouged wadis. "That will be the door into Miniet," said Leitensdorfer. "Once it is quite dark, find us a way into Miniet through that gap, and better, a way out for Hamet and his followers." The huge Sudanese nodded his understanding.

The next morning, as the first light appeared, Leitensdorfer was sitting in the center of the Mameluke camp, cross-legged, dressed in a wandering dervish's tall conical red cap and black robe. His eyes closed, he was chanting the ninety-nine names of Allah over and over again in a high, sing-song voice. Afid sat next to him, like a jet black mountain that had been dropped in the sand. Several hundred Mamelukes gathered around Leitensdorfer, watching and quietly discussing the magical arrival of a Holy Man.

As soon as the sun's edge rose above the surrounding hills, Leitensdorfer got to his feet and slowly removed his long outer black robe to reveal himself dressed in a white shirt, vest, and white leggings covered by a long white skirt. His eyes rose to heaven, he crossed his arms tightly over his chest, then began to whirl in place, slowly and gracefully in a clockwise fashion, his white skirt billowing around him. Afid produced a wooden flute and began to play. Almost as the first notes sounded, many of the surrounding Mamelukes began clapping in rhythm.

Minute by minute, the music's tempo increased until Leitensdorfer gracefully spread his arms, his right hand reaching up to God, his left stretched forward toward the earth. He danced for an hour then slowly collapsed in a trance. The watching Mamelukes were enthralled.

When Leitensdorfer awoke from his trance, there was food and tea set before him. By now, the hundreds of watchers included the Mameluke leaders. Ignoring the food, Leitensdorfer pulled a rope from his pocket and stretched it between his two hands. Then closing his hands, he drew the rope into a loop, pulled out a knife, and cut it cleanly through the middle. He then gathered the severed ends into his hands, clasping them tightly together and raising them to heaven, and began praying, this time in a deep, loud voice. At the climax of his prayer, he shouted *Alham-*

dulillah! and snapped his hands apart. Behold, the severed rope was whole again!

"This is the sinful life of man that God, *subhanahu wa ta'ala*, makes whole!" The miracle was greeted by shouts of acclaim and piety from the watching soldiers.

The Mameluke general, El-Aybak, approached Leitensdorfer, bowed deeply and sat down in front of him. "Why have you been sent to us, oh *Wali?*" he asked.

Leitensdorfer answered, "God, the All Merciful and Compassionate, does not intend that you should be trapped here by these treacherous Turkish dogs. I have been sent to help you find a way out of this trap. It has been revealed to me that the man who will guide you is Hamet Karamanli, the Tripolitan. Take me to him."

Leitensdorfer and Afid were ushered into Hamet's tent. As soon as they had entered, Leitensdorfer pointed instantly at Hamet, sitting among his followers, and cried, "You are the one who is chosen to lead! The rest depart!" Hamet's Bedouins left muttering: "More magic!" Leitensdorfer, of course, had been thoroughly briefed by Eaton on how to recognize Hamet. Afid positioned himself by the tent's entrance as a guard.

Beckoning Hamet to him, Leitensdorfer said in a low voice, "I come from General Eaton. The Americans are ready to support you, and as we speak, Eaton is gathering an army in Daman-hur, outside Alexandria. I have with me," and he pulled out the papers, "a *firman* from Kourschet Ahmed Pasha giving you safe passage to Damanhur." Hamet grasped the papers, scanned them quickly, and nodded his approval.

"General Eaton tells me to say these words to you: 'God, the Merciful and Compassionate, has ordained that you should see trouble. We believe He has now ordained that your troubles should have an end.'"

"What must I do?" asked Hamet.

"Have fifty or so of your best men ready to ride tomorrow morning. We will head overland, so they will need food and water."

"And the rest of my followers?" Hamet asked.

"Leave behind a few trusted men who will know where we go. Given how loosely the Turks guard Miniet, your men can sneak out at night and follow us."

Leitensdorfer spent the rest of the day visiting the sick and wounded in the Mameluke camp, treating them with salves and potions from the medicine box Afid carried, accompanied by appropriately magical passages from the Koran. Magic works, he thought, because men *want* to believe in it. If the belief is strong enough, the simplest trumpery will convince them. Ah well. Fools light lamps during the day then wonder why they have no oil at night. Perhaps my prayers will be helpful; they're certainly better than the medicine I dispensed. All the same, it's wise for a magician not to linger too long after the magic has been performed.

At first light the next morning, Leitensdorfer, Afid, Hamet and his chosen followers stole out of the camp with promises to return as soon as they had scouted out a safe escape route and killed any Turks blocking the way. As soon as they cleared the Turkish lines, they headed north toward the rendezvous with Eaton in Damanhur.

CHAPTER 19
MALTA 1805

His mission with Eaton in Egypt concluded, Kirkpatrick had boarded the *Eagle* and returned to Malta for new orders. He and fellow captain John Dent were sitting in an enclosed bower on the sweeping veranda overlooking the tree-lined expanse of Baracca and the Grand Harbor itself: the one a tumultuous bustle of strolling pedestrians—soldiers, sailors, and civilians from a dozen nations—the other an equally chaotic bustle of shipping. Slightly below them, they could see groups of British naval officers already half into their cups, laughing to the usual audience of young ladies from the better Maltese families in search of a wealthy husband and whores seeking more immediate financial gain.

Kirkpatrick's mind drifted back into Dent's conversation.

"...We were blown off station by a hellish storm two weeks ago. The *Constellation* and *Constitution* came through decently. I sprung a mast, but the *Enterprise* was badly hammered and will be in Syracuse repairing for several weeks. The worst is that the Tripolitans took advantage of the storm to slip several ships out to sea. Their twenty eight-gun frigate the *Crescent*, a fourteen-gun brig, a sloop, and we think, several feluccas are loose in the Mediterranean. These last represent no threat to us, but they could play Old Ned with our merchant ships. I'm off to Cyprus to join up with Hull in forming a convoy of merchantmen. We'll stop at Malta, Syracuse, Marseilles, and Gibraltar to pick up whatever's ready to sail before seeing them safely past the straits and home-ward bound."

"Any chance the Tripolitans will clear Gibraltar and be wait-ing in the Atlantic?" Kirkpatrick asked.

"We discussed that with Barron and Rodgers—in Barron's sickroom with him barely able to share in the discussion. Hap-pily, our treaty with Morocco is still firm. Even if the Tripolitans captured ships, they would be hard pressed to bring them to a friendly port. So I must expect them to attempt something here in the Med."

"Indeed," Kirkpatrick said. He glanced at the veranda below them. "Excuse me, John, here's someone you should meet." He rose to his feet and waved down to a British officer below them at the foot of the stairs.

"Halloa Dacres," Kirkpatrick called. "It's damned hot out there. Come join us!" The British officer waved back. Kirkpatrick called to the nearby waiter. "*Altro vetro del vino, prego, e più vino.*"

"Splendid fellow," said Kirkpatrick as they watched Dacres mount the stairs toward them. "A right seaman. Beyond the nat-ural pride one takes in one's ships and service, not the whiff of touchiness or condescension about him."

"So good of you to join us, Dacres." Kirkpatrick cried, as he rose to meet their guest. "There's the touch of a breeze here and some wine that may amuse you. May I name my particular friend, John Dent, Master Commander of the *Nautilus*? John, this is James Dacres, Premier of the *Theseus*, 74."

"Your servant, sir," replied Dacres, a broad, open smile flash-ing across his face as he shook both men's hands. "Kirkpatrick, you have saved me not just from perdition but the heat of hell to boot." He gestured down at a well-dressed and obviously furious woman on the veranda below them.

"She looks like a termagant, Dacres," said Kirkpatrick. "Pray God we are safe up here."

"If I may offer a suggestion, Dacres," added Dent, "some captures are better burned than taken home as prizes. She seems hot enough to manage that for herself."

They watched as the woman considered climbing the stairs and thought better of it. She gave one last glare up at Dacres, then, with a wonderful toss of sunlit auburn hair, spun on her heel and headed back toward the crowded tables on the veranda. "I believe I'm spared, gentlemen," said Dacres. She sat down at a table of English naval officers, picked up a glass in front of one of them, and drained it, smiling over the rim of the glass at the officer as she did. "Another sailor, another port, it seems," Dacres laughed.

They waited as the waiter poured wine for them. Dacres, another irresistible smile lighting his face, lifted a glass. "I say, Kirkpatrick, I must wish you joy of your new command. We must wet the swab, sirs," he cried, with a salute to the Master Commander's epaulet on Kirkpatrick's shoulder. "To fair seas, complaisant women, rich prizes, and rapid promotion!"

"To us all!" responded Kirkpatrick, echoed by Dent's "Hear! Hear!"

"And there's your *Eagle*," continued Dacres, pointing below them in the harbor where Kirkpatrick's ship stood out among the other vessels at anchor. "With those steep, backward raked masts and black hull, might I say she looks more like a pirate than a ship of war?"

"Why that's why Preble gave him the *Eagle*, of course," said Dent, "piracy being more his true nature."

"When it comes to prizes and prize money, gentlemen," said Dacres, "are we not all pirates at heart? But she does look fast." He turned to Kirkpatrick. "Might one ask how fast?"

"Well," responded Kirkpatrick, suddenly caught between pride and embarrassment, "suppose I was to say she makes fifteen knots with the wind just off the beam?"

"I would say" answered Dacres, "that's faster than any of His Majesty's frigates can sail unless they pump out their water and throw all their guns overboard, followed by their midshipmen." He looked at the *Eagle* with a trained seaman's eye. "In truth, a top speed of fifteen knots? Remarkable."

"Sometimes," said Kirkpatrick, "the wind and sea being favorable, of course." Unable to resist, he then added with an apologetic smile, "We did make seventeen knots coming into Alexandria," and watched the startled look on Dacres' face.

"Why that ain't sailing, you know," said Dacres." "It's flying. If you wasn't a friend, I might think this just another Yankee tall tale." Staring at the *Eagle* now with new admiration, he continued. "Seventeen knots—even fifteen—is twice the speed of most British ships. How on earth do you manage that? Is it those raked masts?"

"That's what many think, I dare say," answered Kirkpatrick. "It's what one notices first about these Baltimore topsail schooners. Certainly a sail maker will tell you that with gaff sails, the rake makes it easier to achieve good sail shape—the more rake the better. Look at the ring-tail boom, if you will. It extends our mainsail twenty five feet past the ship's stern. The rake gives us a much greater sail area for our size than a traditional vertical rig."

"But you know," said Dacres, "If the rake of a mast is more than six to eight degrees, aren't you hampered sailing down wind or with anything less than a light breeze?"

"You're right," said Kirkpatrick. "So I would say it's more a combination of different factors and getting the balance just right. What a casual observer doesn't see is hull shape. I would venture that's the most important contributor to the *Eagle*'s speed. If you look at the transom, there, Dacres, you'll see that we have an extreme rake to the sternpost—eighteen degrees—and a steep deadrise. Her sharpness fore and aft gives her what some call a hollow hull—like cutting through the water with a knife, not pushing against it with a plow."

"That's all very well as it goes," said Dacres, "but I put this to you. Unlike a square-rigged brig, you can't maneuver easily under short sail or stop and back with sails alone. I should think that a dangerous flaw in a warship."

"And so I thought, as well, before I took command of the *Eagle*," said Kirkpatrick. "I started my service and learned the ropes aboard square-rigged ships, as I suspect you did, Dacres. One masters the tactics and sailing qualities that the ship's rig and dimensions make possible. Imagine, though, that maneuvering a square-rigged ship is like steering a heavy wagon through narrow streets surrounded by high-walled buildings. It takes considerable skill, all that backing and filling. But why go to the trouble when one can just race freely across an open plain astride a swift horse? At sea, I think the only walls we encounter are the ones we raise in our own minds, based on what we always do— because that's all we imagine it's possible for us *to* do. It's quite different in fleet battles with rated ships, of course, but for us now in the Mediterranean, speed and maneuverability plus accurate, deadly fire are what it's about." Kirkpatrick stopped himself suddenly. "But there you go. I've just given another damned speech. Pray forgive me. I do seem to get carried away."

"Not at all, not at all," replied Dacres. "I grant you Americans are clever—and untroubled by past practices. There is something, I'm sure, to be said for invention and progress. If not, we'd all be sailing ships like our grandfather's. Drake's *Revenge* or even Anson's *Centurion* would look as curiously antiquated now as the doublets, slops, and codpieces of the old Queen's time on a man, or farthingales and starched Spanish ruffs on a woman. But all that said, I for one would be deucedly uncomfortable abandoning ways that have worked well in the past, or throwing long standing, honored traditions to the winds."

Dacres glanced at his watch and rose to his feet. "Gentlemen, I am afraid I must leave you. A pleasure, indeed, captain" he said to Dent. "My thanks, Kirkpatrick, for the rescue and the delightful glass of sillery. Capital. Just the thing. Perhaps we may continue our conversation, another time? Don't expect to convert me, you know. But that Yankee skimming disk of yours does interest me greatly." After a careful inspection of the veranda below, he bowed to both men and started down the stairs.

"Splendid fellow, indeed," said Dent. "Quite the welcome change from your usual stiff-necked British officer. But I would still make him the exception, not the rule." Checking to ensure Dacres was safely out of earshot, he continued. "I have more news. You would not believe how poorly Barron does. His health seems to flow with the tides, better one day and near death the next. He looks awful, the evilest yellow cast to his skin you could imagine. While you were in Cairo, Commodore Barron shifted his lodgings to Syracuse because of the excellent hospital and doctors there. As soon as he arrived in Syracuse, the Commodore was stricken to his bed. Until the Commodore regains his health, Consul Lear is in charge of all naval operations in the Mediterranean and remains in Malta.

"I wish Barron a fast and full recovery," Kirkpatrick said. "We are now in the midst of a war without a commanding officer. Rodgers does what he can, but Barron won't step down—or just between us, Tobias Lear won't let him. All Lear talks about is arranging a treaty with the enemy instead of prosecuting the war. If Rodgers we're in command, we'd see an end to that nonsense and a return to the energy we displayed under Preble. But now Barron's sending *Enterprise* and *Vixen* to rejoin the blockade. Locking the barn door after the horses leave, I should say. Then there's the matter of securing naval stores to refit our ships. Between the Maltese scoundrels in the shipyard and the fools we hire to deal with them ... "

"What the devil!" Dent cried. Standing before them, as if he'd jumped out of a Genie's flask, was a little ragamuffin of a boy.

Kirkpatrick recovered his composure first. "Look here, you little wretch. We are not interested in your young sister, your mother, your aunts, your cousins, your grandmother, or any other flesh you are peddling. Perform another magic act and disappear this instant!"

"Oh no, sirs. None of that," the bundle of rags in front of them replied. "I have message here for Captain Kirkpatrick. Fine gentlemen below," he pointed toward some English naval officers, regarding them with mild curiosity, "said I might find Yankees skulking in the shrubbery. Their words, good sirs, not your worthless servant's." With that, he pulled an envelope from under his soiled shirt and placed it on the table. It was addressed to Kirkpatrick and sealed with the British consulate stamp.

Kirkpatrick seized the envelope and tore it open to read the invitation it contained. Wordlessly, he passed it over to Dent, who read it just as quickly.

"Well, ain't you the Grand Beejum in the flesh, Kirkpatrick! You are 'requested and prevailed upon to present yourself at the British Consulate this evening at 7:00 sharp to attend to a matter of grave importance.' It carries the signature of the Consul himself. I shouldn't doubt but that they wish to honor you with an earldom, or a knighthood, at least. You will, naturally, require a loyal page to serve you," and with that he rose from the table and bowed elegantly to Kirkpatrick—and they both saw the small boy, still standing in front of them and smiling.

"John?" Kirkpatrick asked with a helpless shrug.

"Again? Peter, you really might wish to consider capturing some of your conquests and sending them back as prizes, not just sinking them." He threw a few coins across the table at the little boy who scooped them up effortlessly. "Now leave us," Dent said.

"I go, worthy sirs. I go—but should your worships change your mind, I have a little sister of fourteen years. On my mother's life, she is a virgin, who..."

"Now look here," said Dent, "you misbegotten goat's spawn fathered by a pox-ridden Greek. My friend here, for all his youth, is the most feared, murderous, heartless monster on the inner sea. By his hand he has slaughtered a thousand Turks, and no one bothers to count the Arabs. He was raised in America by the savage Indians and fed from infancy on a diet of little babies and small boys. He is monstrously sharp set with hunger, and while he might wish you to have more fat on you, dirty as you are, you would serve to take edge off his famine. Unless you wish to feel the flesh torn from your bones, disappear yourself this instant!"

Without another word, their little messenger disappeared.

"So, Peter, can you penetrate this mystery?" Dent asked.

"I haven't a clue," Kirkpatrick said.

"With your infernal luck, Peter, you will be on detached service, running around scooping up prizes on a voyage, while Isaac and I slog along playing nursemaid to a bunch of slow-sailing merchant tubs. If you sat any of these wool-gathering merchant captains on a gunpowder keg with a lighted match at hand, you couldn't get them to move. As for keeping station ... Hmph. We can hope that the *Crescent* or their other ships make some attempt on the convoy, but I fear that's just whistling for a wind. Unless they believe they have overwhelming superiority, we can't expect them to attack our navy."

∞

Promptly at 7:00 p.m., Kirkpatrick was ushered into Sir Samuel's study. General Eaton rose to greet him warmly.

"Why here you are, on the moment. Nothing like the Navy for keeping time, hey? Captain Kirkpatrick, may I introduce you to Consul Briggs?" Sir Samuel rose, returned Kirkpatrick's bow, and took him by the hand.

"Come, captain. We have been enjoying an unusually fine burgundy. Will you please join us?"

When they sat down, Sir Samuel nodded toward a third man who had remained seated. "This gentleman, who shall remain nameless, has information of great interest to General Eaton's planned mission. I pray you begin, sir." Kirkpatrick looked at the third man for the first time, noticed the stranger's penetrating stare, and instantly felt like a bug being dissected.

"Gentlemen," Grey began, "we understand the... ah... difficulties you have been experiencing in securing the funding to support your affair with Hamet and Tripoli." Kirkpatrick's nervousness turned to anger as he sensed the mockery just below Grey's politeness. "Happily, we make be able to offer you a solution. We have learned that Napoleon intends to buy the Turks' loyalty with a treasure worth more than two hundred thousand pounds. A nondescript Lebanese merchant ship has put to sea with the treasure from Marsala, in Sicily, to rendezvous off the island of Lampedusa with a Tripolitan ship, the *Tripoli*. From there, the *Tripoli* will take the treasure to Alexandria. Do you know this ship, by any chance, Captain?"

"Yes, sir," said Kirkpatrick. "I saw Lieutenant O'Bannon's report on the Tripolitan warships that he observed in Gibraltar in '01. With her strangely painted hull, the *Tripoli* will be unmistakable. My thought would be to wait off Alexandria."

"Then I see no obstacle to your seizing this ship and its cargo. For reasons I will not disclose, His Majesty's government wishes that this treasure not reach Mohammed Ali and the Turks. Nor must we be seen to have been involved in this affair. Your absolute discretion regarding this conversation is required. But the treasure, once captured, would go a long way to furthering General Eaton's plans, which..."

"Sir, you can count on my discretion and resolve in this matter!" Kirkpatrick interrupted. "But surely that much gold will attract attention, if for no other reason than its bulk." The silence that followed his outburst deafened him. Briggs had turned his gaze to a minute inspection of the dregs in his wineglass; Eaton stared at him in shock, as if Kirkpatrick had just broken wind in a drawing room. The stranger just looked at him.

"A fine observation, captain, really," Grey said, "and one, it appears, that has already occurred to the French, which is why the treasure will be delivered in gems: diamonds, rubies, emeralds and the like—easily transported and hidden. It is a bribe just as welcome as gold. You will look for a metal strongbox, perhaps a third the size of a seaman's chest, hidden in the Turkish captain's quarters. Once you secure the treasure, you are to take it immediately to General Eaton. I trust you can find the general's lodgings?"

"Yes, sir."

"Good. We are settled then," said Grey. "Captain, I'm sure you have pressing matters to attend to?"

Kirkpatrick saluted the officers and turned quickly toward the door, aware that he had been not only dismissed, but dressed down in front of General Eaton. He stepped into the corridor, closing the door behind him more sharply than he should have. "Fool!" he said to himself bitterly, "I will never learn to curb my tongue!" He heard a soft cough behind him and spun around toward the sound, realizing in horror that he had been speaking aloud. General Eaton had followed him out the door, and stood observing him, a humorous smile on his face.

"Captain Kirkpatrick," Eaton said, "that was certainly an awkward moment in there, but please remember, you follow my orders and serve America's purposes, not England's. I have the utmost confidence in your ability to succeed in this matter." He placed a hand on Kirkpatrick's shoulder. "God speed and good sailing, captain, and let you come back to me with news of a stunning triumph."

"I will not fail you, sir," said Kirkpatrick. Had he been praised by the President, it could not have done more to lift his spirits.

CHAPTER 20
❧ MALTA 1805 ❧

Peter Kirkpatrick and John Dent had returned to the bower in the veranda for a late supper.

"... That's as much as I can tell you, John. It seems we are to be paymasters for General Eaton's expedition, but before we can distribute the money, we must collect it. Where would you think to intercept the *Tripoli?*"

"You have the advantage of knowing where they must arrive, Peter, if not when, and thus can let them come to you—although it would help to know if he was making for the eastern or western harbor. Was I the *Tripoli's* captain and as anxious to be rid of my burden as he must be, with the wind as it is this time of year I should think he would head straight for the Great Pass, and avoid the coastal shoals altogether." Dent pulled a scrap of paper and a pencil from his pocket and quickly sketched a map showing the deep water channel that stretched out from Alexandria through the treacherous shoreline that surrounded the city. "Here he will make his choice, I would guess, for east or west. What do you think?"

Kirkpatrick pulled the sketch to him, spun the paper to orient it, and made an *X* at what might be ten miles off the edge of the Great Pass. "Here he must come, and here we will be. He may sail with thousands of leagues of sea room to hide him, but the door into Alexandria is small enough to be easily guarded."

"So how will you get the treasure to Eaton?" Dent asked. "Lieutenant Lane's Marines and a division of the crew?"

"I think not. A large, heavily armed party would attract attention, and between the rival Turks and Mamelukes who patrol different parts of the city at night, far too much curiosity. I'll take six men with me. Dressed as locals, we'll slip ashore at dusk, then go down Shari Faransa past the El-Shorbagi Mosque complex and cut through the back alley leading to Eaton's quarters in the *Place des Consuls*," Kirkpatrick said.

"Well then, I wish you good luck and fair seas," Dent said.

As the two Americans rose to leave, their small messenger from the afternoon crouched behind the low wall surrounding the arbor. Once he saw the Americans were safely away, he scurried down the veranda steps and turned into an alley. The man who had hired him handed him a gold coin and asked, "So. Your news?"

Captain Vincents and Burton Grey were meeting in Briggs' study. Sir Samuel had declined to join them. "A capital plan, I dare say! The best thing!" exclaimed Vincents. "The Americans will rob Napoleon's treasure from the French and we will rob it from the Americans."

"Quite so," said Grey. "You will, of course, be dressed in Arab robes. You don't speak French, I suppose?" Captain Vincents looked back at him with benign puzzlement as if he'd just been asked if he had wings and could fly. "I thought not," said Grey. "Then do your best to disguise your voice."

"And if they resist? That might lead to unpleasantness," said Captain Vincents.

"It is the business of you and your men to see that no such thing happens," Grey responded. "I have given you the route they are directed to take to General Eaton's quarters. We have ensured that the treasure will be guarded by no more than six men, including the captain, dressed like you, in native costume. Station your men, armed with pistols, along the route so that they can flow, one or two at a time, into whatever crowd of townspeople are accompanying the Americans. Even at the evening hour picked for their departure for Eaton's, there will be enough people on the streets for your men to blend in innocently. They will come down the Sharri Al-Horreya. Before they reach the alley leading to Midan Tarir, which they have been directed to take, each of your men should be walking next to an American. A pistol to the head of each American should quell any thought of foolhardy resistance on their part. Be sure to take their weapons. The captain will have the treasure on him. We have arranged to have a door in the alley unlocked, on the left side; it's the only door you will see. Pull him in, remove the treasure, and let him loose. Your men by then will have disappeared back into the crowd. Without weapons, the Americans will hardly pursue them, and they will doubtless be more concerned for their captain."

"He has the reputation of a hot-tempered man and surely will not give up the treasure without a struggle, regardless of the peril to his life."

"Then you have my permission to knock him over the head with your pistol," said Grey, "and let the blame go to the French."

Tal-Patann sat in Chameau's rented room in the Ras At-Tin, overlooking the old western harbor. "What a complete piece of *demerdement* you have managed to contrive in Alexandria," said Chameau. "With no El Habibka to contend with, you have been outwitted by imbeciles!" He waited for Tal-Patann's response. Getting none, he continued. "Fortunately for us, the American

Consul Lear's gullibility exceeds your stupidity. The Americans have somehow learned of the shipment of treasure. According to the man I have placed in Lear's close circle, they intend to capture it at sea, bring it to Alexandria, and then take it to Eaton so he can use it to raise an army against the Pasha of Tripoli. That must not happen; we have our own plans for the Pasha, and that treasure must not wind up in the Americans' hands. Have you five or six ruffians you can command who will follow orders and kill without needing to know the reason or purpose?"

"I have the very men for the job," answered Tal-Patann. "They would slit their mother's throats for money."

"Fine," said Chameau. "If they turn out to be competent, I may hire them to slit yours, as well. Now here is what you will do. The treasure will be aboard a Tripolitan ship. Their captain thinks the money is promised to the Pasha of Tripoli. I will look for their ship arriving in the Western Harbor. If the Americans are successful in seizing the treasure, their ship will pass the western Harbor to enter the eastern Harbor used by foreigners. Once we know who has the treasure, we will know what to do. If the Tripolitans elude the Americans, I will handle the receipt of the treasure as planned. If the American ship shows up, then you and your men will intercept the treasure and bring it to me." Chameau paused for a moment. "No. I think I will go with you and your men to ensure there is no more failure on your part. Now see to your men, and make sure you are in position to watch the entrance to the eastern Harbor. We will arrange to meet in the alley behind the Abu El-Abbas Mosque."

CHAPTER 21
ঌ THE EAGLE 1805 ঌ

The *Eagle* was holding station off the entrance to the Great Pass leading into Alexandria. Kirkpatrick stood by the wheel, enjoying the lift and surge of his ship on yet another brilliant morning. He checked the shape of the clouds and weather to the west for the hundredth time. If the *Tripoli* has made a smooth crossing, Kirkpatrick thought, she will appear tomorrow. This will be my first real test in a ship against ship battle; success or failure will sit upon my shoulders and no one else's. I think—rather I hope—I am ready for the challenge. The real question is whether the men believe I'm ready.

When Kirkpatrick had abruptly assumed command of the *Eagle* following Dickie Somers' death, he had steeled himself to the inevitable comparison with the *Eagle*'s former captain. The fact that we were friends don't signify, thought Kirkpatrick. In the crew's minds the question will be, do I measure up to Dickie?

Kirkpatrick had discretely inquired about Somer's attitude toward punishment. With a captain like Dickie, Kirkpatrick thought, they will consider fair what they have become used to. Happily, I'm of his mind when it comes to discipline and punishment. What did Preble tell us so often: "When a captain can only maintain discipline with the lash, he is whipping the wrong man."

So he had instantly abandoned the notion of making his mark by improving the crew's seamanship. By now, every man on the

Eagle knew the ropes, and could hand and reef a sail and pull an oar in a true seamanlike way. More than that, Kirkpatrick recognized that his topmen seemed to know what his command would be before he gave it, so quick was their response in trimming sail. Kirkpatrick had wondered uncharitably if they ever thought to themselves: Captain Dickie wouldn't 'a done it that way. So with seamanship out of the question, Kirkpatrick had decided to make himself a very tartar when it came to gunnery.

All his officers and gun captains well knew the competitive standards for rates of fire among the various nations' navies in the Mediterranean. The official, but optimistic, British standard was three broadsides every five minutes: optimistic because the Admiralty was notorious for "powder pinching" in restricting the allotment of powder and shot for the navy. British captains would start a months-long voyage with 100 rounds for each gun—if they were fortunate. Unless British captains had their own private funds to pay for the ammunition required for practice or were lucky in taking prizes, captains guarded their supplies for use in battle. Most British captains limited practice merely to the dumb show of running the great guns in and out. British disregard for speed of fire applied as well to accuracy. Rather than attempt long-distance shooting, most captains were content to bring their ships alongside the enemy and batter it out, yardarm to yardarm, with the inevitable cost of increased casualties. If they cared more for their men, Kirkpatrick thought, they would train them better.

French practice, for the most part, emphasized accuracy over speed. French gunnery could be accurate—devilishly accurate in fact—but slow: a French ship that could manage three broadsides in six minutes was doing very well indeed. The Spanish trailed the French both in speed and accuracy, and the Barbary nations paid no attention to gunfire at all, preferring to win battles by boarding their enemy and overwhelming them in hand to hand combat.

Kirkpatrick knew Preble was convinced that America would be at war with England within a decade. "We are on a collision course with our former masters," Preble would often and adamantly remark. "We can never hope to equal them in number of ships, so we must become more deadly in battle: bigger, faster, stronger ships and more lethal gunnery. Every American ship must achieve or better the rate of fire of the very best British ships, and be able to sustain that level amidst the deafening noise, blinding smoke, and chaos of battle."

Preble's words echoed in Kirkpatrick's mind as he thought of the impending fight with the *Tripoli*. So it was no more than expected routine when the *Eagle* beat to quarters after breakfast for gunnery drill. The ship's carpenters had banged together targets of empty barrels, broken spars, and discarded canvas to be towed behind the ship's launch. As Kirkpatrick readied the ship for gunnery practice, he was pleased to observe that the level of competition among the gun crews was, as usual, very high: not only for the prize of an extra ration of grog in the evening, but more for the opportunity for the winning crew to lord it over their shipmates—until the next gunnery practice. Kirkpatrick had placed a board painted with the winning gun's name in each competition above the main hatch where all could see. He knew it was the source of healthy rivalry, spirited mockery, and active wagering among the *Eagle*'s crew—and, he suspected, an equally enthusiastic lottery among his officers.

Kirkpatrick had planned a surprise for today's drill. He walked down the starboard battery until he came to the aft-most gun, *Serapis*, named after the British ship defeated by John Paul Jones in the Revolutionary War. The gun captain, Natty Wilson, was an old growler who had served with Paul Jones in that victory.

"Wilson," Kirkpatrick cried, "I have bad news for you, I fear. It turns out that the trollop you so diligently serve in Valletta has given you a monstrous case of the clap, and you must report to sick bay on the double."

Kirkpatrick's announcement was greeted by brief rejoinders from the seven-man gun crew: "Old Natty had the clap from his mother the day he was born, sir!" "He's served her up with a brace of bastards; turnabout is fair play!"

"Now look you here, men," Kirkpatrick cried, instantly regaining their attention. "For this drill you must do without your gun captain. Wilson, you must stand aside. You may observe, but must say nothing to help or guide your crew." In the silence that followed his command, Kirkpatrick went down the line of the starboard battery, gun by gun, here removing another gun captain, there a loader or the strongest member of the crew charged with hauling the heavy weapon back against the bulwark for firing. He repeated the instructions with the port-side gun crews, often with an equally bantering explanation for each man's sudden, enforced absence. When he reached the last, forward-most port gun, he called out to the gun crews:

"Men, each of your crews is short a man; he has lost, if not the number of his mess, perhaps for this drill the number of his grog, as each of you will, unless you can immediately re-assign his duties among you! Officers, be ready with your watches and tally boards. The practice will start in two minutes!"

For the next hour, the *Eagle* sailed forward through a dense cloud of cannon smoke as batteries raced to hit the towed targets with the greatest possible speed and accuracy. At the half hour, Kirkpatrick cried to his First Lieutenant, "Mr. Christopher, about ship!" and the *Eagle*'s topmen and sail trimmers leapt into action to bring the Eagle smoothly onto the starboard tack and bring the larboard battery into play. After an hour, the shrill call of bo'suns whistles signaled the men to belay firing. Once his hearing, and that of his men, had recovered from the deafening cannon fire, Kirkpatrick addressed the crew.

"Sharply done, *Eagles*; sharply done!" he cried. "I threw you a nasty turn there and you responded well—very well. This will be our regular practice from now on. God forbid a man ever goes down, but should that happen, each of you must know each other's duties so well that regardless of who remains, you can still serve your gun with speed and accuracy or help another gun crew in need. But Wolinsky," he addressed a loader who had taken command of the forward starboard gun, who was now grimacing from the pain of crushed toes, "If you wish to keep both legs you were born with, stand back when you pull the lanyard! And *Truxtons*," he called out to another crew, "too eager, too eager by half. Remember to time the ship's upward roll, and let the target come to you!" Then Kirkpatrick said something he imagined would never be heard on a British ship.

"Officers, report to me with your tallies. We will announce the winner shortly. Gun captains, while we are comparing results, meet with your crews to review how you handled the challenge I threw at you and determine how you will improve your work as a team. I will expect a report from each gun captain after supper. Now Mr. Christopher, if you please, you may have the men stand down."

The following morning, the *Eagle* was now nine leagues out of Alexandria, sailing easily through moderately rolling swells on a close reach under topsails and fore-and-aft mainsails. Breakfast had just been cleared when then the lookout cried, "Sail to starboard, four points off the starboard bow!" Kirkpatrick and Thomas Christopher called for their glasses and caught the glint of sails just above the horizon.

Kirkpatrick checked the breeze, looked aloft to see how the *Eagle*'s sails were drawing, and said, "Thomas, let's hang out more laundry. I think we should chase this rabbit down." Within a minute, stu'nsails blossomed on the *Eagle*'s windward topsail and t'gallant and she drove through the sea with greater force and urgency. Two hours later, their prey, now obviously a brig about their size, was well within sight, still four points off the *Eagle*'s bow to windward. "What do you make of her?" Christopher asked.

"I saw Lieutenant O'Bannon's report on the Tripolitan warships he observed in Gibraltar in '01," Kirkpatrick answered. "Those garish colors: yellow hull, white streak, and heavy Spanish rigging can only mean the *Tripoli*. She carries fourteen 9-pounders—a broadside of no more than sixty-three pounds—but she's crammed with men. Lieutenant O'Bannon thought upward of a hundred and twenty boarders beside the crew to sail her. Her captain is Kemal Reis."

"Kemal Reis? Why, that's the greatest pirate of the whole damned lot," said Kirkpatrick. "A Scottish renegade who turned Turk. His name is a byword for treachery and murder. He has more innocent blood on his hands than human blood in his veins. We'll see to him."

"Shall we fetch her wake?" asked Christopher.

"I think so," said Kirkpatrick. "If we show a British ensign at our forepeak and come up easily on her leeward side, they'll think nothing's amiss. See to the British ensign, Tom, and have our flag at the peak as well, cased and ready to fly."

In response to the British flag, the *Tripoli* reduced sail to its fore topsail and head sails, allowing the *Eagle* to come up to her. Kirkpatrick had ordered the topsails brailed up, so the *Eagle* now sailed under fore-and-aft sails only. The starboard guns were double shotted with round ball and grape, and he had sent the three best shots among his Marines into the rigging with ship's boys as loaders. The remaining Marines were at their battle station under Lieutenant Lane.

"Eagles!" Kirkpatrick cried to the crew ranged in stations on the deck before him: "We know their game. They will fire one volley, give a great shout, doubtless to terrify us, and then seek to board. It serves them well against helpless merchantman. But I think they have caught no merchantman here, rather an American ship that will pay them dearly for their arrogance! We mean to take her as a prize, so sweep her decks clear of men, but as you value your lives, do not touch her hull."

The two ships drew abreast, within pistol shot. "Well, she is garish ... and ugly," Christopher said to Kirkpatrick. Look at her taffrail there." To mount stern chasers, the *Tripoli* had cut down her aft railing, giving her a decidedly down-at-the-heel look. "She appears, for all the world, like a dog slinking along with its tail between its legs."

"And a mangy dog at that," said Kirkpatrick. "Look at the lubberly way they have furled their courses." The *Tripoli*'s furled sails hung in loose, uneven baggy bundles under the yardarms. "They carry their clewgarnet blocks, old style, near the center of the yardarm and haul the sail by buntlines and clewlines. Ugly isn't in it. And they've made Irish Pennants out of the gaskets instead of tricing them up neatly. They are certainly no sailors. Let's see what sort of fighters they turn out to be."

Kirkpatrick picked up his speaking trumpet. "What ship is that and whither bound?" he called in French. Hearing no reply, he called again in English.

Back came the response they had expected. "His Supreme Tripolitan Majesty's Ship *Tripoli*. We have come out seeking Americans, but sadly haven't found any."

"Allah has smiled on you with fortune then," called out Kirkpatrick, then to the midshipman standing next to him, "Strike the British ensign, show our colors, and fire a warning shot!"

The *Eagle*'s single shot was met with a poorly aimed, ragged broadside from the *Tripoli*, followed by the expected loud cry of defiance from the boarders massed on her deck.

The *Eagle's* response was a deafening broadside from her starboard double-shotted battery. Unlike the solid shot used for long guns, American carronades fire a hollow ball that explodes into shrapnel as it hits home. At that close range, the *Tripoli's* deck turned into a horror of metal fragments, musket balls released from the grape canisters, and a lethal cloud of wood splinters from the shattered bulwarks. The two ships, now rocking almost motionless alongside each other, exchanged broadsides, the Americans firing at the tongues of flame from the *Tripoli* that pierced the grey pall of gun smoke settling over both ships. After fifteen minutes of battering, the *Tripoli's* port broadside had been reduced to sporadic fire from a single gun.

Wind filling her sails again, the *Eagle* surged forward. The *Tripoli's* decks had been turned into a wreckage of shattered bulwarks and shot-away rigging. Blood ran freely over her scuppers.

"She strikes! She's ours!" Christopher yelled, as the *Tripoli's* green and white striped flag tumbled to the deck and a cheer rose from the *Eagle's* crew.

Well she might, thought Kirkpatrick. "Helm hard a-port. Gun crews stand down." he cried, and the *Eagle* gathered speed to cut in front of the *Tripoli,* not less than fifty feet away. Suddenly, the *Tripoli* turned into the wind, her huge lateen sail released from its brails. She lunged at the *Eagle,* her flag again rising to the pinnacle. Up from her protected hull swarmed dozens of boarders, clustering into her bow, screaming in rage.

Show your wings, *Eagle,* Kirkpatrick said to himself, and with his wish, a gust caught his ship's undamaged sails and drove her forward. As she passed the *Tripoli,* the aft 24-pounders fired double loads of grape into the men massed in the *Tripoli's* bow. The first rows of boarders simply disappeared in a red cloud.

"Two points to leeward," Kirkpatrick called to the helmsman, bringing the wind square back on the *Eagle's* starboard beam. "Pick up speed, then come about. Let's pull the rest of her teeth!" The *Eagle* sped ahead, gracefully tacked, and came up along the *Tripoli*'s undamaged starboard side. As the two ships drifted together, the *Eagle*'s fire smashed into the *Tripoli*, broadside after broadside, until the enemy's guns were silenced. Her mizzen mast collapsed and in a tangle of wreckage and with it, down came the *Tripoli*'s flag again.

"Have a care! She means to board us again," Kirkpatrick cried. Sure enough, the *Tripoli* put her helm over and tried to make another pass at the *Eagle* but failed. Boarders—now fewer of them—again crowding into her bow. This time, the *Eagle*'s entire broadside, gun after gun, tore into the helpless mass of men. The *Tripoli,* her decks swept clean of the living and her helm unmanned, drifted past the *Eagle*. A lone figure, obviously European, his arm in a sling and his shirt red with blood, picked his way through the tangle of rigging and bodies and called out to the *Eagle*, this time in English.

"Mercy! Mercy, in the name of God the Compassionate. We truly surrender. You have slaughtered us! Here is my flag." With that, he stooped behind him, pulled up the tattered Tripolitan flag, and dropped it into the sea,

"Lower a boat, then, and come aboard."

"I cannot, sir. I have no boats left. You have destroyed them all and the men who would row them as well."

"Then we will board you. But mark you. Attempt another scurvy trick, and you are the first man to die. Mr. Lane," he called. "Have your men aim at that scoundrel. If you see the sign of resistance, shoot him down!"

Kirkpatrick, Christopher, and ten men rowed across and climbed into the charnel house that had once been the *Tripoli*. As he mounted her side, Kirkpatrick looked below him to see sharks gathering around the ship. The deck of the *Tripoli* was a scene from Hell. The deck was slippery in blood, and strewn with bodies and parts of bodies. Maimed men, many with arms and legs severed or cruelly laid open, lay where they had fallen. A desolate party of the survivors worked along the deck, picking up the wounded to carry below and throwing the dead or those past saving overboard. From below came the most unholy tumult of voices, crying in pain, groaning, and, Kirkpatrick imagined, loudly cursing their fate.

Kemal Reis limped forward to meet them, pulled his sword, and offered it hilt-first to Kirkpatrick, who took it, and threw it into the sea.

"I will not disgrace myself, sir, by accepting your sword." Then, pulling out a pistol and pointing it at Kemal Reis's head, said, "Your cabin, now, sir, and none of your damned treacherous ways."

They entered the undamaged cabin, and with his pistol, Kirkpatrick gestured Kemal Reis to the cabinets in the stern. "You have something we want, I believe. In a metal-bound chest. Produce it now or die in the instant."

Kemal Reis moved to his chart desk, opened a drawer, and took out a key. He fumbled left-handed for a few moments with the lock of a cupboard before Kirkpatrick strode forward, grabbed the key, forced the lock open, and saw a metal-clad strong box inside. He turned to Kemal Reis.

"Bring that box out and place it on the table."

"But my wound," Kemal Reis replied, pointing to where a Marine rifle ball had ruined his shoulder.

"Damn you and damn your shoulder. Either the box on the table or your dead body."

Kemal Reis managed painfully to wrestle the box on to the chart table. Kirkpatrick yanked the key chain from Kemal Reis' neck and opened the box. There indeed were the seven bags of precious stones. "Now sir," Kirkpatrick said. "Americans do not kill prisoners of war, nor, unlike you cursed Turks, do we torture them. But you are not a prisoner. You are an acknowledged and attainted renegade, a pirate, and a murderer, guilty of monstrous crimes and rapine beyond measure. I would venture there are only two men here who know the contents of this box. Now there will be one. As I am your judge, my verdict is that you forfeit your life for your crimes." With that, he shot him in the head.

Kirkpatrick mounted the deck and saw Christopher directing the *Tripoli's* survivors as they tossed the bodies of their dead comrades over the side to the waiting sharks.

"There is no fight left in them," Christopher said, "so we put them to work."

"Good. Tell me, Tom, what is the butcher's bill here?"

"Forty-three dead, another twenty-one more will not see the next morning, and some thirty less seriously wounded." He paused and shook his head. "For our tally, but three wounded, and none seriously."

"You may add another to the list of their slain," said Kirkpatrick. "You'll find him in the cabin. I will cross back to the *Eagle* and send back the surgeon with lint and bandages. There may be something he can do for the wretches who remain alive." He looked at a pitiful group of survivors huddled around the *Tripoli's* shattered binnacle. The murder dashed out of them, he thought, they might almost pass for men.

The next morning, Christopher and Kirkpatrick sat in the *Tripoli's* cabin as the prize crew that would take her back to Malta finished knotting, spicing and repairing the rigging damaged in the battle.

"I wish you a safe journey, Tom," said Kirkpatrick. "I saw you looking at the treasure, and I, too, imagined the shares that might come to us, after Barron, of course, received his cut. But there's nothing in that. Giving the money to Barron would be like placing it in Lear's pocket, and anyway, I would never fail in my duty to the general."

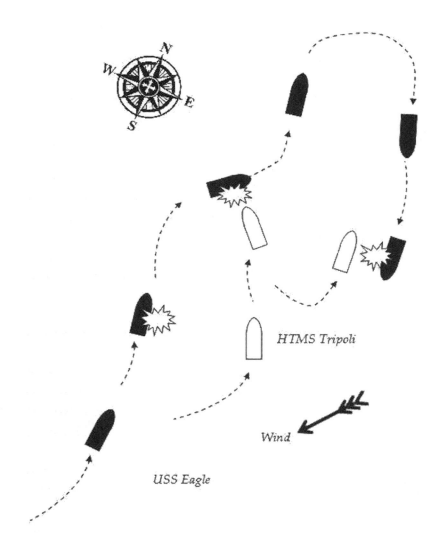

CHAPTER 22
࿏ ALEXANDRIA 1805 ࿏

As soon as the *Eagle* had safely made her anchorage in the eastern Harbor, Kirkpatrick dispatched Lieutenant Lane to get the Mameluke costume he had worn in Cairo from his room in the embassy and pick up five burnooses from one of the *suqs* on the way. Lieutenant Lane returned as dusk was approaching, carrying several large parcels.

"So, Lieutenant, I trust your shopping trip was successful?"

"I have your Mameluke outfit, sir, including the chainmail vest—which I hope you don't need. As for the rest, the Brits at the consulate fitted me out."

"They don't know about our mission?" Kirkpatrick hastily asked.

"Oh no, sir." A large smile lit up Lane's craggy face. "I told them some of the boys were going *gishta*-hunting." Seeing the puzzled look on Kirkpatrick's face, he added: "*Gishtas*. Beggin' your pardon, sir, that's whores in the local lingo. I told 'em we wanted to improve our odds."

"A good story, Lieutenant," Kirkpatrick said. "They would believe no less of US Marines. Did you locate the alley where we turn past the El-Shorbagi Mosque?"

"As you ordered, sir. It's 263 paces past the fountain at the southwest corner of the open space in front of the mosque. The building to the left of the alley has a purple and gold awning and barrels—oil, I think—stacked out in front. There's a big chunk out of the balcony by the opposite building; we can't miss it."

As soon as the sun had set, while there was still light, Kirkpatrick, Lieutenant Lane and four Marines set out, armed with cutlasses and pistols. Kirkpatrick had transferred the treasure to bags hung around his neck under his robe. Lieutenant Lane and another Marine led the way, Kirkpatrick following ten yards behind with Sergeant Townley. Two more Marines trailed them twenty yards back. They encountered no problems proceeding down the busy Shari Faransa; Kirkpatrick's costume ensured that passersby gave him ample room. Navigating the El-Shorbagi Mosque complex was just as easy. At this hour after prayers, the courtyard in front of the mosque was largely deserted. They found the fountain without trouble and headed down the narrow street past it toward their turn at the alley. By now, the buildings around them cast the street into deep shadow. The few merchants they saw were closing their shops for the night.

They entered the alley, now walking in a tight group, when armed men burst out of the building behind them. Kirkpatrick and the Marines pulled out their pistols and spun to face their attackers. Before they could act, a voice cried out: "Halt, or you die where you stand!" A fusillade of shots rang out from the roofs of the buildings on either side, and the attackers behind them crumpled to the ground.

"Unless you wish to share the same fate as the thieves we just killed," the voice called out from above them, "you and your men must drop your weapons. Put aside thoughts of resistance. At this range we won't miss." Kirkpatrick and the Marines scanned the rooftops above them, trying to count their attackers. Six? Ten? He couldn't tell.

He saw two men in Arab garb step out of the shadows at the end of the alley ahead of them. Three of their new attackers entered the alley behind them, going to each of the men they'd shot and finishing off the wounded. "Save this one," he heard one say. "He's their leader." They dragged him off.

The Marines, still holding their pistols, looked to Kirkpatrick. His mind raced through his choices, all of them bad. If we try to put up a fight, we'll die in the instant and they'll still have the treasure. I can't throw away my men's lives for nothing. After a moment's further thought, he shook his head and unbuckled his sword belt, letting it fall to the ground. "We have no choice," he called out to the Marines. "Do as they say." He placed his pistol next to his sword and reluctantly, the Marines followed his example. Their new attackers quickly bound and gagged them. Their leader pulled aside Kirkpatrick's robes, found the bags, and cut them free with his knife. Wordlessly, he took the bags. Their captors ran back up the alley and disappeared.

The voice called out again from the rooftop: "We've left your bonds loose, captain. You can release your men after we've gone. Consider remaining alive ample compensation for the loss of the treasure."

Kirkpatrick, still dressed like a Mameluke, stood before General Eaton in his quarters, feeling as embarrassed as someone who had showed up at a wake dressed, by mistake, for a costume party. He wished a stray shot from the *Tripoli* might have crippled him or that he'd died defending the treasure.

"So let me understand," Eaton said. "You arrive in triumph, having captured the *Tripoli*, and send me word you have the treasure safe and will bring it to me this evening? And then you appear, dressed in motley, to announce that not only were you robbed at gunpoint, but that then the thieves were themselves despoiled by a second set of robbers, who took the treasure, but let you survive to bring me this disastrous news? What, were you set upon by four men in buckram suits who then were accosted by eleven men in kendall grey?"

"I don't know about that, sir," Kirkpatrick stammered. "The first group of thieves looked like common street ruffians. We were ready to defend ourselves when the second group wiped out the first group in a fusillade of rifle fire while we were spared. Our escape was blocked and the second group had men on the rooftop with rifles. Had we attempted resistance, we would have suffered the same fate. General, you know I would gladly have given my life ..."

"No, Kirkpatrick," Eaton said. "This was a sorry business, but I think the blame you give yourself will be much harder than any criticism coming from me." He paused, then went to a sideboard, and poured brandy into two glasses. Handing one to Kirkpatrick, the general raised his glass and downed the brandy in a gulp. Afraid he might choke attempting the same thing, Kirkpatrick just sipped his. Eaton walked to the window looking out at the night that had enveloped Alexandria. Kirkpatrick just waited, in more inner pain than he had ever felt before in his life. After what felt to Kirkpatrick like an eternity of silence, Eaton turned back to him. His face was free of anger. "Your plan was sound, Kirkpatrick, and there was nothing you could have done to change things. I cannot imagine how it became such common news, but between the Turks, the Mamelukes, the French, and, I am afraid, especially our friends the English, we seem out of our depth here. I much prefer the clarity of open battle where courage and the sword can triumph over knavery and politics. Happily, that battle still lies ahead of us. Sometimes, Kirkpatrick, destiny gives us the challenge we need, not the one we wish for. Go back to your ship. I judge that you will not easily put this failure behind you, but for my part, I do, even as we speak. You must do the same. It is over and done, and cannot be repaired. I would rather have you committed to what we must yet accomplish than tormented by what may not have been in the fates to give us in the first place."

"Well, Sir Samuel, what a sorry theatrical farce this has turned out to be."

It was a brilliant morning. The early morning sky had unfolded in translucent reds and roses. Now the newly risen sun was painting the Mediterranean in sheets of shimmering, molten gold against a background of sapphire blue. The breathtaking beauty, so unlike the thick morning sky in England, was lost on Grey and Briggs. They had waited up all night only to discover that Grey's well-conceived plans had failed utterly. They were now taking both solace and coffee on Sir Samuel's veranda overlooking Alexandria.

"Indeed, Grey. Had Captain Vincents been set upon by Macheath, Jemmy Twitcher and Crook-Finger'd Jack, this misfortune could not have been more complete."

"But at least Gay's play made him rich, and Richard Rich gay. I think this farce has just made us beggars. Our brave worthies were captured without a shot by mysterious Arabs, who then bound and gagged them, killed the gang of thieves bent on despoiling the original thieves, the Americans, and left with the treasure, having spared the Americans in the bargain. I'm amazed Captain Vincents didn't report that these mystery men just escaped by mounting flying carpets."

Briggs took a quiet pleasure in seeing Grey's cold, implacable self-confidence quite diminished. "Well you have this to be thankful for, Grey, that while every water carrier and *suq* merchant in Alexandria knows all the details of this burlesque, the Americans won't talk, and Mohammed Ali and Pasha Ahmet have no one to blame. I made inquiries early this morning, and it appears the French won't be talking either. The leader of the ruffians who made the first attempt was a gentleman we have been watching for some time, a Maltese in French pay named

Tal-Patann. He, at least, will trouble neither us nor the Americans any more. Now all that is required is for us to be discrete, and there is a good chance we all will escape being made the target of Sheridan's gibes in the coming London theater season."

"That would, indeed, be a mercy," said Grey. "I would rather be flogged than pilloried on stage by that damned Whig, Sheridan. But as for Tal-Patann, we are well rid of him. The Frenchman he reports to, a man named Chameau, is still in Alexandria. I think it might be instructive to pay him a call."

"As you think best," said Briggs. "But what, now, do you think of the Americans' prospects?"

"I suspect they are none the wiser for this adventure," said Grey, "but no poorer either, since they lost a treasure they never anticipated having in the first place. If I may confess myself chastened, I would be interested in what else you have learned."

"I understand that Leitensdorfer," Briggs said, "or whatever his real name is—he appears to have several—appeared in the Mameluke camp, charmed the commander, and somehow managed to extricate Hamet Karamanli from the Mamelukes in upper Egypt. I would guess them to be four days away from joining Eaton in the desert outside Alexandria. Their prospects have been what they always were: a puppet Pasha Hamet, whose vanity exceeds his courage and ability; questionable, even treacherous allies; an American government and bureaucracy whose support shifts with the changing wind; and hundreds of miles of desert to cross at the start of the season of relentless sandstorms. This desert has eaten many armies before them. To answer your question, I think their prospects are that they will be tested beyond anything they could have imagined."

Following the ambush in the alley, Doyle and his ten men had rejoined Dihya and the rest of the Tuareg patrol of fifty men a two-day ride south of Alexandria. They were camped in desert country, amid dun-colored rocky outcrops that rose from the sand like the spines on a lizard's back. The dense, early morning fog covering the ground had finally been burned away, and the sun rose hot in a brilliant blue sky. Dihya and Doyle had taken their coffee outside so they could talk in private. He placed the camel saddles he had grabbed from the stack down on a small knoll overlooking their camp, and he and Dihya sat down, leaning against the tall saddlebacks.

"So you robbed the Americans, and yet you still help them?" Dihya asked.

Doyle laughed, "Should you, a warrior princess of the *Imagzighen,* legendary for their skill in stealing camels and horses, object to thievery? I just robbed the robbers, who stole from the French, and prevented two other groups of scoundrels from getting the gems and diamonds for themselves. The treasure is already in the hands of the Baccris' agent in Alexandria where it will purchase more modern rifles and ammunition and buy grain and wheat against the years of bad harvests. I thought, briefly, of leaving the Americans some of the treasure to support their attack against Tripoli, but they don't need it. They are sufficiently well financed to hire the mercenaries they need in Alexandria; the city teems with them."

Doyle turned back into his thoughts, and the two were silent for a while. Below them the morning patrol was preparing to ride out. As the troopers mounted, their camels, braying noisily, rose on their back legs then lurched upright. Doyle looked at the desert around them: "So now," he continued, "the Americans seek to plant the seeds of freedom here, in a part of the world that, for thousands of years, has known nothing but conquest, tyranny, and slavery. I suspect they will find it rocky, infertile soil."

"You say the Americans preach freedom," Dihya said. "You have told me of your childhood. What freedom did they give your people?"

"Less than they give their black slaves. For the Iroquois killed by their diseases and wars, no life; for those driven out of their ancestral homes, no liberty; and for those doomed to be a forgotten people in a hostile world, precious little happiness to pursue. I suspect 'freedom' for Americans means the right to do whatever their power makes possible for them to do. Had the French known how dangerous the idea of freedom is, they never would have supported the rebels; had the English known, they would have done well to have sent competent generals to put down the rebellion. Whether the Americans are able to live up to their own promise remains to be seen. But for the present moment, we have our own freedom to attend to. Hamet is a weakling, and his allies would sell their mothers for gold. The Arabs may need some stiffening. I think it is time for El Habibka to appear."

"You will take with you our *harka*—who look like Arabs but fight like devils?"

"Yes. I think they will be an unwelcome surprise for Jusef Karamanli's Bedouin allies."

"You know of course, *Igider*, that I will go with them and fight alongside you."

"Of course, my *Tizemt*," Doyle laughed. "I would have better chances ordering the *Khamsin* to stop blowing in the season of winds than to order you not to come."

"We are a strange couple. I'm particular about men—or should I say how I feel about men. Many women seek men to fill an emptiness they feel inside themselves. I have no such emptiness that needs filling." She paused for a moment and smiled wickedly at him. "Well, that's not entirely true, but the emptiness you fill isn't in my spirit." She became serious again. "Men sense that need in women and welcome it. And for their part, men seek continuously to dominate their women in order to assure themselves that they are actually strong. Because their constant fear of weakness never disappears, men's need to control never goes away. You aren't like that. I think that's why I love you."

"Only that?" Doyle said. "I would have thought there would be other reasons. My charm, my wit ..."

"Certainly none of those," she answered. "But there must be some other reason ... Ah. I have one. For an old man, you are surprisingly good in bed .... most of the time." She gave him another wicked look.

"I would say we are good together," Doyle replied. "But this lovemaking thing. A man my age must stay in practice or he risks forgetting how to do it completely. Perhaps tonight when we camp, unless you have something better to attend to."

She laughed, "You know what I want to attend to, *Igider,* and it's not your mind."

From the Journals of El Habibka
I have been through many changes. Through each change I did not know where the journey was taking me. And I still have a hundred more changes ahead of me.

Rumi

CHAPTER 23
❧ ALEXANDRIA 1805 ❧

Chameau had managed to survive the catastrophe in the Midan Tarir. An impulse had alerted him to lag behind Tal-Patann and his hired ruffians when they closed with the Americans. That premonition had saved his life, but not the treasure, at least part of which he had fully intended to deliver to the Turks. Chameau's destination today was the camp of Sheik El-Tahib, with whom Eaton was negotiating to procure camels to carry the supplies of his army in the attack on Tripoli. Over the years, Chameau had developed a deep loathing for all things Arabic in general and for camels in particular. Especially camels. So his misery, as he bounced along on top of a particularly malicious beast, viciously intent on biting his legs, was complete.

After two hours of agony, Chameau arrived at El-Tahib's camp: a noisy, dusty, seething mass of foul men and fouler-smelling beasts. He gingerly lifted himself down from his mount, narrowly avoiding yet another snap of the camel's teeth, then lashed out savagely at the camel's head with his riding crop. "See that I have a different, docile beast for the return to Alexandria!" he ordered El-Tahib's aide, El-Nakahmet, who had guided him to the camp.

Accompanied by the aide, Chameau limped painfully to El-Tahib's tent and entered without ceremony. The sheik was sitting at a small rough table cluttered with paper. "Have you considered my offer, sheik?" Chameau asked.

"Yes, *Franzwazi*," El-Tahib answered, just as contemptuously. "I care nothing for your plans. If all Infidels were to be swept from this land by plague—or jihad—my prayers would be answered. But I will happily see that the Americans are destroyed—for the money you have promised."

Chameau tossed a purse onto El-Tahib's table. "Here is a third of the payment. You get the rest when you bring me word that the American's bones are being picked clean in the desert by vultures and kites." With that, he turned awkwardly, brushed through the tent flaps, and started back toward the line of tethered camels for the ride back to Alexandria.

"He has requested a different camel for the return trip, *Effendi*," said El-Nakahmet.

"See that the Infidel gets *El Shaitan*," said El-Tahib to his aide. "And may he return to Alexandria with no more than bleeding stumps for legs."

It was close to sunset when Chameau finally reached his lodgings in Alexandria and struggled up the stairs to his room, pausing every few steps to catch his breath. He felt like weeping from exhaustion and pain. As tired as he was, he did not notice in the dim stairwell light the missing "telltale" of hair he had left at the base of the door to alert him if someone had entered his quarters. But some sixth sense, an unconscious awareness that the door was opening much faster and easier than it should, caused him at the last second to step back and shove against the door. So the dagger that would have struck him squarely in the back as he entered glanced off the door's edge and cut into his left arm instead. His pistol was useless—he hadn't bothered to check the priming—so he pulled his knife, and sprang into the room.

Chameau and his attacker circled each other, feinting and looking for an opening to strike. His attacker lunged first, too soon, thought Chameau. Chameau stepped back and aside, avoiding his attacker's killing thrust but not quickly enough to escape another cut, this time across his stomach. Chameau's reward, however, was the opening his attacker's lunge created for Chameau to slash him deeply across the neck and shoulder. Both men paused, eyeing each other and now breathing heavily. Both of us are too old for this game, thought Chameau.

They circled again, this time more slowly and warily, Chameau seizing the advantage by moving steadily to his right, forcing his adversary to steadily retreat, guarding his left side. Chameau feinted three attacks in rapid succession; his adversary over-reacted each time, opening up his body as he did so. An amateur, Chameau thought. If I were a younger man, he would already be a corpse. As Chameau had planned, the other man kept backing up until he reached the low Ottoman behind him, tripped, and fell. In an instant Chameau was astride him, and a single stab to the jugular finished off his adversary. Chameau collapsed alongside the dead man, gasping for breath. In the dim light from the lamp in the hall he could just make out his attacker's features; he was a European of middle age Chameau had never seen before.

As Chameau's breath began to slowly return to normal, so did his innate sense of caution. He looked around at his ransacked room. This man may not be alone. I have no support here. I think my work in Alexandria is done. Good luck to that scoundrel El-Tahib, and even better luck collecting the rest of his money. I will give the American and British dogs this round; there is much more of the game to play. Chameau rapidly gathered his private papers and a shoulder bag already stocked with clothing and provisions from their hiding place beneath a loose floorboard. He soaked his bed clothes with oil from a lamp, struck a match to ignite the fire and waited to see that it was burning well before heading for his escape hatch: a window leading out to the flat roof of the next apartment. Minutes later he was back on the street, heading for the port and the boat ready to take him back to Malta.

In spite of Grey's confident assurances, Briggs had been troubled by Grey's decision to search Chameau's quarters. He had sent Captain Vincents with instructions to follow Grey, but under no circumstances to be observed by him. Captain Vincents saw Grey enter Chameau's lodgings, but was too far away to provide warning when Chameau suddenly appeared out of the darkness and began climbing the stairs. Captain Vincents heard the soft sounds of a scuffle through Chameau's open second story windows, and uncertain as to what to do, did nothing. Only when he saw the smoke coming from the window did Captain Vincents jump into action, racing up the stairs, pistol at the ready. When he pushed the partially ajar door open into the now fiercely burning room, he saw Grey's body lying near the door. Grabbing the body under the armpits, he dragged it out of the burning building to the safety of the street, then to a neighboring alley where he hid it under a pile of refuse, and hurried back to give his report to Briggs.

"Mr. Grey is dead, Sir Samuel," Captain Vincents announced, when he burst into the British Consul's study. "He was killed in a fight with the Frenchman. I rescued his body, but saw no sign of Chameau. I presume he, too, was killed and died in the fire, since I saw no one leave the building."

If Captain Vincents had been expecting praise for having acted quickly to extricate Grey's body from the fire, Briggs instantly changed that impression. "Take some men," Briggs said tersely, "recover Grey's body, and bring it here. But do have a care to bring a rug or some other devise with you to hide the corpse if you are stopped by the watch. As a rule, neither Turks nor Mamelukes care much if foreigners kill each other, but Mr. Grey deserves the semblance of anonymity in death, since he prized it so greatly in life. See if you can manage that, captain, with greater success than your last two assignments."

CHAPTER 24
❧ ALEXANDRIA 1805 ❧

As soon as Commodore Samuel Barron had left Malta for Syracuse to be near its hospital, US Consul Tobias Lear, as the de facto commander of American military forces in the Mediterranean, had made the Commodore's office his, hanging the signed portrait General Washington had given him prominently behind his desk. Rather than the American army uniform his honorary rank of colonel entitled him to wear, today he was dressed in a finely tailored dark green suit of the best merino wool and an elaborately brocaded yellow waistcoat, set off by an equally fine neckpiece of expensive Florentine lace.

Lear's normally sour mood was becoming increasingly dyspeptic each time he re-read the latest communication from Naval Secretary Smith, newly arrived in the diplomatic pouch for Commodore Barron. Lear, of course, had opened the letter in Barron's absence.

> My Dear Commodore Barron:
> You are well aware of my reservations regarding Eaton's expedition to depose Pasha Jusef Karamanli and put his brother Hamet on the throne of Tripoli. Were Eaton to fail, and at present we have no assurances that he will not fail, we damage our chances of a negotiated settlement with Pasha Karamanli to free the Philadelphia hostages. Should Eaton, by some stroke of fortune succeed, then we are obli-

gated to maintain a considerable naval force in the Mediterranean to support the puppet regime we have put in place.

I am mindful, as well, of Consul Lear's deep skepticism about Hamet Karamanli's ability to gain the support and loyalty of a people who were well-enough contented some years ago to see him deposed and replaced by his brother. Were we to take responsibility for his regime, we might soon enough find ourselves searching for a replacement puppet. These people change rulers the way a sot changes his linen. No sooner is it donned than it is soiled.

So were the policy left to me, we would continue to provide Eaton with just enough support to ensure that if he fails, we are blameless, and should he succeed, we still may negotiate a favorable settlement. Unfortunately, there are other voices in Washington, and they have caught the President's ear. Preble has been outspoken in his support for Eaton (and less than lukewarm regarding your leadership). Preble struts about like a hero, and not only the mob, but serious men who should know better, believe him. It seems, as well, that Eaton has his powerful advocates within the Army.

It is my duty to inform you that both the President and Secretary Madison have now concluded that only military force will compel Pasha Karamanli to accede to our demands, free the Philadelphia captives and forever exempt the Unites States from paying any tribute to Tripoli. They believe that once Pasha Karamanli is brought to his knees, you may negotiate a treaty without any price or pecuniary conditions. They have instructed me to tell you that if, as a final measure, you need to offer some compensation for the prisoners' care during captivity, it should be merely a token sum—perhaps $20 per prisoner—to amount to $6,000 at most.

The upshot is that you must carry out a policy that I fear can bring small advantage to our country and less fame. As the United States' naval commander in the Mediterranean, you are therefore directed and required to ensure that the support for Eaton and Hamet return to the status quo ante bellum, or should one say anti bedlam. *The written orders accompanying this letter will serve as your authorization for doing so. You will secure the arms, munitions, and materiél in Eaton's original contract and seek the most expeditious means to find him and equip him as needed. His support should include, as well, the full $20,000 to establish Hamet's regime. In the event Eaton conquers Derna or Benghazi, a final assault by our fleet will be launched against Tripoli itself with the intent of securing Pasha Jusef Karamanli's deposition—or death, whichever his subjects determine is most appropriate. That final assault, however, should wait until June when you will have received reinforcement of two more frigates, the John Adams and Congress, as well as a dozen of the gunboats Preble has designed and commissioned to be built to bombard the fortress at Tripoli. That will bring the forces under your command to six frigates, four brigs, two schooners, one sloop and the gunboats with over five hundred Marines and 1,000 sailors for the land assault. If we are to use military force, nothing less than a complete victory is required of you and the men under your command.*

Our personal reservations aside, these are your orders. Both of us serve at the President's pleasure. So long as Mr. Jefferson is president, our duty is clear. I have done mine in sending you this unwelcome news; you must do yours in carrying these instructions out.

I remain, yours,
Samuel Smith, Sect'y of the Navy, &etc.

What madness, what utter folly is this! Lear fumed. "Rokku!" he yelled for his secretary. There was no immediate response. "Rokku!" he called again, "You impertinent excuse for a competent man! Come here this instant! I will not call a third time! If I must come to seek you, I will bring my cane!" Seconds before Lear, in his impatience, would have done just that, the door to his office opened and his secretary popped in, an apologetic smile on his face.

"A thousand pardons, excellency," he said. "The necessary …" he pointed in the direction of the privies and shrugged his shoulders in innocent apology.

Lear ignored his explanation. Insolent, lying bastard, he thought. "Rokku," he said, "what appointments do I have for the balance of the day?"

Without needing to look at Lear's diary, he said, "Salvatore Bufuttil, Hamet's agent in Malta, at 1:00, and Captain Hull at 3:00."

"Bufuttil at 1:00 and Hull and 3:00," Lear reflected. "Perfect," he said, then turning to Rokku, "Now leave."

By himself again, Lear considered his options. This letter and the accompanying orders must never reach Barron, he thought, but how to manage that? I can't replace them with a forged letter and orders; Smith will have a copy. So they must disappear. He looked at the door separating his office from Rokku's desk. In this part of the world, he said to himself, nothing is safe or secure. He took out his pocketknife and gently pried up the now broken wax seal from the diplomatic folder. He then lit a candle, just slightly melted the underside of the two halves of the wax seal, then replaced them back on the folder. He made sure that the bottom half was only slightly out of alignment with the top, so that the tampering would not be immediately noticeable unless one scrutinized the seals. Once the wax was dry, he crossed to his safe and put the folder in with the rest of his secure correspondence. Secretary Smith's letter and the orders for Barron went into the secret compartment on the side of his desk. When the inquiry was raised about the existence of Secretary Smith's letter and Barron's orders, the disturbed seals would tell the story, and the identity of the spy who opened the folder would be evident—especially if he were no longer present to defend himself. Lear cast a look at the door separating him from Rokku, smiled, enjoying his cleverness for a moment, then got up, and walked out of his office. "I am leaving for lunch, now," he called to Rokku as he passed. "When I return, see that I am not disturbed except for the Bufuttil and Hull appointments."

Hamet's aide Bufuttil appeared, predictably late, at 1:30. As Rokku ushered him in, Lear rose, and crossed his office to greet him effusively.

"An honor, Signore Bufuttil," Lear said, taking Bufuttil's hand. "A pleasure, really. You come at a propitious time, when we all hunger for reports of Hamet's success. Please make yourself comfortable." He walked Bufuttil to the chair placed in front of his desk. Its legs had been slightly shortened to place whoever sat there at an uncomfortable disadvantage. Lear sat down behind his desk; the small wooden platform he had placed behind the desk for his chair allowed him to look down upon those who sat in front of him.

"Forgive my eagerness, Signore," Lear began, "but what news can you give me of Hamet? Are the people of Tripoli rising to support him?"

Bufuttil searched Lear's face for a clue as to how best to frame his answer. Getting none, he began. "Hamet Karamanli and Eaton are still making their way across the desert."

"Yes?" Lear answered, his face expressionless waiting for Bufuttil to continue.

"And we have yet to hear from them," Bufuttil stammered, then hurriedly continued, "but there can be no question that Hamet's loyal subjects will follow him with the greatest zeal and devotion. No doubt at all, excellency!" As they followed him into exile in Egypt, Lear thought.

"A cornerstone of this plan, as you know, Signore Bufuttil, is the loyalty of the people of Tripoli to their rightful ruler," Lear said. "What then, might be a realistic estimate of the size of the army Hamet will gather to him as he approaches Derna?"

Still unsure of how to properly—and safely—couch his answer, Bufuttil took a breath and surrendered to enthusiasm. "By the time he reaches Derna, which we believe has already risen in Hamet's support and expelled Jusef Karamanli's regent Mustifa Bey, the Tripolitans whose loyalty Hamet commands are sure to exceed three thousand men."

He was rewarded by a friendly, encouraging smile from Lear. Bufuttil continued with the pleased enthusiasm of a child, "And that does not include the people of Derna, Bengazi, and the tribes to the west before he reaches Tripoli itself. As we know, the American siege of Tripoli by sea has utterly turned the inhabitants of that city against the usurper Jusef."

"Why, this is the very best of news!" Lear exclaimed, "More than we might have dared hope for. With such an army behind him, facing a crippled and dispirited foe, Hamet's triumph is a foregone conclusion! How splendid! But in all goodness, Signore Bufuttil, you suggested five thousand men. Might Hamet's support exceed even that number?"

"There can be no question, excellency," cried Bufuttil, echoing Lear's excitement. "A whole nation awaits Hamet's appearance like the coming of the *Mahdi*."

"Then since the present is so happily secure," said Lear, "let us talk about the future." He got up from his desk and pulled a chair to where he could sit facing Bufuttil. He reached his hand across and patted Bufuttil on the knee. "I am so pleased, Signore, for you, Hamet, and the oppressed people of Tripoli. But here is my thought. Since Hamet's triumph is already foreordained, should we not turn our attention to not just his conquest, but his rule?" Bufuttil had already started nodding in agreement. "My country has pledged $20,000 to Hamet in loans, to be secured by the yearly tribute money from Denmark. I wonder if some of that money might now, in this present situation, be better used to support Hamet in the months after he takes the throne?

A man such as yourself, with your expertise in this part of the world, knows that for any ruler, there are alliances to be secured and loyal followers to be rewarded. Would you say, Signore, that should be even more true for a ruler newly come to power like Hamet?"

"Of course, excellency," said Bufuttil. "That is exactly how things are."

"We have already given General Eaton $10,000 to support Hamet's invasion. Would it then not make sense to you, as Hamet's representative, to agree to set aside the remaining $10,000 to assure Hamet's success after he ascends the throne?"

"Your excellency is a wise man," said Bufuttil. "That is the very thing. I could not have conceived a better idea myself! Hamet is fortunate to have such an ally as America."

"It is settled, then," said Lear. "I will see that the appropriate orders are given." He rose from his chair, offering Bufuttil his arm. "Come, Signore Bufuttil," he continued, "Such a bold, thoughtful plan deserves to be celebrated. Will you join me in drinking to Hamet's triumph? Some brandy, perhaps?"

After a series of toasts, to President Jefferson, Hamet, the valor of the American Navy and Army, the memory of the illustrious President Washington, the confusion of their enemies, and the future prosperity and happiness of the people of Tripoli, Lear escorted a now somewhat unsteady Bufuttil to the door of his office, embraced him, and bid him farewell. As soon as Bufuttil had left the antechamber, Lear turned to Rokku.

"Come." Lear said. "I have orders for Captain Hull, under Commodore Barron's seal, that must be written before Hull arrives at 3:00."

For several weeks on his way home from American headquarters, Rokku had dutifully checked the empty niche in the wall of St. Paul's Street for the chalk mark that would tell him to meet with Tal-Patann. This evening, the mark was there. He hurried to the regular rendezvous spot, a non-descript café on the Triq Il-Lanca in a poor, run-down quarter of Malta where he was unlikely to be recognized. He ordered a bottle of red *Gellewza* wine, a thick pâté of fava beans, garlic, and cheese, and waited for Tal-Patann to appear. After a few minutes, a stranger pushed through the hanging beadwork over the door, spotted him, came to his table and sat down. Not seeing a menu board, the stranger asked, "What won't poison me here?"

"I'm having *bigilla*," Rokku said. "The fried *lampuki* won't kill you—or the *stuffat tal-fenek,* that is, if you like rabbit. The stranger ordered the fried fish and a tankard of local beer. Both men ate in silence for a while.

Without preamble, Chameau began the conversation. "Tal-Patann is dead."

"*Il-mewt ma tahfirha 'l hadd.* Death comes to us all," said Rokku, then added. "But he would be a hard man to kill. How do you know he is dead?"

Chameau reached into his pocket and dropped a ring on the table, the small garnet ring Tal-Patann had always worn on his left hand. "He was killed several weeks ago in Alexandria by American agents."

"Anyone can take a ring off a corpse, friend," said Rokku. "Tal-Patann and I had a countersign."

"*Mitt jien miet kulhadd,*" said Chameau, in harshly accented Maltese, "when I die, everyone dies."

"*Ta wara jsakkar jekk irid*—and let the last man alive shut the door," Rokku said, completing the countersign, then after a pause, "so now what?"

"The people who paid to get information about the American Lear still have interest in that business," said Chameau. "There would be no change in your payments."

"And no change in Lear's insults and beatings," Rokku said. "With Tal-Patann gone, I think the value of my information has become more expensive."

"What do you Maltese say? 'When a miser dies, his heirs kill a pig in celebration.' The government will take his property once they learn of his death, but his income can now come to you."

"Good enough," said Rokku. "One man's death is another man's life. So what do you want to know?"

"What can you tell me of Lear's plans regarding Eaton?"

"I think Lear cooks the sauce before he catches the fish," said Rokku. "It's not clear to me that the Pasha of Tripoli, Jusef Karamanli, will live long enough to sign the treaty Lear is so anxious to create. But this is a long conversation. Can you get into Tal-Patann's lodgings?"

"I can," Chameau answered.

"Good," said Rokku, pocketing Tal-Patann's ring. "Let us continue the conversation there ... perhaps we may find a few trifles among Tal-Patann's possessions that would do better in our hands than in the government's? *Ruhek 'l Allah,"* he added as he and Chameau rose from the table. "His soul to God, his body to dust, and his property to those who survive him."

CHAPTER 25
❧ DAMANHUR 1805 ❧

"This is outrageous, Isaac!" Eaton cried, on hearing Hull's report of his meeting with Lear. "In spite of the specific instructions from the President to support this venture, the stands of arms, the hundreds of Marines and sailors, the artillery, and most important the money to equip our expedition, instead of this aid, only you, your ship, and the resources you have on board are our total support for this enterprise?"

They were seated in Eaton's tent in the cool shade of Damanhur: the oasis Eaton had chosen as the staging ground for his invasion of Tripoli. The camp was a noisy confusion of shouting men and braying camels. Hull could see bundles of supplies being packed into camel loads, overseen by European soldiers in uniforms he did not recognize.

"These are Commodore Barron's directions, William," Hull answered. "Actually Lear's, but it amounts to the same thing. Lear told me he has been in touch with Hamet's representative in Malta, Salvatore Bufuttil, who assures him that Hamet will raise an army of several thousand Arabs to his cause, and that far from having to conquer Tripoli, he will be welcomed by the local populace as the hero freeing them from his brother's tyranny. The Navy may assist in the final capture of Tripoli from the sea, but Lear is convinced that no American troops should be risked, or are, in point of fact, needed, to achieve victory."

"No American troops? The insufferable fool!" exclaimed Eaton. "This from a man who has never faced an enemy in battle? But surely Barron cannot agree!"

"My *written* orders from Commodore Barron, in Lear's hand, of course, now empower me to supply you with such stores, ammunition, or money as may be spared from the *Argus,* taking receipts and vouchers for the same—if it should be found necessary. As for the money, Lear told me that, again according to Bufuttil, no more than $10,000 would be required to support the conquest of Derna and Bengazi, as a loan to be repaid, according to Lear, from the spoils taken at Derna, Bengazi, and Tripoli. I have $3,000 with me, with the promise of the balance when you reach Derna. Lear is convinced that all we will need to do to ensure the capitulation of the local ruler is to make a show of force for the population of Derna. Then Hamet may gather his army for the push on to Tripoli itself. In Lear's mind, if Hamet is to become the next ruler of Tripoli, he should be able to muster sufficient support among his people to make the use of American troops unnecessary."

"But this is madness! At best, Bufuttil is no more than a buffoon, willing to say whatever he thinks will please the ears of the person he is speaking with at the moment. And I have darker concerns, Isaac, that he, in fact, has been purchased by the French. What do Rogers and Decatur say of Lear's taking charge so highhandedly?"

"Rogers is beside himself with frustration. He would be pressing home the attacks begun by Preble, but is forestalled by Lear. As for Decatur, he merely remarked how odd it was to have a civilian who had never faced an enemy or fired a shot in anger placed in command of the navy in the midst of a war. I have heard that Decatur has written directly to President Jefferson on the conduct of our efforts against Tripoli. Given the enthusiastic public celebrations of his destruction of the *Philadelphia*, Decatur believes his words may carry influence with the President. But in essence, I fear we can expect no help from Commodore Barron. John Dent called on poor Barron recently and told me that the Commodore's mind is so distracted with his illness that he cannot remember things from one day to the next and will often lose the thread of discussion in the midst of a conversation. He is given to picking aimlessly at the covers of his bedclothes as if the forgotten subject of the discourse were written there. He is fed soft food and softer information—when his health will permit him to accept either. But tell me, pray, how do your recruiting efforts progress here?"

"I had hoped for success. Alexandria is awash in out-of-work mercenaries eager to ply their trade. But the Turks complain that I am trying to take their best soldiers from them," Eaton said. "I had several hundred promising Maltese signed up, but was forced to release them by the local Pasha. I suspect this is all more French meddling. The French, at least, still have money for bribes. Had I the funds, even as little as $10,000, we would have no trouble finding men. To date I have enlisted some twenty-five Piedmontese artillerymen to man the field pieces you tell me you do not yet have and thirty-eight Greek infantrymen. Without more money for recruiting, and, of course, for the arms and supplies to equip more men, we are left with local Arabs—whatever Hamet can muster—and you can provide yourself."

"I wish I had better news for you, William. Over half of my Marine contingent was invalided back to Syracuse, quarantined by the plague. I can spare you six privates, a sergeant, and Lieutenant O'Bannon."

"So few," mused Eaton, "so few. Washington launched his daring stroke against the Hessians at Trenton with two thousand men, Arnold captured Quebec with one thousand, and even brave Leonidas fought at the end with three hundred fierce, unyielding

Spartans. If it must be just seven United States Marines, then they will have to do. What remains to be seen, then, is … "

His thoughts were stopped by a cry from the sentry on a small bluff overlooking the camp. "Riders from the south! Attention in the camp, there! Horsemen approaching!"

Within a half hour, the dust cloud boiling up from the south had turned into a galloping stream of splendidly mounted Arab cavalry, shouting *Allah Akbar!* and firing off their muskets as they rode into camp, with a beaming Leitensdorfer riding next to Hamet Karamanli.

"You come in good season, colonel," Eaton cried, as Leitensdorfer and Hamet dismounted, knocking the dust from their robes. He pointed to an area to the east of the camp, sheltered by palm trees. "If you would be so kind, colonel, have Pasha Karamanli's men make their camp by those trees; they will find ample water and forage for their horses. See if they need refreshment for themselves, then join us in my tent." Then he turned to embrace Hamet.

"Greetings, your Highness!" cried Eaton in his usual flawless Arabic. As the Arab horsemen had surged into camp, Eaton had made a rapid calculation of their numbers. "If the rest of your forces, excellency, are but half as warlike in their appearance and so well horsed as the vanguard that accompanies you, the fate of the usurper your brother, is sealed!"

Hamet turned away from Eaton and looked at his troops now making camp, then looked back toward Eaton, not meeting his eyes.

"Unfortunately, general, these fifty men *are* my army. I led them on what was supposed to be an expedition and we kept riding north. When the Mamelukes learned we had deserted, they locked up the rest of my supporters in chains. The best I can do now is to recruit from the local tribes, who, of course, will need payment for their service."

Eaton took a moment to reflect on this latest setback and turned to Hamet. "A brave American, excellency, in the darkest days of our own struggle for freedom, wrote 'Tyranny, like hell, is not easily conquered; yet we have this consolation with us, that the harder the conflict, the more glorious the triumph.' Please join your men and see to their comfort; you have had a hard ride. Then I would beg you to meet with me, Captain Hull, and Colonel Leitensdorfer so we can begin planning the stroke that will replace you on your throne."

When Eaton's sentry ushered Hamet into the tent, the brave warrior who had entered camp at the head of his men, eyes flashing and head held high, had vanished. A broken man collapsed into the chair Eaton led him to. Eaton turned to Leitensdorfer and Hull. "Pray give his excellency and me some time in private," he said, exchanging glances with both of them. "I will call you when we are ready for our conference." He looked at the slumped form of Hamet. Much, much less than I'd hoped, he thought, and worse than my greatest fears. Eaton pulled his chair facing Hamet, and waited patiently until Hamet became aware of his presence and lifted up his head to reveal a face lined with sadness and stripped of all hope.

"You had a hard ride, excellency," Eaton began.

"No, no" said Hamet. "Not the ride." He dispiritedly waved his arm in a circle to encompass the almost non-existent army Eaton had assembled. "This— this— nothing. I had expected so much more. Barely a hundred men with which to conquer a country? No. I have let myself be lured, once more, into a cruel dream of attaining the impossible. I am grateful for your efforts on my behalf, general, but now my loyal followers are reduced to the fifty men with me, I cannot go back to the Mamelukes, and Egypt will be closed to me. It is finished. A blind man could see that the stars are aligned against me."

"In truth, excellency," Eaton replied, desperately searching for a way to rekindle Hamet's hope, "who else but God the Merciful and Compassionate knows how the thread of men's lives will run out?" He caught the glimpse of an idea. "If we set upon a great and noble undertaking and fail, the fault is not in our stars, but in ourselves." He spread his hands in front of Hamet's face, moving them up and down like the scales of a balance. "Hamet and Jusef," he said. "Jusef and Hamet. You have fought for your name and honor, sword in hand, accompanied by loyal followers who have stayed true to you for years through your exile. Your brother lies back in indolent luxury, hated by those who suffer under his harsh rule. Which of these two men should be weighed more precious in the scale of honor and nobility?" Having caught both his theme and Hamet's attention, Eaton warmed to his task. "Hamet? Jusef? Why should his name be sounded more than yours in the ears of man and God? Who deserves more of his people? Who, in the time of judgment, can account more favorably for his deeds in this life? Should you kneel before an idol of straw while your people cry for a ruler with fire in his belly and strong steel for a spine? I know that brave man is in you. Let him come forth now at the time of greatest need."

As he spoke, Eaton had watched carefully as the light returned to Hamet's face and his body straightened. "Excellency," he continued, "let me invite in my friends. Colonel Leitensdorfer you know to be a man of extraordinary talents and powers; Captain Hull commands the full resources of the naval power that has brought your brother Jusef to his knees. What can the four of us, in the brotherhood of battle, *not* do—if we but set our wills to see it through?" He held out his arm for Hamet to rise, and the two men walked together toward the door of the tent to call in Hull and Leitensdorfer. I've struck a fire again inside of Hamet, Eaton thought. I hope the flame lasts at least until we are out of Egypt and into Tripoli.

As Eaton left the tent to summon Captain Hull and Leitensdorfer to meet with Hamet, Hull stopped him. "I overheard the whole business from outside the tent," Hull said. "That was certainly remarkable. Do you plan to use similar magic to conjure up an army, now? Sewing dragon's teeth, perhaps?"

"Dragon's teeth?" Eaton mused. "No, Isaac, I suspect nothing quite so mythical. It's true the French have interfered to keep me from recruiting more Europeans, but this part of Egypt is full of Arab mercenaries looking for work."

"We both know how Lear has stripped you of money, William. How in God's name will you pay for the troops? More magic?"

"Happily not," said Eaton. "Briggs, in his goodness, has advanced me letters of credit that should pay for a force of two hundred additional Arab soldiers."

"But meaning no disrespect, against what security?"

"My own personal pledge."

"William," Hull cried, "you cannot be thinking of risking your own fortune in this venture!"

"Isaac, when you stand on deck in a battle, facing the enemy's cannon and musket fire, or when you board an enemy ship, do you not risk something even more precious than money? A man can always replace lost money; it's harder to replace lost courage and faith."

"Well, I can't argue with you there," Hull acknowledged, "but only two hundred Arab soldiers? William, that's no army!"

"Let me ask you, when the entire naval squadron shows up in front of Tripoli now, do they fear your cannon fire—or just the threat of it? If I can launch any kind of army into Tripoli and take Derna, Jusef Karamanli's fear itself will sew the dragon's teeth that will devour him."

"And how will you procure these dragon's teeth of yours?"

"From the same rascal that is providing me with camels to carry our supply train," said Eaton, "a sheik named El-Tahib."

CHAPTER 26
❧ MALTA 1805 ❧

Summoned by Tobias Lear to naval headquarters in Malta, Kirkpatrick was by now in a furious mood. He had approached Rokku three times in the past hour, asking to see Lear, and been placidly rebuffed. "I understand you have an appointment, captain; after all, I keep Consul Lear's calendar for him. Regrettably, he is still busy with his current visitors. I'm sure he will see you when he's free."

Lear was concluding a meeting with peace emissaries between Pasha Jusef Karamanli in Tripoli and the Americans: Don Joseph De Souza, the Spanish Consul General, and the banker Leon Far-fara. For today's meetings, Lear was wearing the full uniform of a colonel in the American Army, cut and fashioned, like his civilian clothing, by his tailor in Florence. Lear's gold epaulets sparkled in the sunlight.

"I can assure you, Don Joseph," Lear was concluding the meeting, "that President Jefferson's and Secretary Madison's support for Eaton's mad scheme continues to wane as we learn more about Eaton's grandiose posturing and Hamet's utter unfitness for successful rule. So long as Naval Secretary Smith maintains control, the way is clear to do what all sensible people recognize must be the only solution to freeing the American hostages held by Pasha Karamanli: arrange for a peaceful settlement and a new treaty that will, once and for all, protect American commerce from the depredations of the corsairs. I will gladly pass your wise assessment of Hamet to Secretary Smith. We can count on him to see that the real truth behind all this foolishness reaches the right ears in Washington. In the meantime, Pasha Karamanli's offer to restore Hamet's imprisoned wife and children to him is gracious indeed."

The meeting over, he walked De Souza to the door, arm in arm, Farfara ahead of them. "Please convey my latest counter-proposal to Pasha Karamanli, Señor De Souza. As a gesture of good faith, I have agreed to the release of Hamet's family to us and the details of how that transfer may be made. The ransom figure I offer is, I think, fair and reasonable, especially in light of the commercial concessions you have suggested as an inducement. I thank you for both your efforts on behalf of peace and the wise counsel you so graciously provide. In the meantime, I have to deal with yet another of Preble's impetuous, undisciplined hotheads."

As Lear opened the door to his office to show De Souza and Farfara out, Kirkpatrick, long past patience, jumped to his feet. Lear looked at him without emotion. "I will see you in due time captain," he said, and went back into his office and closed the door. At his desk, Lear wrote for a few minutes, and then called for his Maltese secretary, Rokku.

"Rokku. See that Consul De Souza's report is included with this week's dispatches to Washington, and add this note," he said, handing his secretary the sheet of paper he had just written. "You may put it in the usual ciphers." He paused for a few more moments, then added, "Now you can show Captain Kirkpatrick in."

Kirkpatrick was ushered in by Rokku and saw Lear sitting behind his desk. What a presumptuous ass, Kirkpatrick thought, sitting up there craning his neck and preening like some great bloated bird.

"Have a seat," Lear gestured toward the chair in front of his desk.

"No, thank you," said Kirkpatrick. "I prefer to stand. I have been sitting for more than an hour, as you know." He walked forward to stand in front of Lear's desk.

Without preamble, Lear pushed a folder across his desk. "I have orders for you."

"As you should know, *Mister* Lear, I take orders from my superior, Commodore Baron," Kirkpatrick said.

"Commodore Barron is confined to his bed. In his absence, you will take your orders from me." We'll see about that, thought Kirkpatrick, and picked up the folder to read its contents.

"So. I am to go, Mister Lear, on what looks like a wild goose chase to pick up Hamet Karamanli's family off the beach in a nameless cove outside of Tripoli. Are these orders legal?"

"You recognize the letterhead, I believe," said Lear, "and Commodore Barron's seal. I should think you would also recognize the uniform I am wearing. I notice you did not salute when you entered—a regrettable, but unsurprising breach of normal discipline. And you should be addressing me as 'Colonel Lear.'"

"I recognize the uniform, Mister Lear, but not the man wearing it." Kirkpatrick felt the anger welling up in him. "Tell me, sir, have you ever faced enemy fire? Have you ever commanded troops in battle? For that matter, have you ever commanded troops at all?" Without waiting for Lear's answer, he continued: "We both know you have not. So your uniform is a costume, sir, something one might expect on a play actor—or a mountebank."

Lear continued looking at him placidly, without speaking.

"Your title, sir, is a sham, and as Commodore Barron's replacement—well, you are what you are. A word a man might use is scrub, and a damnable, cowardly scrub at that. If you were a man of honor, you would know how to respond. Your silence suggests that you are not." He *has* to take offense, Kirkpatrick thought, the little fox-faced shit.

Lear allowed the silence to build between them, then said, with no apparent emotion, "Men can call me what they wish; it does not touch me. What does, signify, *captain*, is that you have been given legal orders and must obey them, or face consequences which I am sure you are well aware of. Regardless of your contemptuous self-esteem, there is still discipline in the navy. You may leave now. Rokku!" he called. "You may show the captain out."

CHAPTER 27
✦ THE EAGLE 1805 ✦

Two days later, the *Eagle* lay anchored off shore in a small bay to the east of Tripoli. The bay, three miles deep and four across, curved around them from high headlands to the east.

Kirkpatrick and his first lieutenant, Thomas Christopher, stared at the shoreline through their glasses. The bright full moon clearly lit the beach a half mile away. "Will our passengers make their rendezvous, do you think?" asked Christopher.

"Damned if I know," Kirkpatrick answered. "You know, I dislike everything about this mission. We may be on some wild goose chase concocted by Consul Lear." His temper flared as he recalled the meeting. "But I tell you what it is, Tom—this Lear is no more than a grass-combing, lubberly, spineless coxcomb! Absolutely without honor. I couldn't challenge him to a duel, of course, but any officer and gentleman must respond to an insult. I gave him every opportunity to provoke me, so that I might then in good conscience call him out. But he refused the bait." Kirkpatrick pitched his voice in a high falsetto. "'Men can call me what they wish,' he said. 'It does not touch me.' Then he dismissed me as easy as kiss my hand. Kiss my arse, I should say." Kirkpatrick walked away from Christopher to let himself cool down. Taking his night glass, he once again scanned the shore, then turned back to Christopher, who had prudently remained silent.

"Well, bugger him, anyway. So here we are, Tom, waiting for Hamet Karamali's wife and children to appear. If our guests *are* going to show, it is near midnight now and we are certainly on time." As if in response to his thoughts, a light flashed from the palm trees that rimmed the shoreline. "Three, one, two, one," Kirkpatrick counted. "Send the countersignal," he ordered the signalman next to him. The *Eagle*'s lantern flashed out the reverse sequence. "Send away the cutter," Kirkpatrick ordered. The *Eagle*'s cutter, with a crew of twelve, armed with muskets and a 4 pound swivel on the bow, pulled away from the *Eagle* and headed toward the shore.

Kirkpatrick, Christopher, and the other officers scanned the shore as the cutter closed the distance. "The site is well chosen, at least," Kirkpatrick observed. "There's little surf. The beach slopes gently up."

"There," Christopher cried. "Two points off the starboard bow past the tree line." Out from the shadows under the palm trees they saw a party make its way toward the incoming cutter.

"What do you make of them?"

"Three men, three women—I suspect by their size they are women but I can't make out features—and perhaps two children."

"That would be Hamet's family, then," Kirkpatrick said. "So this wasn't a wild goose chase." They watched as the cutter closed to within two hundred yards of the shore.

Christopher had continued to scan the shoreline. The light cloud cover from earlier in the evening had blown away and the moonlight now began to filter through the shadows under the trees. "Captain!" Christopher exclaimed. "Look into the tree line. What do you see?"

Kirkpatrick trained his glass away from the party on the shore. Sure enough, the shadowy space under the palm trees now seemed to be lit by hundreds of fireflies.

"That's moonlight reflecting off metal!" Kirkpatrick cried. "This is a goddamned trap! Those are armed men in the shadows. Fire a gun to alert the cutter. Our carronades are useless at this range. Put a shot from the bow chaser into those trees."

The *Eagle*'s starboard 9-pounder boomed out. Seconds later, hundreds of mounted men surged onto the beach, shooting their muskets at the Americans as Hamet Karamanli's "family" scurried for cover. From higher up the hill, a field piece, then another, began firing at the cutter, the first ball falling short, the second close enough to douse the boat crew with spray. The cutter returned one round of grape from its bow chaser, then spun around and began racing toward the *Eagle,* spreading its sail to gain more speed.

"Silence those shore guns there," Kirkpatrick cried to the bow chaser crew. Then to Christopher, "Make ready to haul anchor. We'll work closer to shore and show those treacherous devils what it means to ambush an American ship."

"Ahoy on deck there!" came the cry from the masthead lookout. "Sail to the northwest!" Kirkpatrick and the others whipped around. A frigate was entering the bay, sailing by now well clear of the western headlands.

"Damn your eyes," Kirkpatrick yelled up at the lookout. "You should have kept a proper watch instead of skylarking over the business ashore. That ship has been in view for ages." He turned to his bo'sun. "I want that man's name tomorrow. He will learn attentiveness to duty the hard way. Mr. Christopher, can you make out a flag on that ship?" Kirkpatrick asked. "It's certainly not one of ours."

The strange frigate was now well in sight, sailing close hauled with the wind on the port beam. "Look at the old-fashioned cross-jack rig on her mizzen," Christopher said. "No European ship carries a sail like that anymore. It must be the *Crescent.*"

"Cut loose the anchor!" Kirkpatrick cried. "Make all sail— helm to starboard!" The *Eagle*'s crew leaped into action and the ship turned to run along the shoreline to the east. Kirkpatrick turned back to Christopher: "What do we know of this ship?"

"She's one of our tribute ships—American built, more's the shame of it," replied Christopher, "so she'll be stout. Campbell sailed with her to Algiers in '97 to turn her over to the Dey, who sold her to the Tripolitans," replied Christopher. "James Hackett built her as small as her rate would allow, but she still carries a main battery of twenty 18-pounders and eight 24 pound carronades."

Perhaps I was a bit hasty with my boast about teaching them how to conduct an ambush, Kirkpatrick thought. If we were the real prey and the cutter just the bait, we are well and truly caught in the trap. He quickly gauged the speed of the cutter racing back toward the *Eagle* and the speed and position of the *Crescent*. All my choices here are bad. If we hope to beat the *Crescent* to the eastern lip of the bay and the open sea, we must leave now ... but that would mean abandoning the cutter crew, which I will not do at any cost. By the time we pick them up and get under way, those devils will be able to batter us with their long guns at their pleasure. At this range our carronades won't touch them.

The cutter by now was ranging up along the starboard side, squeezing every bit of speed out of its sail to catch the *Eagle* as she gathered headway. A line snaked out from the *Eagle's* stern to the cutter and missed. "Ease the main sheet, there! Lively does it!" Kirkpatrick called, and as the wind spilled out of the sail, the *Eagle* momentarily slowed. This time, the line just barely reached the cutter, and a man lunged forward to secure it, almost falling over the side. The cutter's crew made the line fast, dropped its sail, and was pulled alongside the *Eagle*, its crew scrambling up the netting that had been hung over the weather rail.

"Eagles," Kirkpatrick cried. "You see what we have here. These rascals have laid a pretty trap for us, and think to serve us ill. We must put up with a bit of a drubbing until our guns will bear. But then, they will find that they thought to snare a sparrow but caught an eagle instead—and an American eagle at that!" A loud "huzzah" erupted from the crew.

"Hold her due east," Kirkpatrick ordered, as the *Eagle* blossomed with sails, rapidly gaining speed. He stared at the approaching enemy, the white of her sails bright in the moonlight, trying to gain some sense of her qualities and a measure of the man commanding her. They were at the innermost part of the bay that, like a gourd, widened near the shore and narrowed at its entrance. We are in a bad way, here, he thought. The *Crescent* sits at the apex of a triangle and we sail along its base. No matter what we do, all their captain needs to do is hold position on us. So we must make him give us sea room, and hope not to get blown out of the water in the process. As if her captain had read Kirkpatrick's mind, the *Crescent* reduced sail to keep her leverage over the *Eagle*.

He turned to Christopher. "What do you make of her?"

"She has reefed courses and gallants set on her main and foremasts and damned if I know why, but they've brailed up their mizzen topsails. Her head is lifting up. I would think her too slack, carrying too much lee helm by far. She will have a devilish time tacking against this tide."

"Then that is what we must force her to do," said Kirkpatrick. "We need to gain enough room to gybe back toward the western opening of the bay—or at least make them think that's what we intend." As the *Eagle* raced eastward, the *Crescent* continued sailing on the wind, maintaining its position to cut the *Eagle* off from escape.

The *Crescent*'s first ranging shot from her forward gun hit just ahead of the *Eagle*. Decent practice for a Turk, thought Kirkpatrick. Then the first broadside hit home, shattering the port cathead, striking a great ringing blow to the anchor, and punching several holes in the *Eagle*'s side.

"Below decks there," he called into the speaking tube by the binnacle. "What damage?"

"Three inches in the well, sir, but holding steady," came the reply. "We'll have patched the shot holes above the waterline in a few moments more."

Kirkpatrick looked forward. The *Eagle* was sprinting ahead now, all sails drawing well, her sharp bow knifing through the low southerly swells in rhythmic bursts of spray that glinted in the bright moonlight. Kirkpatrick's eyes traveled up the sharply raked masts. No other nation makes a ship that sails like this, he thought, or a crew that fights like this.

With the eastern shore rising ahead of him, he prepared to gybe and bring the *Eagle* around before the wind to head northwest. He silently thanked his friend Dickie Somers for the many hours drilling the *Eagle*'s crew; over the next hour, they would need every bit of skill they possessed. "Star and bar shot in the port-side guns, Mr. Christopher," he ordered, "round shot in on the starboard." Unlike European navies, American warships carried a devilish arsenal of armament specifically designed to shatter masts and spars and shred sails and rigging, including Kirkpatrick's favorite, star shot: long iron rods tethered to an iron ring that, when they left the cannon, turned into viciously whirling scythes. "First we'll cripple her, then we'll gut her."

Kirkpatrick gauged the speed of the wind and the angle to the far western headlands. "Helm a-starboard," Kirkpatrick cried. "Handsomely does it!" and the *Eagle* gracefully pivoted to point northwest. As the *Eagle*'s stern turned through the wind, the crew brought the mainsail boom amidships to ease her into the new tack, sheeting out and easing in the foresail, jib, fore staysail, and jib topsail to leeward and hauling the braces of the square topsail and t'gallant. If the *Crescent* didn't alter her course, they would pass astern of her.

"We've made our move," said Christopher. "Now what will they do?"

Kirkpatrick's mind flashed back to the blood-soaked carnage on the deck of the *Tripoli*. I can't let that happen to this ship, or these men. "If they tack," he said, "on this course they will cut us off, and then cut us to pieces. If they're clumsy and miss stays, they'll have to wear around and try to head us off to the west. Of course, we'd gybe again, and they'd wear again, each time opening up more room downwind for us to escape."

Kirkpatrick watched the *Crescent* respond; time stood still. So did his breathing, and that of every man aboard the *Eagle*. They saw the *Crescent*'s helmsman make his first mistake, jamming her hard a-lee, and slowing her progress. The *Crescent*'s crew was just as untimely abrupt in shifting the jib sheets and spanker boom. "Too soon! Too soon!" Christopher cried. The *Crescent* struggled into the face of the wind. "They are hauling their after yards too slowly," Kirkpatrick answered, "they will miss stays!" Indeed, the *Crescent* fell off before the wind and started drifting backward. "They are making a stern board," said Christopher. "Pray God they ruin their rudder." They watched the *Crescent* continue wearing around awkwardly before the wind, repositioning herself to block the *Eagle*'s escape to the west, but surrendering precious sea room as she did so.

"We're too weatherly for this kind of maneuvering duel. They'll lose it—and I think they know that." Kirkpatrick said. "So let's see if her captain has anticipated our next move. "Ready to gybe, again," he cried, and at the right moment, the *Eagle*'s hands quickly brought her back on a starboard tack, this time heading east just enough to clear the far headland.

As the *Eagle*'s bow started swinging to the right, the *Crescent* wore again, her crew scurrying to haul around her sheets, tacks, and braces. Now both ships were on a parallel course toward the eastern opening of the bay. The next few minutes would determine if the *Eagle* lived or died.

"Mr. Strand," he called to the helmsman, "put her over as if we intend to gybe again, but be ready to bring her back on the starboard tack on my command."

"Now, Mr. Strand," Kirkpatrick cried. "Helm a-starboard!" and the *Eagle* headed up before the wind and regained the previous port tack. The *Crescent*, matching their move, wore yet again. "That's well!" Kirkpatrick cried to the helmsman, then gauging the distance to the *Crescent*, "Gybe now! Helm a-port! But steady!" More like a graceful dancer than a warship, the

Eagle spun to parallel the *Crescent* again. The *Eagle*'s carronades, swiveling forward on their sill pivots, had the entire length of the *Crescent* in range; as she turned to counter them, the *Crescent* could only bring part of its broadside to bear.

A moment later, the *Eagle*'s side erupted in a sheet of fire, sending bar and star shot ripping into the *Crescent*'s rigging. In the space of a heartbeat, the guns the enemy was able to bear smashed into the *Eagle*, this time with deadly accuracy. Some have likened the whirr of incoming fire to the sound of ripping silk or canvas. Kirkpatrick was aware of a sudden stillness, as if the air were being sucked away from the *Eagle*. Then the deafening, shocking concussion of the *Crescent*'s shot came aboard, smashing wood, shattering metal, and loosing a deadly cloud of splinters. The *Eagle* staggered under the blow, then righted herself. Kirkpatrick's first thought was always surprise to find himself still alive and miraculously unwounded. His second thought was for the *Eagle*'s helm. "Does she steer?" he cried. Except for some missing top spokes, the wheel was undamaged. Quartermaster Fox had been knocked to the deck but Strand was still at his position at the wheel, now without a face. Fox struggled to his feet, seized the wheel, looked into the horror of what had been the helmsman's head, and vomited. But the *Eagle* was under control again.

The *Eagle* had suffered greatly from this last stroke. Kirkpatrick could see dead and wounded scattered across the deck. Two of the forward carronades had been blown loose from their lashings and their ports battered into one. Unlike long guns, carronades were mounted on slides and not wheeled carriages, so they were less apt to career wildly across the deck. But the crew was still struggling to secure them, throwing hammocks under their slides to stop their mad progress. The main boom had been shattered at the trucks, and the mainsail flopped wildly back and forth, threatening to rip itself free. Kirkpatrick saw Christopher run aft with three men. Timing their move to avoid being hit by its sharp, shattered end, they passed a line around the boom and make it fast again to the mast.

Thick, acrid cannon smoke veiled the two ships from each other. "Now is the moment," Kirkpatrick cried. "Helm hard a-starboard!" For all the chaos on deck, the crew's training and the leadership of its officers took hold. The *Eagle* turned and shot across the *Crescent*'s wake. The breeze blew the cloud of gun smoke to leeward, and there was the *Crescent,* two hundred yards away, her rigging in shambles and her unprotected stern exposed to the raking fire of the *Eagle*'s undamaged starboard battery.

"Starboard battery, fire as you bear," Kirkpatrick cried. "Straight and true into her guts!" At this distance, the *Eagle*'s heavy 24 pound carronades, "right smashers" as the crew called them, were lethal. The *Eagle*'s first shots blew apart the *Crescent*'s stern gallery. Unaccountably, her glass windows hadn't been struck, and so shards of broken glass were added to the hail of wooden splinters and shrapnel that tore into the after gun crews. Each succeeding shot ripped a gaping wound in the *Crescent*'s stern, then probed through the opening, deep into the bowels of the stricken ship.

He watched the frantic activity on the *Crescent*'s afterdeck. Miraculously, she still had helm. Kirkpatrick could see her crew struggling to take in her spanker. She's turning up to run ahead of the wind. As the *Crescent* turned slowly, the *Eagle* gybed again to cross and rake her stern a second time.

"Sir, they must strike to us," Christopher said. "They are helpless to defend themselves."

"Hell and damnation, Tom! If this were a Christian ship, a civilized ship, there would be no question of seeking to avoid further needless carnage. But remember what they did to James Decatur. The miserable bastards feigned surrender, then shot him dead when he stepped aboard to take possession of his prize. It was the same with us and that scoundrel Reis. No, sir. Not with these devils. We will give no quarter." The *Eagle* could muster only five cannon from her port battery, but these were served with an angry will, each shot going home. A dull coughing sound came from deep inside the *Crescent*, and the first tongues of flame began licking upward from the shattered main deck, eagerly feeding on the wooden wreckage of the hull and turning the remaining rigging into a flaming torch. The crew of the *Eagle* could see panic erupt on deck as the crew began fighting to take possession of the *Crescent*'s one remaining boat.

"Make sail for Syracuse," Kirkpatrick ordered, in response to another questioning glance from Christopher. "The *Crescent* is dead. They have boats, or at least one boat, and there certainly will be wreckage to cling to. Let them manage their own survival. We are done here."

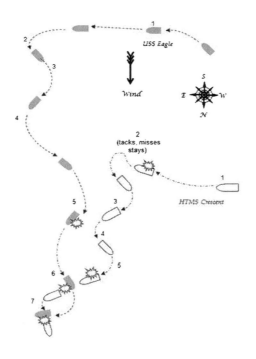

CHAPTER 28
⮞ THE LIBYAN DESERT 1805 ⮜

On March 6, Eaton's army began its march towards Derna, five hundred miles away. Since Kirkpatrick was without a command for the month or more it would take to repair and refit the *Eagle* after her battering by the *Crescent*, Commodore Barron had finally given him permission to accompany the march—but only after a strong appeal from Hull.

During the day, the column stretched haphazardly across the desert for several miles, with the supply camels and their drivers and Hamet's foot soldiers inevitably lagging behind. Eaton's night camp, at least, had the semblance of proper military discipline. At the end of each day's march, as the supply camels finally caught up with the front of the column, the food, ammunition, and supplies were unloaded and arranged in triangular-shaped barricades against the night winds with the tents placed inside the shelter of the barricade. The army's precious supplies were put under the guard of the Greek soldiers commanded by Captain Ulovix and Lieutenant Constantine on rotating four-hour shifts. To Eaton's relief, these two men had turned out to be highly capable officers. Eaton's and Leitensdorfer's tents, the tent shared by Kirkpatrick and O'Bannon, and most important, the army's money chest, were guarded by the Marines.

At Eaton's orders, the *Argus's* Marine detachment, six privates, a sergeant, and Lieutenant O'Bannon, were in full uniform: blue coats with red collars and the distinctive conical shakos that

231

them apart from European soldiers. The Greek and Piedmontese mercenaries wore the uniforms of whatever armies they had last served with—or deserted from—often augmented by Arab burnooses for desert travel.

The Marines were divided between smokers and chewers. Private Davy Thomas was one of the chewers. He let out an expertly guided stream of tobacco juice into the dying coals of the dried camel dung fire over which they'd cooked their meager supper: the last of the salted beef they'd brought with them from the *Argus*.

"Looking at this here scraggedy-arsed detachment, I doubt the Grand Boombah of Tripoli himself would ever suspect he's being invaded by a crack force of United States Marines. Most of this army looks like it was outfitted by Ali Kharr the Rag Man."

Private John Witten loosed his stream of tobacco juice at the fire, narrowly missing the spot where Thomas's missile had sizzled in the embers. "By a 'crack force of United States Marines,' I suppose y'be referring to the seven of us?" he replied.

"Who else?" Thomas answered. "Hell, I'd say each of us can thrash at least twenty Hadjis, so that rascally bastard in Tripoli is actually facing a hundred forty of the meanest devils in the world."

"What d'ye think about the Greeks and cannon cockers?" asked Private Ed Cissell, nodding his head toward the fires of the Greek mercenaries and Piedmontese artillerymen.

"Which the Greeks ain't so bad in my book," replied Whitten. "I mean they ain't Marines—who else is? But they've been fightin' the Turks since their great granddaddy's time, and there's some proper hard cases among them. How about that big 'un Christow who almost nailed y' in the snot locker with the butt of his rifle during bayonet drill yesterday?"

"Piss on it. I let him look good to boost morale,." Cissell answered. "So say they're only half as tough as us. That still brings us up to near battalion strength."

"Sure, but you know who gets the short stick when things get hot. Once the real *zarba* starts flying, the question is, if we lead, will they follow? Or will we get left by ourselves with our arses hanging out?"

"I tell you what it is," Thomas interjected. "I can't figure what *zift* thought this one up: seven Marines against the whole goddamned nation of Tripoli. And while we're amusin' ourselves here, you got five hundred good Marines *shalekhing* in their hammocks at night aboard ship or runnin' around Valetta and Syracuse chasin' *gishtas*. If those lads were with us, nothing would stop us 'til we reached the Atlantic Ocean."

"Are y'not forgetting Pasha Hamet's Arab troops?"

"Right y'are," replied Whitten. "Which it is as fine and proper a collection of dick skinners as I've ever seen. It's all about money with them. They wouldn't get up to wipe their arses without they got paid to do it."

"I dare say it was slick of the generalissimo to have us dump our own money into the expedition's strongbox so it would still sound full. I just hope we get it back."

"Yeah," Whitten replied to Private O'Brien. "But I saw you dump your extra brass buttons into the box to ante up."

"The *gishta*-bait? So what's the odds? If it will work with whores in Alexandria, it will work with camel drivers."

"Well, I'm keeping mine," said Whitten. "Between my spares and what's on my uniform, so long as the rag heads can't tell the difference between polished brass and gold, I'm a rich man."

"I think the only money we'll have will be brass buttons before we're done," Cissell concluded. "That Greek Christow told me that the head camel driver, Sheik El-Tahib, went on strike today. It seems he wanted payment in full for the whole march or he wasn't going to go on. The Old Man faced him down by saying all the money owed him was secure in the strongbox and he'd get it at the end of the march to Derna. That held him—for now."

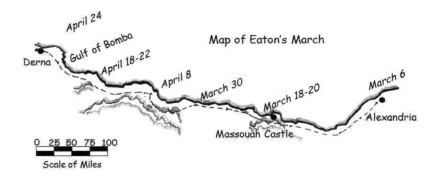

CHAPTER 29
❧ THE LIBYAN DESERT 1805 ❧

Eaton's rag tag army had entered the vast Libyan desert—more truthfully, the desert had simply swallowed them up. They traveled across barren desert plains whose edges disappeared in shimmering mirages—a narrow strip of tantalizing water on the horizon that kept retreating from them as they marched forward. They descended into valleys rimmed by tortured black rock formations, inhabited only by swarms of desert flies.

At sunrise each day, the sky would gradually change from dull gray emptiness into a strange yellow light that threw elusive, elongated shadows behind camels and men, then a reddish purple glow—until the hot sun exploded above the eastern horizon. By mid-morning all the color had been burned out of the sky.

By now, the Marines had adopted the habit of the more experienced European soldiers and wore Bedouin-style head scarves against the flies and constant windblown sand and dust. They baked under a relentless sun during the day and shivered at night in the desert chill. They carried their water with them in *girbas*, goat skins the Arabs had liberally coated, inside and out, with rancid camel fat. The first few days, some of the Marines vomited when they first tasted the foul, brackish water. After a week, they eagerly swilled it down as if it had sprung crystal-clear from pure mountain streams.

Eaton always forged ahead on horseback, accompanied by O'Bannon or Leitensdorfer, following the map Doyle had marked in search of the next water. Eaton's ability to interpret a map that was largely guesswork to begin with, guiding the army through country he had never seen before, was little short of miraculous—and dangerous.

They were in the third day of their march. O'Bannon had joined Eaton for that morning's scout. They rode for a while through open desert without speaking, the only sounds the soft plop of the horse's hooves and the creak of saddle leather. Finally, O'Bannon spoke. "General, have you noticed the silence around us? It's, well ... " he struggled for the right word ... "it feels huge—even oppressive."

"I feel it, too," Eaton said. "No wind whispering in the trees, no murmur of water in a brook, no chatter of voices, no sounds of animals, and, I might add, no rhythmic slap of waves against the sides of a ship. Nothing we would associate with a living world. But I find because there is so little to hear—or see, for that matter—that it sharpens my other senses. I feel I can often sense where the next water will be." Eaton became silent again, and O'Bannon returned to his own thoughts.

They descended into what seemed like a riverbed that had been dry for centuries. O'Bannon looked at the reddish brown cliffs rising above them. "The only things that live out here, general," remarked O'Bannon, "are snakes, scorpions, and bandits. I was thinking that this would be a fine place for an ambush."

Almost as the words left his mouth, two shots rang out, the musket balls plunking into the ground ahead of them. "Climb!" Eaton yelled, and pointed to the cliff above them. Both men spurred their horses up a steep, winding trail cut in the surrounding rock wall until they gained the ridge at the top. The plain around them was empty. Their attackers had disappeared.

"If you have any more premonitions like that, Lieutenant, tell me sooner than later. I think we should stay to the high ground—

with some distance between us. I'll keep looking for water; you look for anyone trying to stop us from getting to it."

After two more days of sniping attacks in which, thankfully, no one had been hit, Eaton's patience ran out. That evening, he called Kirkpatrick and O'Bannon to his tent.

"Gentlemen," he began, "I have decided to put a stop to the brigands taking pot shots at us. Captain," he said to Kirkpatrick, "You will ride with me tomorrow morning ahead of the column, looking for water. That means we will make ourselves targets to smoke out our attackers. I hope that does not make you uneasy," he said with a smile. Kirkpatrick was about to respond, thought better of it, and just nodded his assent.

"Lieutenant," he said to O'Bannon, "You will take your Marines—I will see they have horses—and ride before daybreak to where the captain and I will travel in the morning. I'll show you the route when we're done here. Hide yourselves well. When the captain and I are attacked, as I am sure we will be, we will charge our assailants and drive them into your trap. Have I made that clear?"

"Aye, aye, sir."

"Good, then." Eaton laughed as the thought struck him: "It seems that the British are not the only army with its own Horse Marines!" Then he became serious: "I expect this to be hot work, with no quarter given. You should so advise your men."

O'Bannon looked straight at him: "Aye, aye, sir."

The next morning, Eaton and Kirkpatrick were riding less than a mile ahead of the column, along a flat plain dotted with tall stone outcroppings rising above the desert floor. "This is perfect ambush country," Eaton said to Kirkpatrick, "but that cuts two ways. Given their past practice, the bandits should strike very soon. How are you feeling?" he asked.

The abruptness of the question surprised Kirkpatrick. "The way I feel before any battle: relaxed," he replied instinctively. "In truth, there are a dozen ways a man can be killed in a sea battle. I don't think about it." He paused: "And here we're merely at risk of a lucky..." He was interrupted by the sound of a shot, the musket ball smashing into Eaton's saddle bags. Eaton struggled to bring his horse under control.

Kirkpatrick pointed towards a puff of powder smoke rising above a low outcrop fifty yards away to their left. "There, general! See the smoke?"

"I'm glad we're taking care of this nuisance," Eaton cried. "Their aim is improving. Let's ferret them out!"

Eaton and Kirkpatrick spurred their horses directly at the outcrop from where the fire had come. As expected, their attackers ran for their camels and prepared to flee. O'Bannon had placed his men well. The seven Marines emerged one hundred yards behind their attackers, blocking their immediate escape. At fifty yards, O'Bannon cried "Halt, aim, and fire!" and the Marines reined in their horses to bring their rifles into play. Their first volley brought down two men and one of the camels. As the bandits milled around in confusion, Eaton and Kirkpatrick hit them at full gallop. Eaton shot one man with his pistol, hacked another out of his saddle, and wounded a third. Kirkpatrick missed with his shot, but slammed his horse into the man's camel, knocking him from the saddle; he dispatched a second with his sword. The remaining four bandits fled for their lives—right into O'Bannon's squad. It was fast, cruel, and bloody. As the dust and shouting subsided, Eaton found O'Bannon: "Did any escape?" he cried.

"No, sir, we got them all."

"Are your men all right? O'Bannon looked around quickly. Private O'Brien had lost his mount, but was standing; the other Marines were still mounted. "All accounted for, general!"

"Then see to the wounded," Eaton said. He dismounted, walked over to one of the wounded bandits, and shot him with his second pistol. "There can be no thought of prisoners, gentlemen," he cried. "We must send rascals like these a message they will not misinterpret." He walked up to a young assailant, perhaps no more than fourteen years old, lying in terror on the ground, but apparently not seriously injured.

"Lieutenant O'Bannon," he called out, "put this man under guard. We will spare him for a messenger." At O'Bannon's order, Private O'Brien placed his bayonet over the boy's chest, impassive to the boy's weeping cries for mercy. As the wounded were finished off, Eaton cried, "Strip the bodies. We will leave them here for the vultures and jackals. Take their camels and weapons and burn their clothing." Then as an afterthought, "But take their boots; we may need them."

As the Marines completed their grisly work, Eaton went back to the boy. "Tell your people," he said in Arabic, "We are Americans, not helpless travellers you may rob with impunity. Your friends have suffered the fate of anyone who attacks Americans." He pointed to O'Brien, standing over the boy in his blue coat and tall, conical black hat. The look of death was still on his face: "See that uniform and remember it. Should you repeat this folly, we will follow you to your wretched camp and put everyone to the sword, sparing no one. Do you understand?" The boy nodded through his tears. Eaton grabbed the nose rope of a camel, and with cries of "*Adar-ya-yan!*" forced it down to its knees, placed the boy on the bloody saddle, and yanked the camel back upright. He sent the boy on his way with a blow from the flat of his sword. "*Emishi!* Go, and carry our warning back to the rest of your rabble!"

There were no further attacks.

For the first week, Eaton's skill in finding fresh water was unerring. Each night they camped by the ruins of old forts, equipped with large, spring-fed cisterns or deep wells. One evening, after the men and animals had taken their fill and the water bags had been replenished, Kirkpatrick stood with Eaton, looking at the perfectly aligned stonework of the well's sides disappearing below into the darkness. Kirkpatrick tossed a stone into the well and waited several seconds before they heard the splash.

"Judging from the amount of rope we had to use to fill the goatskins, general, I'd guess these wells are more than seventy-five feet deep. Who in the world do you think built them?"

"Anthony's Roman legionnaires," answered Eaton. "These are the remains of Roman forts, built a day's march apart. People forget that the Roman legionnaires weren't just the best soldiers the world has ever seen; they were also the best engineers." He looked at the ruins around them, then ran his hand over the rough weathered stones on the well's rim.

"This was the kingdom he and Cleopatra meant to enjoy together. Eaton looked up at the star-strewn sky above them. "Such great dreams. How does it go? 'Let Rome in Tiber melt, and the wide arch of the ranged empire fall! Here is my space.' And now the grave that clips them together lies only in our imaginations. So much for dreams. But this stonework has held up for almost two thousand years. I wonder if we Americans will leave a legacy like that behind us. People we can't imagine, in a time far distant, will say, 'Ah. The Americans were here.'"

He picked up a piece of rubble, and like Kirkpatrick, let it fall into the well. They both listened for the sound of the splash from the well's depths. He turned to look at Kirkpatrick. "Happily, our task is easier, captain. We just need to make sure that that rascal Karamanli in Tripoli and the rest of the thieving Barbary pirates know that the Americans have come."

CHAPTER 30
☙ THE LIBYAN DESERT 1805 ❧

By March 13, once they had left the ancient Roman forts behind, their march settled into a routine of just walking forward, a step at a time, with little thought of the ground that they'd covered or the miles ahead. Men marched in silence: talking required too much effort, especially for throats parched by the relentless heat. Every now and then, a man might look up with tired, blood-shot eyes at the far-away line between the bluish white of the sky and the dull yellow of the sand. Finding no relief in the distance, his sight and consciousness would return to the next few steps he needed to take. When they finally made evening camp, after seeing to the unloading of camels and the arrangement of their gear with their last reserves of energy, men just collapsed and lay on the ground.

As night fell, men gathered around the dinner fires, eating in exhausted silence. Then slowly, following the gradual appearance of stars in the darkening sky, life returned: one soldier would start talking or singing quietly, his nearest companions joining him. Men looked up at each other as if to ask: 'Are you all right?' 'So you made it through today?' It became a game—a desert game of make believe—each man trying to be a little more cheerful than his neighbor to give him a renewed sense of confidence and strength for the next day.

Kirkpatrick had left their tent to do the inspection rounds that evening and O'Bannon had returned to his journal.

Dear Father Heard:

It has a while since I've written—or have even had time to think about writing. At the present moment I have more of it than I want.

We have been marching through wild, unknown country; a sad, depressing sameness of desolation with no house or even sign of human habitation, no trees—such plants that one does see are dry, brown, desiccated thorns. We go forward without the knowledge of where, when, or even if we will next find water. What we do find is usually foul and brackish, and so meager in quantity that all we can do is momentarily slake our thirst, with no chance to refill our water skins. Imagine placing one's cup under a small trickle seeping out of a rock fissure and waiting five minutes for enough to collect in the cup to afford a single swallow of water. There is moss—foul smelling, to be sure—clinging to the rocks around these tiny springs. Some of the men take it and squeeze the moisture out of it into their parched throats. And it's worse for our horses. Before we reached camp today, they had gone the entire three days without water. And we still have three hundred miles of this hell ahead of us.

The general has been a pillar of strength for us. He refuses to yield to the dangers and privations we encounter now as a matter of course. And somehow, in this parched land, he finds water, scarce as it may be. If he were to strike a rock and cause a stream to flow, like Moses in the Bible, I wouldn't be surprised.

I have come to respect the strength of the general's second in command, Colonel Leitensdorfer, as well. We call him "colonel"—actually, I think his highest rank was as a sergeant in one of the many armies he served with. All the more reason for a Marine lieutenant to listen to him. He kept to himself on our journey to Cairo, so I had little opportunity to take his measure. Now, the worse things get, the more unshakable his sense of humor. I think he would laugh at his own death wound. He amuses the men with magic tricks. Last week, in one of our halts, he contrived to pluck an astounding collection of objects out of Private Whitten's ear: a cartridge, a stone, a cockroach, and the best of all, a huge, black, vile-looking, wriggling beetle. We all got more pleasure out of it than poor Whitten, I'm afraid.

And the colonel is a deep man, given to deep thoughts. We were riding through the heat on one of our "dry days" when I asked him if anyone lived in this godforsaken wilderness. Oh yes, he told me, large tribes of nomads, herding thousands of sheep, regularly pass through these lands—his greatest hope is to find such a group with whom we can buy or barter fresh food. I asked him why anyone would choose such a place as this. He quoted some sort of scripture to me: there are lands that are full of water for the well-being of the body, and lands that are full of sand for the well-being of the soul. I asked him which he preferred. He said: "I'm sure God will attend to my soul—who am I to tell Him how to go about His business? So I try to take care of the well-being of my body—that's more than enough work for any man." He makes me laugh. That's a precious enough blessing.

But what a country of cruel, unpredictable contrasts this it. Yesterday we found a small ravine with a stream running through it—an actual flowing body of water. Of course we made camp next to it. The men had started fires to cook our evening meal of rice. (When this expedition is over and I return to civilization, I may never eat rice again!) Then the rains came. An unspeakably violent thunder storm crashed upon us, lightning splitting the sky, dumping torrents of rain, drowning our fires, and drenching our gear in minutes.

The general sprang into action, driving us to break camp and move to higher ground, which we did: wading through mud to haul our sodden supplies to the top of the ravine—where we were exposed to the full fury of the storm. The wisdom of his actions became apparent shortly after, when the entire ravine turned into a swollen torrent. It would surely have carried away our tents and supplies, and probably some of us in the bargain. We spent the sorriest night you can imagine, huddled under such shelter as we could contrive—no thought of pitching tents in the fierce wind that accompanied the storm. The next morning the wind abated and we were able to erect our soaked tents and crawl inside them like drowned rats. We are still trapped in our tents—hence the opportunity to write. The rain has continued without let up. Peter, next to me, has fallen asleep. He has the gift of being able to do that anywhere—probably standing up.

The cruelty of it all is that all this water will go to waste; we have nothing to catch it in except our hats. Sometime—today, tomorrow, the rain will stop and we will resume our march and reenter hell.

This is more morose a letter than I expected to write. But then, who knows if you will ever have the opportunity to read it?

Chapter 31
❧ The Libyan Desert 1805 ❧

On March 18, Eaton led them to the first sign of civilization since they left the last of the old Roman forts. Kirkpatrick, riding at the head of the column with Eaton and the other officers, spotted it first as he crested a hill: a tall pile of stone rubble, barely distinguishable in the distance from the weathered sandstone rock outcrops around them.

"What is that, general?" he called out. Eaton turned in the saddle to face him.

"We have reached Massouah Castle. Look there," he pointed toward a cluster of Bedouin tents in the flat ground beneath the castle. "We should be able to barter for fresh food with those people."

"General," Kirkpatrick asked as they rode forward, "Are these the remains of buildings?" Around them, lines of low, rough stone walls in clear rectangular patterns rose out of the surrounding sand.

"We are traveling through a ruined city, sure enough," said Eaton. "I would think," he added, pointing to his right, "those fields once grew grain in abundance."

Kirkpatrick continued to stare at the geometrical lines of rubble around them: "This city must have been huge. We are clearly riding along what must have been a major avenue. What in the world caused all of this to fall into ruin?"

"Look at the ground," Eaton said. As their horses walked forward, they kicked up miniature whirlpools of dust. "Drought did this. The water disappeared and the city died."

"Any idea of whose city this was?" Kirkpatrick asked. By now they were close enough to see the remains of crenelated towers and the shape of an arched entryway at the end of a causeway spanning what would certainly have been a moat.

"It looks medieval. Norman I'd say, more than Arab—perhaps going back to the Counts of Sicily. Hard to tell, though. This part of the world has seen so many conquerors rise, fall, and eventually be forgotten."

Nearing the castle, they cantered through the cluster of black Bedouin tents, scattering dogs and sheep, gathering a cavalcade of noisy children, and triggering high-pitched ululations from the tribe's women as they passed.

Eaton dismounted amid the growing crowd clustering around them. I don't like this, he thought. He turned to O'Bannon: "Have the Marines take our provisions and the strong box into the castle. I'll set up headquarters there." Then to Leitensdorfer, "Colonel, if you would be so kind, find the headman and see what kind of piratical terms he would demand for some of these sheep. Dates and figs would serve us as well," he added.

Several hours later, the last of their straggling camel supply train arrived. Eaton had the escorting Greeks bring their food inside the castle as Hamet and his followers had made camp two hundred yards away by a small stream. Leitensdorfer returned with precious new supplies of goats, sheep, skins of butter, and dates. He also brought bad news.

"That she-jackal El-Tahib is raising mutiny again, general," he reported. "He claims that Hamet only contracted for them to come as far as Massouah Castle here, not all the way to Derna. He insists on the full sum of eleven dollars per camel now, or they will turn back and leave us here. He's also asking to be paid for the contracted hundred and seven camels and not for the eighty he actually provided. When I questioned Hamet about this, he dissimulated, so it seems Hamet lied either to El-Tahib, you, or everyone. But this time, El-Tahib seems resolute."

"Why the devil damn him black!" Eaton cried. "I'll show him what 'resolute' means!" Eaton ordered the Greek bugler to blow "To Arms." When the Marines and European soldiers had formed into ranks, he marched them inside the castle and directed them to set up defensive positions. As his troops scraped out rifle pits and knocked firing holes through the castle's wall, accompanied only by Leitensdorfer he marched through the sprawling Arab camp to Hamet's tent. Hamet's personal guards, clustered around the tent, barely made way for them to pass, nervously fingering their weapons and casting uneasy glances back at Hamet's tent.

"Excellency!" he roared. "What is this new treachery that scoundrel El-Tahib is bringing to us now?"

Eaton's cry brought the Arabs around them running. In less than a minute, Eaton and Leitensdorfer were surrounded by a yelling mob of armed men. I'd better be good here, thought Eaton, one misstep and Leitensdorfer and I are both corpses—and I suspect the other Christians will join us shortly.

He looked at the mass of dark, bearded faces around them: some anxiously concerned, most contorted with rage. "We are not among friends here, I think," he said quietly to Leitensdorfer. "Sorry you came, Eugene?"

Leitensdorfer stood next to him, calm and untroubled. "Wouldn't have missed it for all the world."

Hamet came out of his tent, accompanied by a defiant El-Tahib. I must woo Hamet away from this wretch. Eaton thought. "Excellency," Eaton's voice, now softly reached through the din around them to touch a thoroughly frightened Hamet: "As I know you will be a wise and just ruler of your people, you know how precious the bond of truth is between comrades. You and I both know what was agreed to." His voice rose in quiet intensity. "Your journey and ours does not end here, but at Derna, and then Tripoli itself. Will you now cast aside the suffering and loss of the past five years you have so bravely endured—and the hope of your family, held captive by your brother the usurper—to abandon your quest in a sad moment of weakness—at the feet of this coward, liar, and traitor, El-Tahib?" Hamet looked up, awareness, if not courage, again in his eyes.

Turning to El Tahib, Eaton's voice now carried strongly over the shouting around them: "And you, treacherous, perfidious *ibn haram* that you are" ... he sought for a suitably strong curse. "*Yela'an sabe'a jad lak!* May you and all your forefathers to your seventh great grandfather be cursed to burn in unending flames of Hell itself!" Eaton turned to address the Arabs around them. "I give you my word: if you will not go on, then here my men and I and will stay, with all the food, ammunition, and money. I have already dispatched a rider to the coast to meet with our re-supply ships at Oz Kerr, two days from here. He will return with a strong relief party of Marines." Let's hope they believe that, he thought.

He faced El-Tahib again, his eyes fierce and unrelenting: "I tell you what your treachery will bring down on you and those foolish enough to follow you! I will extract my followers and leave you, your thieving tribesmen and camels to find your own way back to your villages. Know that if you demand more payment than we agreed upon to complete the entire march to Derna, that payment will come not in gold but in hot lead!" With that, Eaton spun on his heel and turned back with Leitensdorfer toward the castle, leaving behind a more resolute Hamet and a fuming El-Tahib. As the Arabs gathered around made way to let them pass, Eaton saw that O'Bannon had brought the Christian troops out of the castle and placed them in formation at the castle causeway, with bayonets fixed. Not so many of us, Eaton thought.

As they reached the edge of the Arab encampment, a lone figure detached himself from the crowd of Arabs and walked toward them. During the confrontation with Hamet and El-Tahib, Leitensdorfer and Eaton had prudently removed their side arms in order to avoid lighting a match that would have set off an explosion. As the veiled stranger approached them, both men viewed him with apprehension.

"That was quite impressive, general, especially since most of it was pure bluff," said Doyle, pulling back his face veil, "especially confronting them unarmed."

"Well not entirely unarmed, Henry" Eaton said, pulling back the sleeves of his burnoose to reveal a throwing knife strapped to each wrist, ready to spring to Eaton's hands with just a pull on the handle. "Good of you to join us."

"A pleasure, as always. Although calling El-Tahib an *ibn haram* might still be considered a gross insult to real bastards like myself," Doyle laughed. "But I think you've won back Hamet—until his next crisis of courage."

Seeing the stranger approaching their two leaders, O'Bannon and Kirkpatrick had run forward, their pistols at the ready. Ignoring Doyle, O'Bannon confronted Eaton: "General, forgive me for speaking so plainly, but that was madness! The two of you alone in that mob!"

"Better two of us at risk than all of us," said Eaton, calmly. "With all the food and ammunition in the castle, had things gone sour, you might have had a chance. In the open..." His voice trailed off as he nodded his head towards the hundreds of Arabs behind them. "But I thank you for your concern. Now, I think this business may not be over. Pray do gather your men and make sure our defensive posture in the castle is as strong as you can make it." O'Bannon saluted and turned with Kirkpatrick to rejoin their troops.

Leitensdorfer had been regarding Doyle with an amused smile. "Well, well, well. It seems our mysterious *djinn* has popped out of his magical bottle once again. So Doyle, do you bring us three gifts this time?"

"Only two," said Doyle. "The first concerns the message one of my scouts will bring in a day or two. It seems as if the population of Derna has risen against the well-hated Governor Mustifa Bey, slaughtered all his Turkish Janissaries, and declared the city for Hamet."

"In God's name," cried Eaton. "Is that true?"

"Of course not," said Doyle. "But since we are in the land of lies, I thought it useful to add one of our own. That story should add a little martial courage to your brave Arabs. My second gift has to do with that *fatah*, El-Tahib. Given his ability to create mischief, I have added two of my best men to his camel drivers. They will serve to bring you news of further troubles while also creating as much mischief of their own for El-Tahib as they can.

"My last news is hardly a gift. It would seem that you Americans haven't quite caught the trick of maintaining secrets. Pasha Jusef Karamanli has somehow received detailed news of your march and has dispatched a relief column to reinforce Derna: two thousand or more Tripolitans, commanded by the Mameluke Hassan Bey and supported by Arab cavalry from the Bey of Bengazi. The good news is that they represent almost all of the loyal troops available to Jusef, so Tripoli is now ripe for the taking. The bad news is that if you don't seize Derna before Hassan Bey can reinforce it, judging by the brave heroes you've assembled for this adventure," he looked back at the Arab encampment, "it won't make a difference. Now, since you've made the fortress a safe place for a proper white man like myself, let's go in and look at your maps while we wait for Hamet to decide what to do about the ultimatum you gave him. Knowing your fondness for coffee, general, I've even brought some with me."

CHAPTER 32
❧ THE LIBYAN DESERT 1805 ❧

Eaton sat with Doyle, savoring their coffee inside what might have been the great hall of Massouah Castle. Their small fire cast flickering shadows along the ruined stone walls rising above them.

"If I may be permitted an observation, William," Doyle said, "the army you've assembled to overthrow Jusef Karamanli seems a little—how should I put it—mixed in its loyalty."

Eaton easily caught the humorous irony in Doyle's tone. Well, Eaton thought, his doubts are no greater than mine. "'Mixed' would be a generous description," replied Eaton. "A sane man would rate our chances poorly. But then, a sane man wouldn't attempt what I'm doing."

"And I'm helping you. What does that say about me?" Doyle laughed. A good question, thought Eaton. I wish I knew the answer.

"In the next few days," continued Doyle, "you'll cross the Egyptian border and enter Tripoli. Perhaps it's time to see what kind of local support Hamet can raise."

"I have been thinking about that," said Eaton. "Sometimes ideas can be more powerful than armies—or their leaders. Perhaps we need to get Pasha Karamanli's subjects excited about the *idea* of Hamet as their new ruler: a proclamation for example, that your scouts might spread ahead of our army."

"The very thing, William. A proclamation. One can't launch a proper revolution or *coup d'état* without one."

Eaton rose, went to his campaign desk, pulled out paper and a pen, and sat down cross-legged by Doyle. "Let's see," Eaton began writing, reading aloud to Doyle as the words poured onto the paper:

To the inhabitants of the kingdom of Tripoli—Brothers, sons of Abraham, faithful believers of the faithful messengers of Truth—

"I'll start with an expression of religious solidarity," said Eaton, "something to the effect that the religion of America—"

"With your 'One God,' of course," added Doyle—"

"Indeed." Eaton ignored Doyle's sarcasm as he wrote:

This peaceful American faith is the orthodox faith of the prophet Abraham, blessings on him, and thus the sister religion to Islam.

"Then we must blackguard Pasha Karamanli. Let us remind his subjects, in case they have forgotten, what a monster he is." Eaton wrote:

Pasha Karamanli is known by all true men to be a bloodthirsty scoundrel, a fratricide who, to secure his unlawful right to the throne, killed one brother, even in his mother's arms, and exiled the other. He has surrounded himself with hypocrites and vagabonds, leeches on the poor nation of Tripoli, stealing the people's wealth to line their own greedy pockets.

"What else?" he asked, looking up at Doyle.

"You can mention," Doyle said, "that:

His pirate ships which brought this calamity on the people of Tripoli are captained by scoundrels escaped from Christian countries to evade the punishment which their crimes have merited.

"Splendid," said Eaton, writing quickly. "Then we must note how Pasha Karamanli has brought his country to ruin by spurning the many peace offers America has graciously extended. What do you think of this?"

He leads you into war with no advantage to you whatsoever. He does not hesitate to drench your land with your blood, provided that he be able to gain money by it!

"Perfect," said Doyle. "Just the very thing. You might add something like:

Like a Turk, he scoffs at your sufferings, saying: O what value are these Moors and these Arabs! They are just beasts which belong to me, worth a great deal less than my camels and my asses.

"That should offend the pride of his subjects properly," laughed Eaton.

As Eaton wrote, Doyle continued. "Then you might brand him with the mark of Cain, and say that:

He bears the mark of the first murder upon his forehead. The wrath of God has been aroused against his treachery. God, the Merciful and Compassionate, has seen fit to use America as the instrument of His righteous wrath, that the cruel reign of the usurper be ended and the people of Tripoli released from their suffering—

"To be ruled, instead," added Eaton,

—by Hamet, a just and merciful prince who greatly loves his subjects and will bring peace to this troubled land.

"So," Eaton concluded. "We have appealed to their faith, their fear and their vanity. Let us tickle their greed by describing the riches and abundant supply of weapons, food and money we bring to support those willing to throw off Pasha Karamanli's hateful yoke."

He wrote a little more and then looked back at Doyle. "Let us end on a personal note. I will close by assuring them that as proof of America's fidelity—

I shall be always with you until the end of the war and even until you have achieved your glorious mission, in proof of America's fidelity and our goodwill.

"That should do it!" said Eaton, signing the proclamation with a flourish of his pen.

"You make bold promises," Doyle said. He was still smiling, but Eaton saw the skepticism in his eyes.

"It is said" Eaton replied, "that when Alexander stood on the banks of the Indus, with all Asia in front of him, he threw his sword across the water and waded in to reclaim it on the other side. 'I will follow my sword,' he said. I can do no less. I will have this translated into Arabic, and with your help, it will fly before us, bringing loyal recruits to our cause."

CHAPTER 33
ॐ THE LIBYAN DESERT 1805 ॐ

Their planning done and the maps put aside, Eaton and Doyle relaxed with the last of their coffee. From his pocket, Eaton pulled out two ancient gold coins, worn almost smooth by the passage of centuries. In knocking a firing hole in the wall, one of the Greek infantrymen had unearthed them amidst a pile of broken crockery. Captain Ulovix had brought the coins for Eaton to examine. Eaton looked above him to where the sky was again ablaze in stars.

"One could imagine as many human souls have lived their brief lives here," said Eaton, "and returned to the dust they sprung from, as the stars above us that have looked ceaselessly and indifferently down on our small hopes and empty dreams. Consider these coins, Doyle. They could be Phoenician, Carthaginian, Roman, I dare say Vandal, or any one of a thousand years of other races and rulers who have had their moment here and passed away. Whose face was inscribed here as a monument to his power? And what of the man who grasped these coins and hid them away in hopes of reclaiming them later? Where be his passions now? His lusts? His flashes of anger that set the room to quaking in fear?" He turned one of the coins over in his hand. "All memory of him has been erased just as completely as the inscription on this coin."

"They may not help him now," said Doyle, "but I think you just found yourself a few more days of food the next time you cross paths with a tribe of Bedouins."

Eaton nodded, put the coins in his pocket, and looked back up at Doyle. "You know, this philosophical turn brings to mind yet another of my impertinent, doubtless foolish questions, if I may be so bold."

"Old Eleazer Wheelock often said that there are no foolish questions," said Doyle.

"As did his son," said Eaton, "unless you happened to ask one yourself. I know something of Islam and have heard you described as being of the Sufi sect. I would take it as a great kindness if you might dispel some of my ignorance about the Sufis."

"For me, and I speak only for myself—I would not presume to speak for all the faithful—one begins to understand the Sufis by remembering the tragic division of Islam into two warring camps upon the death of the Prophet, *salla'llahu 'alayhi wa sallam*. The great gift he brought, peace be upon him, was the gift of 'oneness.' One God, *subhanahu wa ta'ala*, all-merciful, all-powerful; one true prophet; one faith; one blessed union with God. But almost before the Prophet, peace be upon him, had ascended into Paradise, the hearts of his followers had turned away from the light. The world of Islam, a word and an idea which, as you know, means both 'peace' and 'submission to God,' was divided between Sunnis loyal to the Umayyads and the Shi'ites who believed Ali ibn Abi Talib, Mohammad's cousin and son-in-law, to be the true successor of the Prophet, peace be upon him. For more than a thousand years, Sunnis and Shi'ites have fought each other with an enthusiastic savagery that one would have thought better saved for killing Christians and other infidels.

"But where does the sect of the Sufis belong?"

"Nowhere, because it's not a sect, and everywhere, because it precedes religion. As Ibn-el-Farid has said, 'our wine preexists the grape and the vine.' The Prophet, blessing on him, has said that men are asleep when they live and wake when they die. Sufis seek to awaken in this life by finding within themselves the essence of God that existed before the world was created." Doyle paused for a moment. "At the risk of my own presumption, may I ask, general, whether you are a Christian?"

"I am—a Congregationalist."

"And the fine Captain Vincents who accompanied us to Cairo—a staunch Church of England man, I have no doubt of it—would he consider you a Christian?" Doyle asked.

"I suspect not," replied Eaton. "If I were a Methodist, I suppose it would be worse, but, as he sees it, I am a dissenter—and a colonial rebel in the bargain—certainly no one he would consider a true Christian.

"And would he allow Roman Catholics to be admitted as being true Christians?"

"Papists?" laughed Eaton. "I should think not!"

"So one might say that you Christians have as hard a time deciding what constitutes true faith as most Muslims. Sufism is based on a different presumption. If God is the creator of all things, then are not all human beings the creation of God? When Sunnis, Shi'ites, Wahhabis, Jews, or Roman Catholics—or even Congregationalists—declare they are the only true followers of God, do they not call the very nature of God into question? How can God both love and hate what He has created? If we are created in God's image and love, then His spirit is within us, even though our human weakness veils us from understanding that spirit. To deny the presence of God in our hearts is therefore to deny God Himself. Sufis say there are as many ways to God as the breaths of the children of God."

"So Sufis are not, then, Muslims?"

"To the contrary. Sufis who truly seek to experience God base their lives on the three-fold foundation of the Muslim faith: *islam,* submission to the law; *imam,* faith in God and his messengers; and *ihsan,* loving the presence of God in one's heart and living one's life as an expression of that love. Submission to the law is like the wax on the cork that prevents the liquid from seeping out of a bottle. So Sufis seek to honor the law, understand the word, but most of all, see and become in harmony with God's presence in our souls. When Muslims pray, we begin our formal devotions, the *tekbir*, by facing Mecca, raising our hands by our ears to push back the illusions of the world, and say '*Allah hu ekber,*' God is greater. I believe God is greater than our human weakness. I believe we are asked to go beyond the weakness of knowledge to faith. Many—perhaps most—Muslims take the commandment of Mohammed to journey to Mecca as an earthly journey to a physical place. I would prefer to say that the Mecca toward which I travel is in my heart, and it was there before I was born."

"But all this," Eaton continued, "sounds quite mystical. How do you put together your inward journey and a life so continuously, and proficiently, I might add, spent in violence and bloodshed?"

"Sufis say, *Alhamdu lillahi 'ala kulli hal.* Praise belongs to God in every state of being. While we are in this world, we must act in this world. For some, contemplation is the highest form of action. For others, it is the blindest form of self-deceiving inaction. What matters is *how* action is done, not *what* action is done. The Prophet, blessings be upon him, has said, 'Do what you should do when you should do it. Refuse to do what you should not do. When it is not clear, wait until you are sure.' That is how I attempt to live my life."

"And are you sure of me?" Eaton asked.

"I am sure of your intentions. The desert will judge your actions."

Late that night, after a final inspection of the sentry posts, O'Bannon stood for a while in the castle's ruined entrance, looking down at the Arab camp stretched out below him. It was quiet, with only a few fires still glowing among the scattered tents. The star-strewn sky stretched above him endlessly. Unable to sleep, he returned to his tent, gave a quick look at Kirkpatrick, snoring peacefully, then picked up a lamp and his journal and settled comfortably among the fallen stones by the castle's arched gate. He had continued the practice of writing letters without any knowledge of when, or even if, his letters would reach their destinations.

> Dear Father Heard:
> This will be the most unusual letter you have ever received from me—assuming of course, I survive to post it. You know how inseparable I am from my fiddle. To play the airs and tunes from home—and I suppose I mean Ireland as well as America—is a joy I rely upon to keep me sane. Of an evening (after the infantry drills I continue to insist we conduct each day, hungry, thirsty, tired, or no) I take out the fiddle and play. These old songs have echoed in many lands, but here, under a sky so packed with stars that to look at their depth and vastness makes one feel insignificant, by the crackle of a camel-dung fire, the solitary song of a fiddle is both extraordinarily comforting and inexpressibly lonely.
> But we make the most of it. The men insist on the same old favorites, "Soldier's Joy," "Liberty," "Whiskey at Breakfast," and "Hogs in the Corn." John Whitten accompanies me on a Jew's harp while David Thomas and James Owens have fashioned bodhrans out of local tambours, and for a pair of Welshman, they can actually play a bit. I can count on Sergeant Campbell to request a Scots tune or two, which he insists, of course, on accompanying in a voice that would raise the dead from their sleep. He named one of the mules we have commandeered to haul our supplies "Maxwelton." I didn't get the joke until he asked me to play "Maxwelton's Braes Are Bonny."

He repeated the joke, laughing until he cried. I can tell you, he's a fine Marine noncom, but his brays are certainly anything but bonny.

Then it's on to the dancing. Of course Private O'Brien dances, and 'a fine one he is for the reels,' as they would say. So there we were, serenading the empty desert, and up comes the general's chief scout, none other than the mysterious Katir Al-Hareeq who accompanied us up the Nile. I've told you he drifts in and out of camp at night like a wraith with intelligence for the general. So this Al-Hareeq stood and watched for a while, as O'Brien was working himself into fine form. Then he threw off his burnoose and joined him in dance. I was so dumbfounded I almost stopped playing. Step for step he matched O'Brien, with a sureness and sweetness of style not to be seen outside of Ireland. One song led to another—at first they competed, and when it was clear that both were masters, they just danced together, beautifully.

At one point I looked out beyond the fire and became aware that all our troops—Greeks, Piedmontese, and a surprising number of Arabs—were clapping in rhythm and bursting into sustained applause. It was quite extraordinary. Finally, when their legs would no longer stand and I had burned half the hair off my bow, O'Brien and Al-Hareeq stopped and embraced each other in joyful exhaustion. What happened next, Father, goes beyond all sense or reason. Al-Hareeq gathered his burnoose, walked up to me, and said, in pure Gaelic, "And would you not be one of the O'Bannon's of County Tipperary, a descendant of Brian Boru O'Bannon of famous memory? I have seen the Leim ui Bhanain, near Roscrea. The grand castle it is, to be sure. We are both a long way from home, Lieutenant. May the last echoes of your fiddle reach heaven just a heartbeat before you arrive." And that was that. Off he melted again into the desert. Now that he goes about often with his face unveiled, I've finally had a good look at him. More mystery, he's clearly not an Arab. His skin is darker than one might expect in a European, but for that, you might expect

to meet him on a street in Dublin. Oh, then this last mystery, strangest of all. I found out what language he uses when he and the general
want to speak without others understanding them. It's Iroquois.

From the Journals of El Habibka
All wisdom can be stated in two lines:
What is done for you—allow it to be done.
What you must do yourself—make sure you do it.

Khawwas

CHAPTER 34
∞ THE LIBYAN DESERT 1805 ∞

The next day, the army camped by an oasis with an abundant supply of fresh water. Doyle and Eaton rode to the crest of the next hill, beyond which stretched the mountains of the *Auk Bet Salaum*, blue and purple in the shimmering heat.

"Here's where we part company, William. I need to ride south to muster the Tuaregs who will join you at Derna. Once they're underway, I'll get back to you as quickly as I can. Until then, you're on your own. Let's go over the route one last time." They dismounted and once again consulted Eaton's map.

"You'll need to ascend and work your way along the foothills and then over that range," said Doyle, indicating the mountains rising ahead of them. "There's precious little water from this point until you descend again to the coast here, about ninety miles," he pointed to the map, "where you will meet up with Hull."

Eaton shook his head and then looked back at Doyle. "It doesn't get easier, does it?"

"No," said Doyle. "You should make it through the mountains. Whether you have an army with you is anyone's guess."

Eaton just nodded, his mind already on the challenges ahead of his army. "You know," Doyle continued, "had I stayed in America, you and I would probably have fought each other, if not at Fallen Timbers with Wayne, then in the south. We would have been enemies."

Eaton looked up at Doyle. "I know. Given what happened to the Mohawks, the entire Iroquois Nation, and the western tribes in the Northwest Territories, who would have blamed you? Disease, defeat, and devastation were the gifts we brought your people. If I were one to worry, I could imagine that you have brought us this far just to lead us into starvation and thirst in those forbidding mountains."

"You may manage that on your own without my help," laughed Doyle. "But rest assured. When I told you that part of my past died when I left America, I told the truth. I work for my own purposes now—and for money. From what I see of your situation, I'm glad the British have guaranteed my fee." He vaulted into his saddle and swung his horse's head to the south. "I'm off to see if I can gather some troops you can actually rely on. I'll rejoin you somewhere around Bomba—if you make it."

Eaton stayed on the crest of the hill until Doyle's figure, now just a distant speck and a dust cloud, disappeared among the southern foothills. He looked back down at the growing, shapeless confusion of Arab tents, men and beasts on the plain below, and at the pitifully small detachment of Christian troops, and repeated Doyle's parting words: "If we make it." He mounted and spurred down the hill to rejoin his army.

After making the rounds to check on the sentries at nightfall, Lieutenant O'Bannon returned to their tent. Kirkpatrick was futilely trying to fashion new soles from a strip of leather for the ruined dress Wellington half-boots he had regrettably chosen for a five hundred-mile march across a hot, stony desert.

"Well, brother," O'Bannon said, "I see you are attempting another miracle cure with those boots of yours. I stand in awe of your perseverance. If I may be so bold as to be allowed a suggestion, perhaps there's a better use for those boots in their present condition. They look so much like sieves now, or perhaps a badly mended fisherman's net, there is more hole to them than boot."

Kirkpatrick gave him a friendly glare.

"So consider this," O'Bannon went on. "You know how much you complain about, how shall I say, the fragrance of your feet after a long day's march. I must confess I don't find it all that pleasant either. So don't you see, if you were to walk into an oasis, stream, or even a small pool, the free passage of water through those boots would allow you to bathe your feet and still remain fully shod. Of course, there's the added benefit of not having to shake your boots out in the morning to ensure that no scorpion has crawled inside. There are so many holes in your boots, a scorpion would have no place to hide." He ducked the boot Kirkpatrick threw at him and stepped back outside the tent. He returned moments later with a bundle that he tossed into Kirkpatrick's lap. Kirkpatrick pulled out a pair of Arab boots and looked up at O'Bannon.

"I think they're your size," O'Bannon said. In response to Kirkpatrick's look, he continued: "They're from one of the men we killed in that ambush several weeks ago. They were thrown into one of our supply bundles. Sergeant Campbell found them; he's been giving out replacement boots to the Marines who need them. I figured if these were good enough for a Marine, they might serve you. Knowing your delicate sensibilities, I made sure to get you a pair without any blood on them."

"So I'll be marching in a dead man's boots," Kirkpatrick said as he eagerly started pulling the boots on. "Let's hope that's just a figure of speech." Kirkpatrick stood up to walk outside and check the fit. O'Bannon sat down by his bedroll, adjusted the light from the lamp, picked up his journal and began writing.

Yesterday we experienced a near tragedy. At mid-day, a rider brought the news that the population of Derna had revolted against Pasha Karamanli's governor, killed or dispersed his troops, and offered their city to Hamet. It was all a ruse to encourage Hamet and his men. It worked, but not in the way any of us expected. The news of Derna's revolt triggered the most extraordinary outburst by our Arab troops. They mounted their horses and camels and rode like madmen, through and around the camp, yelling at the top of their lungs and firing their muskets into the air. Unfortunately, the sound of their yelling and gunfire thoroughly alarmed our camel drivers and the Arab foot soldiers who accompany them at the rear of our column. They believed the main force ahead of them had been attacked and were about to be overwhelmed by Pasha Karamanli's troops, and determined to "kill all the infidels" and make their escape. The dozen or so Christian troops who were at the rear, guarding the baggage, were convinced they were about to be slaughtered by the frightened Arabs milling around them.

Fortunately, a few cooler heads among the Arabs suggested that they postpone the massacre until a rider was sent forward to discern what was really happening. The rider came back with the news that had set off all the hubbub in the first place. So they, too, exploded into their own unruly celebration. Happily, however, they exhausted their ammunition firing at the sky, and not our Christian troops. But the rumor will, I hope, buy us a few days of less anxious marching.

Since nothing else in this cursed land is what it seems, I shouldn't have been surprised. I have become hardened to the discomforts one lives with aboard ship, primarily the experience of being constantly wet: bedding and clothing soaked from one day to the next and always the trouble of keeping one's gear from mildew and rot and one's weapons free of rust. In the desert, we just exchange a wet hell for a dry one. Had it not been for our friends among the Greek soldiers who have served in this miserable climate and country before, we would all be in the sick bay. Except that here, in this empty land, there is no sick bay and no choice but to keep pushing forward.

Without experiencing it, one can't imagine the heat, sand, and dust that we contend with. We are turning into parched scarecrows—just skin and bones. All of us suffer from nose-bleeds and dry, hacking coughs. Waking in the morning, it sounds like a hospital for incurable lung diseases. Our fingers, noses, and even our eyes are raw and chapped. No matter how well we cover ourselves, the sand and dust find their way into our ears, arm pits, and crotches, constantly chafing the skin as we march. One so desperately wishes for the relief of washing— at least one's face and eyes—but there is precious little water even for drinking.

I never thought I would miss the lice that are our constant companions aboard ship, but they would be a welcome change from the burrowing sand flies we are plagued with in the desert. We have taken the practice of pairing up with a partner and examining each other for these miserable vermin at the end of each day's march. The Greeks tell us they can cause dangerous infections and fever, which happily, we have all avoided.

It is a relief to write these complaints, since I will never utter them in front of my men, The one constant in our trial is General Eaton. Wherever he leads, we will follow. If he wants to lead us into to hell, we'll gladly go there. My task is to do all that I can to make sure once we get there, we'll be ready.

Weariness or thirst regardless, whenever our march sched- ule permits, we drill. I've organized the Marines and Chris- tian mercenaries into seven-man squads led by Sgt. Campbell, Peter, and the Greek and Piedmontese officers. I mean to turn them into lethal killing machines. In addition to tightly coor- dinated bayonet attacks, I have them practice firing at targets and reloading on the dead run. I am confident in the Marines' discipline, but have wondered if the hired troops would follow my orders. As it turns out, my concern was groundless. Compared to our Arab "allies," there aren't many of us, but the general's made us a fighting force. We'll do our duty at Derna—if we ever get there. Well, the general's alerted us that we have two hard day's march before our next water, so I will stop now and hope to write more later.

CHAPTER 35
ॐ THE LIBYAN DESERT 1805 ॐ

The two day's hard marching promised by Eaton turned into a week. Eaton's caravan, now stretching from the lead elements to the stragglers fifteen miles behind in the rear, plodded forward through the mountains. Their food supply was down to a piece of hard bread and a cup of rice per man per day—when they had water to cook it in—supplemented by wild fennel, sorrel, and such roots as they could find by foraging. O'Bannon had given up on his infantry drills and Eaton had placed their disappearing rations forward, under the guard of the Marines. It was the only way to keep his Arab troops from stealing all of it and leaving them to starve.

Their march had deteriorated into a struggle to survive. What drove them forward was the unrelenting need for water. Each day when they made camp, squads of men, Christians and Arabs alike, spread over the flint-hard ground, scrabbling with shovels to unearth even the smallest pool of brackish water. On the fourth day they came upon a well only to find that bandits had dumped the bodies of their two victims into it. They boiled and drank the water anyway.

On the seventh day, Kirkpatrick and Leitensdorfer, riding just ahead of the main body of troops, crested a rocky escarpment. Ahead of them sloped a long descending plain. Far in the distance they could see the sparkling blue of water.

"By God," cried Kirkpatrick. "We made it! That's the Mediterranean! Once this is over, I'll be damned if I ever leave the sea again." He swiveled in his saddle to look at the mountains behind them. "And that's what we crossed. Good thing we didn't know how bad it would be or we might never have started." His eyes caught sight of a strange shape above the horizon to their left. "Colonel, what in the world is that?"

A pink and copper-colored wave of boiling clouds, stretching for miles on either side, was rising behind them to the southwest. Above it, the sky was turning a dark violet, blocking out the sun.

"*Merda!*" cried Leitensdorfer. "*Porco dio*! It's a sandstorm." He pulled out his pistol and fired a shot in the air for Eaton and the men at the head of the column. Within minutes, Eaton, O'Bannon, and their scouts had joined them on the escarpment, roughly reining in their horses from a gallop as they stared at the monstrous wall of sand rushing toward them.

"General, this is bad," said Leitensdorfer. "This storm could swallow up our army." The scouts needed no orders to alert the caravan. They had already spun their horses around and were racing back down the slope they had just climbed, shouting a warning.

"Where's our best chance of survival?" asked Eaton.

"The Arabs will fend for themselves," said Leitensdorfer. True enough, as the word spread, they could see Hamet's troops and the camel drivers dismounting and pulling their animals to the ground as bulwarks against the force of the storm. Leitensdorfer pointed to the low, rocky ridge behind them. "Against this wall."

Captain! Lieutenant!" Eaton yelled. "Get our men and supplies mules up here now!" Kirkpatrick and O'Bannon spurred down the slope. By now, the men below could plainly see the ominous sky above the storm. The sixty-five Marines and European soldiers—running, slipping, and stumbling in the loose sand, hauling and driving their now panicky mules—surged over the lip of the escarpment.

Eaton's voice rose above the frenzy of shouting and cursing. "Barrack the mules and horses and take shelter away from the storm! If you can't get behind an animal, get as close to the ridge here as you can!" As his officers brought order to their men, Eaton turned to Leitensdorfer. "How much time do we have?"

"These storms can travel at sixty miles per hour. I'd say at most five minutes."

"What must we do now?" asked Eaton.

"Have the men cover their heads and faces completely with cloth. The smallest particles of dust nearest the ground can clog the mouth, nose, and lungs. We will be breathing sand, not air in a few minutes. If the men aren't protected, they'll suffocate." As they turned to run toward the men, Leitensdorfer called after them, "If they can, have them take cartridge grease and stuff it in their nostrils."

Kirkpatrick, O'Bannon, and Eaton worked their way down the line of men huddled in the lee of the escarpment. "We've done what we can, Kirkpatrick," Eaton called out above the storm's steadily increasing din. "Take care of yourselves. I hope to see you when we get to the other side."

Kirkpatrick ran to his horse, being held by Private Whitten. The two men wrestled the horse to the ground with its back to the wind, covered its head, and scurried to tuck in behind it. Both men were wearing burnooses; they tore at them to free up cloth to protect their faces. Whitten reached his hand across to Kirkpatrick. "Your nostrils, sir!" he yelled, and smeared cartridge grease up Kirkpatrick's nose, then disappeared into the folds of his burnoose.

I have to see this, thought Kirkpatrick. He craned his neck above his horse's heaving flank to watch the sandstorm hit. The pinkish-grey boiling wall of sand, now towering over 100 feet above him, raced up the side of the escarpment and exploded over the top. At the last second, Kirkpatrick ducked behind the horse; covered his eyes, nose, and mouth; and buried his face in the horse's belly as the world turned black around him.

Kirkpatrick had been momentarily deafened by cannon fire before. The roar of the storm was indescribably louder, like a huge weight trying to push all thought out of his mind. The hot sand and dust swirled through and past the cloth covering his face, blinding and choking him. He brought one hand quickly up to cover his mouth while he grabbed at the hood of his burnoose to draw it even tighter around his head. This must be what it feels like to be buried alive. Time compressed to the interval between each tortured breath.

After what might have been a half hour or two hours, Kirkpatrick's consciousness slowly returned. I'm still alive. He tried to move his feet, but they were covered in sand. In a moment of panic, he realized he couldn't see, then reached up and clawed the caked sand and dust off his eyes.

Through a red haze, he saw sand-covered mounds, where there had once been men and animals, begin to shake and move. Miraculously, his horse was still alive, breathing in deep, rasping gulps of air. Kirkpatrick kicked free of the sand around his legs and rolled over to see if Private Whitten had survived. A ghost, grey from head to toe, stared back at him through red-rimmed eyes.

"You look horrible, Private," Kirkpatrick said.

"Beggin' the captain's pardon, but you're no beauty yourself," said Whitten. Both men collapsed back to the ground, laughing and coughing uncontrollably.

Eaton crawled over to where Leitensdorfer was emerging from his mound of sand. "So, Eugene, you Muslims believe things happen, *inshallah*, as God wills them. Did God bring this storm to test us, or just to punish us?"

"I don't know," Leitensdorfer replied, trying to spit the sand out of his mouth. "But when I see Him, I'll ask Him. I don't know what God has planned for us, but I certainly hope your luck in finding water doesn't fail. One cannot slake a great thirst by saying the word 'water.'"

For the next half hour, Eaton helped O'Bannon and Kirkpatrick and their men dig out of the sand: thanks to Leitensdorfer, all had survived. When Leitensdorfer had regained enough strength and his horse had recovered, Eaton sent him down the hill to see how the Arabs and the troops with the supply caravan had come through the sandstorm. Then he mounted his own horse.

"Captain, Lieutenant," he called out to Kirkpatrick and O'Bannon. "See what order you can make out of our supplies." He pointed down the slope. "You may have to dig them out. I'm going to find water," and he spurred his horse forward, scrambling over the escarpment to the plain above.

Eaton's luck held. He led them to a river bed, a half-mile ahead, where they found springs of bitter, alkaline water. What followed was a panicked stampede of hundreds of men and animals, fighting to reach the muddy, trampled waterholes. One of their horses was trampled to death in the crush. They butchered and ate it.

CHAPTER 36
❧ MALTA 1805 ❧

Captain Hull had been summoned to Syracuse, in one of Commodore Barron's rare moments of improved health, to discuss plans for the reinforcement of Eaton's army. Before leaving, Hull had instructed John Dent to bring Lear to the meeting in the *Nautilus,* but to delay Lear's departure from Malta for Syracuse as long as possible. Dent did all that his years at sea dealing with wily bo'suns and crooked ships' chandlers had taught him. It took Dent's crew three days to repair a nonexistent leak suffered in the storm the *Nautilus* had fought coming into Malta, then another day to load, unload, and re-load stores for Eaton, with Dent checking and challenging everything in the quartermaster's bill of lading. Finally, Dent decided that a good part of the ship's rope and cable needed to be replaced. Since he hadn't been authorized to receive new cordage, he simply had his men take down standing rigging and replace it, with as much clumsiness, dropped, or mislaid tools as they could manage. Finally, he could delay no longer and sent a message to Lear that the *Nautilus* was ready to put to sea.

Dent's message arrived as Lear was meeting again in his office with Pasha Karamanli's negotiators, Spanish Consul De Souza and Leon Farfara, the money lender—reviewing the final details of the peace treaty De Souza would present to Pasha Karamanli on behalf of the American government.

"The thing to impress upon Pasha Karamanli, is that these conditions represent not only the most favorable and honorable peace that he may expect to achieve from the United States." Lear leaned forward over his desk, his eyes fixed on De Souza: "Failure to agree to these terms will subject him to invasion and the loss of his kingdom. Let me review the main points. We agree to exchange our hundred Tripolitan prisoners for members of the hostage crew of the *Philadelphia* of comparable rank and pay $300 each for the release of the remaining two hundred officers and men. In the future, any prisoners captured by either party shall not be made slaves."

Farfara coughed to get Lear's attention. "If I may, your excellency, that last language may be uncomfortable for Pasha Karamanli. Would you be troubled if the Arabic translation of the treaty modified the word 'slaves' to 'prisoners of war'—a more acceptable phrase, perhaps?"

"Do they mean the same thing in Arabic?" asked Lear.

"I am sure of it," quickly answered Farfara.

"Then let the language of the translation be as you think best," said Lear. "The version I will send Washington will still prohibit Tripoli from enslaving Americans." He handed a paper across to De Souza. "Here are the gifts I suggest making to Pasha Karamanli and his chief negotiators as an inducement to their signing the treaty. Since we are reestablishing our consulate in Tripoli, I think it only reasonable to make the Pasha a personal gift of $5,000 as is customary. I have authorized an additional $6,000 in diamonds and other valuables for Pasha Karamanli's sons and chief ministers. Would you think that sufficient, De Souza?"

"More than sufficient, excellency; generous, I would say." He paused for a moment. "It has been a time honored practice for countries to pay Tripoli a $10-per-head tax for each freed slave in addition to any ransom. May I assume that custom will be honored with the release of the *Philadelphia* prisoners?"

"That would be another $3,000 or so, I take it," said Lear. "Fine." Seeing the look in De Souza's eyes at all the money being placed on the table, he added, "I would not have you think America ungrateful for the services you have rendered our country, De Souza. I am authorizing expenses of $1,555 for Farfara and a comparable amount for you." Lear settled back in his chair with look of contentment. "The United States knows how to reward loyalty, gentlemen. Have I omitted anything?"

"There is another matter," said De Souza, his eyes fixed attentively on Lear. "The draft treaty also stipulated that no further yearly tributes would be paid by the United States to Tripoli."

"Well, of course," replied Lear. "That's why we went to war in the first place."

"Would you not think," said De Souza, "that the depredations of the American fleet on Tripoli are such that the Pasha would never consider angering your country again? Surely you have taught him a lesson. I wonder of this clause, which might set an unfortunate precedent for other countries to follow, might now no longer be necessary. It is troublesome to Pasha Karamanli; and, in truth, we are arranging a treaty to free prisoners taken fairly in war, not to change the balance of power in the Mediterranean. If other countries wish to modify their treaties with Tripoli, why, is that not their business?"

"Indeed, indeed," said Lear, his expression of self-approval still unchanged. "Certainly reasonable. You need not insist on this concession from Pasha Karamanli when you bring him our offer. Then I believe," he continued, "we are clear on the details, De Souza. If Pasha Karamanli should try again to alter them, you may tell him that Eaton makes great progress and the rebellious Arabs are flocking to Hamet's standard. I would also let it out that we are expecting reinforcements to the naval forces already outside Tripoli. Unless he signs this agreement, Pasha Karamanli can expect an armada of twenty American ships outside his walls and an invading force of 1,000 Marines."

Lear looked for the first time directly at the money-lender Farfara. "You will see that the transfer of funds we have agreed to is accomplished?" Without waiting for a response, he added, "Then our business, sir, is completed. I need to speak in private with Consul De Souza. You may go now."

Farfara smiled back at Lear, but remained in his chair, then turned to De Souza, and almost apologetically said, "Hamet's family?"

"Of course!" cried De Souza. "How thoughtless of me! Excellency," he now addressed Lear, "there is one small detail whose resolution would, I am sure, guarantee Pasha Karamanli's full compliance with the terms of this treaty. Señor Farfara, if you wouldn't mind?"

"Excellency," Farfara addressed Lear, his eyes on the papers in front of him. "Hamet has long been a thorn in Pasha Karamanli's side. Hamet's present rebellion, supported by the United States, I might add, threatens the security of the Pasha's reign. Even if the Pasha settles matters with the United States, Hamet's danger to the realm must be removed. As you know, the Pasha now holds Hamet's wife and children hostage. Were they to be freed, as the draft treaty provides, Hamet would have no reason not to resume hostilities against his brother. To prevent the resumption of Hamet's attempts against his brother, the United States, as part of the treaty, will naturally withdraw all support for Hamet." He glanced quickly at De Souza, and seeing De Souza's nod, continued. "May I also suggest, with all respect, that to ensure Hamet's good faith, the return of Hamet's family be delayed for four more years, subject to evidence of Hamet's peaceful behavior?"

"Do you agree with this, De Souza?" asked Lear.

"I think it a small concession," De Souza said. "I know the misfortune of Hamet's family has received some sympathy in

America, thanks to Eaton, but things are managed differently in this part of the world. No Turkish ruler would free political hostages like these so long as he had need of them. My goodness, that is why one takes hostages in the first place! Hamet has waited twelve years to be rejoined with his family. Four more years—assuming his good conduct, of course—is not that much longer."

"I certainly hold no love for Hamet" said Lear, "but Eaton has made a great deal of his family's plight, and there was that attempt earlier to free them, however badly it turned out. Once this concession becomes known, it will be unpopular in some quarters in Washington and quite possibly the source of embarrassment to President Jefferson."

"If I may offer a solution," said De Souza, "perhaps the clause regarding Hamet's family could be inserted in the Arabic translation of the treaty and, how shall I say, omitted from the English version? Simply an oversight. Pasha Karamanli will have the assurance he needs, with no evidence to the contrary to arouse objections in America. Once peace is declared and Eaton's support removed, Hamet will become a wandering exile again with few friends. People will forget about him soon enough."

"I like it, De Souza," said Lear. "No one in America is apt to see, read, or much less understand Pasha Karamanli's copy of the treaty in Arabic. A wise solution to a troubling issue, if I may say so." Then turning to Farfara, he said, "You may leave us now. I have other important matters to discuss with Consul De Souza." Both men remained seated as Farfara excused himself and let himself out of the office.

"A nasty, grasping, Christ-killing scoundrel, if you ask me," said Lear, with a nod toward the departed Farfara.

"Well, you know, the Jews manage money for the Turks and Arabs. Were it not for them, these arrangements would be impossible, and for good Christians, distasteful. So long as he profits from it, he is trustworthy."

Lear dismissed the subject with an impatient wave of his hand. "I would still watch him closely, for all that. But we have other business, do we not?"

De Souza had brought the latest information from Dr. Cowdery, the *Philadelphia's* surgeon. Throughout the American hostages' long captivity in Tripoli, Dr. Cowdery had managed to add secret reports in invisible lemon juice to the letters he included with the other prisoners' mail. As America's representative in Tripoli, De Souza brought the mail with him each time he returned to Malta.

"So what does Cowdery tell us about the current situation in Tripoli?" asked Lear.

"Why, to answer that question, excellency, I would have had to lift the seal, steam open Cowdery's letter, hold it over a candle to briefly scan its contents before the lemon juice faded again, and then reseal everything as if it had never been opened."

"And when you did that," said Lear, "what did you learn?"

"You are a very fox among vixens, excellency," De Souza laughed and summarized the contents of Cowdery's secret message for Lear: Having sent his last remaining loyal troops to relieve Derna, Pasha Karamanli had stripped Tripoli of soldiers to defend it, and stripped it, as well, of money, courage, and hope. Pasha Karamanli offered to send his family out of Tripoli before the Americans invaded, and his family balked, preferring to be captured by the Americans than thrown on the mercy of the Arab population. Pasha Karamanli sent his son-in-law to recruit soldiers from the outlying country, but the local villages refused because his incessant taxation has so impoverished and enraged them. His son-in-law returned empty-handed. Then Pasha Karamanli had a proclamation read throughout Tripoli calling for the citizens to gather on the beach so that he could exhort them to defend their homeland. He expected a muster of ten thousand fervent volunteers. The pasha waited for an hour on a dais, looking at an empty beach. He returned to his palace with his personal body guard close around him.

"In Cowdery's opinion," De Souza concluded, "Pasha Karamanli's Tripoli is an empty husk, a hollow shell, an overripe fruit waiting to fall. He thinks one salvo from the massed American fleet and the appearance of just one hundred Marines on shore would send the pasha to his death and bring Hamet Karamanli to the throne in triumph. That is his message."

"Then that is a message Barron will not receive," Lear said. "De Souza, I wish you a safe and speedy voyage back to Tripoli, and a satisfactory conclusion to our negotiations with Pasha Karamanli. Since no one knows of the whereabouts of Eaton and Hamet, feel free to give the most glowing account of their success. That threat should provide Pasha Karamanli all the inducement he needs to agree to our terms."

At the door, Lear took De Souza by the arm. "Remember this, however. Eaton is a madman, but madmen can still be dangerous. It defies reason that Eaton might actually capture Derna and compel Pasha Karamanli to step down, but stranger things have happened. Should Eaton succeed, all our efforts will have been wasted. I must trust you to be persuasive with the pasha."

Once De Souza had departed, Lear opened the dispatch case, removed and cut open Cowdery's letter, looked at it for a few moments and handed it to his secretary, who had been taking notes during the meeting with De Souza. "Rokku, you are a clever rogue. Might you be able to imitate Dr. Cowdery's hand well enough to reproduce these pages and create a new secret message, in lemon juice, of course? It can merely imitate and confirm the other messages we have sent Barron. I can provide the official stationery."

Rokku considered the request, then nodded agreement.

"It needn't be perfect, of course," said Lear. "Barron's eyes are bad, and I will read the contents to him anyway. Do make sure,"

Lear added, "that you give me the originals. That way, regardless of what Barron does or says, I am safe. Get it done now. I have been told by that damned Captain Dent that we will catch the tide in two hours. Curse him for an imbecile anyway! With captains as incompetent as this, small wonder that our sole chance of success here is by politics and diplomacy."

CHAPTER 37
☙ THE LIBYAN DESERT 1805 ☙

On April 16, they reached the coast just a day's march from the Gulf of Bomba—and the rendezvous with Hull's *Argus* with its precious cargo of food, materiél, and funds to pay the troops and camel drivers. Damn El-Tahib's almost incessant delays and mutinies, Eaton thought. We're already a week past the scheduled meeting time with Hull. Hull may have appeared on time, waited fruitlessly, and finally sailed back to Syracuse. If that's the case, we're all dead men. That's a fear I'd better keep to myself.

Eaton and Leitensdorfer had ridden ahead with Kirkpatrick to reach the sea and hopefully catch a glimpse of Hull's ship. They returned at midday, with no sight of a sail, to find that Hamet, at El-Tahib's urging, had made camp and was refusing to march on until a courier brought back word of the American supply ship. Eaton knew that there could be no question of delay. They were out of bread and down to the last of their rice. Fearful that the Arabs might, in their present desperation, try to seize the remaining food, Eaton ordered Lieutenant O'Bannon to form the Christian troops around the food tents. They quickly mustered in a rough square with fixed bayonets, the Marines in the first rank with Captain Ulovix and a line of Greek infantry behind them, and the rest of the Greeks and the Piedmontese completing the other three sides of the infantry square. Eaton, with Leitensdorfer and Kirkpatrick, stepped in front of the Marines as Hamet and

El-Tahib strode forward to meet them. Behind Hamet and El-Tahib was an angrily shouting swirling mass of over two hundred mounted Arabs.

"General," Hamet began. "My chiefs all agree. We must have rest. We cannot go on."

"Well then, if you prefer famine to fatigue, you may stay here. We will continue to march forward to meet the supply ship and will take the remaining food with us! Lieutenant O'Bannon," Eaton cried out. "Take your men through the manual of arms to show these cowards and weaklings what men they are dealing with!"

"Order Arms!" O'Bannon cried, and the rifle butts of the Marines and Ulovix's Greeks slammed to the dusty ground.

"Trail Arms!" At the word 'arms,' the soldiers raised their rifles slightly off the ground, inclining the muzzle and attached bayonet forward.

"Order Arms!" The rifles were snapped back.

"Port Arms!" Again on the word 'arms,' as one man, the soldiers raised their rifles with their right hands diagonally across their bodies then, in rhythm, snapped their left hand down to grasp the small of the stock by the trigger guard.

"They mean to attack us!" yelled someone from the Arab ranks, mistaking the Christians' parade drill sequence for the command to aim and fire. Most of the Arabs had dismounted to observe the parlay between the chiefs and Eaton. Now they sprang into their saddles and started to charge the outnumbered Christian infantry. This has gone terribly wrong, thought Eaton. He stepped forward, crying "No! No! This was just a demonstration. You've seen us do this before! We aren't attacking!" In the noise and confusion, his cry went unheard.

"Ready!" O'Bannon cried out. The Marines and Greeks brought up their rifles, continuing to hold their position resolutely. O'Bannon's eyes were focused on the charging Arabs, gauging the distance before giving the order to fire to maximize the shock of the first volley. Shit, he thought. We won't be able to stop them.

"Take Aim!" he yelled. "Shoot the horses, not the men! The horses!" he repeated. A little further, he thought. Come to it. Fifty feet from the line of infantry, just at the point of giving the final command, the onrushing riders suddenly wheeled— before O'Bannon gave the command "Fire!" They withdrew a short distance, still shouting angrily and waving their muskets and swords. Hamet, whose face was now ashen, and a still defiant El-Tahib, had remained standing sixty feet away as the charging horsemen had swirled around them.

"Excellency!" Eaton cried out to Hamet. "Have you taken leave of all senses? This will be mutual slaughter of us your staunchest allies, of your Arab troops, and of your dream of regaining your throne!"

El-Tahib started to counter with an angry insult, waving his pistol. Kirkpatrick snapped. He crossed the few yards separating him and El-Tahib and standing inches from El-Tahib's startled face, started screaming at him. In a panic, El-Tahib stepped back, raised his pistol, and shot at Kirkpatrick. The pistol did not go off. Pulling his sword, Kirkpatrick used the flat of the blade to knock El-Tahib to the ground and stood over him with the point at El-Tahib's throat. At that moment, some more moderate men among the Arab troops spurred their horses into the open space between the two forces. They yelled at their comrades, "This is madness!" "The Americans are our friends!" "They have come to free us from the tyrant Jusef Karamanli!" "For God's sake, do not attack!"

As the Arabs milled about in confusion, Eaton and Leitensdorfer pulled Hamet back inside the line of Marines and began talking passionately with him. Kirkpatrick stepped back from the still-terrified El-Tahib, kicked dust into his face, spun on his heel, and marched back to rejoin the others. After a tense hour-long stand-off, Hamet emerged to announce their agreement. The Americans would issue a rice ration to all the Arab troops. The march would resume the next morning and continue without further delay until the army had made their rendezvous with the supply ship.

As the Arabs dispersed and the Marines and Christian infantry stood down with relief, O'Bannon turned to Kirkpatrick. "Good thing you guessed that El-Tahib's pistol wasn't primed," O'Bannon observed. "That was a close moment. We were ready to support you, but should his pistol have gone off, you would have been dead before I could call 'Fire.' After that ..." O'Bannon just shrugged. We could out-face twice their number under normal circumstances, he thought. But once blood was spilled ... We're still a handful of Christians; they hate us like dogs. We would have been slaughtered to the last man.

Kirkpatrick didn't respond for a moment or two. "Perhaps I need to moderate my temper a bit," Kirkpatrick remarked.

"It *is* a thought," O'Bannon answered. "But who is it that should say? Had you not cowed them into submission they might have still attacked us. For all that, any dark night they could murder us all in our beds. The more they fear us, I think, the safer we are."

Throughout the next day, the exhausted army straggled out of the mountains onto the bleak, windswept coast at Bomba. A hard shingle beach curved around the broad bay. There was no water, no fodder for their animals, and no sign of Hull. The sun glinted off the tossing whitecaps of an empty sea. As night approached, Hamet, El-Tahib and the other Arab chiefs held a counsel of war from which they angrily excluded Eaton. They emerged after an hour of shouting to confront Eaton and his officers at the water's edge. El-Tahib was in the lead with a thoroughly beaten down Hamet lagging behind him.

"Now we see what American promises mean, general," El-Tahib cried bitterly. "You have led us to our deaths. The shame on us for having believed the lies of a cursed infidel."

"No," retorted Eaton, stepping forward to confront El-Tahib, "the shame on you for causing the delays that have brought us here a week after our appointed meeting time with the supply ships. You have no sense of patriotism, truth, or honor. Your religion is not the faith of the Prophet, blessings be upon him, but in the money you have sought to extort from us at every step of our march. I have found you at the head of every commotion and rebellion which has happened since we left Alexandria." He waved his arm towards the empty ocean. "Captain Hull will not fail us. He keeps his promises—a claim, miserable oath-breaker that you are, you can never make. You may do as you please: go back to Alexandria or into hell." He turned to Hamet. "Do not despair, excellency, nor trust the lies of this scoundrel. A day—no more—and our relief will be here."

He turned away from the Arabs, who once again erupted into angry argument, and pulled Kirkpatrick and O'Bannon aside. "Those were brave words. The facts are that we have no more food. The rice we ate last night was the end of our pitiful supplies. And there is no water in this accursed place."

Eaton looked at the bluff rising above them. "Take our Marines—they, at least, have preserved their discipline—find what wood you can and light a signal beacon on the hill there. Keep it burning all night. We must pray that Hull is close enough to see it and come to our aid. We won't last another day. Then gather all the Christian troops together and see that each man has plenty of ammunition."

They passed a bad night, the Arabs continuing to argue noisily and yell curses at the Christian troops huddled by the shore, the Marines manning the signal fire on the hill.

Kirkpatrick had drawn the last watch before dawn with Private Owens. He awoke from a troubled sleep to a brilliant morning sunrise—and an empty sea stretching for miles in front of him. A cold north wind blew across the barren hill. The signal fire had burned down to glowing coals. Owens called over to him. "You awake, captain?"

Kirkpatrick grunted a response as both men stood to stare at the sea, shading their eyes from the morning glare.

"I think this is our last day, captain. Where do you think the general will want us to make our final stand? Down by the water or up here? Rather than sacrifice any of their precious camels, I think the Hadjis down there would just as soon kill and eat us."

Kirkpatrick didn't respond, his eyes now fixed on the horizon. "Owens—look there to the east, below the sun. Am I going crazy with hunger and thirst, or is that a speck of white?"

"It could be a sail," said Owens. "Pray that it is a sail."

"The fire!" Kirkpatrick cried. "We need smoke!" He shouted down to Eaton. "A sail, general! We need wood!" Within minutes, the signal fire was blazing again, and the Marines threw grass on it to send a plume of smoke rising into the sky.

So in the end, Hull did not fail them. He had arrived at the rendezvous date of April 4, and seeing no sign of Eaton, sent a boat ashore. The officer and men returned saying they had seen no signs of people and no tracks big enough to suggest an army had passed that way. So Hull waited, circling back to the rendezvous spot every few days. His patience was rewarded when he returned and saw their signal. One of Doyle's scouts had found good water a mile to the west. The army limped on to its new camping place: a wide beach with easy access for the ship's boats, rising to a broad plain that easily accommodated the Arab forces and the camel train. When they arrived, the first of the *Argus's* boats started landing life-saving supplies on shore: thirty hogsheads of bread; one hundred sacks of flour, beef, and salt pork; rice; dates; and for the Marines and their European comrades, casks of brandy and wine.

CHAPTER 38
ᚚ DERNA 1805 ᚚ

Within hours after the rendezvous with the *Argus*, the *Nautilus* and *Hornet* arrived with the needed powder, rifles, ammunition, flints, and new uniforms and boots for the Marines. The *Nautilus* had also brought the promised $7,000 in gold. With it, Eaton paid off El-Tahib and his mutinous camel drivers. "Here is the money we promised you," he said, dumping the bags of coin at El-Tahib's feet. "As you see, we keep our promises. You, scoundrel and thief that you are, never made a promise you did not intend to break no sooner than the words left your lips. I am confident that this army will now march forward into victory and the enduring honor that will follow. You may now slink homeward to the enduring ignominy that you deserve." El-Tahib departed with his camel drivers. No one bid them farewell.

By nightfall, a sense of order had returned to Eaton's camp: tents were up, the replenished supplies were neatly stacked, and Eaton's men were relaxing after what had been a day-long feast. From Hamet's camp on the plain beyond the beach, music and singing, and the occasional firing of a musket, proclaimed that the Arabs were also celebrating their delivery. O'Bannon, Sergeant Campbell, and the European officers had decided to stand guard duty: the men had been served brandy and wine and told to stand down. Eaton sat in front of his tent, in a camp chair Hull had kindly brought from the *Argus*, talking with Hull, Kirkpatrick, and Leitensdorfer. Next to his tent, an American flag, fixed to a boarding pike, now danced in the evening breeze above a crackling fire.

"Rider coming in!" a voice called from the crest of the hill above the beach. The Americans watched a horseman pick his way carefully over the crest of the hill and on to the shingle. As Doyle dismounted, Eaton rose and left the fire to welcome him. "Welcome! You come in good time," he said, wrapping Doyle in a strong embrace.

"Glad to see *you* made it, too, general," Doyle said, smiling openly. He nodded a friendly greeting to Kirkpatrick and then Leitensdorfer. "Eugene! It is good to see you!"

"Trust me," said Leitensdorfer, "It's good to be seen, after what we've been through."

Eaton led Hull forward to meet Doyle: "Allow me to introduce Captain Hull of the *Argus*. He needed all of his hundred eyes to find us, which thank God, he did. Isaac, this is Henry Doyle, whose native scouts saved our lives a number of times—although he is known by a number of names, including," and he grinned at Kirkpatrick, "Katir Al-Hareeq."

Hull bowed, "A pleasure, sir."

"My pleasure, indeed," said Doyle.

"Gentlemen," Hull continued. "I pray you give me leave. Captain Dent was unable to secure the field pieces you will need for the assault on Derna, so we will need to figure a way to use carronades from one of the ship as artillery. I must return to the *Argus*." After a round of farewells, he walked down the shingle to the waiting ship's launch.

"May I offer you something?" Eaton asked Doyle, walking him back to his tent. "You won't take sprits, I know, but there's hot water for tea and tea leaves in that canister there. I think you'll find a cup you can use next to it. Forgive me if I continue with my stronger medicine." Doyle spooned tea leaves into the cup, poured hot water over them, and squatted down in front of Eaton's tent, Arab style. Eaton refilled his cup of brandy and returned to his chair, the other Americans pulling up the supply boxes they had been sitting on.

"I imagine you have news?" Eaton asked. "You usually do."

"The relief column of a thousand or more Tripolitans," Doyle said, "commanded by the Mameluke Hassan Bey and supported by Arab cavalry from the Bey of Bengazi, is less than a week's march away. My troopers are about the same distance behind me. It looks like we're all in a race to get to Derna."

"If it's a race, then we need to see how quickly we can get our army back in fitness," said Eaton. "Come Eugene, let's find Lieutenant O'Bannon and Captain Ulovix."

Eaton and Leitensdorfer left; Kirkpatrick remained in front of the fire with Doyle.

"So you are the same Katir Al-Hareeq who accompanied us up the Nile," Kirkpatrick said.

"Allow me to apologize for my deception. For me to guide you to Derna, I needed to take not just your measure but that of General Eaton. Men talk more freely around someone they think can't understand them."

"And what assessment did you make of us?" Kirkpatrick asked.

"I judged that you would be able, with luck and strong leadership, to do what you have actually accomplished: bring an army across five hundred miles of desert to attack Derna. You're a navy officer; that must have been a very different kind of voyage for you."

Kirkpatrick shook his head: "'Different' isn't in it. Hell might be a better word. Once this mission is over, I'm damned if I set foot in a desert again." He rose, went to the brandy flask next to the general's tent, poured himself another cup, and sat back down. "Yet you are at home here."

"I've called many places home. But unlike you, the sea hasn't been one of them. One travels by sea, of course, out of necessity.

But what did Sir Samuel Johnson say? 'Being in a ship is like being in jail, with the added risk of drowning.' If I may ask, how did you come to join the Navy?"

"My father was an artillery officer in the Revolution who died in 1785 from wounds he received at Yorktown. I was four years old. Since my closest friends, Steven Decatur and Dickie Somers, had decided to join the Navy rather than attend college or become apprentices, I signed on as a ship's boy at age fourteen."

"I, too, never knew my father," said Doyle. "It is a curious thing. As a child, I would often look in a mirror, searching for some resemblance or echo of a father in the men I met. Not knowing where one comes from can make it difficult to understand who one is." Doyle paused, knowing that when you wanted someone to give you information, the best questions were no questions at all—just silence.

"I must have been an impossible nuisance as a small boy," Kirkpatrick said. "I would go to any man I knew who had known my father. I would pester him mercilessly, I'm sure, about a man I would never meet. To their credit, as I recall, they were patient with me, doubtless out of respect for my father. After some time, a picture of my father as a good man did emerge. But it is *their* picture. I would have wished to know what he thought of himself."

"And perhaps thought of you?" Doyle asked, gently. Kirkpatrick just nodded. Both men were quiet again for a time.

"Have you brothers or sisters?" Doyle asked.

"I am my parents' only child," said Kirkpatrick. "My mother told me that before she met and married my father, she had lived in the Mohawk country of New York. Her family had been killed by marauding Indians and the Mohawks took her in. She had a son, but always seemed reluctant to talk about those days. For obvious reasons, I never pressed her for details. She said her son died in the war."

"That's a lot of loss and sorrow for a woman to contend with," said Doyle. "May I ask if she is still alive?"

"Mercifully she is, and in reasonably good health," Kirkpatrick answered, "I'm sure she would have preferred me to choose a less dangerous career. But thank you for inquiring."

"I am grateful for the opportunity to get to know you," said Doyle, "especially because when you attack Derna, I will be fighting with you." Seeing Eaton and the others return, he added, "I need a few more minutes' conversation with the general before I leave. But let us talk again."

CHAPTER 39
❧ DERNA 1805 ❧

Well refreshed after several days of good food and the resumption of O'Bannon's drilling, Eaton's troops set out on the last push to Derna, having agreed to rendezvous again with Hull's ships outside the town to unload their artillery for the attack. Hamet's forces were now increased by hundreds of local tribesmen eager to settle scores with the Turks in Derna. For the better part of the day, they had marched amidst rich farmlands, fields of barley and other grains interspersed with orange and plum orchards and vineyards. To the north, through gaps in the low coastal hills, they could see the Mediterranean shimmering in the bright sunlight.

"The desert changes like the ocean," Kirkpatrick said to O'Bannon, riding next to him at the head of the Marines and the other Christian troops. "For forty days we trudged through searing hell; today we're in paradise." He pulled two plums from a tree next to him and gave one to his friend. "When we neared Derna, Grand P'shaw Hamet proclaimed that any man who touches the harvest will lose his right hand." Kirkpatrick took a juicy bite of the plum. "He seemed serious enough laying down the law to the Arab troops. Do you think that edict applies to Christians as well?"

"It's a fine point, I'm sure," O'Bannon answered, biting deeply into his plum. "I talked it over with the other Marines. We decided that eating hanging fruit was definitely out of bounds, but fallen fruit was fair game. Look behind you."

Kirkpatrick turned in his saddle. Sure enough, the first rank of Marines deftly knocked the ripest fruit to the ground to be picked up by those that followed. The Marines happily shared their bounty with the other infantrymen. Normally proud, standoffish, even quarrelsome toward foreign troops, the Marines had gradually accepted the Greeks and Piedmontese with whom they'd suffered in the desert as allies, if not true brothers in arms.

They had been climbing gently rolling hills since noon. Ahead of them, Eaton, Leitensdorfer, Hamet, and a few aides rode ahead. Suddenly, two of their scouts crested the hill in front of them. One raced toward them, another peeled back to intercept Hamet's Arab cavalry. Eaton raised his arm in the signal to halt.

"Derna is just over this next rise," the scout announced. Eaton and the others cantered to where the orchards gave over to a grove of cedars at the crest of the hill. There they dismounted and climbed to the top, crouching low amid the cedar scrub.

Derna stretched below them on a point of land jutting into the sea from the surrounding mountains. Built on the site from the ancient stone of the Roman trading post called Darnis, the old walled city formed a rough diamond, laid out on the four points of the compass. Most of Derna's ten thousand inhabitants lived in the newer town that had risen up outside the old walls to the north and west, linking the old citadel to the crescent-shaped harbor perhaps a half mile away. Cutting through the city from south to north ran the Wadi Derna, a mountain-fed river that for centuries had irrigated Derna's lush fruit groves, vineyards, and gardens.

Eaton turned to Leitensdorfer. "You've visited Derna before, Eugene. What do we have here?"

"You can easily see the mosque to the north there within the citadel walls," Leitensdorfer said. "The other set of turrets to the west is the governor's palace. If you move your glasses to the east, you can see the harbor fort and shore battery through the palm trees along the shoreline."

"They appear to have fortified the buildings between the town walls and the harbor fort," Eaton observed. Kirkpatrick and the others spotted the rough breastworks closing the gaps between houses on the northeast quadrant.

"They had to," Leitensdorfer replied. "The old walls between the town and harbor were torn down years ago as the town grew."

"Those look like musket loopholes in the houses there," O'Bannon added.

"Not surprising," said Leitensdorfer. "Most of Mustifa Bey's staunchest supporters live in this part of town. He is, you know, Jusef Karamanli's cousin and brother-in-law. I'd guess two-thirds of the population varies from lukewarm in their allegiance to Jusef Karamanli's regime to near rebellion."

"Tell me, what artillery do they have?"

"The harbor defenses mount eight 9-pounders," Leitensdorfer said. "They are commanded by a renegade Italian and will give a good account of themselves, I suspect. Fortunately, the guns can't be trained on this side of the town. Mustifa Bey has a 10-inch howitzer on the terrace of the governor's palace, but if they used it against us they'd be more likely to blow up their own troops."

"And what force of troops does Mustifa Bey command?"

"He has some two hundred Turkish Janissaries, well-detested by the local Berbers and Arabs. The Turks will fight hard to preserve their own skins. He has, as well, another six hundred or more Tripolitan foot soldiers, all secure in their loyalty."

"May we hope to lure them out into battle on the open plain by any means?"

"According to Doyle, Hassan Bey's relief column is no more than three days march from Derna—Mustifa Bey need only wait us out until we are caught between two fires. I would say we have no more than a day or two to take the town."

Eaton continued to study the town's defenses. "A tough nut to crack—and our nutcrackers are still on board the *Nautilus* with Dent."

Eaton lapsed into thoughtful silence. Kirkpatrick and O'Bannon backed down the hill until they were out of sight of the town, then rose to their feet.

"So Presley," Kirkpatrick began, "what do you think of our chances tomorrow?"

"If we can close with them, regardless of the numbers, we can break them," said O'Bannon. "You remember the fighting when we attacked the Tripolitan gunboats? You and Decatur routed twice your number on the first boat and three times your number on the next. I was with Trippe when eleven of us dispatched a crew of thirty-six Arabs and Turks. They are great ones for the bravado and bluster but have no stomach for an organized assault pressed home with sword, tomahawk, and bayonet."

"And what of Grand P'shaw Hamet and his army of rascals? What do you expect from these great heroes?"

"They are a sorry lot, to be sure. Did you see Hamet when he learned his brother's relief force was just a day or so away? His face turned the color of a camel's arse. I fear the most we can expect of him and those mercenary thieves he recruited is a diversionary charge—and hope that they don't keep charging all the way back to Alexandria."

With his army now arrayed on the plain to the east of Derna, Eaton sent a message to Mustifa Bey under a flag of truce, urging him to spare his forces and the people of Derna needless suffering by allowing Eaton's army to purchase supplies and pass Derna without opposition. In return, Hamet offered to give Mustifa Bey a position in the new government he would create after Jusef Karamanli's fall. Eaton's letter was returned with a terse scrawled response on the bottom:

"My head or yours. Mustifa"

Punctual and reliable as usual, Hull, accompanied by the *Nautilus* and *Hornet,* appeared as dusk fell that evening, bringing the artillery for the following day's attack.

CHAPTER 40
❧ DERNA 1805 ❧

The next morning they all watched as Dent, with his crew at the sweeps, navigated the *Nautilus* to the foot of a 40-foot-high cliff overlooking the vulnerable breastworks at the northeast corner between the town and the harbor fortress. Their initial attempts at anchoring the ship solidly enough to take the strain of hoisting cannon to the cliff top were frustrated; the ground near the cliff was sandy, offering poor purchase. Only when the *Nautilus's* two anchors were supplemented by other anchors from the *Argus* and *Hornet* could the work begin.

Meanwhile, the *Nautilus's* bo'sun and his mates had been busy since sunup splicing together long coils of the finest white cable. From the top of the rock, Kirkpatrick supervised a crew of the Greek artillerymen in properly staking out one end of what would be a complex network of rope and tackle stretching back down to the *Nautilus* and anchoring two gun emplacements to receive the 24 pound carronades they would use to blast apart the enemy's breastworks.

After what seemed an eternity of preparation, with Eaton and the other officers nervously switching their attention from the slow progress of the work below them to the mountains to the west, hoping not to see the arrival of Jusef Karamali's relief force, a line was thrown down to the *Nautilus*. This was made fast to a heavy hawser, and by means of well-anchored tackles, the first of the system of supporting ropes was pulled to the top. Several hours later, the bo'sun's pride and joy of an aerial railway was ready, a carronade was hitched to the messenger running from the *Nautilus*'s capstan to the summit, and to cries of "Steady now!" "Steady as she goes!" "That's well!" the first carronade made its slow, bobbing ascent to the top, followed by its mountings and munitions.

By 1:00 in the afternoon, the first carronade was ready to fire and Eaton was completely past whatever small morsels of patience he had left. He sent word to forego sending the second cannon, to release the *Nautilus* to join the bombardment of the harbor battery, and to prepare to begin the attack.

By 1:30, the ships were in place. Lieutenant Samuel Evans brought the *Hornet*'s 9-pounders within one hundred yards of the enemy's battery. The *Nautilus* maneuvered a half-mile off shore to the east to enfilade the batteries and support the infantry in case of an enemy counterattack. Hull anchored the *Argus* so its broadside of eight 24-pounders could attack both the battery and the citadel itself.

Before dawn, Eaton had placed the Marines, the Greek infantry, the remaining Piedmontese artillerymen, and several dozen Arab foot soldiers in a deep ravine some hundred yards from the northeast breastworks. Eaton and Kirkpatrick rejoined their men, sprinting through musket fire to take shelter in the ravine.

Hamet had led his cavalry, now numbering a thousand, to the southwest to capture the citadel, prepare to attack Mustifa Bey's forces from the rear, and block attempts at relief should any elements of Hassan Bey's advance force appear. At Eaton's command, a rocket was fired from the ravine and the bombardment began with a deafening roar from the American ships, answered by brisk, resolute fire from the fort's batteries.

A thick, acrid gray pall rapidly settled over the fortress and harbor. From the cliff, Eaton's lone fieldpiece blazed away at the breastworks, seeking to open gaps through which the infantry could charge.

Within thirty minutes, the ferocity and accuracy of the American barrage had silenced the shore batteries. Rather than abandon their positions in a rout, however, Mustifa Bey's artillerymen had managed an orderly retreat, bringing two of their 9-pounders with them to support the musketeers facing Eaton's small detachment. Now, to the withering hail of fire from hundreds of enemy muskets was added the crash of shrapnel, pinning Eaton and his attackers in the ravine. Just at that moment, the overzealous carronade crew on the cliff shot away the ramrod. Without any way to load the cannon, Eaton's one source of covering fire fell silent.

Kirkpatrick huddled next to O'Bannon near the top of the ravine, their faces turned away from the constant spray of sand and dirt kicked up by the relentless fusillade raining on their position. They looked at the troops huddled below them. Some of the Arab foot soldiers and new recruits from the Derna population were clearly cracking, and there were grim, even fearful looks on many of the European soldiers' faces.

"We're in a bad way here, Lieutenant," he shouted to O'Bannon. "In about five minutes this army is going to get a whole lot smaller."

At that moment, Eaton, as if he had read Kirkpatrick's mind, rose to his feet, seemingly impervious to the hail of musket fire. "American Marines," he cried. O'Bannon's men snapped their eyes around at the sound of his voice, carrying strongly above the din. "Today you write the first glorious chapter of a history that will earn you undying honor as the finest fighting men in the world. In years to come, many battle honors will adorn your banners, but none so bravely won as those you are about to gain here in Tripoli!" He then turned to the European troops.

"Men of Greece, descendants of the heroes of Thermopylae and Marathon! Men of the Piedmont! You know the tyranny of slavery and the oppressor's lash. But in your hearts burns a love of freedom—a fire so strong that nothing can stand before it. We few, we happy few, we band of brothers; have we come this far through the hell of the desert not to seize the glory that is in our very grasp? If we are marked to die, then we are enough to do our nation's loss; if destined to live, why then the fewer the number, the greater each man's share of honor. One resolute charge and resistance melts before us!

"Lieutenant O'Bannon, have you our country's flag?" Eaton cried. Sergeant Campbell shook out the American flag mounted on a boarding pike. "Then let the flag of freedom forever banish with its bright light the darkness of tyranny! Bayonets and cold steel, my boys!" he cried. With that, Eaton sprung to the top of the ravine, twirled his sword above his head like a Turkish Janissary, and charged the enemy. The Greek drummer and bugler, utterly caught up in the passion of the moment, sounded the call for "Charge."

As one man, the Marines, Kirkpatrick, and the Greeks surged out of the ravine, the American flag flashing in the sunlight. With a loud shout the Piedmontese followed, sweeping up the Arab foot soldiers in their enthusiasm.

The next few minutes were a blur to Kirkpatrick. He saw Private John Whitten drop next to him from a musket ball in the face, just a few steps from the lip of the ravine. How any of them survived that first few seconds in the open, exposed to a curtain of fire, was a mystery—or a miracle.

But what the defenders saw, thanks to the uniforms with which Eaton had equipped the Greek infantrymen, was a nightmare surge of ravening blue-coated American wolves, the bloodthirsty beasts of Tripoli, merciless, razor-sharp bayonets glinting in the sunlight, charging under that strange flag Arabs and Turks had come to loathe and fear. The army of Mustifa Bey, outnumbering their attackers ten to one, fired one panicky volley. Then, first one at a time, and then by squads, and then in companies, they bolted from their positions.

Kirkpatrick pushed through a hole in the barricade, just a few steps behind Eaton and O'Bannon. He shot a janissary in the chest left-handed, ducked under a sword thrust from a second, and slammed his shoulder into a third who was about to stab O'Bannon from behind, smashing the hilt of his sword into the man's face. Then they were clear of the barricades, sprinting through the groves of palm trees after the fleeing enemy. Some of the braver of Mustifa Bey's troops paused to fire at their pursuers from the cover of the trees, and short, brutal battles broke out among small groups of men.

Now O'Bannon's relentless training took over. Firing and reloading on the run—that weeks ago had been a clumsy fumbling with cartridge, ball, and ramrod—was now an unconscious reaction. Their tactics, drawn from the American's success against the Turkish gunboat crews in Tripoli Harbor, were simple: throw the enemy force into disarray by concentrating the whole force of each squad on separate clusters of enemies, rather than immediately launching into individual combat, their enemy's preferred tactic. The first three men in each squad—preselected—would shoot anyone they thought was an officer or leader. Then the squad would press forward in a concerted bayonet attack. When the enemy broke, as experience had taught them would happen, they would turn on any other groups still holding firm, until the whole enemy force panicked and ran. Then they could drive the fleeing enemy ahead of them.

To his right, Kirkpatrick saw another Marine, Edward Seward, go down, perhaps just wounded. A blue-clad Greek stood over him, lunging at six or seven Turks with his bayonet. Kirkpatrick and his squad raced into the fray. Three shots rang out and three Turks fell. The fierceness of their attack caused most of the remaining Turks to bolt. But one Turk, a huge fellow, braver than the rest, aimed a scimitar stroke at the unprotected side of the Greek. With a desperate lunge, Kirkpatrick took the blow on his outstretched sword, momentarily numbing his arm and snapping his blade in two. He fell, in a tumble at the feet of the Turk. Without thinking, he switched the stub of his sword to his left hand and slashed the Turk deeply across his bare legs. As the Turk doubled over, screaming in pain, Kirkpatrick drove the broken sword into the man's entrails, spattering himself with the Turk's blood.

It all had taken but a few seconds. Kirkpatrick leapt to his feet, grabbed the fallen Turk's scimitar for a weapon, exchanged a brief salute with the Greek whose life he had just saved, yelled for them to see to the wounded Marine, and rallied his squad to continue the pursuit.

With a sharp cry, Eaton, running 20 yards ahead of Kirkpatrick now, grabbed his left wrist. He had been hit by a musket ball. "I'm fine!" he called out. "Press the attack home! They must not be allowed space or time to recover."

Now down to five men, Kirkpatrick's squad ran, fired, and reloaded as they had been trained. While the accuracy of their fire was of mixed success, the sound of gunfire at their enemy's heels had the desired effect of maintaining the rout. "*Areestehra!*" one of the Greeks yelled. Kirkpatrick's head whipped to his left and he saw the danger. A group of Arabs and Turks had barracked themselves behind a stack of lumber and a wagon and were firing at their pursuers with some purpose.

"Take them from behind!" Kirkpatrick cried, in what he hoped was the right Greek expression. The Greek next to him unexpectedly laughed, and yelled something at his comrades that caused them, in the midst of the violence, to burst into laughter as well. They sprinted past the barracked Arabs and Turks, then circled back. Their approach wasn't spotted, and they caught the enemy by surprise. One volley and a loud battle cry did it. The enemy threw down their weapons and dropped to the ground in surrender. As his men scooped up the weapons, Kirkpatrick paused to catch his breath. Sunlight filtered through the tops of the palm trees throwing bright splotches of light on the ground, now covered with fallen bodies or small knots of prisoners.

They had swept the groves clear of resistance. By now, the remains of Mustifa Bey's forces had cleared the palm groves and were dashing madly across open ground toward the Wadi Derna and the governor's palace. O'Bannon, now in the lead, yelled to Eaton's troops to stop the pursuit. The Turks' and Arabs' flight had taken them right under the *Argus*'s guns. Hull's 24-pounders, loaded with grapeshot, tore bloody swaths through the remains of Mustifa Bey's troops.

"To the fortress!" O'Bannon yelled, and men near him cut to their right and stormed into the batteries. They shot or bayoneted the few enemy soldiers that remained, finding to their surprise, that four of the 9-pounders had been loaded and primed, but not fired. They turned these on the fleeing troops now running through the city streets. A great cheer rose from men of Hull's squadron as they watched the Bey's green and white ensign with its star and crescent come fluttering down from the fort's flagpole, replaced by the Stars and Stripes, flying for the first time over a foreign hostile shore.

At that moment, Hamet's cavalry burst into the open ground on the west bank of the Wadi, trapping the survivors between two forces. By now, local residents had joined in the bloodbath. Kirkpatrick watched as crowds of men hacked officers off their horses and swarmed over small groups of Turks trying to surrender, their swords flashing. Kirkpatrick wasn't sure, but it seemed that black-garbed women had joined with their knives in the slaughter as well. By 2:00, a little more than a half hour after Eaton had signaled the charge, resistance was ended. Eighty men had routed a force of eight hundred.

CHAPTER 41
❧ DERNA 1805 ❧

Two days had passed since the capture of Derna. Mustifa Bey with a few followers had taken refuge in the harem of a local sheik. Too late to prevent the capture of Derna, Hassan Bey's relief army had finally arrived and begun to set up camp outside of Derna to the west. Eaton had set up headquarters in the harbor fort, under the protective cover of Hull's ships. Hamet and his followers remained on the open plain to the east of the town. Eaton and Leitensdorfer had ridden out to observe them.

"Since the capture of Derna," Eaton said, "we have seen troops of Bedouins ride in each day to swell the numbers of Hamet's forces, with all the expected ritual cheers and waste of ammunition one expects. But nothing touches the celebration on seeing the renowned El Habibka ride in with his three hundred tough-looking troopers under that striking dark-green banner with its single gold crescent. One would have thought the Prophet himself had re-appeared to lead them."

Eaton and Leitensdorfer had spent the better part of the morning on a small knoll above the plain, watching Doyle's cavalry drill: practicing controlled charges in tight formation from a walk to a trot to a canter, and only for the last fifty yards breaking into full gallop. Then they instantly wheeled by squads to re-form and attack in the direction they had just come from.

"But for the burnooses," said Leitensdorfer, "I would think we were watching Radetzky's Hungarian Hussars on the parade ground." After an hour of close-order formations, Doyle had put his men through individual drills, firing their weapons at targets and riding at a brisk canter, scooping up stones from the ground as they bent over their horse's shoulders. The competition among his men was loud and enthusiastic, with scornful laughter and insults directed at those who failed in their tasks. The exercises completed, as his officers and men retired for the morning, Doyle joined Eaton and Leitensdorfer.

"I must say, Doyle, that those are exceptionally fine troops you've brought with you," remarked Eaton. "One notices, of course, the superb horses, but I also saw they carried two swords along with their carbines. I wondered at that."

"A trick I learned from the Hussar formations I encountered when I was in Turkey, general. As good as the Mamelukes are individually as horsemen and fighters, they were repeatedly routed in battles against Hussars. The Hungarians favored a checkerboard formation with lancers in the first two ranks, and saber-armed troopers behind them. When we attack, we hold the same staggered formation: 'a horse-length apart, a horse-length behind.' My first ranks use their long swords like lances to break up the mass of the enemy, leaning out over their horses so their weapons will hit the enemy before they can bring their own scimitars into play. It's one thing to charge a man for close swordplay on horseback. There the advantage always goes to the better horse and the more skilled rider able to circle to his enemy's unguarded left side. But staring at a solid mass of horsemen coming at you that you know will be able to strike you or your horse before you can defend yourself—that takes a lot of resolve."

"And then," observed Eaton. "as you pass through the enemy's lines, the curved sabers of the remaining ranks are aptly suited for the cut and slash attacks that disable men and horses—I like it!".

"You know the jumble of a cavalry collision, I'm sure, general. To get through the enemy's line to instantly wheel and re-attack, which is when you break most opposing formations, a horseman needs to dodge enemies, the fallen bodies of men and their mounts, and fear-maddened riderless horses. I've long held that the point of a successful cavalry charge is not the initial shock, but the ability to get through to regroup and return to the attack."

"So your long, straight swords are, in effect, like short lances," offered Leitensdorfer, "much like those of Napoleon's cuirassiers."

"Exactly. And used the same way."

"Might I, in all kindness," asked Leitensdorfer, "examine your long sword?"

"Of course," said Doyle, getting up and walking over to his tethered horse and removing the long sword from its saddle-mounted scabbard. "This straight sword is the traditional weapon of the Tuaregs," he said. "I think you'll find it a well-balanced weapon."

He passed it across to Leitensdorfer, whose service with the various armies he'd then deserted from had allowed him to sample a wide range of Christian, Turk, and Arab weapons and tactics. Leitensdorfer skillfully gripped the sword with palm and fingers facing up, as he'd been taught. "Just over thirty-six inches, I'd say, about the size of an English dragoon's and slightly smaller than a French cuirassier's." He took a few practice lunges. "I like how the weight is balanced back toward the *garde*. Much easier than to keep the weapon extended at full arm's length and control the point for the thrust." He examined the straight hilt of Doyle's weapon. "If I may say, however, without any thought of disrespect, I prefer the heavier closed *garde* of the French sword. It helps keep one's hand in the proper position." He handed the weapon back to Doyle.

"A fair point," said Doyle. "But then, the Tuaregs have used this sword for hundreds of years, and grow up with them as boys. So habitual use is easier for them than it might be for a group of Napoleon's raw recruits swept up from farms and city streets."

"And because your men carry both weapons, long sword and saber, you can deploy them as the occasion demands. Quite ingenious," Eaton said. "I see they carry carbines as well, but when we met you on the Nile they had muskets."

"Different purposes, general. On the march, we carry muskets, and when we can get them, rifles, because of the distance their ball will carry and their accuracy. When we anticipate a cavalry battle like this, we switch to the shorter carbine."

"What weapons do you use?" continued Eaton.

"Given my contacts, it has been easiest to get standard British-issue Pagets. A better choice when I can get them are the French Jean LePage rifled carbines. You will see our practice against Hassan Bey's cavalry when we attack them. The rear ranks fire a volley at the front of the enemy's ranks when they are between fifty to seventy-five yards away, creating gaps for our first ranks."

Eaton could not contain his appreciation. "I dare say no monarch in Christendom, nor Pasha either, could so equip an army as well as this!"

"I dare say," said Doyle, "that no monarch could afford to. I have enjoyed financial success from, well, let us say my business endeavors, but I am fitting out five squadrons of one hundred men each, of which, at this point, only three are fully battle-ready. Attempting to do this for thirty thousand cavalrymen would make a pauper out of Croesus. Now gentlemen," Doyle rose to his feet, "I must take my leave. We have a busy afternoon ahead of us."

"More drill?" asked Leitensdorfer.

"Indeed," said Doyle. "You have noticed that with Arab or Turkish cavalry, the battle is all about the mêlée, a chaos of individual combats. My experience has been that tight formations, trained troops, and good tactics will beat individual skill and bravado every day—although I may say you will not find my Tuaregs to be unskilled at close combat either."

"I applaud your leadership," said Leitensdorfer. "What did Napoleon say? 'Two Mamelukes can defeat four Frenchmen, but one hundred French cavalry will not fear the same number of Mamelukes. A thousand French will always rout even twice their number.' Such is the power of tactics, order, and maneuver."

"You know, Eugene," Doyle responded, "in the public fancy, a cavalry charge conjures up the image of two massed, opposing squadrons hurling themselves in fury against each other at full speed, to loud huzzahs and the blare of bugles. Nothing could be further from reality. To begin with, unless a horse is quite maddened by fear or excitement, it will shy away rather than smash headlong into another horse. Men are, with rare exceptions, no different than their mounts. Among European cavalry, I would say that as high as seventy-five percent of the time, one opponent will refuse the attack at a distance, before they can actually see their enemy's eyes. Even when they do charge each other, almost invariably one group or another will turn away before the final collision. In the end, what makes the difference is not physical strength but moral strength. The squadron with the firmer character and better discipline imposes its superior will on their foe. Most casualties are then suffered by a retreating enemy when those fleeing are exposed to the sword thrusts of the enemy behind them."

Eaton, who had never participated in a major cavalry battle like the one awaiting them the next day, had been wholly engrossed in Doyle's analysis. "I eagerly look forward to watching your men in action. By all reports, when Mustufa Bey's Mamelukes attacked Napoleon's army at Imbala, they didn't relish their first taste of European cavalry tactics. We'll see how Hassan Bey's Arabs enjoy them tomorrow at Derna."

Doyle politely excused himself and walked down the short slope to rejoin his men. "So, general," Leitensdorfer said, "We can expect Doyle's Tuaregs to give a good account of themselves tomorrow. Have you noticed that our leader, the intrepid Hamet, seems to have a bit more courage since Doyle's, or should I say, El Habibka's, arrival?"

"I'm pleased you noticed it," said Eaton. "I think tomorrow will be their fight. O'Bannon keeps pleading to lead what remains of our army into the battle, but you know badly we were mauled in taking Derna. We're down to five of his Marines. Only eighteen of our Greek fighters can take the field. As for the Arab infantry, they will follow El Habibka with greater enthusiasm than O'Bannon or, were I fit for combat, me. No, we will stay in the citadel and hope to provide such covering artillery as we may."

"Well, at least we will see nothing of Hadgi Ismain Bey's Bengazi camel corps in this fight," Leitensdorfer said. "In their sortie against the town two days ago, it would appear our gunfire has somewhat discouraged them. I've never seen anything quite like a 24 pound ball striking a camel charging at full stride. It's like when one shoots target practice with pistols aimed at a filled pig's bladder, but a hundred times the explosion. Spectacular isn't in it."

"I hear rumors," Eaton added, "that when Hassan Bey commanded the Bengazi camel corps to use their precious camels to shield an infantry attack from gunfire, Ismain Bey and his men decamped, and for good measure, took Hassan's money box with him. But look." Eaton gestured to where Kirkpatrick was climbing the slope toward them from the town. "Here comes our young Hotspur, doubtless to beg permission to join Doyle's troopers in the attack."

Kirkpatrick strode up to Eaton and Leitensdorfer, stopped in front of them, and saluted. "General, I understand that we are deprived of the honor of participating in today's battle." He cast a quick glance at Leitensdorfer, who was smiling openly. "None of us knows how today will go for Hamet but we are still a handful of Christians amidst a population that views us as infidels, facing a still numerous enemy. The officers and men under you wanted to give you this expression of our trust and loyalty. It's in French, since that was the one language all of us understand." He pulled out a document from his coat and began reading.

> *Sir,*
>
> *In view of the desire and the courage which animates us all to participate in the glory of an expedition which is worthy of such a warlike nation, we are coming today to state to you again the zeal which we have to take part in it. We could not serve a better chief. The heroic ardor and the talents with which you are endowed can only ensure the happiness of your men. We offer our services in this campaign, to strictly carry out your orders, to exact respect for the honorable flag of the United States of America, and to encounter the enemy wherever he may be.*
>
> *Everything assures us of a complete victory under your command. We are only waiting for the moment to win this glory and to fall on the enemy.*
>
> *We believe you are assured in advance of the sentiments which we are proclaiming. Yes! We swear that we shall follow you and that we shall fight unto death.*

With another salute, Kirkpatrick handed the document to Eaton, who sat back in amazement. "Eugene," he asked Leitensdorfer. "You knew about this?"

If anything, Leitensdorfer's grin was now even greater than Kirkpatrick's. "If you look at signatures on the document, general, you will see my name below Lieutenant O'Bannon's and Captain Kirkpatrick's and right above Captain Ulovix's and Lieutenant Constantine's."

Eaton slowly reread the testimonial from his officers, then looked up at Kirkpatrick and Leitensdorfer. "Gentlemen, you humble me. This is too much honor. Too much by far. What is the old saying? 'A general without courageous men willing to follow him is just a fool on a walk by himself.' Not Alexander, not Caesar could be any prouder than I am of men and officers who serve with such loyalty. But let us return to the citadel and see to its defenses. Should the day go against Hamet, there may still be work for us to do. Besides, my wound is starting to trouble me again. I shouldn't think but that a glass or two of the brandy Captain Hull so graciously provided us with would serve perfectly as a tonic for the pain."

Chapter 42
❧ Derna 1805 ❧

The next day, Hamet's army, now numbering close to twelve hundred men, rode out to meet the more numerous force of Hassan Bey. Beyond the most rudimentary agreement on a plan of attack, Doyle had not attempted to influence or organize Hamet's strategy. Once the battle began, there would be no strategy, just a dust-obscured, clashing swirl of men and horses spread out in violent confusion across the plain outside of Derna.

Doyle had positioned his three hundred men slightly in front, to the right of Hamet and his personal guard. The rest of Hamet's men were massed on both sides of their leader, in a wide, narrow crescent, facing Hassan Bey's army of Arabs and Turks. Above them flew Hamet's own green and white flag proclaiming him pasha of Tripoli.

Dihya, as she promised, had accompanied the Tuaregs to Derna. Dihya was armed like the rest of the Tuaregs, her only concession to Doyle being a light coat of chain mail worn under her burnoose. They had fought together before; Doyle had learned not to worry any more for her safety than he would for his. "Will he fight?" Dihya asked, glancing back over her shoulder at Hamet.

"I think he will," answered Doyle. "After so many years of hopeless, penniless wandering, it is as if Hamet has awoken from a bad dream, or recovered from a devastating illness. Eaton may be right: miraculously, Hamet may actually make a strong Pasha.

The next few hours will tell. But I suppose we had better get this business started; otherwise these two grand armies may spend half the day looking at each other waiting for someone to make the first move."

With that, Doyle spurred his horse into the open plain between the two armies and approached the center where Hassan Bey's flag proclaimed his presence. In a strong, commanding voice, he proceeded to hurl the vilest insults he could at Hassan Bey, his ancestry, his illegitimate birth as the diseased spawn of a coupling between unclean beasts, and his unmanly preference for small boys and old men over real women. Doyle paused for a moment. *"Omak zanya fee erd!"* he yelled. "Your mother committed adultery with a monkey!" That should do it, Doyle thought. Hassan Bey listened to Doyle's tirade for less than a minute then angrily signaled his army to charge. With a roar from both sides, the center of both armies, perhaps 600 men on each side, surged forward toward each other, with the wings of both armies holding back to exploit whatever advantage the first attack of cavalry produced.

As planned, the Tuaregs turned to their right, trotting their horses to take a flanking position against the lead elements of Hassan Bey's vanguard, Doyle cantering to his position in the front. The Turks spread out before them, quickly losing all sense of formation as the fastest riders sprinted out ahead. On command, Doyle's men slowed to a walk, smoothly wheeled from column to staggered echelon formation, and began moving forward at a slow trot. One hundred yards from the leading exposed edge of Hassan Bey's charging troops, Doyle ordered a canter, his men still keeping a tight formation. Only at thirty yards from the enemy did he signal "Charge." The Tuaregs spurred into a gallop, hitting Hamet Bey's men on an angle at full speed. The Tuaregs slashed into the spread-out Turks like a scythe through wheat, splitting Hassan Bey's vanguard in half and cutting men down from their saddles as they passed. Hassan Bey's front elements were immediately swallowed up by Hamet's charging Arabs. The rear elements of Hassan Bey's Turks, seeing the carnage ahead of them, turned out of the way and galloped from the field, away from the Tuareg charge.

Doyle regrouped his men, leading them at a slow trot to the left toward Hassan Bey's right wing. In contrast to the wildly galloping, surging fighting now on the field behind them, they seemed to be moving in slow motion, their deliberate, ordered pace almost terrifying to the enemy unsure of their next move. Seventy-five yards from the end of Hassan Bey's line, Doyle cried "Three lines by sections!" They wheeled again into a hundred-man front, three lines deep. "Carbines!" Doyle yelled. The second line unhooked their carbines and checked their priming. "Advance at a walk!" was the next command, and both lines started moving toward the now anxious Turks. Unable to take the pressure, the Turkish commander signaled his charge, and Hassan Bey's right wing, three times the number of Doyle's force, surged forward in a gallop.

"Ready to fire!" Doyle ordered, and a moment later, "Fire!" The Tuareg's second line loosed a deadly fusillade into the front line of their charging enemy, spilling horses and riders in tumbling confusion.

"Advance at a trot!" was the next command, and Doyle's troops began again the careful, measured sequence that would lead into a decisive, crushing charge. Less than fifty yards from the oncoming Turks, Doyle's Tuaregs kicked their horse into full gallop, the long swords of the front line pointed like lances at the enemy. As Doyle had predicted the day before, the Turks in Hassan Bey's right wing wavered, then turned their horses to avoid the oncoming shock.

A feverish flight of pursued and their pursuers spread out across the plain. Doyle was now in the midst of the flowing, eddying maelstrom of the battle. Ahead, a Turk he had been chasing suddenly spun his horse to the left, right in front of Doyle. As Doyle swerved to avoid contact, the man nimbly ducked his horse behind Doyle's, taking a slashing swing at Doyle's unprotected back as he passed, opening a small wound. Now he was on Doyle's unprotected left side, closing quickly. Ahead, Doyle saw another of Hassan Bey's men charging straight at him, pinning him momentarily between two enemies. He twisted in his saddle to meet the attack to his rear from the nearer of the two men when the pursuing Turk's head simply flew off his body and the headless rider and horse galloped past Doyle. Right behind the dead man rode Dihya, blood on her sword.

She flashed Doyle a quick, knowing smile, and spurred her horse forward. Doyle tucked in behind her, avoiding his oncoming opponent. As they worked through the now fleeing, now counterattacking Turks, Doyle marveled at Dihya's horsemanship. Where the men around her collided in anger, Dihya floated in the space around her; where their swords clashed, hers danced. With her there is no difference between horse, rider, and the riding itself, he thought.

Then he and Dihya popped through the vortex of men and horses into the open space beyond, turning to face the fray still raging behind them. Doyle concentrated on bringing his breathing under control. I don't want Dihya to see me winded, he thought. In front of them, clusters of Doyle's Tuaregs were coming through after them, most unscathed. Doyle turned to Dihya. "Thanks for back there. You were wonderful. " She smiled and nodded again. "I have seen you fight with fury to protect your—"Doyle instantly corrected himself, "our people. But back there you seemed, I don't know, both completely in the fight and disengaged at the same time."

"Yes," Dihya said. "This is your fight, not mine."

"Then why are you here?" Doyle asked, confused.

"Why to protect you, of course." Her radiant, relaxed smile this time melted his heart. "Now I think we have more fighting to do," she added.

Doyle's men had cut through Hassan Bey's scattered left wing and then reformed to the rear of the remaining Turks now desperately engaged with Hamet's full force. Above the swirling dust, they could see the gleam of Hamet's banner.

"This last charge should do it," Doyle cried. "One more volley—then crush them." The remaining Turks were hit from behind by surprise and broke in panic.

Doyle and Dihya cantered up to where Hamet, surrounded by his personal guard on a small knoll, sat proudly on his horse. Below them on the plain, the confused turmoil of the battle was now sorting itself out. It was a complete rout: the survivors of the main body of Hassan Bey's Turks were now in full flight toward their encampment to the west. Smaller clusters of Turks were still engaged with pursuing Tuaregs and Arabs. As Doyle and Dihya approached, they could see Hamet's eyes glinting with excitement—his face was flushed with the joy of victory. The blood on his robes and sword signaled that this time, Hamet had not merely been a spectator in the re-conquest of his throne. Doyle and Dihya pulled up their horses next to Hamet in a flurry of dust, their robes billowing around them.

"Excellency," Doyle cried, saluting Hamet with his sword. "The day is yours! Congratulations on a complete triumph! Hassan Bey will not be able to take the field again. Most of his men will not stop running until they return to their homes."

"The day would not have been won without you and your men, El Habibka," Hamet graciously replied, returning Doyle's salute, his face flushed with the excitement of victory. "If we were the sword, you were its point. The triumph is mine; the greater valor is yours."

"Today you won a battle, excellency. Tomorrow you begin to regain a kingdom." With a bow to Hamet, Doyle and Dihya turned to rejoin their men. They had abandoned the chase and were reforming in disciplined ranks.

As they neared their Tuaregs, Doyle turned to Dihya. "Rather like winning a game of chess in a sandstorm, I should say."

CHAPTER 43
⫷ DERNA 1805 ⫸

"I never would have expected Hamet to have that much fire in his belly—or steel in his spine, for that matter. Hull's ships could provide no covering fire. This victory was his alone." Leitensdorfer was speaking as the American officers were taking breakfast on the quarterdeck of the *Argus,* planning the coordinated attack by Hamet's forces and the navy squadron against Tripoli.

With fresh provisions from Malta so readily available, Hull had spread out a feast: croquettes with Béchamel sauce, plates of assorted cheeses, fresh fruit, olives, sausages, a Sardinian *torta di carciofi*, Fiesole omelets, rashers of bacon and platters of boiled ham, all accompanied by steaming coffee and bottles of well-chilled 1801 *Veuve Clicquot*. It was a brilliant morning. The *Argus* rode easily in soft swells; under the protective shade of the sail Hull had rigged over the quarterdeck, they could see the American flag flying next to Hamet's over the harbor fort.

"They look good together," said Hull. He raised a glass of champagne: "Here's to the courage of the men who raised those flags in victory. May we next see them flying over the pasha's palace in Tripoli!" A chorus of "Hear! Hear!" acknowledged his toast.

"I have lately had good reasons to correct the unfavorable opinion I at one time entertained of Hamet's military enterprise," Eaton said. "Though not a great general, Hamet has shown himself capable of winning a decisive battle. After all, some aspire to greatness, some are born to it, and some have greatness thrust upon them. This latter destiny may yet be the case with Hamet. Now, Tripoli lies before him like an open door."

They were interrupted by a cry from the *Argus*'s masthead. "Below on deck. D'ye hear on deck there? Sail to the northeast!" The officers, naval and military alike, jumped to their feet and crowded the *Argus*'s seaward rail.

"Peter," Hull called out. "Be so good as to light aloft with your glass and tell us what you see."

Kirkpatrick scurried to the very top of the mizzenmast and trained his glass on the approaching stranger.

"She's big," Kirkpatrick called down. "The pasha has no ships like that, nor none of the other Barbary states, either." He waited a few minutes as more of the ship rose over the horizon. "The *Constitution* or *Constellation*," he shouted. "I'm sure of it."

"Then come down, if you please," Hull called out. Being a practical and experienced captain, however, he also passed word to ready all the ships in his squadron to make sail quickly, should the unknown ship inexplicably prove to be hostile.

Within two more hours, it was clear to all that the new arrival was, in fact, the *Constellation,* under Hugh Campbell. The excitement among Hull's flotilla was infectious, and had spread into the town itself. As the huge frigate neared the harbor, dwarfing Hull's brig and the schooners, the inhabitants of Derna went mad with joy.

Kirkpatrick and Leitensdorfer had returned to the harbor fort where the Marines and European soldiers were garrisoned to help O'Bannon ready the buildings to accommodate another five hundred Marines and sailors. "If this were a Christian town," Kirkpatrick remarked, "we would be deafened by the triumphant peal of bells from every church and cathedral. Here we must make do with gunfire."

True enough, hundreds of locals flocked through the streets, joined by units from Hamet's Arab cavalry who had left their stations, racing through the narrow streets and squares, firing their weapons into the air. The women added to the din with their high-pitched ululations. Kirkpatrick noticed some residents were boisterously waving crudely made American flags. He could hear the same cries coming from the throng like a chorus. "What are they shouting?" he asked Leitensdorfer.

"Long live the Americans! Long live our friends and protectors! Long live our liberators!" answered Leitensdorfer. He listened a little longer. "The women are singing *"Din din Mohammed u ryas melekan manhandi,"* which means 'Mohammed for religion and the Americans for courage.' There are, of course, the odd 'Death to the usurper Jusef!' thrown in," Leitensdorfer added. "These people are very earnest in their politics. When we appear outside the harbor of Tripoli in a week or so, it is the strangler's silken cord for Jusef Karamanli."

Kirkpatrick, O'Bannon, and Leitensdorfer watched as the *Constellation* gracefully backed her foresails, turned into the wind, and dropped anchor. Her masts, soaring as much as 200 feet above her deck, seemed to blot out the sky. A gun sounded, and Kirkpatrick saw signals break out from her signal halyard.

"Captains Report," he read. "Gentlemen, I know I don't have a ship at present, but surely the *Eagle*'s repairs will have been completed to allow her to take part in the final assault on Tripoli. I beg you excuse me." Without even waiting for the hastily granted assent from O'Bannon and Leitensdorfer, he started sprinting down the steps toward the water batteries, yelling for a boat crew as he ran.

A grim-faced group of men heard Campbell's news in the main cabin of the *Constellation*. Eaton could barely contain his rage on learning of the shameful bargain Tobias Lear had struck with Jusef Karamanli. "So, if I take you right, Captain Campbell, by Lear's treaty, we have agreed to ransom the freedom of the *Philadelphia* captives for $60,000, without a shot having been fired by the mightiest naval force ever assembled by the United States in foreign waters. A mere third of that unearned tribute, $20,000 in troop payments and materiél, coupled with a resolute show of force before Tripoli, would have brought the usurper to his knees. Tripoli is indefensible from the landward side. Pasha Karamanli is out of money; his people flee the city in terror. He cannot recruit more troops. The army we have battered into submission here at Derna *is* his only, final hope for success. But rather than spend $20,000 on absolute, irrevocable victory, we have allowed ourselves to be outfaced and hoodwinked by this Prince of Lies, this Tyrant of Straw! The jackal has defeated the lion."

"It is a bad business," said Captain Campbell. "Rodgers—the other captains—none of us had any sense of what you had accomplished here. The only intelligence we received was of Hamet Karamanli's shortcomings in rousing the populace against his brother's regime. It gets worse than that," Campbell added. "The word in Malta was that reinforcements will be arriving early in June: the frigates *Congress* and *John Adams* and ten of the gunboats Preble ordered, and that we should delay any action against Tripoli until their arrival. There was some talk among the Commodore's staff that these reinforcements were carrying additional money to establish Hamet Karamanli's regime."

"Small wonder, then," Eaton said, "that Lear was so urgent in bringing this shameful deal with the pasha to a rapid conclusion. In another month, all the glory he sought as the architect of 'peace' and the liberator of the *Philadelphia* captives would have been jerked from his grasping fingers."

"Gentlemen," Hull spoke now for the first time. "It seems to me these matters are more the subject for a formal hearing or tribunal than for our general discourse. I have no doubt that in due time, such an investigation will follow what has transpired here. But this treaty has been signed and sealed. We are, I regret to say it, obliged to carry out its provisions, our personal reservations notwithstanding."

"So we must leave Derna," Eaton cried, "striking the flag of our country here in the presence of an enemy who have not merited that triumph. We came here, four years ago, to demonstrate that the resolve of our Republic was such that it would never bow to tyranny, wherever that evil specter raised its brutal visage over an oppressed people. So much for our resolve. So much for the honor of our Republic and the brave men who have given their lives in the cause of freedom. So much for the sacrifice of Somers, Caldwell, James Decatur, Wadsworth, Dorsey, Israel, and the Marines and brave followers who died at Derna."

Kirkpatrick could feel his blood run hot as he listened to Eaton. Looking around the cabin of the *Constellation* at the other captains, he could see in their dark faces and averted glances the same sense of helpless frustration and unearned shame. Damn Smith and the Naval Department, he thought, for replacing a great commander like Preble with a feckless invalid like Barron. Damn Barron for not having the decency to step down in favor of a fighting captain like Rodgers, or for lacking the sense of timing to have perished swiftly from his illness. But most of all, let a special place in Hell be found for Tobias Lear, who sacrificed the honor of his country and demeaned the lives of its heroes for his personal gain.

Eaton now turned to the plight of Hamet, his army, and the population of Derna. "You all heard the cries this afternoon as the *Constellation* arrived. I wonder, as we leave the inhabitants of Derna to the cruel mercies of their former ruler, the tyrant Jusef, how high they will hold us now in their esteem?"

He pulled a letter from his pocket. "Here, gentlemen, are the last words I will send Commodore Barron. I fear they are suited to be the epitaph of this expedition. "How many years must pass," he read, "before another enslaved people trust our resolve enough to again proclaim 'God Bless America?' The bravest man would weep to witness the unbounded confidence placed in the American character here, based not so much on our history, for we are still a nation young in deeds, but in our promise. Do we dare reflect that this confidence will shortly sink into contempt and eternal hatred? Havoc will be the legacy we leave behind us; not a soul of those who trusted our word can escape the savage vengeance of the enemy."

"But Pasha Karamanli has sent a personal delegate on board the *Constellation* to assure the residents of Derna that if they re-swear fealty to him, their rebellion will be forgotten," Campbell said. "It is a condition of the agreement signed by the Pasha and Lear."

"So is the stipulation that Hamet's family, held hostage all these years, will finally be freed," Eaton replied. "Do any of us truly believe in these chimerical fantasies? If a snake could speak, would you trust its utterances?"

"So what must we do?" Hull asked.

"Clearly, if we pull out in the face of a large enemy force, we doom Hamet's army to whole scale slaughter and the town's inhabitants to a bloodbath of rapine and pillage. Let us therefore make a brave show of what we, in all honor, *should* have done, and what Hassan Bey, in all terror, assumes we *will* do. We learned of Lear's peace treaty to our unwelcome surprise today. No rider could have brought the news across the desert faster to the enemy. Let both our allies and our enemies assume we are planning the ultimate attack that will break open the road to the gates of Tripoli. Replenish the supplies, hand out extra ammunition and rations to Hamet's forces, then pass the word for a grand attack upon the morrow. Under the cover of darkness and the great deception of American fidelity, we will stealthily withdraw our Marines and European mercenaries. I will speak to Hamet myself and break the tragic news. He really has no choice other than to board the American ship that takes him into exile from his family, his country, and his dreams."

"May I speak, sir?" Kirkpatrick asked, mindful, for a change, of his low rank among those assembled.

"Your service has earned you the right to be heard," Eaton responded.

"We may safely extricate our troops and Hamet's immediate retinue, but we leave Hamet's army and the inhabitants of Derna to slaughter. Let the *Constellation*, with its immense firepower, cover their retreat. At the very least, Hamet's army and those citizens of Derna who wished to avoid the resumption of Pasha Karamali's rule could make their escape in the morning into Egypt free from pursuit. Hassan Bey's troops have experienced fire from our sloops and brigs. Nothing in their most feverish nightmares will have prepared them for a broadside or two from the *Constellation.* They will feel the world has come to an end."

"But Peter," Dent said, "You know we can't see over the coastal hills to direct our fire. We couldn't support Hamet's troops yesterday for fear of subjecting them to friendly fire; how is this different?"

"Let me direct the fire," Kirkpatrick volunteered. "From the top of the hills to the west of town, I can see the entire plateau. If we mark our maps with numbered grids, I can certainly communicate the proper targets with signal flags."

"We can cover you with a squad of Marines," O'Bannon offered.

"You're kind, Presley," said Kirkpatrick, "but enough American lives have been squandered here. The Greeks are paid for their work. They may not be Marines, but they have proved themselves to be fierce fighters. I would feel safe in their care."

"So we are agreed on this shameful action," Eaton concluded. "Make your plans, gentlemen, as you think best. Colonel Leitensdorfer, may I ask you to manage the charade with our European troops? They must not know our true purpose until right before they board the boats that will bring them to the *Constellation.*" He rose from his chair and stared for a moment at the cluttered table in front of them as if he wished to smash everything on it. With a shake of his head, he continued. "In a few minutes we shall lose sight of this devoted city, which has experienced as strange a reverse in so short a time as ever was recorded in the disasters of war: thrown from proud success and elated prospects into an abyss of hopeless wretchedness. Six hours ago the enemy was seeking safety from the people of Derna by flight. Now we drop these people into the hands of their enemy for no other crime than too much confidence in us! And the man whose fortune we have accompanied thus far experiences a reverse just as striking. Hamet falls from the most flattering prospects of a kingdom into exile and beggary!"

As the officers dispersed, Eaton signaled to Kirkpatrick to join him.

"Captain Kirkpatrick," Eaton began, once they were alone. "I must beg of you to carry out a difficult task for me, if you will. I will tell Hamet of his newest tragedy. He has been lied to and betrayed so many other times that I doubt he will actually be surprised. But I cannot in all conscience, face Doyle. You have struck up a friendship with him, have you not?"

"Friendship may be too strong a word," Kirkpatrick said, "but I think he regards me with some kindness."

"Then will you do this for me? I am the first to lead men into an enemy's fire, but this shame, my shame, our country's shame, is ..." Eaton just shook his head without finishing his thought.

"I will do it," said Kirkpatrick, strongly. "You may count on me, general."

Eaton returned his steady look. "I have, I do, and I will. You are the man I thought you to be when I asked you to join this expedition, Peter. He reached out for Kirkpatrick and the two men embraced. Eaton pulled back and again looked Kirkpatrick in the face. "Thank you," was all he said.

Kirkpatrick caught up with Leitensdorfer as they were boarding boats to return to Derna. "How can I carry this message?" he asked.

"It's a heavy message," said Leitensdorfer. "I suggest you carry it lightly. You are not the same impetuous young man whom I knew in Cairo. Remember that. Be who you are now. No mirror ever became iron again; no bread ever returned to wheat; no wine ever changed back into grapes."

Kirkpatrick had borrowed a horse to ride to Doyle's camp. The men there stared at his now familiar uniform but did not challenge him. Kirkpatrick was struck by the military orderliness of the encampment in contrast with the clutter of an Arab camp. To his right, a small group of men practiced their swordsmanship under the direction of a trooper Kirkpatrick took to be a sergeant. He followed the landmark of Doyle's flag waving above the tents until he came to Doyle's quarters. Dismounting, he approached the guard.

"I am here be speaking El Habibka, with General Eaton compliment," he said.

The trooper raised his eyebrows at Kirkpatrick's Arabic, but nodded and went inside the tent. A few minutes later he emerged and gestured for Kirkpatrick to enter.

As Kirkpatrick's eyes adjusted to the soft, yellow light within the tent, they were drawn to the person seated next to Doyle.

Sitting on the cushions was the most beautiful woman he'd ever seen. She was dressed simply and casually in what looked to be men's-style clothing, so Kirkpatrick caught a sense of an attractive, even sensuous figure. Her long hair was jet black, her features strong and fine: the word "noble" entered Kirkpatrick's mind. He was reminded of Irish women he had seen, although her skin was darker. He guessed her to be of above average height, only slightly shorter than himself. Her eyes were a startling emerald green.

Doyle rose, walked welcomingly toward Kirkpatrick, and made the introductions. "Captain Kirkpatrick, I have the honor of presenting Princess Dihya of the Tuareg people and the clan of the *M'Tougas*."

Kirkpatrick snapped his heels together, then bowed ceremoniously. Not sure of what language to use, he said to Doyle, "Please tell her I am both charmed and greatly honored."

Doyle spoke a few sentences to the princess in a tongue Kirkpatrick didn't recognize. Dihya looked at Kirkpatrick and smiled; his heart instantly stopped beating. Jesus, Kirkpatrick thought. If a man had a woman like that waiting at home, why the hell would he ever go to war? If I did have that kind of woman, I'd hide her face behind veils when we went out in public, like the Arabs.

Doyle watched Kirkpatrick's reaction to Dihya with amusement for a few moments, then broke the spell. "Captain. This is a welcome surprise! May we offer you refreshment? Some tea, perhaps?"

"No," Kirkpatrick said. " I'm afraid I bring bad, even tragic news."

"Then, by all means, join us," he motioned back to where Dihya had remained. "This sounds like news we should hear sitting down."

When they were seated, Kirkpatrick turned to Doyle. "I don't know exactly how to say this." He paused. "It appears that while we were marching across the desert, the American general consul for the Mediterranean, Tobias Lear, had been secretly negotiating a separate peace treaty with Pasha Karamanli."

"I know Lear," Doyle said. "The news is ugly, unwelcome, but predictable."

"Shortly after our initial victory at Derna, the treaty was signed," continued Kirkpatrick. "The American hostages have been released; a state of peace now exists between the Unites States and the Kingdom of Tripoli and its present ruler, Pasha Jusef Karamanli." Kirkpatrick almost spit the words out as he said them. "Hamet, of course, is once again a stateless refugee."

Doyle rose and walked away from them. His attention seemed fixed on some place or object far away. "So what now for Hamet?" Doyle asked in a flat voice. Dihya remained seated, her eyes carefully following the interchange between the two men, even though she couldn't understand their words.

"We are providing him with protection," said Peter, his voice just as expressionless. "He and a few of his chosen followers will be taken aboard a Navy ship and transported to a destination they choose."

Doyle turned back to them. "He'd better hope that your protection is more trustworthy than the support you promised him to reclaim his throne," he said. "And his followers?"

"We will provide them, and any citizens of Derna who wish to leave, covering fire so they may begin their escape back to Egypt in safety."

"And then you leave," said Doyle. "They are on their own." It was not a question.

It took Kirkpatrick a while to respond. "Yes."

Doyle looked at Kirkpatrick more kindly now. "Captain, may I call you Peter? I know that this disgrace is none of your doing; in fact, I would think it is the last thing you could possibly have envisioned or wanted. I can only imagine the pain it cost you to have to bring me this message." He reached out a hand to help Dihya up. She clung to him for a moment, knowing that something terribly wrong had just happened. Doyle spoke to her quietly. Her face went grim. Doyle gently freed himself from her embrace and walked with Kirkpatrick to the entrance of the tent.

"I intend no rudeness, Peter, but I am sure you have preparations of your own to make. It now seems that we should ready our men for departure as well. So farewell and Godspeed." He reached forward, and in American fashion, shook Kirkpatrick's hand, then placed his hand over his heart. As Kirkpatrick turned to leave, Doyle added: "Have the kindness to send my deepest regrets to General Eaton. You may say that it was an honor for me to have served and fought with him. A great honor. Whatever my thoughts of the nation that sent him on this mission and then abandoned him, his character as a man is, in my eyes, untarnished. Sadly, he is far from the first brave soldier to be disgraced by his country. Please give him that message.

"I will," said Kirkpatrick. Obeying an impulse, he stepped back to embrace Doyle; Doyle strongly returned the embrace. As they stepped apart, still in the strange awkwardness of the moment, Doyle looked at Kirkpatrick piercingly, and simply said, "Yes," he nodded. "Yes." And so they parted.

Dihya was waiting by Doyle's side as he turned back from the entrance. "We will be busy in a few minutes, but may I ask you if you were surprised by this news?"

"Disappointed. I, too, fell under Eaton's spell for a while. But not surprised. America may be a new nation, but they have proved themselves apt, eager students of the old arts of political corruption, self-interest, and betrayal."

CHAPTER 44
⮿ DERNA 1805 ⮾

Before dawn, Kirkpatrick went ashore, accompanied by Lieutenant Constantine and twelve Greek volunteers. They climbed up a bluff to the northwest of town overlooking both Derna and the hundreds of white tents comprising the remnants of Hassan Bey's army. Hamet's forces were still camped to the east of the city, from where Eaton had launched his initial attack. Thus they could still be supported by the *Argus, Nautilus,* and *Hornet.* Concerned about the dangerous shoals and shallow water surrounding the harbor at Derna, Captain Campbell had the *Constellation* towed at night to a position opposite Kirkpatrick's signaling position. Her 24-pound long guns could easily enfilade Hassan Bey's position, even though they could not see it, and also provide covering fire for the retreat of Kirkpatrick and his men. The *Constellation'*s boats were already in the water, manned and ready to bring Kirkpatrick and his men back to the ship.

By daybreak, Private Christow and Kirkpatrick had set up his signaling post on the seaward side of a slight depression on top of the bluff where he would be invisible to both Hassan Bey's army and the town. Lieutenant Constantine placed his men to provide covering fire should they be discovered. Over the years, erosion had turned the landward side of the bluff into a steep, treacherous slope up which their attackers would have to scramble in order to attack them. What none of them had noticed in the early morning light was a deep *wadi* one hundred yards to the east of them leading down to the desert floor below. They hadn't seen the men posted at the lip of the *wadi,* sent to track the *Constellation*'s movement, who had scurried back to report as soon as Kirkpatrick and his squad had appeared at the top of the bluff.

Eaton's deception had held long enough to bring Hamet and a handful of his closest aides to board the *Constellation* at night under the guise of a strategy conference for the feigned attack to be launched in the morning. But by the time the European troops began embarking the following morning, the population had become aware that something was amiss. In small groups, and then in great numbers, they crowded the waterfront, calling out to Eaton to deny what their eyes could tell them was the disgraceful truth—they were being abandoned.

The retreat was covered by the Marines, O'Bannon's veterans of the march to Derna and another twenty from the *Constellation*, their bayonets fixed again, but this time against people who had, hours before, considered themselves America's allies. Under a barrage of rocks and refuse, accompanied by shrieks, curses, and cries of despair, O'Bannon and the Marines were the last to step away from the shores of Tripoli.

At 9:00, as the Americans and Europeans were boarding the boats to return to the *Argus,* the *Constellation* began firing ranging shots at high elevation, aiming first at the empty desert between Hamet's and Hassan Bey's forces, carefully adjusting distance and direction following Kirkpatrick's signals. At 9:30, the *Constellation* launched the first full broadside from her starboard 22-gun main battery at Hassan Bey's camp, already in a terrified frenzy as the artillery fire walked across the desert toward them. The effect of the 24 pound balls smashing into the mass of milling men, horses, camels, and equipment was staggering. As the *Constellation*'s thundering broadsides roared over their heads, Lieutenant Constantine ran across the depression to Kirkpatrick's position. "Should we retire, now sir?" he asked.

"Not yet, Lieutenant," said Kirkpatrick. "Let's make sure Hamet's forces are well away in their escape." He and Private Christow ran back with Lieutenant Constantine to join the other Greeks now peering over the edge of the bluff, staring and pointing at the turmoil erupting within Hassan Bey's camp. "We leave here, sadly, in defeat," Kirkpatrick said to the men around him. "But these bastards will at least have something to remember us by." Someone has to pay for Lear's treachery, he thought. Those poor souls down there will have to do.

The first musket volley from the fifty men Hassan Bey had sent up the *wadi*, aimed at the backs of the unsuspecting, unprotected Greeks, killed Lieutenant Constantine and four of his men outright and wounded five more. The ensuing fight was vicious and brief. Groups of Turks swarmed the remaining Greeks, slashing them down while others finished off the wounded. Kirkpatrick and Private Christow, fighting back to back, held out the longest: Kirkpatrick because the Turks had been ordered to take him alive as a prisoner, Christow because his huge size and fierce bayonet thrusts kept his attackers momentarily at bay. In the moment Kirkpatrick tripped over the body of a fallen Turk at his feet, Christow was felled by a dozen musket shots. Before Kirkpatrick could regain his feet, he was knocked senseless by the blow from a musket butt. Bringing their wounded but leaving the Greeks where they fell, the Turks quickly retreated off the top of the bluff, taking a dazed, securely bound Kirkpatrick, bleeding from a dozen wounds, with them.

After thirty minutes without a response from the *Constellation*'s repeated signals, Captain Campbell's concern had turned to outright worry. He ordered the *Constellation*'s boats to go ashore, with a strong contingent of sailors and Marines, while repositioning the *Constellation*'s guns to cover the removal of Kirkpatrick and his men. Two hours later, the boats returned, empty. Captain

Campbell leaned over the rail to call down to the first boat, "Your news?"

"The top of the bluff was littered with the bodies of the Greeks, Captain," the midshipman answered. "We buried them where they fell. There was no sign of Captain Kirkpatrick, sir." He held up Kirkpatrick's bloody coat and hat. "This is all we found."

Charles Mayberry, Campbell's First Lieutenant, asked the question all the officers were thinking. "Shall we assemble a rescue party to try to find him, sir?"

"This ship's entire company is three hundred eighty-two men," Campbell answered. "There are still more than a thousand Turks out there, and a desert for them to hide Captain Kirkpatrick in, if he survived. We must pray, I fear, that he did not. This is a damnable business, but there can be no consideration of rescue. Mr. Mayberry," he called. "Ready to warp the ship around to the open sea. We sail for Syracuse."

As Kirkpatrick drifted in and out of painful consciousness on the floor of Hassan Bey's tent, a fierce argument had erupted among the Turkish and Arab chiefs over who would have the prize of him as a prisoner—and the money he might draw in ransom. Hassan Bey listened to the quarrelling chiefs for a few minutes, then pushed his way into the circle among them, crying, "Enough! There will be no ransom for this dog. A thousand Americans would need to die to atone for the misery and suffering they have caused us. We have only one American prisoner, so he must die a thousand deaths, one at a time. There is only one place where that can happen: in the marble quarries in the Hoggar mountains to the south, the Sepulcher of Wet Bones."

He kicked Kirkpatrick awake. "My judgment, you miserable creature, is that you be condemned to a living hell until your body and spirit finally surrender in death and madness. Let me tell you what awaits you in the Sepulcher of Wet Bones. When you pass its gates you become one of the living dead. There will be no word of your imprisonment, no one will know you suffer there, and thus there can be no thought of ransom from your friends. There can be no escape, not from the guards, and certainly not from the empty wild and waterless desert that surrounds the quarries. Those wretches who attempt escape are dealt with as a lesson to the rest. First, the skin is flayed off them and salt poured on their exposed flesh. Then they are blinded, their tongues ripped out by burning pincers, their eardrums shattered, and their private parts cut off. Then they are thrown from the top of the prison to be impaled on a sharp iron hook set in the walls. There they may hang for days, the madness of unyielding pain overtaking them, the blessed gift of death constantly tantalizing and eluding them, until they finally perish in their torment. There their corpses hang until the birds of prey have picked their skeletons clean of flesh. That is your fate." Before he had finished speaking, Kirkpatrick had fainted again.

The next day passed like a nightmare. Kirkpatrick's wounds had been roughly tended to and sewn up. He had been given a meal of water and dates to prepare him for the journey over the desert to the quarries. The remains of his uniform had been stripped off him, and he had been given a loincloth and a rough robe to cover himself with. At daybreak he and his six guards set off, his guards on camels and Kirkpatrick walking and stumbling behind them, his feet in fetters, his hands tied to one of the camels by a long rope. "He should suffer," Hassan Bey had ordered, "but he must not be allowed to die."

As the miles unfolded, Kirkpatrick passed from increasingly hopeless misery to a dull, almost unconscious desire simply to survive the next hour, one painful step at a time. The sun beat on him like a fiery hot, bronze sword. Whenever he fell in exhaustion, his guards would halt, give him water and a few minutes rest, pull him to his feet, and resume their journey. At midafternoon, his guards crested the top of a long ridge of dunes to see the oasis they had marched toward already populated by several dozen tents. Their leader immediately pulled his camel to a halt. "Tuaregs," he called back in a near whisper to the other guards.

"No need to speak softly," a voice called from a dune to their left. "We have watched you approach for the last hour." Five men stood up from the brush next to them, their carbines pointed at Kirkpatrick's guards. Another three appeared behind them, their carbines also at the ready. "I am sure you seek fresh water, fodder for your camels, and rest from your journey. Please join us—but leave your weapons on the top of the knoll here. Oh yes, and bring your prisoner with you." Hassan Bey's Turks, closely watched by the Tuaregs, rode down to the oasis. They dismounted in the welcome shade of the palm trees surrounding the large pool of water in the center of the grove. They were in the midst of a camp of Tuareg warriors, whose leader stepped out of his tent as they arrived.

"Welcome," he said. *"As-salaam ahlakum.* Make yourself comfortable; there is water here for all. As to your prisoner, he looks as if your journey here has fatigued him. We will, in all hospitality, tend to his needs. He certainly is valuable to someone, but his value disappears if he is dead." The Tuareg's leader motioned to his men to carry Kirkpatrick into his tent. Hassan Bey's guards looked at each other in confusion, but without protest, as their prisoner was taken from them. After they had watered their camels, quenched their own thirst, and eaten, the Tuareg leader emerged, walked over, and squatted down next to them.

"Your unwilling companion interests me. Whose prisoner is he?"

"He belongs to His Excellency, the Sheik Hassan Bey, brother-in-law of Pasha Jusef Karamanli. We take him to the pasha's marble quarries to the south."

"Why that's a long, hard walk to get to a bad place. I tell you what. Let me make you a fair offer. I will trade one of my excellent *demi-méhari* camels for your prisoner. Given the miserable condition of your prisoner, that's so one-sided a trade I'm almost ashamed to make it. You can take the camel to Pasha Karamanli, or keep him for yourself and tell the pasha that, *inshallah,* the prisoner's wounds proved too much for him and he died along the way."

"On our heads, Effendi, we cannot do that!" cried the head guard.

"On your lives you must," answered the Tuareg. "If the trade of your prisoner for a camel doesn't agree with you, why then we can just kill you and keep both your prisoner, our camel, and, of course, yours as well. Let me give you some time to choose between your oath to Pasha Karamanli and your worthless lives." With that, he rose and went back toward his tent. When he returned, the guard's leader announced that the exchange of their prisoner for a fine camel was more than fair.

"Excellent," the Tuareg answered. "Then once you and your camels are refreshed, leave this oasis. The very sight of you is offensive to my eyes."

Having disposed of Hassan Bey's Turks, Doyle walked back into his tent, where Kirkpatrick lay, dressed in a clean white caftan, his wounds tended and his body bathed.

CHAPTER 45
❧ THE LIBYAN DESERT 1805 ❧

As Kirkpatrick struggled into wakefulness, his dream returned. Once again, he was lying in pain on the hot sand. But this time, he felt himself rising, his strength returning, his body somehow soaring into the air to join the bird that hovered above him. He opened his eyes and looked down at his body and felt the soft cushions beneath him. He was in a Bedouin tent, enclosed in curtains of white gauze. Surely I have died and gone to heaven, Kirkpatrick thought. I just didn't expect it to be an Arab heaven. The curtains parted and the man he first knew as Katir Al-Hareeq, then as El Habibka, entered and sat down next to the bed.

"How do you feel?" Doyle asked.

"I'm alive, it seems," said Kirkpatrick. "That's an improvement over what I felt a few hours ago. But as used as I've become to not understanding anything that happens in this country, I'm at a loss to understand why I'm here, or for that matter, why you're here. It would appear that you've rescued me from those damned Turks."

"It was easy to guess their destination when you left Hassan Bey's camp, and given the slow pace of you and your captors, easy enough to get here first and prepare a welcome for them."

"But what of my Greek soldiers and the *Constellation*? I remember we were ambushed, but little after that."

"The Turks killed all your men, and when the *Constellation's* rescue party found no trace of you, they had no choice but to set sail and depart. You are all alone here, and your friends must think—or hope—that you died in battle. But I am curious to know if you wonder why I have taken the trouble to save you."

"Curious, yes, and deeply grateful. The future they had planned for me in the quarries didn't sound very appealing." He tried to sit up, winced from the sudden pain, and settled back into the cushions. "That wasn't a good idea. And speaking of which, it would appear that we Americans have made a sorry mess of this whole business."

"Yes and no," said Doyle. "Suppose you had defeated Jusef and installed Hamet as Pasha? Jusef would have had to be killed; that's how they do things here. Would you have had the stomach for that? Would your government indefinitely provide the thousand troops and the naval squadron needed to keep Hamet in power? Perhaps it's a blessing that Eaton failed. I can't imagine the United States wanting to support a colony in North Africa."

"So our sacrifice meant nothing."

"Who's to say? You may need to come back to the Mediterranean and blow up a few more cities, but you have exposed the Turkish rule in North Africa for the hollow shell that it is. You may need to nail the coffin, but the age of Barbary piracy is dead. The Barbary States don't have the power to stand up to a modern military force. You proved that; and in the process, you have announced to the world that, for better or worse, America is here and will need to be reckoned with. You could have accomplished less."

"And now what?" Kirkpatrick asked.

"Well that depends on what happens next," Doyle replied. "Do you remember our conversation about your childhood?"

"I do," said Kirkpatrick.

"You spoke of your mother living among the Mohawks in New York and the son she lost in the war." He reached inside his robe, pulled out a locket on a chain and handed it to Kirkpatrick. "Tell me if this face is familiar to you."

Kirkpatrick opened the locket and stared at the portrait inside, a miniature version of one that had been by his mother's bedside as long as he could remember. "But this is my mother!" he cried. "How the devil did you come by this!"

"She gave it to me when she left the Mohawk Valley with Samuel Kirkpatrick, right before the war broke out." Doyle paused to let Kirkpatrick absorb the shock of that revelation. "She had begged me to go with her to Kirkpatrick's people in Philadelphia. I knew him to be a decent man who would care for her, but I knew my place was with my adopted people, the Mohawk tribe of the Iroquois."

"But she told me you had died in the war," Kirkpatrick said.

"I know," said Doyle. "I asked Joseph Brant to get a message to her that I had been killed in the fighting around Fort Niagara. I could not consider ever seeing her again. My life would have been forfeited if I ever returned to America and was recognized. In truth, I had no desire to return to an America that had destroyed my people and stolen their land. In any event, given what I became and where that work took me, correspondence would have been almost impossible. I regret it sadly now, but at the time, I thought it better for her to think I had died, so that whole part of her past could die with me. After what she had been through, a fresh, clean start with Kirkpatrick would be a blessing for her."

"No mother rejoices at the death of a son," Kirkpatrick said quietly.

"I know," said Doyle. They both were silent for a while.

"So now I have a brother," said Kirkpatrick, "who shows up as if by magic."

Well," laughed Doyle, "knowing me now as you do, how else might you have imagined me to appear?"

"And did you know who I was when we were together on the Nile going toward Cairo?" asked Kirkpatrick.

"You and Lieutenant O'Bannon spent so much time exchanging life stories while I pretended to sleep nearby—yes, I knew."

"But you then had the deviltry to pretend you didn't understand us and made me go through all that preposterous business of tortured French, sign language, and grunts—and that 'friendly' conversation before the battle," exclaimed Kirkpatrick, "one might call that a scurvy trick for a brother to play."

"To the contrary, younger brother," Doyle laughed, "I would say that as your older brother, I had a long-postponed duty to plague you as mercilessly as my imagination might let me. I had a lot of lost time to make up."

"We both have a lot of lost time to make up," said Kirkpatrick. "I grew up without a father, wishing for a brother who I believed had died before I was born."

"There are so many questions to explore," said Doyle. He thought for a moment. "This may seem a strange beginning, but let me ask you, what do you love the most?"

"The sea," was Kirkpatrick's immediate response. "On land, and with people, I feel awkward, unsure of myself, impetuous. It is like the clumsy person always getting into trouble is someone else. I don't like that side of me very much. But at sea—it's difficult to express it—at sea, with a good ship and a good crew, I am home. It's not that the sea is easy, or kind. The ancient Greeks, believing the sea was ruled by the angry, unpredictable God Poseidon, were right. In one moment the sea is your lover, giving the gifts of unspeakable beauty and freedom; in the next it is your killer. I'd never thought about this before, but perhaps I love the sea for what it lets me be and become.

"Fools ignore the power of the sea, and it usually eats them," Kirkpatrick continued. "Cowards fear it and stay safely on land. Madmen seek to control or conquer it. My study, my goal if you will, is to become one with it. When I was a young midshipman struggling to learn what Truxton was trying to teach us, I was confounded by how much I needed to master: the rigging, sailing, and working of a ship; winds, tides, and the weather; navigation—so much. Gradually it is becoming now not something that I study, but a part of me. I often see the sky, feel the changing air pressure, sense the movement of the sea and wind, and just know what the sea will do. The low clouds masking the setting sun on the horizon—as a boy I would have to scurry to my books and first look up the name of the clouds, then the weather patterns associated with them—it was all a jumble. Now—I don't know if this makes any sense—Henry, but I don't think about it, I just, well, flow with it." Realizing he had been giving a speech, and perhaps not a very coherent speech at that, Kirkpatrick paused and looked at his brother. "Why are you smiling?" he asked Doyle.

"You sound just like my old teacher, *Tiyanoga,* talking about the forest. What did he say so many years ago? 'When you move, see with your feet, listen with your eyes, and look with your ears. Let the forest come to you.' It is the same with what some call the 'sea of sand,' the desert. You and I grew up apart, yet it sounds as if we had similar teachers. If I may ask another question, what will you do when we take you back to Alexandria?"

"I will leave the Navy," Kirkpatrick said. "I care about and enjoy my men and my ship—but a government and high command that could allow something like this to happen—so much waste—so little regard for merit or bravery or sacrifice." He shook his head. "No. I need the freedom of my own ship and crew and an ocean to explore. But there I go, blabbing again..." He became silent.

Doyle reached over and patted Kirkpatrick's uninjured arm. "I think you should rest now. We have many hours of talk ahead of us. I will send someone to refresh your water and look in on you. Sleep well." With that, he rose and started to leave the tent.

Kirkpatrick called out to him. "Henry, could you stay a moment? I have another question I need to ask you." Doyle came back to the bed, sat down, and waited patiently for Kirkpatrick to begin.

"Ever since I came to North Africa, I've had the strangest dreams. In Cairo, and again on our march, I've seen myself lying on the sand in this oasis, at the point of death from my wounds and fatigue. I'd obviously never been here before—so how was I able to imagine what would happen to me?"

Doyle thought a bit before answering. "You need to know that I have had the same dream of rescuing you here in the oasis many times, the first when I was a ten-year-old boy among the Mohawks."

"That's impossible," cried Kirkpatrick. "That would have had to be years before I was conceived and born. I didn't exist when you dreamed about me!"

"I know," said Doyle. "But tell me about your dream, anyway."

"It starts in different ways. In Cairo, I emerged into this oasis from catacombs beneath the city. During our march, one time I dreamed I had fallen overboard off the *Eagle* and no one saw me. I was left behind to drown in the ocean." He paused. "This sounds like the ravings of a madman—or a drunkard."

"Trust me. You are neither. Please continue."

"Well, instead of drowning, in my dream I sank beneath the water and somehow gained the ability to breathe. The next thing I knew, I was swimming effortlessly alongside a huge dolphin that seemed to be guiding me. I followed him into what seemed to be a dark shape under the water and then emerged again in the oasis at the point of death."

"Did you dream of being rescued?"

"Yes," said Kirkpatrick, "and always the same way." He shook his head in embarrassment. "I dreamed I was a wounded bird, surrounded by hungry jackals moving in to kill me. Some larger bird appeared above me. It dropped down, picked me up, and carried me to safety. To here," he added. "This exact spot in the desert."

"What do you want to know about this dream?" asked Doyle.

"Well, obviously how I was able to dream something that hadn't happened yet—to see the future—but," he paused again, "in your dream, how did you rescue me?"

"I was in the body of a hawk. I spotted you in the desert, flew down, and plucked you away from the jackals. We dreamed the same dream."

"Decades apart from each other and before I was born?"

"Yes," said Doyle. "For the Iroquois, especially the Mohawks who raised me, the physical world we inhabit, with all its confusion and uncertainty, is a shadow world. The real world is the timeless world of the spirit. In our dreams, if we dream truly and explore those dreams, we enter that real world."

"So our dreams allow us to predict and change the future?"

"Sometimes. In the dream world—as in the shadow world we live in—there are evil forces that seek to control and misguide us for their own aims. Learning to dream truly demands that we distinguish between good, healing spirits and those that seek to destroy us and others. For the Mohawks who raised me, dreams provide that life-giving contact with the real world. The spirits tell us of what *may* happen in the future. Sometimes we may be able to change that future or lessen some part of it; sometimes we must learn to endure it. Our happiness depends on what we do with our dreams."

He saw the look of puzzlement on Kirkpatrick's face. "Think for a moment about what white people—Americans, English, French, and the rest—attempt to do. Their lives are spent in a frantic search for control; they even invented a philosophy to justify that passion to make a world they don't understand bow to their desires. They call it 'Reason.' So tell me, Peter, you've had a fiery baptism in an attempt to control things. How has that worked for you? For Eaton? For Hamet and the people of Derna?"

Kirkpatrick just nodded.

"We will talk again. Until then, consider this: we both dreamed the identical dream that actually took place here in this oasis. Was that real?"

CHAPTER 46
❧ THE LIBYAN DESERT 1805 ❧

Doyle was with Dihya in her tent. She rose and poured them both tea.

"So, *Igider*," Dihya asked, "what is this *awlagh,* this dead rabbit, you have given me to nurse back to life?"

"*Ilayetmas.* It is truly as I told you. He is my brother."

"On your father's side or your mother's?"

"He is my mother's second son."

"Then he is truly your brother and must be saved. But he is *azerwal,* one of the Americans?"

"Yes, his father was an American, Dihya."

"And thus by magic, this blue-eyed American crosses the western seas to arrive at an oasis deep in the great desert where he is rescued by a brother he never knew existed—who happens to arrive there as if by chance just in time to free him from the Turkish devils who had taken him prisoner." She laughed at her own words. "I tell you, *Igider*, this tale would be more believable if it were spun by Scheherazade in the *Alf Layla wa Layla.* Surely his father was not some American farmer. Your mother must have slept with a *ziri*—a spirit disguised as a moonbeam— or one of the *amalu* shadow demons. But to speak seriously, all this was in your dream, *Igider*. You have the second sight—as I do. True visions must always be trusted, even when they are not fully understood."

"And this is a true vision. I saw this oasis when I was a boy of ten years and had not traveled more than fifty miles from my home. And I saw my brother in my dream—or at least his spirit."

"So we are now at the place toward which your journey of many years was leading you. But he is only an American. From what you have told me, they do not dream. I understand why you are here. But what brought *him* here?"

Doyle paused to sip the tea. For a moment, he was lost in his thoughts. "It's strange, Dihya. When I left my home twenty-five years ago, there was no such thing as an American; there were only loyal British subjects—and rebels against their lawful sovereign. Now all of us have to deal with this strange new creature, the American, that none of us really understands." He lay back on the cushions in reflection, looking up at the white walls of the tent.

"Mention a new idea to an Englishman and he'll give you a dozen reasons why it's improper and shouldn't be done. Broach the same idea to a Frenchman and he'll tell you a thousand reasons why it's impossible and can't be done. Propose it to an Arab and he'll just say *inshallah,* it will be done if Allah, the Merciful and Compassionate, decides that it will be done. But the Americans—the impulsive idea and the confident deed are instantaneous. The notion that they might be wrong or have misunderstood the complexity of what they have leaped into so wholeheartedly—they are wholly innocent of such reservations. They are young in the world and have a young man's impatient self-assurance, rather like my brother Peter, I might say." He rose to refill his tea, then sat back down next to Dihya. So it's no surprise that they are here in the Mediterranean, testing their fledgling power against the Barbary Pirates, having first blooded themselves against the French. I suspect the English will be next on their list. It's no surprise, either then, that Peter would be in the forefront of that effort, or that his headlong, willful enthusiasm would lead him, unconsciously, to this oasis. In a sense he was already here long before we arrived."

"Once he has recovered, and I think he will recover—like you, his spirit is strong—what will you do with him?"

"I will keep him with us for a while. He needs to heal, and there's much to learn about each other and what brought us here. I will offer him what I know he will not be able to accept: the chance to join us and be part of our world. When it is time for him to leave, we will escort him in safety back to Alexandria and the rest of the journey he is taking with his life. I think the harder question is what will I do with myself?"

"What do you mean?"

"Will I let him into my life? One's acquaintances, no matter how friendly the relationship, live outside one's spirit; the people you love enter in and become inseparably part of you. I knew holy men in India whose spirit was so huge that they could love all humanity. That's a gift I was not given. So I love a very few people. Of course, I love the *Imagzighen,* but that's different. As for individuals, you, with all of my soul—but not many others."

"And people in your past?" she asked.

"When I leave a place, I shut the door." He stood and stretched, then looked in the direction of Kirkpatrick's tent. "But to turn again to my brother, he represents much that I hate. I said the Americans were like young men; actually they are like strong, willful children who break whatever they touch or play with. Peter may grow out of that. In some ways, we are very much the same. So we will always be friends. My question is: do I let him into my heart?"

"What does your spirit say?"

"That I didn't save him in order to leave him—that there is more to our story together. I just don't see it yet."

"When you're ready, *Igider*, it will appear."

That evening, Doyle and Dihya returned to Kirkpatrick's bedside carrying hot water, salve, and fresh bandages. They both watched him as he tossed in bed, still in the midst of a dream, until he woke. Wordlessly, Dihya went to him, helped him rise to a sitting position, and gently cleaned and dressed his wounds. Doyle laughed to himself watching Kirkpatrick's expression as Dihya tended to him. *Oh my goodness. I think the boy's in love. Well, who would blame him?* When she was done, Dihya gave Kirkpatrick another heart-wrenching smile and left with the soiled bandages.

"She's an amazing woman," Kirkpatrick said. "You're lucky to be with her."

"Yes she is, and yes I am. Now, I thought I might inquire about some food. Are you hungry?"

"I'm not sure. I think I'm famished. How about a roasted lamb for starters? Then perhaps a camel?"

Doyle laughed. "How about some herbed broth and then couscous?" He stepped to the entrance to the tent and gave orders to one of his servants. When Doyle returned, he rejoined Kirkpatrick on the bed.

"I'm sure you have more questions for me."

"Only a thousand," Kirkpatrick said. "I guess a place to start would be your own boyhood with our mother ..." after a pause he added, "and your father."

"My father was Sir William Johnson, whom the People called *Warrahiyagey*. A giant of a man, physically and spiritually. He came to America a penniless Irish immigrant and built an empire on the fur trade. An intuitively brilliant commander, his colonial militia and Iroquois allies routed a larger force of French regulars, Canadians, and Indians under Baron Dieskau, saving New York and western New England from French conquest. An irresistibly persuasive diplomat, the sphere of his influence stretched from the Mohawk Valley and all the council fires of the Six Nations, to Albany, New York, Boston, Philadelphia, and London. He created Crown policy; broke British commanders and governors who opposed him; removed one British Prime Minister; and on his own, added Kentucky, Tennessee, and western Virginia to the thirteen colonies.

"He had two overarching passions: the first—uncompromising and unconquerable—was protecting the safety and security of the Mohawk people and thus that of the entire Six Nations from the military threat of the French and the greed and stupidity of the English. Let me tell you a story about him.

"Two years after his victory over Baron Dieskau, the French sent an even larger army under the Marquis de Montcalm down Lake George to attack Fort William Henry—a stronghold my father had built at the southern end of the lake. The British, under siege and outnumbered three to one, sent a frantic call for help. My father and over fifteen hundred colonial militia and Indians arrived five days later at the camp of General Webb in Fort Edward, just fourteen miles from Fort William Henry. The offered to join Webb's thirty-five hundred British troops in relieving the beleaguered garrison. Webb refused to move.

"My father, dressed entirely in the Indian attire he preferred when doing battle, his face painted in red and black, angrily burst into Webb's headquarters with a handful of Mohawk chiefs. Webb, so typically British, knew he was confronting a newly knighted English baronet, but couldn't see past the war paint on what he took to be an utterly mad colonial. His answer to my father's plea was: 'I do not wish to expose myself to complete defeat.' Then he turned, in placid arrogance, to leave the room. Before he could get to the door, an Indian buckskin legging struck him in the foot. My father had unlaced one of his leggings and thrown it at Webb. Within seconds, each of his Mohawk chiefs did the same.

He cried out to Webb: 'You will not go?' Webb responded 'No.' My father unlaced his other legging and threw it at Webb, the Indians following his example. He stepped menacingly toward Webb and asked again: 'You will not go?'

"Webb just as angrily answered, 'No.' One garment at a time, my father and his Mohawks disrobed, hurling their deerskins at Webb each time he answered 'No' to my father's repeated question. Finally, when they were down to just their breechcloths, they raised their tomahawks. A final time, my father asked: You will not go?' Webb's terrified silence gave them their answer. They threw their tomahawks to the floor and departed with their forces back to the Mohawk Valley. The garrison at Fort William Henry, deprived of reinforcements, their fort crumbling under Montcalm's artillery barrage, surrendered—and were massacred by Montcalm's Indians as they marched out under a flag of truce."

"Any soldier would follow a leader like that," said Kirkpatrick. "And what was his other passion?"

"Women. He loved them, and they found his personal force irresistible. His detractors claim he fathered three hundred illegitimate children among the Indian and white women he loved. I think the real number is much higher."

"My mother?"

"I am one of his many bastards," said Doyle, watching Kirkpatrick's response closely. "She never apologized for what she did in bringing me into the world; I never asked her to."

Kirkpatrick digested that, and then looked up at Doyle. "And what of my father? Did you know him?"

"I knew him when I was a young boy. He was a widower on a small farm near Johnson Hall. He never held my birth against our mother—he just loved her. The times we were together he treated me as if I were his son. When we say someone was 'a good man' after his death, it is usually a polite, empty compliment. In your father's case, it was simply true. He never made a promise he did not mean to keep and never broke his word."

"I do so wish I had more time with him. And now I've met you. What happens to us, Henry?"

"We are brothers, Peter. Blood brothers. I cannot see into our future yet. But I do know what's next for you: a light supper. Dihya will probably put some of that lamb you crave into the couscous. She likes to see her men well fed. As for us, we have the rest of our lives to discover our future."

From the Journals of El Habibka
You are my brother. I am a prayer. You're the 'amen.'

Rumi

HISTORICAL EPILOGUE

While this novel is a work of fiction, the historical framework of William Eaton's epic march, the betrayal of Eaton and Hamet, the pointless sacrifice of the victory at Derna, and Lear's shameful treaty with Tripoli is sadly true.

Nevertheless, the peace won by deceit held for seven years. Then, in 1812, with war between England and the United States imminent, the English prime minister, Lord Liverpool, offered to create an alliance between England and Algiers, the strongest of the Barbary States. As part of the agreement, England pledged to refit and rearm the Algerian fleet and gave the Algerians permission to attack American military vessels and commercial shipping. Algeria accepted the offer eagerly.

On the pretext of insufficient tribute, the Dey of Algiers expelled the United States consul and his suite, in effect declaring war on the United States. The US Consul to Algiers, now none other than Tobias Lear, was able to extricate himself and the other American staff only after paying the Algerians an additional $25,000 on top of the yearly tribute—with borrowed funds at twenty-five percent interest. Fortunately, the threat of war that very year had sent most American merchant ships scurrying for home. The US Navy had recalled its warships, so all Algeria had to claim for its declaration of war against the United States was the capture of a single small brig, the *Edwin*.

That all changed in 1815. With the end of the war with England, American merchant ships once again took to the seas and the US government as eagerly looked for import duties to replenish its depleted treasury. So in March, 1815, Congress authorized President Madison to deploy whatever naval force he deemed necessary to protect American shipping in the Mediterranean—or implicitly anywhere else on the globe. Included in the authorization was the power of the naval commander on the scene to declare a de facto state of war, as he thought appropriate, with any nation or power threatening American interests.

The commander of the first American squadron to be sent to the Mediterranean was Stephen Decatur, famed for his daring destruction in 1804 of the captured *Philadelphia* in Tripoli. His stunning victory in the *United States* over the *HMS Macedonian* in 1812 and his heroic battle in the *President* against a superior British force at the end of the war had added to his laurels. For the mission against Algiers, Decatur commanded a fleet of ten ships, including the *Constellation*, the former British frigate *Macedonian,* and a brand new "super frigate," the *Guerriere*, named after the British frigate sunk by Isaac Hull in the *Constitution* during the war.

Decatur would be followed, several weeks later, by a second, even more powerful force under Commodore William Bainbridge, including America's first, newly built line of battle ship, the *Independence,* and another new "super frigate," the *Java*, named after the British frigate sunk by Bainbridge in the war.

In a perhaps apocryphal story, when Decatur's squadron made its stately entrance into Gibraltar, a group of British officers asked a visiting American to name the ships. "The first," the American allegedly said, "is the *Guerriere*, the second the *Macedonian*, the third the *Java*, the next *Epervier*," naming British ships captured or sunk by the American navy in the war. "The next ..." he began, "Oh damn the rest!" was a British officer's retort.

On arriving in the Mediterranean, Decatur made short work of the Algerians, capturing the Algerine flagship *Meshuda* and killing the Algerine admiral, Rais Hamidou, then taking a second Algerine ship, the *Estedio.* Decatur's squadron arrived off Algiers on June 28. Five days later, Decatur had forced a complete surrender and treaty of perpetual peace, unfettered trade, and nonaggression between Algiers and the United States. He then worked his way down the Barbary coast to Tunis, from whom he secured the same terms, finally arriving off Tripoli in August of 1815. This time, Decatur's offer to Pasha Jusef Karamanli was simple: pay the United States $50,000 in reparations, return the prizes seized by the Tripolitans, and free European prisoners—or Tripoli would be destroyed. Pasha Jusef Karamanli had had his fill of the American Navy and Stephen Decatur ten years before. The Pasha managed to whittle the reparations down to $25,000, all the ready money he claimed to have on hand. As the band of the *Guerriere* played "Hail, Columbia" on the shore of Tripoli, Decatur celebrated yet another peace treaty, dictated, he said "at the cannon's mouth." By the time Bainbridge arrived with his squadron, Decatur had won a lasting peace for America with the Barbary pirates.

Returning to Gibraltar in the *Guerriere*, this time without escorts, Decatur ran into the remains of the Algerine navy: four frigates and three sloops of war all rigged for battle. Not sure if the Algerians knew about the treaty, or would respect it if they did, Decatur ordered the *Guerriere* cleared for action and maneuvered his ship to seize the windward weather gauge. The Algerine ships formed in two parallel lines and sailed past the *Guerriere* downwind at point blank range of the *Guerriere's* 24-pound main battery and 42-pound carronades. The passing crews watched each other in tense silence, but no shots were fired. As the last Algerine ship passed, her captain called out in Italian, *"Dove andante?* Where are you going?"

Decatur answered, *"Dove mi piace.* Where I please." And now he was speaking for America.

ACKNOWLEDGEMENTS

The genesis of *Blood Brothers* occurred when, as a ten-year-old, I read Kenneth Robert's *Lydia Bailey* and was captivated by the story of William Eaton's heroism and ultimate betrayal. This novel began emerging fifteen years ago when I read James Thomas Flexner's *Lord of the Mohawks,* and the character of Henry Doyle showed up in my consciousness asking—demanding actually—that I tell his story.

In time the two threads of a bastard child raised by the Mohawks in the 1770's and Eaton's epic march across the Libyan desert to attack Tripoli in 1805 merged into the novel *Blood Brothers*. From Henry Boyle's dreams I knew he had a half-brother, Peter Kirkpatrick. It took a little longer to find him and discover his place in the story.

Readers who have loved P.C. Wren's masterful trilogy of the Foreign Legion in North Africa (*Beau Geste, Beau Sabreur, Beau Ideal*) will recognize the source of the name "El Habibka" and the idea of training desert nomads to fight like European cavalry.

Anyone who writes in this genre owes unrepayable debts to both C. S. Forester and Patrick O'Brian. It took considerable discipline not to bring Stephen Maturin into this story: he would instantly have recognized Burton Grey for the scrub that he turned out to be.

Like any other writer of historical fiction who stirs together real and imaginary events with actual people and invented characters, I am indebted to my sources for helping provide the context for *Blood Brothers.* The authors and works that inspired this book are listed in the Appendix under "Sources." For readers interested in the actual history of America's first attempt at nation building in the Islamic world, these are wonderfully written books and authors to get to know and enjoy—as I have.

Writing a historical novel like this is akin to sailing around the world. In point of fact, Magellan managed his circumnavigation five years faster than I did. Happily, I didn't have to make the voyage alone. Over the years, many friends have read the manuscript in its various stages and provided wise insights and loving support. To Ann Cromarty, Patty Cronheim, Dock Murdock, Kevin O'Brien USMC, Priit Vesilind, Merrill Weingrod, and Jenny Behr Wilson: thank you for helping make this story and its characters come more fully to life. Joseph Borlo was invaluable in catching factual inaccuracies and anachronisms, challenging the political and religious underpinning of this novel, and providing encouragement worthy of our long friendship.

Michael Peterman, of Trent University in Canada, lent his skilled writer's eye and impatience with lazy writing to the first close reading of the final text.

I am grateful to Sidney Moody, formerly of the Associated Press and author of *'76: The World Turned Upside Down*, one of my favorite books about the Revolutionary War, for introducing me to Eugene Leitensdorfer. Cervantes or Rabelais could hardly have invented a character more fascinating than this real-life rascal.

Walter Carell, a wise horseman who learned "boots and spurs" cavalry tactics at Valley Forge Military Academy, provided helpful insights on the collisions of men and horses in the mêlée of a battle.

Nat Wilson, master sail maker, graciously lent me his copy of a rare manuscript: the log of the *USS Constitution.*

The model for Peter Kirkpatrick's ship, the fictional *USS Eagle*, is an actual replica of an 1812 Baltimore topsail schooner, the *Pride of Baltimore*. Jan C. Miles, captain of the *Pride*, provided extraordinarily gracious and helpful advice to an amateur sailor like me in figuring out the sailing complexities of an early 19th-century warship. Any technical inaccuracies that appear in *Blood Brothers* are solely the result of my lack of expertise.

David Cameron and Nancy Sherwood of EarthSea.com, good friends to Native People, provided my first understanding of the beliefs and rituals that would form the basis of Henry Doyle's character and contributed helpful feedback on the details of Henry's childhood.

Thanks to Richard Martin for creating the artwork for the book's cover and to Jenny Legan and the Create Space publishing team for helping me navigate the unknown waters of bringing this book into print.

In today's world, marketing a book takes one inevitably into the world of websites and social networking. Thanks to Mark Brodie of MIB Productions and Gene Samson of Samson Media LLC for their expertise in helping bring this book to the attention of readers.

I was blessed to be born into a family that loves books and writing; it's no surprise, then, that so many members of my family have become professional writers. My brother, Peter Behr, for decades a journalist and editor for the *Washington Post* and now a feature writer *for www.eenews.net*, has made this journey with me from the start. Simply put, this novel would not exist but for his unflagging encouragement and insistence that I find the truth within my characters and story and tell it simply and honestly.

Mary Behr, my daughter and copy editor, waged what I hope has been a successful, patient war against the insidious typographical errors that seem to arise of their own volition in a manuscript. I am grateful for her painstaking attention. I wish I'd made her job easier.

I owe a huge debt of gratitude to my editor and niece, Alex Behr, an award-winning fiction writer in her own right. Her wise directives are advice all authors should heed: place the reader in midst of the action; don't just create a sense of place, let your characters live in that space; bring the inherent tension within the characters and story to life on each page. I have tried to live up to that standard.

Finally, living with a writer is rarely easy, especially one who far too often commandeers the kitchen table—or any other still uncluttered space—when the mass of research books and manuscripts has buried his desk. Heartfelt thanks to JoAnn Behr for both encouraging and putting up with me over the years it took to finish this book.

APPENDIX

SOURCES

In telling this story I have taken necessary liberties with the factual record. The history itself makes for compelling reading. I am indebted to the following sources:

THE MOHAWKS

James Thomas Flexner's *Lord of the Mohawks* (1979) is a richly detailed, comprehensive biography of Sir William Johnson and the Mohawk people.

All of Tom Brown's works, but especially *Nature Observation and Tracking* (1983), contributed deeply to the background for Doyle's woodcraft as a boy raised by the Mohawks.

My major source for Doyle's experience with dream rituals of the Iroquois comes from Robert Moss's *The Interpreter* (1997) and *Dreamways of the Iroquois* (2005).

EATON'S CAMPAIGN

Most of the details of desert travel come from *Travels in Nubia by the late John Lewis Burckhardt* (1819) and A.M. Hassanein Bey's extraordinary *The Lost Oases* (1923).

Some details of the behavior and appearance of the Turkish and Arab people come from William Spencer's *Algiers in the Age of the Corsairs* (1976).

Glenn Tucker's *Dawn Like Thunder: The Barbary Wars and the Birth of the US Navy* (1963) is a delightfully narrated account of the real story behind America's first, failed attempt at nation building and Eaton's heroic march. All of us who write of this time and characters stand on his shoulders.

Joseph Wheelan's *Jefferson's War: America's First War on Terror* (2003) contains its own rich details about Eaton's exploits, the naval campaigns in 1801 to 1805, and the successful return of Decatur's fleet in 1815 that put a final end to the Barbary pirates' attacks on American ships.

I am also indebted to A.B.C. Whipple's *To the Shores of Tripoli: The Birth of the US Navy and Marines* (1991) and Richard Zacks' thoroughly annotated, gripping account, *The Pirate Coast: Thomas Jefferson, The First Marines, and the Secret Mission of 1805* (2005).

Frederick C. Leiner's *The End of Barbary Terror: America's 1815 War Against the Pirates of North Africa* (2006) is equally authoritative on the final chapter of America's first foreign war.

Lieutenant Presley Neville O'Bannon's letters are entirely my own creation. In addition to the above sources, the background I used for his character comes from Trudy J. Sundberg and John Kenneth Gott's *Valiant Virginian: Story of Presley Neville O'Bannon, 1776-1850* (2009).

The US Navy in the Barbary Wars

Dean King and John B. Hattendorf's rich anthology of period sources, *Every Man Will Do His Duty* (1997), was an invaluable aid in capturing the language and details of sailors, sea battles, and shipboard life.

Henry Gruppe's *The Frigates* (1979) provided my first vivid insights into the ships that fought in the Barbary Wars and the captains who commanded them. I also came across a copy of John Harland's *Seamanship in the Age of Sail* (1984), a goldmine for anyone writing about the ships of this age.

I am also indebted to Howard I. Chapelle's *History of the American Sailing Navy* (1949), Robert Gardiner's *Frigates of the*

Napoleonic Wars (2000), Brian Tunstall and Nicholas Tracy's *Naval Warfare in the Age of Sail* (2001), Donald L. Canney's *Sailing Warships of the US Navy* (2001), and Karl Heinz Marquardt's *The Global Schooner* (2003).

In addition to the invaluable suggestions of Captain Jan C. Miles of the *Pride of Baltimore,* Captain Daniel Moreland of the tall ship *Picton Castle* introduced me to the complexities of sailing traditional square-rigged ships. Other sources include Darcy Lever's *The Young Sea Officers Sheet Anchor* (1819, Dover Publications 1998), and *Eagle Seamanship: A Manual for Square-Rigger Sailing*, revised by Lt. Edwin H. Daniels Jr. USCG (1990).

SUFISM

My still-imperfect understanding of Sufism was guided by Idries Shah's *The Way of the Sufi* (1968), James Fadiman and Robert Frager's *Essential Sufism* (1997), William C. Chittick's *Sufism* (2000)—a beginner's guide for someone who is trying to understand Sufism with a "beginner's mind"—and the teachings of Sheikh Tosun Bayrak al-Jerrahi. Doyle's descriptions of his religious beliefs are my own fictional creation.

OTHER REFERENCES

The quarrel between the American sailors and British officers in Chapter 1 comes from the memoirs of Commander Anthony Garner, R.N. in Dean King and John Hattendorf's wonderful collection of contemporary sources, *Every Man Will Do His Duty,* 1997.

The duel described in Chapter 6, in which Decatur serves as Kirkpatrick's second, actually involved Midshipman Joseph Bainbridge.

Burton Grey's diatribe against Americans in Chapter 10 is drawn from a note in King and Hattendorf's *Every Man Will Do His Duty*. The actual statement by Michael Scott (1829-1830) is more generous than Grey's and worth repeating: "I don't like Americans. I never did and I never shall. I have seldom met with an American gentleman, in the large and complete sense of the term. I have no wish to eat with them, drink with them, deal or consort with them in any way. But let me tell you the whole truth—nor to fight with them, were it not for the laurels to be acquired by overcoming an enemy so brave, determined, alert, and in every way so worthy of one's steel as they have always proved."

The background for the discussion of cavalry fighting in Chapters 41 and 42 come from a marvelously detailed website: *Cavalry Tactics and Combat in the Napoleonic Wars*, http://www.napolun.com.

Kirkpatrick's sea battle in Chapter 21 is based on Captain Andrew Starrett's victory over the *Tripoli* in 1801. The *Eagle's* victory over the *Crescent* in Chapter 27 is fictional.

Eaton's proclamation in Chapter 32 is based on sources quoted in Zacks' *The Pirate Coast* and Wheelan's *Jefferson's War*.

The name "Sepulcher of Wet Bones" in Chapter 44 comes from Edison Marshall's *American Captain* (1954).

The wonderful story of Decatur's final encounter with the Algerine fleet in the *Epilogue* comes from Frederick C. Leiner's *The End of Barbary Terror.*

THE HISTORICAL
CHARACTERS

WILLIAM EATON: Graduate of Dartmouth College, army officer, Indian fighter, former US Consul to Tunis, and commander of America's first invasion of a foreign country, he was as brilliant a military leader as I have described. In creating the fictional representation of William Eaton, I drew heavily on the descriptions of Eaton in *Dawn Like Thunder* and *Jefferson's War*. Both books cite Eaton's statements and letters extensively. Where his actual words fit the story, I have incorporated them. Eaton's fondness for quoting Shakespeare is my own invention, but one that seemed appropriate given both Eaton's education and fondness for lofty rhetoric. His greatest strength, as a veteran of the Revolutionary War, was his belief in the principles on which our nation was founded. That belief also led to his downfall. If the real story has a true tragic hero, it would be Eaton. Betrayed by his country, then forgotten, he died in 1811 at the age of forty-seven in sad, alcoholic obscurity. He deserved better from his country.

EUGENE LEITENSDORFER: Leitensdorfer's character in this book is almost wholly fictional; the real Leitensdorfer is one of the most fascinating characters in American history. He was all the things said about him in Chapter 3, and astoundingly much more: Capuchin monk, Muslim holy man, adventurer, con artist, faith healer, and soldier of fortune. He deserted multiple wives as readily as he deserted the many Christian and Muslim armies he served in. Hired by Eaton as his adjutant, it was Leitensdorfer who found and freed Hamet Karamanli from his self-imposed captivity to join Eaton's army of invasion. After the failure of Eaton's campaign, Leitensdorfer wound up in the United States, living for a while in the United States Capitol, cooking for himself in an upper chamber behind the old Senate Gallery. He retired on a US government pension years later to a comfortable life as an entertainer, story-teller, and magician in Missouri. When Leitensdorfer's pension was voted on, it is reported that one Senator asked, "By the way, did we ever do anything about old Eaton?"

USMC LIEUTENANT PRESLEY NEVILLE O'BANNON'S character is also wholly fictional, but is drawn on the enormous respect the real O'Bannon earned from all who served with him. The dress sword worn today by United States Marine officers is a replica of the Mameluke scimitar awarded to him by Hamet Karamanli in gratitude for his bravery. He retired from the Marine Corps shortly after his return from the Mediterranean.

O'BANNON'S MARINES: We know the names of six of the seven Marines who served under O'Bannon and Eaton: Sergeant Arthur Campbell and Privates Bernard O'Brian, David Thomas, James Owens, John Whitten, and Edward Stewart. For the seventh Marine whose name has been lost, I appropriated the name of a much respected former mentor Ed Cissel, who served in the USMC in Korean War. The Greek Sergeant who fights and dies defending Kirkpatrick is named after another friend and USMC veteran, the late George Christow. In my fictional account of the historical Marines who fought "on the shores of Tripoli," I have tried to be true to the character of these two exemplary leaders and sadly missed friends.

CAPTAIN ISAAC HULL, USN: As captain of the *USS Argus*, Hull strongly backed Eaton's plan to invade Tripoli. He led the small naval force that bombarded Derna in support of Eaton's attack by land. Hull was one of the young naval officers, "Preble's Boys," groomed by Commodore William Preble during the Mediterranean war, who gained fame by their victories over the British Navy almost a decade later in the War of 1812. As captain of the *USS Constitution* in that war, Hull defeated the British frigate *Guerriere* in a brilliantly one-sided victory. He went on to a long career in the US Navy. Honored by both his friends and former British foes, he died peacefully in 1843. Except for his penchant for splitting his tight britches in battle, Isaac Hull's character in this novel is fictional.

CAPTAIN STEPHEN DECATUR, USN: Decatur entered the service during the quasi-war with France in 1799. He led the cutting out expedition against the captured *USS Philadelphia* in Tripoli harbor in 1804, an act Admiral Nelson hailed as "the most bold and daring act of the age." In the War of 1812, as commander of the *USS United States*, he defeated *HMS Macedonian* in a brilliant, one-sided battle. Transferring his command to the *USS President*, he escaped the British blockade of New York only to run into the British West Indies Squadron of four frigates. In a long running fight, he disabled *HMS Endymion*, but was trapped by the remaining British ships and surrendered to avoid the needless slaughter of his crew. He returned home to national acclaim, only increasing those laurels by his exploits in the Second Barbary War. Following the war, he served as a Navy Commissioner. In 1820, following a personal feud with Commodore James Barron, he answered Barron's challenge to a duel. An expert shot and duelist, Decatur deliberately wounded Barron only slightly. Barron's ball hit Decatur in the stomach and he died several hours later in great pain. Over 10,000 people gathered in Washington to pay their last respects to the greatest of "Preble's Boys." His character in this novel and friendship with Kirkpatrick is fictional.

MASTER COMMANDER JOHN DENT, USN: He began his naval career as a midshipman aboard the *USS Constellation* in her defeat of the French *L'Insurgente* and the battle with the *Vengance*. After serving on the *USS Essex*, he joined the American Mediterranean squadron in 1803, taking command of the *USS Nautilus* and participating in the attacks on both Tripoli and Derna. As a captain during the War of 1812, he was commandant of the naval stations in Charleston, South Carolina and Wilmington, North Carolina. He resigned from the navy after the war, settling in Charleston, where he died in 1823. His character and relationship with Kirkpatrick is also fictional.

TOBIAS LEAR: Former aide to George Washington during his first presidency. Commissioned to write a posthumous biography of Washington, Lear was widely blamed for destroying some of Washington's correspondence that might have cast Thomas Jefferson in a bad light during Jefferson's bid for the Presidency. His service to Jefferson was rewarded by his appointment in 1803 as General Consul to North Africa. Lear opposed Eaton's plan from the beginning and was instrumental in influencing Commodore Samuel Barron to withhold the military supplies, money, and naval support that would have guaranteed the capture of Tripoli. Lear's fictional character is drawn from the accounts and judgments of his many detractors, starting with the Federalist congressmen who blamed Lear for what they considered a cowardly, needless peace settlement. He took his life in 1816.

HAMET KARAMANLI: His failings notwithstanding, Hamet deserved better of the United States. After his ignominious retreat from Derna in 1805, Hamet settled in Syracuse, sustaining himself for a while on a $200 a month stipend from the United States. In spite of letters pleading his case to Jefferson and Congress and passionate support from Eaton, his monthly stipend was terminated by Congress in June 1806. He wound up with $2,400 as a final settlement. Unknown to Eaton and the United States government, Lear had agreed to a secret clause inserted in the final signed treaty with Jusef Karamanli. The clause allowed the Pasha to keep his brother Hamet's wife and children captives for four more years, with their release after that time solely based on Hamet's continuing peaceful behavior. Only in 1807, when George Davis, the new envoy to Tripoli, demanded immediate freedom for Hamet's family, was Hamet reunited with his wife, three sons and daughter. Twelve years had passed since Jusef Karamanli had taken them as prisoners. With the restoration of his family, Hamet Karamanli passed into obscurity and out of America's memory and conscience.

DOYLE'S "SUFISM"

I am not a Muslim, nor do I practice Sufism. I have been, however, a life-long searcher for the presence and spirit of God in myself, others, and the world. My exploration of Taoism and Zen Buddhism led me to Sufism via the writings of Idries Shah, and later William C. Chittick.

The best explanation I can give for why Henry Doyle becomes a follower of Sufism is that one day, when I was well into the novel, he showed up in my consciousness to announce: "I have news for you. I've converted to Islam and have set out on the Sufi path." My response was, "OK. I guess I'd better find out what that means."

As I learned more about Sufism and explored the Mohawk Indian beliefs and practice of dreaming, it became clearer to me why a character like Doyle, raised by the Mohawks, would find Sufism so appealing. For the Mohawks, as for many other Native Americans, the Great Spirit is present in all creation and is a gift to be used mindfully, not exploited mindlessly.

Doyle is his kind of Sufi—but then, every Sufi is his or her kind of Sufi. A Sufi might say: "There are as many ways to God as there are human beings, as many as the breaths of the children of God." Rumi, the Persian teacher and poet, wrote: "Christian, Jew, Muslim, shaman, Zoroastrian, stone, ground, mountain, river, each has a secret way of being with the mystery, unique and not to be judged."

At the time of this story, Doyle is many years and miles removed from his Sufi teacher in India. Since the role of teacher to pupil in central to Sufism, Doyle, in this novel, is often lost. He is the veil that conceals him from himself. "It is easier to drag along a mountain by a hair than to emerge from the self by oneself." (Abu Said Ibn Abi-l-Khayr)

In the sequel to this novel (see the excerpt on the following pages), Doyle is imprisoned in a hellish Algerian prison. That's as good a place as any to find a new teacher.

Readers of the novel in its draft stages commented on the paradox in Doyle's character: his whole life is devoted to saving people whose values align with his spiritual center; at the same time he is a ruthless, cold-blooded killer. That's who he is; the challenge and pleasure of writing the novel is discovering how he got that way and how these two sides merge in his personality.

One clue comes from a Sufi's ability to live peacefully in the midst of unreconciled paradoxes. For Sufis, God is immanently present in all of creation; and because He is God, He is at the same time utterly unknowable and transcendent.

That sense of balance—of dancing in the center of polarized opposites—informs the themes of this book. In narrating William Eaton's incredible march and improbable victory at Derna, I could not help but celebrate his heroism and that of O'Bannon and the Marines and mercenaries who served with him. Their story tells the beginning of our nation's emergence as a world power. At the same time, his betrayal by Tobias Lear and Commodore Barron is just one of many dark chapters in American history in which self-interest and greed have triumphed over the national values we so proudly proclaim.

In the same way, the two main characters—the "blood brothers"—are a Sufi Muslim and an unquestioningly patriotic American. The journey of discovery that brings them together is one all of us should undertake.

FROM THE FORTHCOMING
THE MOST BOLD AND DARING ACT OF THE AGE
A Henry Doyle/Peter Kirkpatrick Novel

Chapter 1
Washington, D.C.
1815

Peter Kirkpatrick walked easily through the piles of rubble and burned timbers cluttering the field outside the Capitol building. The scars of the fires set by the invading British army were still visible in the smoke-stained, empty windows of the gutted House of Representatives building. The Senate building next to it, in the final stages of reconstruction, was swarming with workers. Looking down the muddy expanse of Pennsylvania Avenue, he could see the charred shell of the White House in the distance.

In a city of powerful, self-promoting leaders and politicians, Kirkpatrick's calm strength attracted attention: men first noticed him, then gave him room to pass. As he neared the Capitol, he picked his way through huge piles of lumber, bricks, sandstone, and marble amid an army of workmen, shouting supervisors, and oxen-drawn carts. Ahead, he saw his destination: a large tent stretched between the two buildings housing the United States Congress. On entering the tent, he approached one of the architects poring over plans stretched out on a long table and politely coughed. The man looked up in irritation, saw Kirkpatrick's smile, and respectfully said, "How may I help you, sir?"

"Would you have the kindness to point out Mr. Latrobe to me?"

"He is the tall gentleman there, in the black suit by the table to the rear," answered the architect.

Benjamin Latrobe, Chief Architect in charge of rebuilding the nation's ravaged capital, was impossible to miss. He radiated the strong sense of purposeful intelligence and relaxed charm of a natural leader.

"Mr. Latrobe," Kirkpatrick greeted him, extending his hand. "It is an honor to meet you. Please let me introduce myself. I am Captain Peter Kirkpatrick."

Latrobe took his hand in a warm welcome. "Your servant, sir."

"Upon my word, Mr. Latrobe," Kirkpatrick began, "you would seem to have a monumental challenge ahead of you. I had heard of the destruction of Washington in the war; but seeing it in person—Cockburn's soldiers did devilish work here."

"It was a sorry business. There were no effective troops to defend the capital. The President and Congress fled with the British hot on their heels. Cockburn's men actually finished President Madison's uneaten dinner and open wine before burning the White House. But it could have been worse. They spared private buildings, at least." He turned and nodded toward the Senate building. "We make progress, but I say this as a mere matter of fact and not a complaint, we could make so much more had we the funds. The recent war, however, has stripped the Treasury of money, as wars, unfortunately, will do."

"Then I am come at a good time," said Kirkpatrick, reaching into his cloak and pulling out an envelope. He handed the envelope to Latrobe: "Here is a draft on my bank in Philadelphia for $15,000. During the war, I had the honor of serving my country as the captain of a privateer, and the British were quite generous in supplying us with lucrative prizes. So at least I have the pleasure of knowing that what the British burned, they will now help rebuild."

"Why this is handsomely done, Captain Kirkpatrick," Latrobe cried. "Most generous, I dare say." Then he laughed openly. "May I be permitted to say it is a *capitol* gift?"

"I just wish the British had been even more generous," Kirkpatrick replied. He paused for a moment. "There is, I might add, another purpose in my calling on you."

Latrobe had opened the envelope and was gazing in pleasure at the bank draft. He instantly looked up at Kirkpatrick. "Name any service I may provide for you and it is done."

"I believe you have a man working for you named Leitensdorfer, Eugene Leitensdorfer. He and I fought together in the Mediterranean in '05. I wonder if you might direct me to him?"

"That wonderful scoundrel! Of course," laughed Latrobe. "He managed to get himself appointed by Congress to be surveyor of public buildings. I'm never sure what exactly he does now, since we have so precious few public buildings left to survey, but he does it, whatever it is, with marvelous style." Latrobe pointed to the Senate building. "At this hour you should find him in his rooms on the third floor at the back of the building."

After a mutually warm farewell, Kirkpatrick left Latrobe and made his way through the clutter of reconstruction to the third floor. Finding what he took to be Leitensdorfer's lodgings, knocked on the door.

Leitensdorfer opened it and seeing Kirkpatrick, broke into a joyful shout: "A miracle! A miracle!" The two friends embraced each other, then Leitensdorfer stepped back, still holding Kirkpatrick by the shoulders, to look at him with unfeigned affection. "So the British couldn't kill you after all. We read about your exploits in the war. You so plagued them that had they caught you, they would surely have found some excuse to hang you, Letter of Marque or no. What a pleasure you are for my eyes!"

"No less a pleasure than for mine, old comrade" said Kirkpatrick.

"Come in! Come in!" cried Leitensdorfer. "In surveying the ruins of the White House cellars I found some wine the British missed. Since they would have taken it had they found it, I decided the bottles were legitimate spoils of war. Pray join me in a glass. I am with child to learn of your adventures!"

"And I, yours." Kirkpatrick looked around the surprisingly spacious suite Leitensdorfer had commandeered for himself. "I would say you have done quite well for yourself, Eugene. Surveyor of public buildings indeed. Well, I would have expected no less of you."

"Would it be permissible boasting to add that I have also been granted a lifetime pension as a full colonel for my service in Tripoli, along with a generous land grant in Missouri—wherever that is?"

"Perhaps not permissible, but certainly predictable. And what's this?" Kirkpatrick walked over to a desk covered with handbills and picked one up: "The Illustrious Dervish Magician and Fortune Teller Murat Aga," he read, "Who has Astounded Multitudes, Been Honored by Turkish Pashas, Deys, and Caliphs, and Appeared Before Emperors and Princes of Europe! Now In a Limited Engagement at Tunnicliffe's City Hotel over the Coming Fortnight! Tickets Available at the Door."

"Eugene, this is monstrous," Kirkpatrick laughed, tossing the flyer back on the desk. "Coming it too high by far. Have you no shame?"

"I will acquire shame when men acquire common sense and lose their vanity. So far as I can tell, the chief difference between a Turkish Pasha and an American Congressman is that as a rule, Turks smell better—because they bathe more often and use perfume. But I am like the beggar who approached a rich friend asking for money to buy an elephant. 'You are a beggar,' protested his friend. 'Once you have an elephant, how can you afford to keep him?' 'I came here to get money, not advice,' said the beggar."

"But how did you manage all this?"

"I owe it to the general. When I came to America in '09, I visited him in Massachusetts. He still had some influence in

Washington and wrote the kindest imaginable letters praising my service to the country and recommending me for a position."

"Ah, the general. Not all of us survived that war, Eugene. He died while I was at sea. I never got the chance to bid him farewell."

"If all you have now are your memories, Peter, you are better off for it. When I saw him, two years before he died, he had already surrendered to melancholy and drink. The man who led us across the desert without fear or fatigue was a gout-crippled, whiskey-sodden wreck at age forty-five. The American government did to him what no enemy army ever could—they destroyed his soul."

Leitensdorfer went to his cabinet, pulled out a bottle of wine, opened it and poured them both a glass. "To General Eaton. No man ever deserved more from his country; no man ever received less."

"To General Eaton," Kirkpatrick echoed. As they both sat down, Kirkpatrick turned to Leitensdorfer. "O'Bannon wrote me that you were in Washington. I looked you up not merely for the great pleasure of seeing you once more, but because I need your help. It's about my brother, Henry."

"Nothing has happened to him!" Leitensdorfer cried.

"Unfortunately, yes. He hired out to the British after Napoleon's return from Elba. Some business about the Algerians proclaiming jihad and coming into the renewed war on the side of the French."

"I knew about that—and worried about it, too. Your brother and I correspond, in cypher of course, and he told me he was going to take the assignment. He promised it was his last as a hired spy. I suggested that he might be getting a bit old for the game. But you know your brother. The idea of failure never crosses his mind. What happened?"

"That French bastard Chameau—you remember him from Alexandria—well, Chameau found him out and betrayed him to the Algerians. Doyle's in one of their dungeons. He saved my life in the desert in '05. I'm taking the *Eagle* to Algiers to rescue him, although I haven't the faintest notion of how to do it. But I'm like my brother in one regard, at least: the idea of failure is untenable. O'Bannon's signed on; he's out of the Marine Corps now. Will you join us?"

"With all my heart," answered Leitensdorfer.

THE HENRY DOYLE/PETER KIRKPATRICK SAGA

Prequels to this novel tell the full story of Doyle's boyhood, his failed effort to save his Mohawk people in the Revolution, and his exploits as a British agent in the Middle East and India.

In future novels, Peter Kirkpatrick and Henry Doyle's friendship, nurtured by Kirkpatrick's career as a merchant captain in the Mediterranean, will be tested by the hostilities that break out between America and England in the war of 1812. In that war, Kirkpatrick serves as a highly successful American privateer captain.

Following that war, Henry is captured by the Algerians in revenge for foiling an Algerian attempt to enlist an army in support of Napoleon's return from exile. Kirkpatrick, now facing his opportunity to rescue his brother, becomes involved in America's second attempt to crush the Barbary pirates, this time successfully led by Stephen Decatur in 1815. Kirkpatrick takes advantage of Decatur's attack on Algiers to extricate his brother from an Algerian prison and bring him to safety.

QUESTIONS FOR READING GROUPS

1. Both Henry Doyle and Peter Kirkpatrick grow up without fathers.
   - What characters in the novel take on the role of "father figure" for Henry Doyle? What guidance or insight do they provide?
   - What characters in the novel take on the role of "father figure" for Peter Kirkpatrick? What guidance or insight do they provide?
2. In 1779-1780, the Continental Army, following George Washington's orders, launched a devastating attack against the Iroquois in New York state. The Iroquois lands were devastated and they were forced into exile.
   - What was Henry Doyle's perspective on this attack?
   - How might that experience have shaped his later life?
   Additional Resources:
   http://en.wikipedia.org/wiki/Sullivan_Expedition
   http://www.accessgenealogy.com/native/races/general_sullivan_against_iroquois.htm
   http://www.suite101.com/content/general-john-sullivan-and-the-war-against-the-iroquois-indians
3. Henry Doyle grows up with the Mohawk belief in the power of dreams to reveal the truth about human identity and purpose in life. For the Mohawks (and other Native Americans), the world we perceive in our senses is a "shadow world"—the

"real world" exists only in our dreams. (You may be reminded of Plato's "Allegory of the Cave" in *The Republic*.)

Researchers studying the brain now suggest that up to 90% of our daily actions and decisions may be governed by beliefs in our subconscious mind. In effect, we act for reasons we may not consciously be aware of.

- In what ways might the Mohawk's beliefs actually be a meaningful description of human behavior?

4. In *Blood Brothers,* the characters Henry Doyle, Burton Grey, and Sir Samuel Briggs offer perspectives on American character.

- How does each of them view "America" and "Americans?"
- How might you respond to their characterizations of "America" and "Americans?"

5. What would Hamet Karamanli have to say about his experience with "America" and "Americans?"

6. *Blood Brothers* is set in a violent world in which life was often cheap. How much more "civilized" are people in today's world?

7. While a work of fiction, *Blood Brothers* accurately depicts the political and military choices available to America in dealing with the threat of Barbary piracy. If you were President Jefferson (who authorized Eaton's plan in the first place), what approach would you have chosen:

- Eaton's attempt to overthrow Pasha Jusef Karamanli and put his brother Hamet on the throne to gain valuable concessions for America in the Mediterranean?
- Lear's attempt to secure peace through a negotiated settlement?
- Some other approach?

8. What parts of Eaton's march across the desert did you find the most harrowing? If you had to make such a journey

(assuming an appropriate age and physical condition), how do you think you would have fared?

9. Dihya is portrayed as a minor character in this novel—we know her only through her words and actions, not her inner thoughts (she will play a greater role in the sequels). Her strength and independence reflect the values of her culture, in which women are respected (and although Muslims, allowed to appear unveiled in public).

   • What part does her character play in the story?
   • What core assumptions might she make about her role in her society and relationships with men?

10. The Muslims in *Blood Brothers* are viewed through American and European eyes (largely based on the historical characters' actual reports and journals).

    • How fair and accurate is that perception?
    • What are Henry Doyle's beliefs about Islam?

    Additional Resources (besides those listed in "Sources"):
    http://www.uga.edu/islam/Sufism.html
    http://www.nimatullahi.org/sufism
    http://www.sufiorder.org/

11. For sailors and military historians:

    • What are the sailing qualities of the Baltimore topsail schooners that made them so effective?
    • What were their limitations as warships?
    • What lessons did the US Navy learn in the Barbary War that they were able to exploit in the War of 1812?

Made in the USA
Lexington, KY
17 September 2015